A MYSTERY ON CHURCH STREET

This extraordinary story classically captures the mindset of the 1940s. Addie and her friend Kate reflect the voices women hear as they face confusing dilemmas 75 years later—my first read kept me up into the wee hours. I will refer my readers to *In Times Like These*!
Patricia Evans, author of
The Verbally Abusive Relationship,
Controlling People,
and other books listed at www.VerbalAbuse.com

Wartime brings out the best and the worst in people. I loved the way Addie and Kate, each in her own way, dug down inside to become more than either had ever dreamed. *With Each New Dawn* will inspire you toward resilience and personal growth even as it keeps you riveted with each page turn.
Sonia C. Solomonson, freelance writer and life coach
Way2Grow Coaching

I*n Times Like These* clearly portrays the difficulties for women during WW2. First, there are the challenges of raising food, preserving it, making money stretch, wisely using ration cards and just plain living in fear of the war. But then the overlay of Addie's controlling husband made me instantly empathize with the main character. His verbally abusive and cold treatment of Addie unfortunately is not just a problem from another era. God's provision for her was intriguing. The value of faith, friendship and compassion are evident in this book. I personally enjoyed the food tips and recipes, as well as vivid descriptions of farm life. This may be my favorite book by Gail Kittleson. It is the first in the mini-series, *Women of the Heartland*. Be sure to read the books in order.
Cleo Lampos

Gail Kittleson introduces us to a small town community, under the strains of World War II. The everyday lives of the town folks unfolding their thoughts and concern for the husbands and brothers fighting for their country. The family and friends dynamics in this story keeps the reader wanting to turn page after page. The author knows how to keep the reader engaged. Looking forward to Ms. Kittleson's next book.

K Currie

Kittleson's writing style fosters instant empathy as her quiet heroine, Addie, struggles through daily living in Iowa during WW2. Readers are introduced to Addie through patriotism, friendship, and self-realization. "I've spent my whole life in fear instead of living each day," highlights Addie's growth in overcoming an emotionally abusive husband. Highest recommendation.

Carolyn Cobb

…the pages almost turned themselves. Great period piece exploring family dynamics and interpersonal relationships as well as the growth of self-esteem and the importance of friendship.

Lisa Lickel

Kittleson deftly writes strong female characters facing heartbreaking tragedies. *Until Then* features two: Marian, caught in the Blitz, and Dorothy, a surgical nurse whose work with the 11th Evacuation Hospital has taken her to North Africa, through Sicily and into France. Their stories intertwine in a narrative that touches then heals the soul. Highly, highly recommended!

Literary Soirée

Also by Gail Kittleson

Women of the Heartland Series
In Times Like These
With Each New Dawn
A Purpose True
All for the Cause
Until Then
&
Kiss Me Once Again
a Women of the Heartland story

In This Together
Catching Up With Daylight

With Billy Rae Stewart
Country Music's Hidden Gem

With Cleo Lampos
The Food That Held the World Together
A World War 2 Holiday Scrapbook

A
MYSTERY
ON CHURCH STREET

a novel

GAIL KITTLESON

WordCrafts

A Mystery on Church Street
Copyright © 2023
Gail Kittleson

ISBN: 978-1-957344-67-6

Cover concept and design by Mike Parker.

Map design by Leslie E. Smith and Lance Kittleson, used by permission, all rights reserved.

Published by WordCrafts Press
Cody, Wyoming 82414
www.wordcrafts.net

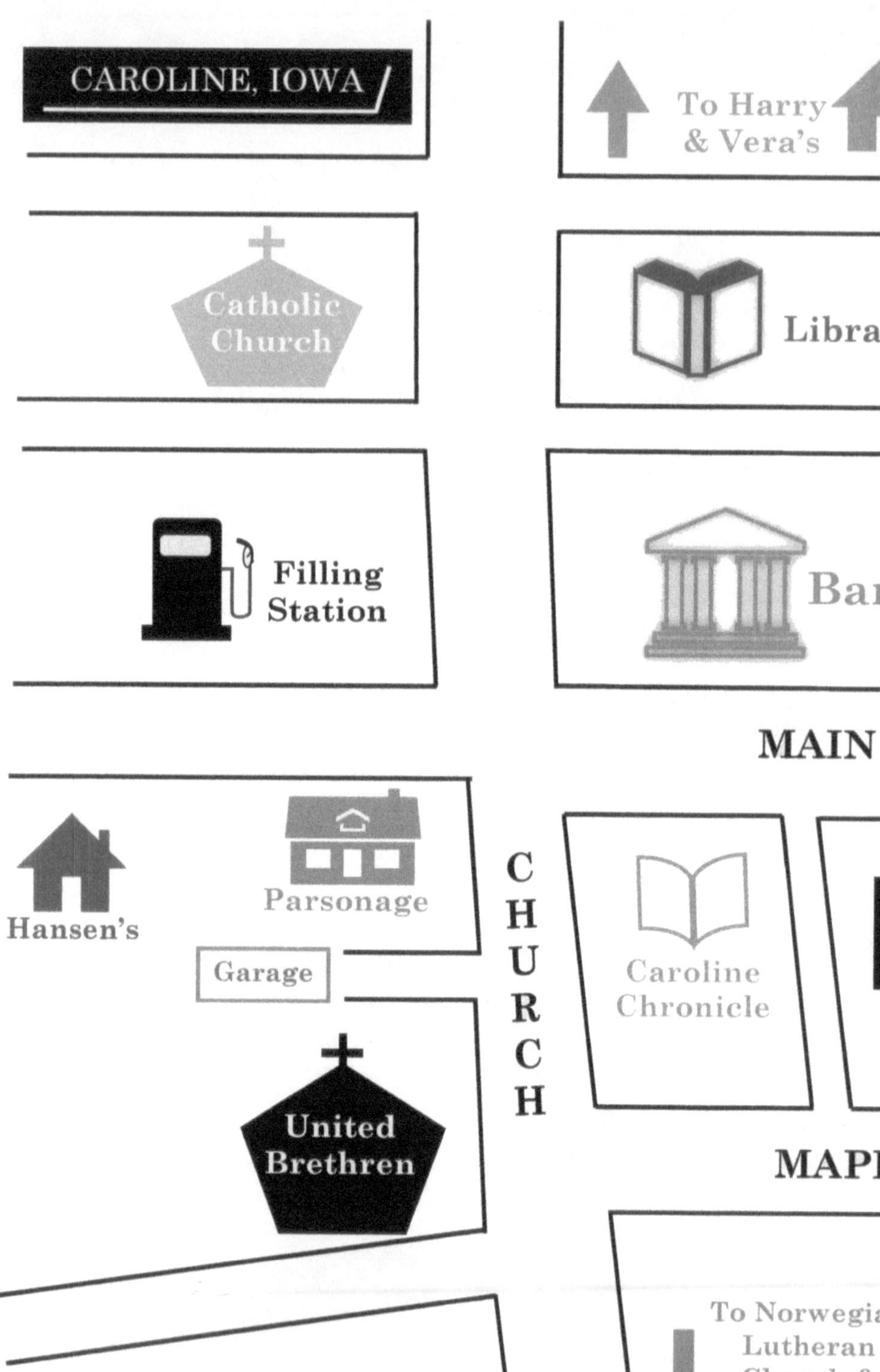

CAROLINE, IOWA
To Harry & Vera's
Catholic Church
Librar
Filling Station
Ban
MAIN
Hansen's
Parsonage
Garage
CHURCH
Caroline Chronicle
United Brethren
MAPL
To Norwegian Lutheran Church & Cemetery

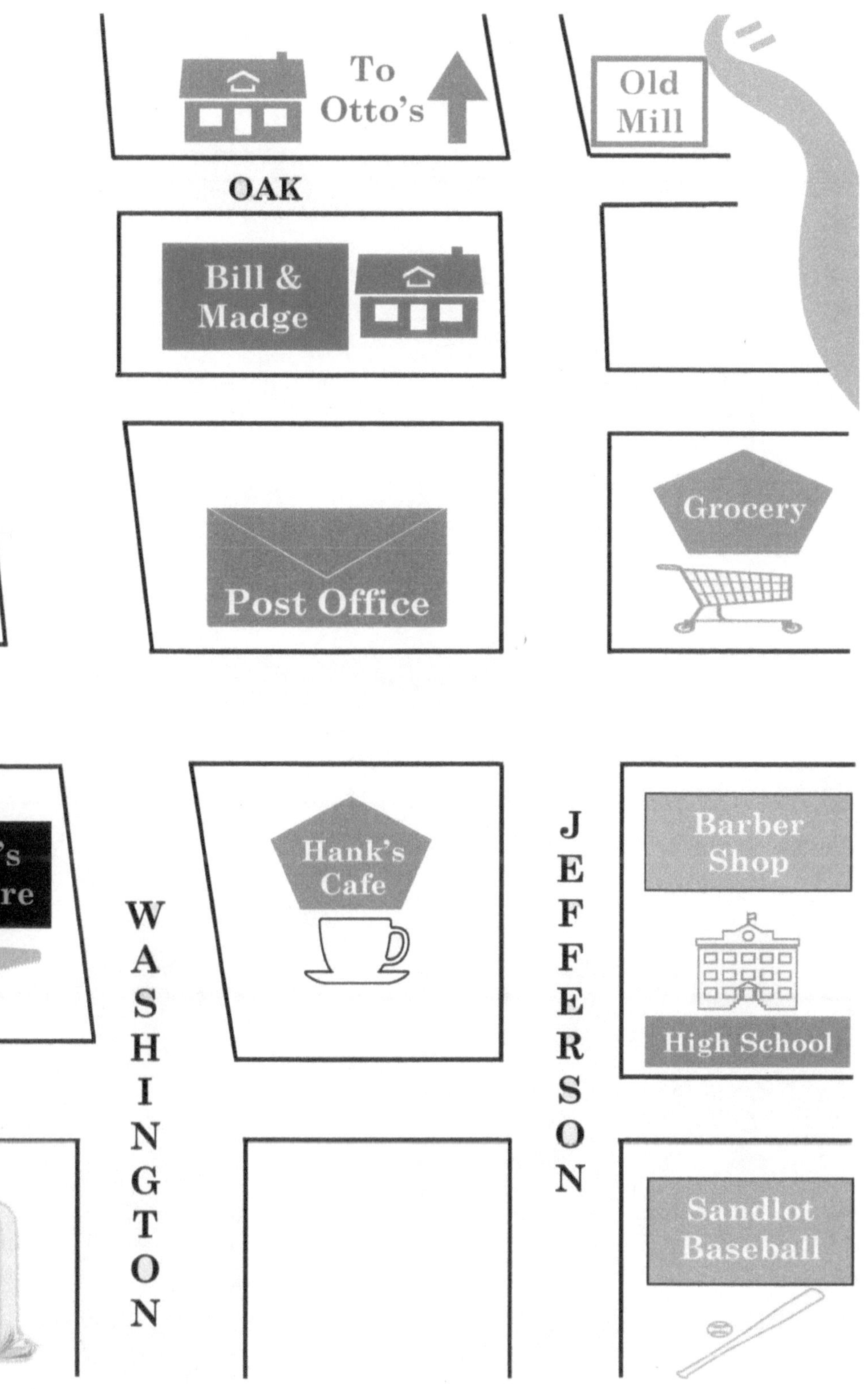

To Otto's
Old Mill
OAK
Bill & Madge
Post Office
Grocery
n's are
WASHINGTON
Hank's Cafe
JEFFERSON
Barber Shop
High School
Sandlot Baseball

Chapter One

A heavy morning mist enveloped the corner of Fourth and Main. Bill McQuestion propped his thermos against the stoop and jiggled the back doorknob of the *Caroline Chronicle* office. After a rough night, he had crept out of bed and downstairs without waking Madge, boiled the coffee and slipped outside.

A cold breeze swept across northern Iowa, normal for late winter. After a few kicks, the recalcitrant door to the press room finally responded, revealing an inky interior.

But Bill knew this space, fathomed its sleepy solitude—a sense of separation from the warring world. No wonder Dad had done most of his thinking here.

Loading wood into an ancient corner stove, Bill shuttled past an aisle of bookcases thick with reference texts and decades-old *Chronicle* issues. When he turned on the ceiling bulb, a tattered history volume called out to him, so he eased into the creaky wooden chair that served his father well until a heart attack stole any chance to say good-bye.

Missing his passing carved a wordless gap in Bill's soul. He once avoided funerals but realized now how they clarified a loved one's death. When his mother passed, having his father's grief to tend helped, but this time, Madge's letter about the heart attack took weeks to reach Bill's unit in North Africa.

When he finally read the news, he had to tuck it away—in his rucksack and in his heart. Now he half-expected his father to round the corner any moment, could almost feel Dad's pat on his shoulder.

"Good to have you back, Son. You're runnin' a mighty fine newspaper here, y' know."

But that part of life—being a son—had come to an end. Another adjustment to make when the bus from Fort McCoy carried him across the state line from Wisconsin a year ago.

An hour later, one long step onto Main Street produced a peculiar terror, but then Madge started waving to him. Seeing her in her red polka-dot dress, his favorite, banished all trepidation and set his ears to roaring.

Racing over, heels and all, she burst into his arms. "Oh, my Billy-boy! You're home!"

Like sunlight on snow, her embrace melted away his misgivings and highlighted her dark auburn hair. Her lavender scent inundated his senses.

Her touch reintroduced him to the present—in a word, redeemed him. Ever since then, he'd been plowing his way through, like stalwart farmers out in their fields each spring, two furrows at a time, or for some who'd graduated to tractors since he deployed, four.

Yes, some things had changed, but after that initial reunion, he faced manageable chunks of time—one day, or sometimes one hour or even a second. Truth be told, the pain in his head and back had tempted him to stay in bed some mornings, especially at first.

But Madge would have none of that, appearing beside him with a cup of coffee so strong no man could stay asleep. Once she helped him sit up, he took his first slurp. Then she brought his clothes.

"Time to get dressed. Fresh coffee cake waiting for you downstairs." In her best no-nonsense manner, she buttoned buttons, zipped zippers and tied shoes, as she had for their three daughters years ago.

Down the stairs and into the kitchen she guided him, no matter how his body protested. There, he sank into a wooden chair at the head of the table, anticipating his reward.

Just a hint of almond in the coffee cake dough, that was her secret. Since he'd stepped off the bus, Madge came forth with information never before divulged, at least not that he recalled.

One day, she said, she'd reached for the vanilla bottle, but poured from the almond one instead. The results surprised her.

Details of her tale stuck in Bill's brain like bookmarks. The long and short of it? Her coffee cake made his mouth water, and the Watkins salesman boasted a standing order every time he knocked on the front door.

"Who'd have thought I could improve on Grandma's old recipe? Just like you coming home, don't you know? Things might be a little different, but you'll always be my Bill. *Different* doesn't necessarily mean bad."

So that's how it had gone—because she declared things so, that's the way they had been. Now, though, instead of her driving him down here each morning in their worn Studebaker, he dressed himself and arrived long before she did.

In this domain, he felt at home. No second-guessing the rules, and the process of setting the press came back right away. Dad might have been right here beside him, nodding at his every move.

The full thermos responded to a twist, and the coffee cup Bill had used for several weeks filled quickly. Another good point about Madge—she left this room entirely to him.

If his stacks of books and papers bothered her, she never said a word. Piles filled nearly every available inch, all laced in printer's ink.

Ahh . . . coffee. The aroma energized him, and his wartime duty only rendered its bitter taste more desirable. True, the government rationed it, but to celebrate his homecoming, the town grocer had vowed never to let the McQuestion household run out.

Word spread, and people donated some of their own ration coupons for the cause. Nice to know folks cared.

The chair remonstrated when Bill leaned back a little. This old history book had so much to offer. Back in the 1800s, someone took time to record Iowa militia units returning from the Mexican War during the early days of settling this state.

They informed the naming of several counties and towns—Buena Vista, Cerro Gordo, Palo Alto, Alta Vista. These examples made sense, but nowadays, who realized they named others for their commanders in the war?

Altogether, fifteen counties out of ninety-nine—a little over fifteen percent—had some connection. Fremont, Butler, Scott, Taylor, Clay, Guthrie, Hardin, Mills, Page, Ringgold, and Worth. Iowa also benefited from over fourteen million acres of land grants to veterans, even though an all-Iowa regiment had never materialized.

War's ways had not changed. Some facts became obvious to the public, others remained obscure.

Imbibing his coffee like nectar, Bill stretched his stiff shoulders and read on. What a luxury—time to read and plenty of books.

Captain Edwin Guthrie of Fort Madison and Burlington's Major Frederick Mills had raised an independent company of 100 men, "Company K," Fifteenth United States Infantry. Under General Winfield Scott, they helped capture Veracruz, fought in the Battle of Churubusco, and occupied Mexico City.

Memories accompanied them home, and words. Yes, this was the way of war.

A key turned in the front door lock. That would be Madge opening up for the new day. She insisted on locking the office at night, though they never bothered with the alley door.

A single grimy window revealed sunlight struggling with an early morning haze. Soon, people would venture onto Main Street. Who knew what March first, 1944 held in store?

Sunday, March 26, 1944

Old Otto's prelude dragged on with the foot pedals stuck. Madge kept a cardboard Jensen's Hardware fan fluttering near her face like a moth, but it did little to ease the heat.

Hot air billowed from the massive iron floor grate at the front of the sanctuary. Didn't the furnace stoker know how many women in the congregation were going through "the pause?"

Another wrong note. Madge jiggled her Sunday shoe from the

toes of her right foot. "Gotta get that organ fixed. Maybe this new pastor can make some changes around here."

A sideways glance at Bill, off in some other world, stirred an uneasy sensation in the pit of her stomach. These past few weeks, he'd been getting better. Why did he have to take a downturn today?

Blast this miserable war!

A trail of perspiration traced her temple. Maybe the new pastor would mercifully shorten his sermon. *Blessed are the merciful, for they shall obtain mercy.* He was mighty for sure going to need that quality here.

Recalling one of the reported fights among the church founders brought a grin in spite of everything. Bill would remember the specifics—at one time, anyway. Seemed one faction believed in predestination down to the bone, while the other leaned just as strongly toward free will.

Originally, Church Street United Brethren stood a mile north of town, surrounded by farms. One Sunday morning a faithful member dropped his wagon hitch a few inches over the property line onto the adjoining land.

Of the opposite theological opinion, that property owner promptly sawed off the wooden wagon tongue. Imagining the ensuing brouhaha tickled Madge's funny bone. How could folks get so cantankerous?

In the aisle near Bill, Percival Wellsby stumbled, and Madge turned to see Agnes bending over her calf. Her moan carried above the music.

"You've snagged my hose, Percival! Now I've got a run."

Her husband's hiss carried like dust mites. "...not drivin' ya home . . . almost out of gas ration tickets."

Madge considered volunteering, but the cranky organ wheezed into silence. The choir hunched like an agitated gaggle of geese.

Old Otto Depperschmidt struck a new chord and *Great is Thy Faithfulness* cascaded over sedate pews arranged in perfect rows on spanking-clean oaken floorboards. Meanwhile, Agnes and Percival found their seats.

These floors sparkled because Madge and Agnes scrubbed them raw on Thursday and buffed them to a high shine yesterday. That new Procter and Gamble dust mop certainly did the trick.

Coupled with the hymn's theme that one thing would never change, the memory eased Madge's mind. She'd purchased that mop without seeking repayment from the board—her sacrifice for Lent.

The idea occurred to her in the hardware store. Mama always required her brood to forego some specific joy during the six weeks before Easter, to better appreciate the Passion.

A debatable outcome, but some habits die hard. On Thursday afternoon as Madge eyed the brooms and mops, inspiration struck. Instead of buying a new Easter bonnet, she'd opt for a decent mop. The tag revealed about the same price, so she plunged ahead, and sacrifice made, hurried to the church basement.

The suffering, almost too transitory to count, would have failed to satisfy Mama. Better to spread out the agony over six weeks, the reason so many folks gave up chocolate. Increased pain does more for the soul, don't you know?

Good point, but Madge gave less than two hoots for Easter bonnets. When the Scriptures mentioned women covering their heads, they certainly didn't specify outlandish *frou-frou*.

Case in point, the display topping Vera Walters' tight Victory Roll. When Bill first spotted it, he clutched Madge's arm, and she patted his hand.

"Just ignore it."

"Hmm."

But temptation wooed her more than once. Surely she wouldn't be the only one staring.

Steeling herself, Madge returned her attention to the hand-hewn oak floorboards, sturdy wood symbolizing eternal faithfulness. This foundation enhanced the carved altar, created through painstaking pioneer labor.

Wasn't it Keats who wrote, "A thing of beauty is a joy forever?"

Good to recall those settlers chopping trees, taking them to the sawmill, and kneeling to piece the finished lumber together. Did they realize the overall beauty they created?

Morning by morning, new mercies I see

In tandem with folks around her, Madge belted out the chorus with gusto. Another thing Mama used to say: "If you're going to attend church, do it with all your heart."

All I have needed, Thy hand hath provided

The final notes of the chorus evidenced dogged determination. Otto invariably found a right key here and there. Ah, well. Some things simply must be endured.

As the organ wheezed into blessed silence, Harry Walters waddled to the podium and flung his arms wide. His jowls trembled. Someone had to preside over the council, the constitution declared, and he ended up in this position more often than not.

This odd assortment of parishioners required a leader. What a mixture of backgrounds and family names—Stuempfle, Walters, Blanchette, Kowalski, Widdowson, Machacek, Wohlforth, Hansen, and Culver.

Such a diverse group, one might expect trouble now and then. A few blocks down, the Norwegian Lutheran congregation had an easier time. Still, steam rose from church council meetings now and then.

Even those stoic Scandinavoian souls had their limits, though unimpeachable family circles guarded aberrations like prisoners of war. Still, news seeped out through inter-marriages with non-members, and once in a great while, their pastor's wife shared a confidence in the *Chronicle* office.

The poor woman's forehead creased as she grappled for a bit of friendly support. Upon hearing Madge's vow not to breathe a word, Mrs. Larson squeezed her hand.

"Thank you for listening. It's not easy, you know."

"Being married to a pastor? Oh, I have no doubt."

But in general, those Norskies stuck together. So how did it happen that this congregation took in everyone from everywhere? A question to research someday.

This morning, a greater inquiry presented itself. What could the district office be thinking, sending someone named Zevenbergen to fill the pulpit? The name sounded way too foreign, some whispered. Way too German, they meant, not that this community lacked German roots already.

"Don't those high n' mighty office folks know we're at war with 'em? And for the second time, too yet."

In spite of naysayers, Madge cherished private hopes for this new pastor and went so far as to look up his name at the library. Discovering it meant *Seven Hills* in the North Brabant area of Holland provided ammunition.

Aha—perhaps not German after all! She made a point of spreading the news.

But this fellow's first name was another thing—Aivars. She almost wished she hadn't read his appointment letter, even though someone left it in plain sight in the church office. She'd just have to ask him what it meant.

In the meantime, she kept reminding folks they were lucky to find a preacher at all. So many had joined the forces as chaplains and were slogging through South Pacific jungles, fighting in Europe, or had gone down with their ships.

No one missed the USS Dorchester sinking in early February of '43, with those four "immortal chaplains" relinquishing their life jackets for sailors.

One of them, Clark Polling, a Reformed minister and son of a Great War chaplain, had been told by his father that chaplains had the highest death rate in the armed forces. Clark wrote home that he didn't pray to live, only to be adequate. He left behind a little son and an expectant wife in Michigan.

Madge's article in the *Chronicle* included Clark's words. From then on, she repeated one phrase daily—*help me be adequate*. With Bill, the sentiment applied as much today as ever.

Front and center, Harry waxed eloquent. Even though she understood the reason for his volume—a childhood bout of scarlet fever—the drone of his voice grated on Madge's nerves.

"We have been preacher-less for twenty-seven months, two weeks and sixteen days to be exact. Blah, blah, blah . . ."

Harry, the banker—all about numbers. Still, his figures caught Madge up short. Had it really been that long? Some quick calculations gave confirmation.

Some elderly ministers did fill in once or twice a month. Harry and Vera always hosted them, which spurred Vera's take-charge attitude.

Recently she'd become persnickety about small matters such as the dishtowels in the kitchen drawers. With such earth-shattering events taking place in the war, who cared? Someone ought to shake some sense into that woman.

Aware of Bill still gazing at nothing, Madge casually took in other members. A few women had splurged on Easter hats early—nothing wrong with brightening things up a bit.

Her reporter's instinct awakened, so she snuck out her notebook. Agnes wore last year's simple white straw with a modest brim. Mira, quiet and gentle, donned a grey velvet number that almost matched her suit.

In a sunny spot hand-picked to show off her good taste, Vera squared her bony shoulders. Perched atop her blue-tinted victory roll, her bonnet left little to the imagination.

Similar to what folks set on their dining tables lately, heaven knew why. Bright red faux tulips with daffodils and fake green leaves encircling a white trellis-like contraption. A blue songbird announced that Vera surely bought the hat out-of-town.

Before she lost her composure, Madge looked away—she'd known better than to succumb in the first place. But as Harry went on and on, the hat pulled her back.

Oh, my. As if one bird weren't enough, another small brownish-red warbler perched on the brim. Below it hung a wispy white veil. A tiny triangular opening had caught on the tip of Vera's sharp nose.

If she hadn't been as starchy as the cuffed white sleeves of her blouse, it mightn't have been so bad. Hadn't wartime restrictions come out against excess fabric? Every week, another constraint crossed Madge's desk.

"Now, let me introduce . . ." Harry ushered the new pastor forward. In the process, an Easter lily on a stand near the pulpit got in the way. Vera started up as if to save the day, and her purse knocked old Sam Shoemaker in the head.

Still, Bill sat like a stone. Madge pinched the inside of her elbow as two other members flung themselves in the general direction of the plant, toppling leeward. Still, Bill sat like a stone.

And then, a miracle. Later, people swore Aivars Zevenbergen's arm grew a foot as he caught the lily and set it on the stand. A few pews down, the mother of the high school's wide receiver, now gone off to fight, surely recalled her boy saving the homecoming game last fall.

As the plant settled down, a unanimous gasp swept the crowd. Madge scribbled furiously. Later, folks would lower their voices as they described this young preacher's crystal blue eyes, pure as the bubbling spring out on Harm Miller's back forty.

As time passed, Madge's astute reporting would enhance their recollections. Providing Bill's mental stupor disappeared soon, that is—these spells rarely lasted more than a few hours. But when she smoothed his hand, he barely noticed.

Last week, he said something about training an apprentice, but the subject died a quick death when they considered possible candidates. Besides, what would he do without the paper?

When the service ended, everyone rushed to greet the hero, but Madge made a beeline for Vera. An inner warning light blinked, but she ignored it.

"Vera, I couldn't help but notice your, er . . . interesting Easter bonnet. Wherever did you find it?"

Vera caressed the blue-feathered bird with her long fingers. "You like it?"

"I certainly have never seen anything quite like it."

A satisfied look softened Vera's features. She leaned forward. "A secret admirer, or so the card said."

"Really? You don't know who sent it?"

"Not at all. Quite the surprise."

"You have no idea who?"

A shadow replaced Vera's smug smile. " Harry thinks I bought it in Albert Lea. She grasped Madge's wrist. "Promise me you won't tell him?"

"No, but . . ."

"Please. I'll explain later." Vera's voice trembled

"Sure."

Was that a flicker of genuine fear in Vera's eyes? Absurd—Harry, now meandering their way, could be a buffoon but would never hurt anyone.

"Harry, I'll be with you in a few minutes." Vera drew in her breath.

"We're having Reverend Zevenbergen for dinner today, and tomorrow, my cousin from La Crosse is comng."

"You have a cousin there?"

"Indeed." Vera's smugness reclaimed her sharp features.

Things had returned to normal—this was the woman Madge had known and disliked for so long. Vera set out, stopping at a cluster of chatting women.

Secret admirer, phooey!

Chapter Two

The sun slid a bleary eye over the horizon, blinked, and returned to sleep. From the porch swing, the initial flash of dawn intrigued Bill.

Funny how war turned things around. Recovered from the Great War's effects, he could sleep through anything, while Madge once stirred at the slightest sound. But now, getting to sleep proved tough, staying there impossible.

As often happened, December seventh came to mind. He and Madge had sat knees to the Philco radio that afternoon in '41 as the announcer noted an attack in Hawaii.

A persistent gnawing in Bill's gut declared that his National Guard unit would deploy, and the monthly meeting revealed its accuracy.

"Be ready for the call," his commander instructed. "We'll most likely be sent with the 134th out of Minnesota—the Red Bulls. No idea where or when. But I'd bet last year's pay our summons will come soon."

Word arrived in a telegram delivered to the newspaper office one February day. Bill hesitated after reading it. No telling how much this would change their lives—his, Madge's and Gloria's, not to mention their two older daughters and so many other families.

He'd stepped out onto the sidewalk then. Sure enough, the clanging at the Guard installation beyond the Minnesota border drifted south to Caroline over oak groves rising from snow-covered pastures.

From that moment on, a fresh tightness niggled his chest. This tension had dogged him through the Great War, but he had come so far from the obsessive watchfulness that accompanied him home.

He'd finally ceased imagining the furnace blowing up in the night, even though he'd done everything possible to ensure his family's safety. And he'd been able to stop rubbing the skin off his left thumb as other catastrophic thoughts haunted him like fireflies in July.

His father welcomed him into the newspaper business, giving a weekly focus to time's passage. Gathering stories about this little burg, selling ads and setting the type created a reliable cycle. If they ever invented another way to put out a paper, he'd still follow this process, stable week after week after week.

The sun appeared again with a show of strength, so Bill moved to the base of the front porch steps. Solid beneath his feet, these stairs. Like Madge, always here, sensible and positive.

His eyes teared at the way she handled everything while he'd been gone. What a strong woman—she made do with whatever life handed her.

Up on the wide dormer above the porch, double windows looked out over the street. Their bedroom curtains blew inward a bit. No sign of a light yet, because his wild dreams had kept Madge awake in the night.

No need to hurry this morning. They'd been up late getting the paper out, and he'd told her he would open today. Hopefully, she could sleep in a little.

Drat his unpredictable nightmares!

Still, she never complained. Her nature remained unchanged when he returned from North Africa half the man he'd been. He'd been sent to a hospital in the South, and knew the Army surgeon expected him to die after they sent him home.

Expecting the worst, he'd wanted to spend whatever time he had left here. With her.

Of course, she set about caring for him without batting an eye. Simply put, she refused to accept anything other than his recovery. Stubborn, her mother always called her.

Presently, a morning breeze brought the waking-up sounds of this little town. A door opened somewhere, a dog barked down the street, the paper boy pedaled by on his bicycle, followed by the *thump* of the *Des Moines Register* against the curb.

The *Waterloo Courier* or *The Globe Gazette* out of Mason City landed on other porches. Bill would buy all of them if he could—nothing like reading the news first thing in the morning.

These everyday events, simplistic on the surface, marked the rhythms of serenity that escaped him during his unit's perilous voyage across the Atlantic and the long months of battling their way across North Africa.

Ah, he'd rather be here than anywhere else in the entire world.

No doubt about it, without Madge's constant watchfulness, he might be long gone. So much he'd have missed—their youngest daughter's graduation this spring, for one thing. Gloria was all smiles about that, and the lilt in her voice cheered him no end.

Damp but bracing late March air filled his lungs. The acrid scent of wood smoke and a tantalizing aroma of brewing coffee tickled his senses.

Florence Hampton was up and about, making coffee in spite of her terrible rheumatism. As twisted as the pear branches in the tree out by the alley, her fingers still fashioned succulent piecrusts filled with apples or raspberries and peaches.

That *clink clink* would be the neighbor on the other side loading up his furnace.

How many pies had Florence brought over since he returned? "Just to remind you how glad we are to have you back, Bill," she'd say with her little-girl-in-mischief grin.

He ran out of words to thank her for those mouth-watering temptations. She waved off his gratitude, saying she wished she could do the same for all of *our boys over there.*

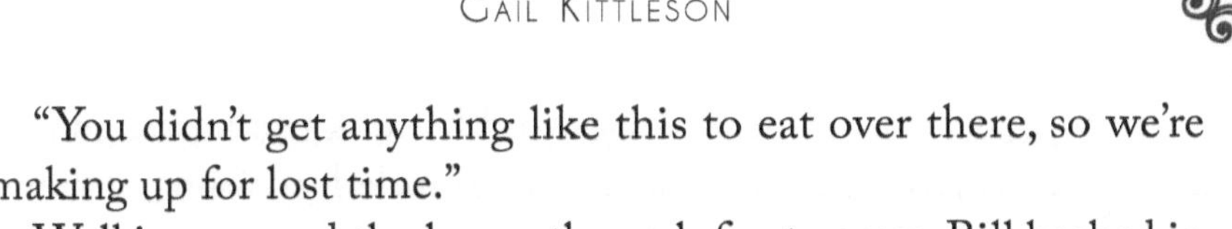

"You didn't get anything like this to eat over there, so we're making up for lost time."

Walking around the house through frosty grass, Bill basked in the early sunlight dappling their ancient pear tree. Stippled with some sort of disease, the poor thing hung on. Should've cut it down years ago, but Madge still held out hope. Always hope.

That was her, never giving up. He sank against the trunk for a few minutes, and her face passed before him. Still so soft and lovely after all these years, and every move she made showed spirit.

The ground might be a little damp, but who cared? He'd spent so much time with a crust over his skin in North Africa that nothing seemed dirty now. What wouldn't he have given for one minute under a shade tree back then?

He closed his eyes and allowed a few memories to enter—at times like this, they arrived mostly through his senses. The putridity of the latrine, always with his unit, except when they went without and everyone did their business helter-skelter.

The desert dryness against his face and hands—Brits wore shorts during the worst heat, but what could ward off the relentless blowing sand? Once, on a mission from one officer's tent to another, not far at all, he'd gotten disoriented.

Sort of like walking through hardscrabble country on a moonless night with a blindfold securely in place. Pelting his skin, the grit slipped between his lips, between his teeth. He'd thought his mouth would never be clean again.

During that storm, he dropped in place, covered his head the best he could, and waited. Images of home came to him then. The girls. His parents. But most of all—and so real he could have touched her—Madge.

For her sake, he would obliterate the horrors these long nights still dredged up. Maybe time would heal, or so they said. For now, he could only carry on—make himself as useful as possible.

At least he could work. So many couldn't. At least he'd come home. So many didn't, or wouldn't.

A cardinal called from the lilacs, and he took in the resonance. Lovely. Everything here looked and sounded positively lovely. When the bird fell silent, he slid back up the pear trunk and continued toward the lot's far corner.

Kicking at a fence post shredded off some weathered wood. Time eventually rendered objects like this useless. Sometimes his body felt that way, but Doc Engel insisted that time would make things right again.

Until then, he'd give life his best shot—that was all he could do, especially when so many from his unit still faced battles as difficult as the one that took him out. Their ongoing struggle in Europe invaded his consciousness mostly by night, but always was with him to some degree.

He would give anything to be whole again, to be fighting beside them. To watch their backs as they had watched his.

Did his old wood saw still hang in the shed? Dad's actually, probably even Grandpa's. Maye he'd pull out that post and cut it for campfires this summer.

But if he started to work, Madge would awaken. She would glance out the window, and seeing him, get her hopes up that the old Bill was indeed coming back.

He sure hoped she was right.

After the Palm Sunday service, planning Pastor Zevenbergen's welcome potluck couldn't have caused more of a stir within the Ladies Aid. Vera Walters rose to new heights, positioning herself like a sentinel at the front door to announce the impromptu meeting.

As the women gathered in the front pews, she organized them into shifts, writing down each name with painstaking care. Of course, they would have preferred to come and go as they pleased, like they always did. But Vera's sharp gray eyes brooked no arguments.

Agnes, the closest thing to a best friend Madge could claim, ran her fingers through her unruly brown curls. A tired sigh escaped as she and Madge left the meeting.

"Why do we put up with this? It gripes me the way Vera bosses us, always dreaming up organizational schemes. I determine not to let her bother me, but nothing seems to cure my peevish attitude."

"I know what you mean. That's just human nature, Agnes. We all bristle at people lording it over us. I can smell that take-charge type a mile away, and speaking of smelling, Vera's perfume makes me want to gag. Don't the war restrictions include that?"

No one lurked within hearing distance, but she still lowered her voice as she and Agnes started out the side door. "Now that Bill's . . . changed, I realize I'm different, too."

Agnes wrinkled her brow. Through everything, she'd always been ready to listen.

"He was never bossy or demanding before the war, but I let him think for me, especially at the office. Then after his dad passed, everything was up to me. Thanks to Bill's old friend from Greene, I somehow got the paper out, and now . . . It's just that—oh, I can't even explain it."

Agnes glanced toward Percival, already drumming his fingers on the dusty hood of the ramshackle Plymouth they'd inherited from his uncle. "That was an awful time, wasn't it?"

In the ensuing silence, she picked at her cuticle. "Sometimes I feel like a pitchfork out in the hay mow, here only to do Percival's bidding." Her tone took on a definite snap, and her violet eyes narrowed.

"Bill's come home so . . . well, you know. But I've grown less patient with being bossed around, especially by the likes of Vera. I can't tell you how many times I've had to zip my lips."

"It's disgusting to go to the one place you expect to find peace and have someone like her lance a barb at you." Agnes touched Madge's shoulder. "But I really have nothing to complain about. Our nephew Jimmy's over there in that horrendous fight through Italy, and my poor sis is beside herself."

Percival performed the loudest throat-clearing Madge had ever heard.

"Bill and I pray for Jimmy every night."

"Thank you—that means a lot." Another throat clearing, louder than the last. "Oh, he's so blasted impatient." Agnes sniffed. "I'd best get going before he blows a gasket."

"'Bye. See you Wednesday at prayer meeting. What are you bringing for afterward?" Without waiting for an answer, Madge changed direction. "I might just switch to your work group for the welcome dinner. Vera will have a fit, but it won't be the first time, nor the last. Some risks are worth taking."

"You're so strong. I guess when your husband comes home like …" Agnes turned to where Bill occupied a bench near the church. "I remember the tears we shed when he left, and when you heard he'd been wounded. Now, we're still together."

"Yes, I give thanks for that every single day."

Agnes hurried toward the auto. Percival muttered and shook his head as she neared, instigating a slow burn in Madge's chest. His insolence made her want to scream.

Then she shook herself. "I'm as riled up as an expectant horse. Always thought age would make me more tolerant, but I get worse by the day."

"Mom, wait for me!"

Late afternoon shadows crisscrossed the schoolyard's front lawn as the most beautiful senior girl headed Madge's way. A golden wave bounced loose from the carefully pinned victory roll Gloria created this morning, and her chocolate-brown eyes blazed.

"Some of us have decided to put on a little play for the pastor's welcome potluck. And guess what?"

"A play?" Madge tried to think of something fitting, but Gloria cut her off.

"I'm so excited! We're doing some scenes from *Arsenic and Old Lace,* and I'm going to play Mrs. Brewster."

"Isn't that about some crazy old aunts and murder?"

"Yes, but it's a comedy. We all agreed everyone could stand a little laughter these days. We're meeting tonight to practice, and guess who plays my husband?"

The sun played hopscotch on Gloria's hair. Madge might have ventured a couple of names but held her peace.

"That dreamy Vern Barker."

"Sounds like a lot of fun, dear. I'm sure Pastor Zevenbergen will enjoy it."

"Hmm? Oh yeah. Hurry up, my petite little mom. Gotta figure out my costumes. Do we have anything up in the attic? What were you doing here today?"

"Just some regular Wednesday newspaper business. April's a busy month—Easter the ninth, and then so many school activities. I had to get the details straight."

Keeping up with her lithe daughter offered a challenge. Those long legs came from Bill's side—sure made reaching the highest kitchen shelf easier. Madge's swirling thoughts flew as fast as Gloria's feet.

The years had gone by far too fast, except during Bill's deployment. Lillian, their middle daughter, had left for munitions work on the west coast in '42, shortly after Bill. Those final months before he returned, time seemed to stand still.

At least Gloria still had friends coming over, and basketball games or homework to do in the evenings. Her generally cheerful nature made such a big difference—she never let circumstances get in the way of enjoying life.

She took the wartime transitions with steady calm, another marvelous quality straight from her father. Sometimes when Bill had been gone, Madge tiptoed into Gloria's room in the middle of the night and always found her deep in slumber.

What a gift, being able to fall asleep like that!

Wise for her age and always courteous, Gloria paused at Mrs. Lawmaster's white picket fence to say hello. Sometimes this youngest daughter seemed even older in her thinking than Lillian. Maybe that came from being the youngest—and from the war.

Their oldest, Judith, lived in Michigan, where her Gerald worked in the Navy shipyards. Busy having babies, she'd not been back to Caroline for years, and gas rationing made visiting impossible these days. During Bill's absence, Madge kept thinking they'd take the train up there when he came home.

But how would he react to a long trip like that? He'd fallen into a comfortable rhythm in the press room each day, and being there seemed good for him. Often in the mornings, she found him reading some history book.

His never-ending curiosity about how places were settled, how pioneers managed the cold weather, and why certain towns grew while others languished held him in good stead. Gave him something to think about besides the war.

As Gloria engaged Mrs. Lawmaster about her flowers, Madge's mind continued to wander. Judith had produced three grandbabies already—how could that be? And they hadn't laid eyes on any of them yet.

About a year ago, Lillian sent word from the California coast that she'd met the man of her dreams, a sailor named Marcus. Her announcement stayed in Madge's mind, word-for-word like a poem from childhood.

His family emigrated from Italy when he was little. Believe me, he loves America as much as we do, even though his family lost their livelihood with all the hatred shown to Italians.

No surprise when Lillian and Marcus married last November. His ancestry didn't bother Madge at all, except she wished she could've met him and his parents.

After the war, they would settle down out West, no doubt. *Bing, bing, bing*—that's the way it happened, but breaking the news to Bill by mail had been tough. He had no favorites and

loved Gloria to death, but something special always bonded him with Lillian.

Surely, a baby would soon arrive in California, but getting there posed an even bigger challenge than a trip to Michigan. A few years back, they'd never even have thought of going so far away, and never dreamed their daughters would, either.

Anyway, it seemed like Gloria represented the one chance she and Bill had to know any of their grandchildren. She never had exhibited an overriding desire to teach or be a secretary. When the ads came out for the Army Nurse Corps, some of her friends went wild, and two of them were following through.

Gloria toyed around with the idea, but without much conviction. Fortunately, she liked helping around the house and office. Maybe she'd stay right here and eventually take over the *Chronicle*.

The way the world had changed, why not stick close to home, marry young and start a family? Home and family had become even greater treasures than before, if that were possible.

Gloria waved good-bye to Mrs. Lawmaster and so did Madge—poor lady, awaiting word from her two grandsons in the Pacific. Bill reported to her every time he heard any new tidbit about those taken captive on the Philippine island of Bataan.

Near home, Gloria ran ahead and skipped up the front steps like a deer. The front door slammed behind her, a reminder of one slight imperfection—impulsiveness. Bill pointed out her ability to make decisions without getting caught up in all of the pros and cons. He called Gloria's bubbly nature *spontaneous*.

That word brought to mind their new pastor's miraculous catch last Sunday. Maybe a young man like him would appreciate a little spontaneity.

With such a serious role to play, he surely needed some fun in his life. He seemed so energetic and healthy—why hadn't he been drafted into the armed forces? She'd heard others ask this question, but so far, no one knew.

Anyway, wouldn't someone who dealt with such dire issues in

his work seek a wife with some spark? Gloria might be setting her sights on that Barker boy, but he'd be off to the war in the blink of an eye.

On the other hand, this new pastor, well-educated and already into his career, would make a far better match. True, he must be in his mid-twenties at least, but so what? Age meant less and less these days.

On the first step, an unbidden thought struck. Would Gloria make a good pastor's wife? She certainly wasn't anything like the bedraggled spouse of their former pastor, with six children under ten, a huge garden, and a household to manage.

Not to mention a rather grumpy husband, from what Madge could see. No wonder his wife always looked frazzled, as if she would rather be somewhere else.

But what about Gloria? Always a good student, her loyalty ran deep. Other girls—and guys—seemed drawn to her. She kept busy with school activities and friendly outings.

She'd known deprivation, too, with Bill gone for so long and Judith and Lillian moving away. Through it all, she'd kept a positive attitude—such a go-getter, as pastor's wives surely must be.

Submissive? Hmm . . . maybe not so much. Gloria knew her own mind and had no qualms about taking necessary action. How often had Madge dragged home from the *Chronicle* late in the afternoon to find Gloria with her homework done and dinner already made?

With a husband out meeting people's needs day and night, self-sufficiency would be a laudable characteristic, wouldn't it? Pros and cons rose and fell as Madge crossed the porch.

So much was changing. Maybe keeping some things the same was good, like the path she'd just taken across their front yard. Some folks had put in concrete sidewalks out front, but she'd hate to give up the well-worn trail they'd used for decades.

Under the generous shade of two tall pines Bill planted years ago, flat limestone slabs led to the house. Hand on the door knob, Madge envisioned the girls when they were little, skipping from stone to stone.

Through the screen door, Gloria's chuckle drifted like springtime freshness. She would already have run into the living room to hug Bill, in his usual position in his armchair.

Now, she would be checking on the roast and setting the table, dependable as daylight after a storm. Hadn't her teachers always echoed the same sentiment? As Madge eased into the front hallway, a singular truth alighted just below her collarbone.

The new pastor and Gloria had no idea they were perfect for each other. Yet. They only needed a little time to get acquainted, and possibly a slight motherly push in the right direction.

Chapter Three

Aivars Zevenbergen filled a wooden table with earmarked books and research notes. Despite an annoying squeak in his desk chair, this quiet back corner behind the sanctuary provided all he needed.

After days of hoping that annoying squeak would magically disappear, he determined to locate the source. Every time he shifted his weight, *whamo*. Whenever he sat down or moved, the sound reminded him he really wasn't in charge.

Last week in Jensen's Hardware, he bought an oilcan and squirted the contents on the hinges to no avail. He tried adjusting the seat with a wrench. Now, the heavy chair sprawled upside-down on his study floor.

"I wonder if this bothered the last pastor, too? Oh well, can't expect everything to be perfect. I have it so much easier than Alex and Martin, over there in the fight."

Thinking of these seminary buddies serving in Europe, Aivars banged on the central rod under the seat. Maybe something would jiggle loose.

After flipping over the chair, he turned his attention to a box he'd shoved out of the way. The credentials his mother had framed stared up at him—he 'd planned to leave them in a drawer back home with his high school mementoes. But his father intervened.

Why hang this plaque—Bachelor's Degree in history? So much had happened since college, and anyhow, how did it qualify him for this job?

True, the ordination certificate testified to such hard work over the past three years—intense study for exams, memorizing, writing and practice preaching. But at times he still felt inadequate.

Dad's advice rang in his head. "Certain members may want to see evidence of your qualifications. Better take these along."

Here in his first official role, reciting Greek or Hebrew passages seemed unimpressive. The question of the hour had become, "How do I channel my knowledge into helping real-live hurting folks?"

Shoved behind the boxes, a framed canvas showed Peter sinking in deep waters and being rescued by the Master of stormy seas. Overhead, storm clouds threatened, and in a small boat, the other disciples rowed like crazy to keep from capsizing.

Ah, Peter. Such an impulsive, emotional fellow.

Grandpa Zevenbergen gave him this painting when he entered seminary. What a fitting present it had made back then, when fears and doubts about becoming a pastor skewed his perspective. Even now, Peter's predicament never failed to lift the spirits.

Grandpa had taught college Latin and Greek, but always expressed a bent for things theological. Discussions with him had led to the momentous decision about seminary.

Along the way, each hurdle had been conquered, and this painting showed exactly what Aivars needed to do now—reach out to people in need. The world went on its way despite people's troubles, but he could stop. He could stand with them through whatever they faced.

They might be threatened by stormy seas, but so was Peter. He may have acted rashly at times, but his quick actions also exhibited courage, so needed in this time of war.

From a single window set high on the south wall, very little of the town of Caroline met the eye, but Aivars had already tramped the streets day and night to glean the lay of the land. Hopefully he would soon know more people and prove an asset to the troops when they returned.

Another window adjacent to his desk let in late afternoon light and gave a good view of the church sign. Plain and wooden,

probably cobbled together by some retired member. Nothing nota-
ble about the name, simple and to the point—Church Street.

But location mattered. Wherever you landed in life, you needed
to be *all there*.

To his right, a beveled oak door led out to the hallway and altar
area. The polished furnishings, homemade and down-to-earth,
reminded him of Caroline's regular folks, for whom the war had
made life anything but easy.

On his left, another door opened to a landing with a stairway
leading to the basement. Dank and dark, the limestone-walled
cellar housed a kitchen and several rooms for Sunday school classes.

He'd been down there many times to mull over possibilities for
the youth group. What might he do to equip these high schoolers for
the future, especially when some of them would soon be off to war?

A short wall opposite his desk boasted some church photographs,
a map of Caroline, and a list of current members serving overseas.
One name already had a gold star—even this isolated farm town
had made the ultimate sacrifice.

Blue stars marked those in the fight right now, seven of them so
far. He'd most likely met some of their parents without realizing
it. This musing sent a shudder through him.

"If only I could've joined up."

Tens of thousands struggled against the Axis powers in Europe,
and tens of thousands more fought the Japanese in the Pacific.
With no end in sight, he ought to be *over there* too.

Army doctors—drat them! Recalling his induction physical and
that cold stethoscope on his chest galled Aivars even now. When
the first doctor called in another for a second opinion, he'd figured
there must be some mistake.

But then they both left the room for a few minutes. Only one
returned to announce his doom.

Such a pivotal experience, but at the time, he almost felt removed,
as though watching the scene from somewhere above. This couldn't
really be happening, could it?

Days passed before he fully absorbed the truth. Because of some obscure condition in his heart, the U.S. Army had bluntly refused him. Why hadn't this shown up in the physical he took before seminary?

What a lousy shock. He cheered on his buddies as they prepared to serve, but with a sad heart. Then one day he noticed Peter in the water and decided to quit wasting time in regret. If he couldn't be there doing his part, he would do his best here on the home front.

With another glance at Peter, he wandered out into the sanctuary, a testimony to his parishioners' pride. They entered this place each Sunday with their soldiers' welfare heavy on their hearts. What might he do to encourage them?

Between the altar and the first pew, an idea occurred. Why not bring photographs of every G.I. in here? The slanted center aisle led to the front door, so perhaps he could post the photographs right at the threshold.

This would require a visit to each family asking for photos, for starters. He set the names front and center on his desk, where they riveted his attention. No use trying to concentrate on the week's lessons now—far more important to pray for these young fellows.

Twenty minutes later, Aivars decided to hang the Shepherd painting and hurried down to the furnace room. Dingy grease and dust, tools and old paint cans welcomed him—reminded him of Grandfather's workshop. He grabbed a hammer and stuck some nails in his pocket.

Back upstairs, dismal old reproductions lined the hallway. Dark greens, browns and grays—probably had been hanging here forever. Hopefully nobody's grandmother donated them and specified where they should hang, because Peter belonged right here.

No question about it—people passed through this hallway often. Knowing even the slightest change by a new pastor could be misinterpreted, Aivars plunged ahead. How could such a small difference cause a problem?

He took down the other frames and shoved them way back in

the closet, along with most of his certificates. No need to tout his training—people would either see his worth or not.

One last look at Peter in big trouble brought a chuckle.

"I'm just like you, you know? I'm putting you opposite my door because I plan to leave it open, and every time I look up, you'll remind me why I'm here."

His mind went back to last Sunday's initiation. Despite all the commotion over the plant, one moment stood out in his mid. From behind the pulpit, he couldn't help but notice a gaunt man clinging to an armrest.

Next to the far aisle, five rows back, about in the center. Beside him sat a highly freckled redhead, probably his wife. She seemed engaged in the goings-on, while her husband might have been in some other universe. Looked too old to be a returned soldier, but one never knew.

Later, Vera and Harry Walters offered some details. Bill McQuestion, a Great War veteran, had been called up with the National Guard early on and severely wounded in a battle somewhere in North Africa.

Vera wasn't sure which one, but considering when Bill returned, Aivars guessed the Allied disaster at the Kasserine Pass. Army surgeons sent Bill home to recover—or to die, some thought.

Vera dramatized her description. "Madge held down the fort at the newspaper office the whole time. Can you imagine how hard it must have been to see him step off the train?

"Besides that, we heard he really wouldn't have had to go. But they needed him for training, and he's not the sort to shy away from duty."

"Sounds like a true patriot."

"Yes, but when he came home, he had a terrible color. although he's recovered now. Well, mostly. He'll never be quite the same, I'm certain. That's the way it happens sometimes—body's whole, but the brain's gone. Isn't that so, Harry?"

"Hmm . . ." A safe enough response.

Here in his quiet office, Aivars pondered the names of deployed men. Bill's topped the list—to have been called so early, he must possess special abilities gleaned in the last war. A middle-aged man in his dad's congregation had deployed early, too, to help train raw recruits.

A sudden bustle and women's voices echoed from the stairwell. Aivars shut the closet door and stepped out to see what was going on. Several women of all shapes and sizes stood on the back stairs, a mix of smiles and seriousness. So much lively energy here, and as his mother would say, that could go either way.

"Oh, Reverend, we didn't mean to disturb you." Vera took the lead, and the redhead he'd spotted on Sunday gave him a big grin.

She shifted a towel-covered basket to her left arm to shake his hand and met his gaze, the sparkle in her eyes awash in an emerald sea. The firmness of her handshake quickened his pulse.

Looking people in the eye impressed him, especially in a woman. So many walked around with pinched, worried faces these days. But not Madge—the chestnut highlights in her undeniably red hair only deepened the green in her eyes.

"No bother at all." He released her hand. "What are you ladies up to this fine day?" He gave an exaggerated sniff. "Do I detect a tantalizing aroma?"

Vera tittered. "Why, that's homemade cinnamon rolls, my very own recipe. We're doing some cleaning downstairs, and I thought I might as well bring the refreshments for tonight."

"Ah, I see." She must mean the prayer meeting—he'd never heard of serving food at one. "Well, I'll let you get on with your duties."

They turned as he stepped back into his office. A second later, a sudden noise alerted him—sort of a quiet shriek, if such a thing existed.

"Oh my—somebody's moved the pictures!" That would be Vera.

"Wow—look at this new one. Don't you just love the story of Peter walking on the water? I feel like that's what I'm doing half of the time!"

That would be Madge, Bill McQuestion's wife.

"But . . . but, Aunt Beatrice gave the other ones to the church before she died. Why, I never!"

His heartbeat thrumming, Aivars froze.

"Well, we can put them up somewhere else, can't we? Lots of empty walls. I say we could use a few changes around here."

"That's right, Madge. And the organ needs fixing. Those stuck pedals drive me crazy!"

Someone added another idea and, diverted from the wall hangings, the women descended. Strange—why had they all traipsed up here if they intended to clean?

Another thing—had that been a snort following Vera's comment about her Aunt Beatrice? Aivars could almost visualize Madge rolling her eyes.

His mother had been right. When the letter came with his call to this church, she took him aside. "I'm delighted for you, of course, but keep in mind that church women can be catty."

"Catty? What exactly does that mean?"

The tabby feline that wandered the halls of his boarding house passed before Aivars. One of the other boarders disliked cats, and the tabby made it plain that she *knew*. Almost as if she had a sixth sense.

"Your father has been caught in the crosshairs with no idea what was going on before the women struck. Trust me, the church kitchen produces some mighty good eats, but it can also lead to territorial battles."

"Thanks. I'll watch out."

"Good. But being a man can be a real hindrance. Try to get to know the women one-by-one, and don't make any assumptions during the first year. You're young and good-looking, so they'll be watching your every move, especially if they have marriageable daughters."

"Oh, Mom. The last thing I need right now is a romance."

"Maybe so, but they don't know that."

They'd laughed together then, but his mother knew more than most about women's wiles. Dad had experienced them first hand, and somehow, she helped him through everything with her quiet sense of humor.

Definitely a spark between Madge and Vera—what was that all about? Come to think of it, he'd sensed something amiss when Vera described Madge the other day. Something in her tone hinted at underlying trouble.

Bill and Madge's daughter Gloria was a high school senior, way too young for him. Did Vera and Harry have an eligible daughter, too? He perused the handwritten list of teenagers on his bulletin board. Not that he could see, and surely, Vera would have shown him a photograph by now.

He shook off these thoughts and tried to concentrate on the week's lesson. Knowing the women were on site motivated him, he had to admit.

Chatter drifted from the basement. Impossible to concentrate, so he headed for the vestibule. Here, even those who never went downstairs could see the local troops. It took half an hour to find a bulletin board. Now, he just needed the photos.

The odor of fresh floor wax lent its mellow scent to these beautiful oak floors. Probably someone down in the kitchen was responsible for this. Perhaps he'd catch whoever it was at work someday.

As he returned to his office, a female voice carried from the back stairway, "I'll lock up when I leave."

Where he grew up, Dad never locked the church. You could slip into the sanctuary and cry your heart out day or night. Only heaven knew how many times he'd wandered in there to pray, and how much good it did his soul.

Maybe in a year or so when people realized they needed to look out for everyone in town, not just their own members, he'd bring up the idea.

Chapter Four

*B*eep *beep de beep beepity beep.* "It's time, America! Time for Walter Winchell!" *Da da DA da da Da da ta da ta DA*

Simulated clatter from a teletype machine followed by someone banging on typewriter keys drew Bill's attention to the big screen of Caroline's moving picture theater. Built in 1910, this town treasure exuded the aura of Renaissance Revival architecture.

In a fusion of light and film, Walter Winchell took center screen. Nothing special about his appearance, but sitting before a microphone in his typical Fedora, business suit and tie, he appeared earnest and energetic.

"Good Morning, Mr. and Mrs. United States." *Rat-a-tat-tat-tatta-tat-tat-tat.* In another clip, a battleship crossed the ocean.

Heads turned throughout the theater. Chatter ceased. This must be fresh breaking news!

Back to Mr. Winchell, a well-known journalist who began describing Nazi Germany's downfall. Listening to his staccato beat made Bill feel weary.

"No doubt the Allies will squelch them entirely, as they did in Tunisia, my friends. And oh! What a day that will be!"

Like the tension in this high-ceilinged auditorium, Madge's grip tightened on Bill's arm. A rubber band doubled . . . no, tripled.

Her reasons for coming this evening made sense. "We need to get out more, have a little fun. Gloria saw *Lassie Come Home* with her friends last week and recommends it. That new actress, Elizabeth somebody, is in it."

So they had come, but now, maybe Walter was giving her second thoughts. She dug into the bag of popcorn they shared—a small luxury.

"Wish they wouldn't show the news."

Bill patted her wrist. "I'm all right, hon. There's just no getting away from the war—it's everywhere."

Remembering his youth, when theaters offered no snacks at all, since they were trying to mimic real theaters with lush draperies and carpets, Bill took a handful of popcorn, too.

"Remember how that guy used to sell popcorn out front? What was his name?"

"Mmm. Let me see. During the Depression, wasn't it?" Madge's forehead broke into thought lines.

"Yep. The melted butter convinced us we couldn't go without—just another nickel. Probably netted more than the movie tickets."

"Tony something, I think."

"Yeah. Italian."

"Started with an *a* ..."

Walter Winchell disappeared, and a few minutes later on the big screen, a young actor named Roddy McDowell played a Yorkshire lad forced to sell his beloved Lassie to a rich landowner with holdings in Scotland.

Thus began the saga of a dog filled with undying love for her master. As Lassie sought her way home, Bill soon found his cheeks as wet as Madge's. So many souls hungry for *home* right now.

Faces of men in his unit surfaced. Still fighting after all these years—would they never rest? Two especially, younger than Judith and Lillian, haunted his memory. As young as he'd been in the Great War, but this combat was lasting so much longer.

He dabbed his face and handed Madge his handkerchief. The sound of her sigh made him wish he could turn back the irrevocable passage of Time.

Once, in another world, they had spent evenings at the movies without a care.

"Marjorie Marie McQuestion, this time you've gone too far!"

The voice garnered Madge's full attention. Only her mother dared call her Marjorie, but she had passed years ago. Agnes nearly spilled her coffee down her front.

Like a dragon from its cave, Vera shot through the kitchen doorway. "Too far, I say. You've lost your sense of propriety, and I have had it!"

"What on earth are you talking about?"

Then Madge noticed the eight-page *Caroline Chronicle* clutched in Vera's hand. Yep, last week's edition, with the hardware's spring sale on the back page. Behind Vera, Harry skulked along like an over-sized June bug.

Her face livid, Vera stomped within inches and waved the paper under Madge's nose. "I've suffered in silence until now. You pretended to like my hat, though I knew you didn't, but did you have to make a mockery of me before the whole town?"

"Mockery? I didn't—"

"Oh, yes you did, and you *know* it." Vera stamped her foot like Lillian used to when something didn't go her way.

Madge glanced around. No help from Harry, who fiddled with his fingers. And in the twinkling of an eye, Agnes had vanished into the kitchen's hazy depths.

At the other end of the basement, Bill spoke with the new pastor while she and Agnes set things to rights in the kitchen after an evening meeting. Hopefully they hadn't heard.

"I meant no harm. I just thought a little good-natured humor might brighten things up. We need all the cheer we can get these days, don't you think?"

When Vera clenched her jaw, the chords in her neck bulged against her pale skin even more than normal. Her eyes scathed Madge.

"If I've hurt you, I apologize."

"Humph. We'll see about that." Vera set her lips and pivoted.

Harry grabbed her arm and hissed, "What's gotten into you? I didn't know you was goin' back home for that silly paper. Madge didn't mean no . . ."

He gave Madge a sympathetic look, exactly the wrong thing to do. Jerking her arm away, Vera rounded on him.

"You think it's all a big joke, don't you?" She surveyed the outer room as if suddenly aware of who might be listening. In that moment, tears glistened on her eyelashes.

A sinking feeling struck Madge's midsection. Vera seemed truly wounded. Why couldn't she see that the weekly column poked fun at everyone and everything, that her intentions had been good?

Then that pesky inner voice started in. *You did want to get back at her, though. Be honest.*

Vera made for the stairs, and Madge followed as Harry backed against the kitchen wall. "With all the dreary war news lately, I just wanted to give folks a chance to smile."

But Vera kept climbing. Madge reached out her hand and uttered an unintelligible syllable as Vera flounced the skirt of her tailored shirtdress.

Harry followed. His heavy footsteps finally reached the top of the long stairway, and the side door banged shut.

A tap came on Madge's shoulder. Agnes clucked her tongue. "That woman! I wondered why she left so early."

"Me, too."

"She overreacted, as usual. Your article struck my funny bone and made Percival chuckle, and you can guess how often *that* happens." Agnes handed Madge some coffee, and it burned its way down her throat.

"But did I get too carried away describing her hat?"

"I wouldn't say that." Agene scrunched her brow. "Well, maybe a little, but you poked fun at *all* of our hats. You made me laugh, and I so appreciated it."

She lowered her voice. "You know, I saw a concoction like Vera's in

Albert Lea a few weeks ago when Percival sold a hog over there. He likes me to ride along when he makes those trips, don't you know?"

Agnes guided Madge back into the dining room and wrinkled her nose. "The hat might not have been quite the same, but I nearly fainted at the price tag." Her eyes widened. "Eight dollars, if you can believe it, more than a week's wages."

"Whew! That's outrageous."

Why would anyone go to such expense? The war board's manufacturing restrictions had jacked up prices beyond reason. With yet another fight looming—Bill was convinced the Allies would soon invade France—finding a pair of good nylons had become impossible.

Who could possibly afford splurging on an outlandish Easter bonnet? The whole thing made no sense, but she'd promised Vera not to say anything about her secret admirer. Well, not exactly— not to tell Harry.

Just then a gleam of light from one of the windows reflected off a thick head of hair the color of ripe oats. Arms crossed, Pastor Zevenbergen seemed deeply engaged in conversation with Bill.

A closer look confirmed the unbelievable. Bill actually immersed in dialogue? Would wonders never cease?

"Well, look at that—our new pastor has Bill talking!" Agnes shook her head. "He's quite the fellow, don't you think?"

"Y-yes." Percival called for Agnes and she hurried off. Now Bill was even gesturing with his hands like he used to.

Five minutes later, the unimaginable was still happening. Madge couldn't help herself and crept a few feet closer.

True, Bill trekked to the office each day to work on the newspaper, but lately, he accomplished his tasks like an automaton. Except when Gloria bounced home from school, he showed no emotion and kept his thoughts to himself.

Evening after evening, he sat in his armchair listening to the current war news. Afterwards, he went up to bed. Then came the nightmares. His back seemed to bother him less recently, but what went on in his head was anyone's guess.

"Hello, Mrs. McQuestion." Pastor Zevenbergen spotted her and gestured her over. "I was just telling your husband what kept the army from making the most of my expertise."

"Oh?"

"Yes, I'm sure folks wonder. Uncle Sam called me up in my second year in seminary—fall of '42. I was ready to go, but the Army doc found something wrong with my heart."

"Oh, no! Is it serious?"

"Not life-threatening under normal conditions, but the stress of combat would be too much, they thought. So they classified me 4-F, I finished my studies, and now I'm here."

"B-better a l-live p-pastor than a d-dead ch-chaplain," Bill stuttered with an endearing grin. "D-don't you th-think s-so, M-Maddie-g-girl?" He reached up for her hand, since she stood behind his chair.

Speechless, Madge wrapped her arms around his shoulders and rested her chin on the crest of his head, where the essence of Wildroot hair cream enveloped her. Her tears must be obvious to the pastor, but at least Bill couldn't see them.

"Oh Billy-boy, do you know how long it's been since you called me that?"

He reached for one of her hands and pulled her around. After all he'd been through, his strength always surprised her. She brushed the tears away as he looked her square in the eyes with that cock-eyed smile she could grow to love.

"Abb-bout as l-long as it's b-been since y-you c-called me B-Bil-ly-b-boy, I rek-kon."

"Always quick with a good comeback."

Pastor Zevenbergen's smile widened. He remained quiet, but she launched into an explanation.

"He hasn't talked like this since—" She stopped for fear of upsetting Bill but needn't have worried. Pastor Zevenbergen cut her off, anyway.

"During my last two years, I studied extra psychology courses, hoping I could help returning soldiers, although I don't pretend to be an expert." He focused in on Bill. "How do you feel your recovery has gone so far?"

Bill said nothing, so Madge started, "He has a shell fragment buried in his back and another in his skull. The doctors decided not to remove either one."

But the new pastor seemed not to hear and kept his eyes on Bill. "Everyone around you knows certain facts about your injuries, but you're the only one who understands the full scope. Can you give us any insights?"

Bill sat up taller. "They told me the shrapnel m-might mix up my thinking a little. That it would take some time for my head to clear. And M-Madge can t-testify to that, eh?" He squeezed her hand. "But she's stood b-beside me."

Heat braised Madge's cheeks. What a wonder to see Bill connecting with another adult like this—to think, he remembered what the Army doctors said so long ago. He'd never told her that—but could talking about the past somehow hinder his progress?

Her anxiety faded as Pastor Zevenbergen replied. "That shrapnel could be what triggers your occasional lapses, since it puts pressure on your brain. But the doctors probably feared further surgery might cause even more damage."

"You nailed it. I'm a certified m-mess."

"The way I see it, we all are in one way or another."

"Maybe so."

A thrill ran the length of Madge's spine. Bill had taken charge and didn't seem to mind direct questions, either.

Until this moment, she had felt utterly responsible for him, as if he were a child. Later, she'd take a long walk to think all this through, but for the time being, relief washed over her like a heavenly gift.

The two men chatted a while longer until Bill fidgeted. "B-better g-get going. This old fella is starting to w-wear out."

He slid forward in his chair, so she hurried to help him. Then she remembered Vera. "I . . . I'm sorry if you two witnessed that scene a while ago."

The young man raised his eyebrows. "Not at all. Believe me, I know how complicated relationships can get."

"I'll straighten it out with her tomorrow. I honestly meant no harm."

Bill reached for her hand. "I t-told you you'd g-get into t-trouble one day, didn't I? G-guess Vera can't t-take a joke."

"That's the way. Just keep talking, Bill. Little by little, your stammer will diminish, and someday, may totally disappear. If a few words come hard, don't push it—takes time for our brains to adjust. Slow and steady, like that old tortoise racing the hare."

Madge pressed her hand to her collarbone. She could have hugged this oh-so-handsome young fellow. The mere mention of things getting better meant far more than she could put into words.

He had evaded her comment and focused on Bill. Smart. And Bill helped him out.

"Madge, here's your basket and towel." Agnes handed them to Madge.

"Thanks, I would have forgotten." Madge slipped the basket over her arm and turned to Bill. "Ready?" She slid her purse onto her arm beside the basket.

He pressed his hands against the seat to push himself up but fell back with a grunt. "B-been s-sittin' on this hard ch-chair too long."

"Here, let me help you. In my opinion, these planning meetings could be shortened." Pastor Zevenbergen slipped his arm under Bill's right shoulder while Madge did the same on the left.

Once he found his feet, the pastor remained at Bill's side as they crossed to the stairs leading to the sanctuary—far less steep than the side stairway.

Bill's stride became strong and steady. He navigated the steps one-by-one, and at the top, the pastor opened the door and stepped out with him and Madge.

"May I have the pleasure of walking you two home?"

"Oh, you don't need to trouble yourself. It's a short walk."

"No trouble at all, Mrs. McQuestion. I enjoy your husband's company. And yours, too, of course. Bill, you remind me of my Uncle Ander, my mother's brother up in Bemidji. I spent many carefree childhood summers with him and Aunt Millicent at their cabin."

"G-get in lots of f-fishing, d-did ya?"

"Sure did. Couldn't keep me off the water, despite mosquitoes the size of hummingbirds."

Bill laughed outright. "That big, eh?"

"Those were the small ones. The bigger ones lived on the other side."

Taking in snippets of their chat, Madge eased in behind them. Houses along the way appeared like scenes from a feature movie. She'd been so tense lately, she hadn't paid any attention.

Before long, the men turned left, and soon their welcoming front porch beckoned. Pastor Zevenbergen took his leave, and she and Bill watched his progress down the path.

Bill pecked her on the cheek. "Well, M-Maddie-girl, I sure do like that young m-man."

"Same here, Billy-boy. Same here."

Long after Bill fell asleep, the skirmish with Vera occupied Madge. No matter how she put her mind to it, she could imagine no way to assuage Vera's wounded pride.

Finally she gave up and switched to considering Pastor Zevenbergen's aptitude for reading Bill. Twice, he made sure they didn't talk *about* him, but *to* him. What a considerate fellow, and so intelligent.

She'd barely drifted off when one of Bill's terrible nightmares struck. He thrashed around in bed, yelled, and nearly fell out. After about five minutes, he whimpered like a puppy, which bothered Madge more than any other aspect.

She wrapped her arms around him until his shoulders stopped shaking. With a heavy heart, she rubbed his neck. Finally, he lay back and eventually eased into sleep again.

Silent tears streamed her cheeks as she sat cross-legged beside him until his breathing settled into a regular pattern. Thankfully, Gloria had been a sound sleeper since infancy.

What horrors replayed in his mind? Battle fatigue, they called this. She'd heard that some returning soldiers never got over it.

"Oh please, don't let Bill be one of them." Her plea slipped out to join the moonlight undulating through the window.

After such a pleasant day, especially talking with the pastor and walking home with his newfound friend at twilight, what could have brought on this nasty episode?

Forcing away this unanswerable inquiry, she stroked Bill's hand, and the warmth of his skin calmed her. Still the same man she married, the father of their girls, their family's provider.

No matter what, having him here meant everything. Compared to some of the scenarios she imagined when word came that the Army had evacuated him to a hospital ship, this was manageable. With that thought, she nestled down beside him. A few minutes later, he flailed the air with his arms, but soon quieted again.

Before sleep claimed Madge, the concern and kindness in Pastor Zevenbergen's eyes floated near, as real as the moonlight. He'd been so helpful today. People in the congregation were facing so many troubles right now—soon, he'd be so busy.

But an idea occurred to her—maybe he would have some suggestions. What would he say if she asked to talk to him more about this?

Chapter Five

Saturday, April 1, 1944

A mound of chopped onions on the yellow linoleum countertop grew by the moment. Passing by Madge and Agnes, Vera wiped her eyes.

"Ooh, they're strong! I don't know how you girls can stand chopping that many all at once." Her tone turned icy. "Madge, I see you decided to come now instead of following my schedule."

Madge kept her eyes on Vera. Bill once told her that staring at someone long enough would force them to look at you.

Sure enough, Vera did. "Were you going to answer?"

"Guess it really doesn't matter that much, does it? Either way, the work is getting done."

Like those British Spitfires in the newsreels at the local theater a few weeks ago, Vera's nose gained altitude.

Agnes stifled a snigger as Vera struck a dignified pose and moved along. "Now ladies, we want the floral arrangements to be just *perfect,* don't we? Fortunately we've had good rains lately, and you all have been *so very* generous with your early flowers."

She walked between the rows of tables, remarking on the arrangements. "Oh my, who brought these tulips? Mine aren't even close to blooming yet. Did you find these precious crocuses down by the river, Lila?"

One by one, the ladies on the decorating committee finished up and left for home. Wilma, who had thawed out a virtual ton of ground beef donated by her parents-in-law, dug into the mound with her hands.

Gradually, onions, tomato sauce, and egg mushed together in her famous meatloaf recipe. At her command, Norma shook in salt and pepper. Wilma dug her hands in again and flipped the mixture onto the counter with a *splat*. Then she formed six large loaves on individual baking pans.

"What did we do before they invented the Frigidaire?" A speck of raw ground beef balanced on the tip of her nose, but Madge thought better of brushing it off.

"And freezers. Bill's aunt swears by her new International Harvester model." Madge scrubbed garden dirt from the potatoes she'd retrieved from the fruit cellar this morning and hauled over in the red *Radio Flyer* wagon.

A gift from Bill's parents when the girls were little tykes, the sturdy wagon still came in handy. Best of all, it triggered memories of her sweet cherubs pulling each other up and down the alley while she and Bill worked in the garden on early summer evenings.

Those golden days were times she would never forget. The older girls might live far away but always stayed close in her thoughts.

"Percival will never fork over the money for a freezer, I just know he won't. He's such a skinflint." Agnes reddened. "Sorry, I know better than to—"

Wilma spoke up. "No, that's all right. We have to be able to speak the truth somewhere. Right, Madge?"

"Absolutely. It's the only way to survive."

Slap . . . slap . . . slap . . . slap . . . Wilma's final pats on the meatloaves lent a note of finality to their work. She wiped her face and scrubbed her hands. Madge and Agnes covered the pans with wet towels and slid them into the fridge—not an easy task, with space so limited.

Wilma rubbed her right shoulder.

"Sore?"

"Yeah. Better get on home and ice it again. I never would've dreamed one silly fall on the ice would still be affecting me."

The stair door opened, and Percival hollered down.

"You about ready down there, Aggie?"

"I'll be right up." Agnes dried her hands on her apron and hung it on a hook beside the Frigidaire. "See you both tomorrow." She mounted the stairs, and Madge turned to Wilma.

"Why don't you go take care of that shoulder and get a good night's sleep? I'll clean up here and meet you early in the morning."

"After getting to know Pastor Zevenbergen, this welcome almost seems like an afterthought." Wilma grabbed her jacket. "But then, you can never have too many potlucks."

She must really be hurting. Madge set the potatoes on towels to dry and peeked into the dining room. Wintered-over geraniums perked up the tottery old tables, and somebody had discovered a lilac bush with enough blossoms for a few vases.

Across the west wall stretched a big sign painted in red letters on brown butcher paper:

WELCOME TO
CHURCH STREET UNITED BRETHREN!

Despite the strong onion essence, a clean geranium fragrance wafted into the kitchen. That fresh smell always took Madge back to her childhood. No matter how hard times became when the banks folded, Mama pulled last year's dilapidated geraniums from the furnace room in late March.

In the back porch, she tended them until the danger of a hard frost had passed. By mid-June, her ministrations wooed the plants into productivity, and they welcomed anyone who stopped by.

Looking around one last time, Madge turned out the lights and climbed the stairs to retrieve the little red wagon. But as she touched the knob, the door flew open, nearly catapulting her into the arms of a startled Vera, whose lips formed a tight thin line.

In the late afternoon light, tiny blue veins showed around her nostrils. Of course, she came back—couldn't be satisfied that they would leave the basement in good order.

"Checking on things?" A heavy tinge of sarcasm rang out before Madge could stop herself.

"No, I just forgot to bring these towels back earlier." Furrows lined Vera's forehead. The pile of feed sack dishtowels in her arms offered silent testimony.

A sudden wave of sympathy took Madge by surprise. Perhaps a little encouragement wouldn't hurt.

"You've done a good job organizing this potluck."

"You don't mean that. I try my best, but everyone resents my efforts."

"Come on, now. Aren't we all supposed to work together?"

Vera sucked in her breath to pass by, so Madge leaned into the framework with a tired sigh. Two steps down, Vera turned, so Madge braced herself. But Vera said nothing.

A moment later she found her voice, but her message faded as she continued. "You have no idea what I've—"

"What?"

A shudder passed over Vera's shoulders, as if the sixty-degree temperature had suddenly dropped below zero. But she said nothing as she set the towels in a drawer.

Mama's words came then. "You never know what burden someone else might be carrying." If only she had something to offer Vera—but what?

"Good night then, Vera."

Silence drifted up the stairs.

"Hey, where you goin'? You're my wife, so you oughta be walkin' with me."

Gloria had just turned the corner of Second and Elm a bit ahead of Madge and Bill. This new habit of an evening walk settled well with him. Invariably, they exchanged a greeting with someone along the way and often stopped to talk for a while.

But who had just called Gloria his wife? They turned the corner and Vern Barker saw them and blanched.

Gloria giggled. "It's all right. Mom and Dad know all about the play." She ran back to peck Madge on the check before joining Vern again. "Time for us to head over to church. See you later."

"I-I'll walk her home, Mr. McQuestion, if that's all right." Vern's sheepish grin tugged at Madge's heart and so did Bill's response.

"Sure. But mind you, no later than ten."

"Yes, sir." Vern's hand shifted a bit, as if he started to salute but thought better of it. If he weren't in the class after Gloria's, he would already have been drafted, like half the other boys her age. And unless this war ended soon, he would most likely be the next to head overseas.

So many of them were risking their lives. When would it all be over? Madge's sigh drifted like smoke as they rounded the next corner toward home. Bill squeezed her hand—he must be thinking the same thing.

The aroma of Sunday supper curled from someone's house. Left-over chicken from dinner, warmed over potatoes . . .

"Hmm . . . Billy Boy, smells like baked chicken, your favorite."

"Yes, b-but I like your homemade c-chicken and noodles even m-more."

His comment brought Madge up short. She'd avoided making homemade noodles and chicken while he had been gone because it made her sad to think of him missing out. But he hadn't mentioned it since he came home.

Until now.

Yes, he returned to her alive, but without the perk in his step and lacking the buoyant smile that could charm her out of a foul mood. Oh, how she missed the easy conversations they once enjoyed, but she'd gotten used to his new lopsided grin caused by nerve damage.

But how she cherished these quiet hand squeezes that told her he understood! *And* . . . he was talking! With a stutter, true. But still . . .

His silence those first few months had been hardest to accept. Before he left, he always had a quip to share—she and the girls had been hard-pressed to keep up with his quick wit.

Maybe it was time to re-think that chicken-noodle meal. She'd do just that as soon as the Yoder family delivered their tri-weekly load of fresh cream and butter to the grocery.

Nothing like homemade noodles over boiled potatoes with butter melting on them. Smothered in chicken and rich broth, what could be better?

Funny how contemplating something so simple lightened her heart. Nearby, Florence, their sixty-something neighbor, man-handled a rake far too big for her, while Carl smoothed out the crushed rock at the edge of their property.

They'd be married forty-two years on June fifteenth—mustn't forget to take over something to help them celebrate. Florence had made a gorgeous baby quilt when each of the girls was born, plus a bevy of lovely meals.

Carl stopped his work and stationed himself near Florence. They chatted about something, and he patted Florence's shoulder.

"They're ahead of us on the yard work—that last ice storm sure wreaked h-havoc on things." Bill stood back to let Madge lead the way on the porch steps, and hope surged through her.

What he said next made her want to shout "Whoopee!"

"I'd b-better get out here and pick up some b-branches after work t-tomorrow. The east side's a big mess."

Ah, the old Bill, noticing what needed to be done in the yard. He'd always been Johnny-on-the-spot to get the job done.

Between the top step and the front door, Madge waited for him. Then she honed in and gave him a hug for the pure joy of it.

Chapter Six

Palm Sunday, April 2, 1944

Palm Sunday dawned clear and fresh, thanks to an April shower the night before. Knowing Bill and Gloria would come over later, Madge walked to church early to start the potatoes and meatloaves baking.

Holding Pastor Zevenbergen's welcome potluck today had its pros and cons. Vera noted this in their meeting. Palm Sunday fit the theme of welcoming someone, but knowing what lay ahead, still carried a tinge of sadness.

Sure enough, her piercing stare greeted Madge from under that preposterous hat. As if their unintended meeting on the stairway had never happened, Vera turned smug.

"It was so early when I got here, I beat the sun."

Madge's inner light flashed yellow and red by turns. Ignoring it completely, she spouted a retort.

"Six of us worked all last evening to make sure everything goes well. Didn't you find things in order when you got here?"

"Well, I never!" Vera drew in her breath.

"Things *were* all set, weren't they?"

Pastor Zevenbergen rescued Vera from having to invent emergency actions she had taken to prevent disaster. For one thing, he missed the bottom step, and only quick reflexes forestalled him from crashing into the Frigidaire.

"Nothing like making a dramatic entrance, right?" His blue eyes twinkled, and Madge gave thanks for his self-effacing humor. No telling how much he had heard, but she let it go.

"I always appreciate you women who come early and stay late. What would the church do without you?"

"I'm sure I don't know." Vera dug a bit deeper. "It sounds as if you certainly have had some experience with churchwomen."

"My brother and I overheard plenty, Mrs. Walters, but during my internship, some wonderful women helped me out of a pickle or two. Their practical wisdom taught me a few things. you can't learn in seminary.

"Besides that, my grandmother and mother are strong women." His grin piqued Madge's interest. "Plus a raft of aunts and cousins."

Tidying the already-tidy serving counter, Vera looked up. "Strong?"

"My family's full of women who know their minds."

"Oh, my, you certainly do have a way with words." Vera clasped her hands together. "But please, won't you call me Vera?"

Madge removed the meatloaves from the Frigidaire and slid them into the oven. Meanwhile, Vera attached her fingers to Pastor Zevenbergen's elbow and steered him into the dining room.

Regaled by a myriad of dessert choices after the huge meal, Aivars could have heaved. But that would never do in the presence of these parishioners, especially at a dinner in his honor. So he loosened his tie and discreetly readjusted his belt.

How had rich desserts become such a part of these gatherings? The women outdid each other, conjuring concoctions that might send a man into heart failure. Given the state of rationing, they must have hoarded sugar in their corncribs or somewhere.

Against all common sense, he plunged his fork into Wilma Stuempfle's red velvet cake. He'd seen her eyeing his plate, awaiting this moment, so how could he disappoint her? Just one or two bites and he'd be home free.

"Ooh, yum!"

That was all it took for Wilma to beam. Someone asked, "You like that cake, eh?"

Who was that fellow anyway? One of his professors had advised his class to pay strict attention to people's names. Nothing won hearts faster than this personal touch.

Easy for him to say, with only thirty names to learn when his new classes started each semester. But within week one, 200 new names vied for position here.

Of course, everyone shook his hand after these first two services and murmured, "Good sermon, Reverend." He was supposed to reply, "Thank you, Edmond." Or whoever.

But did those folks mean what they said? That was the question, and compliments were cheap. How on earth could he discover what they really thought?

More important right now—what was this man's name? Vera's husband, the church council president, and they'd had him out to eat at their house. How could he forget?

Just then, Madge provided the answer.

"More coffee, Harry?"

Harry! Of course.

"You betcha. Fill 'er right up."

Harry's capacity for ingesting food and drink never ceased to astonish. He'd already downed a plateful of fried chicken, baked potatoes, and Jell-O salad, followed by a second of roast beef and gravy, plus a slab of meatloaf.

In the big cities, meat was being rationed, but definitely not here in farm country. Another perk of living in rural America—like always having access to cheese and milk.

Harry consumed two pieces of pie—apple and cherry. Now he was slurping through a bowl of bread pudding swimming in thick cream, one of Vera's contributions.

Earlier, she left the table with a rather chunky blonde woman, but not until she made a point of introducing her visitor to the guest of honor.

"Pastor Zevenbergen, this is my cousin, Helene Miller. She's visiting for a few days from La Crosse."

"Pleased to meet you, Miss Miller." He half-stood and shook Helene's hand. "I hope you're enjoying your stay here."

"Oh, yes. Vera and I have a lot of catching up to do. It's been too long, hasn't it, cousin?"

A shadow crossed Vera's countenance but just as quickly disappeared. "Yes, way too long." Her response lacked the warmth one would expect. Curious.

"Will you be here long?"

"No, I'm afraid not. I must be back for work on Tuesday—important for the war effort, don't you know?"

"Yes. Good. We all must do our part." He wished her Godspeed, and Vera guided Helene away. Something seemed peculiar between those two.

"You, Pastor?"

"Hmm?" Aivars jerked his head up to see Madge with the coffee pot, eyeing Vera and her cousin, too.

"Now that's interesting. I never knew Vera had a cousin until she mentioned her the other day."

"You didn't?"

"In such a small town, you think you know everything about everybody, but you get surprised sometimes. Well, never mind. Would you like more coffee?"

Tucking away Madge's reaction, Aivars covered his cup with his hand. "No thanks. If I put one more ounce into my stomach I'll burst."

"My sentiments exactly. That's why I found something to do."

"What a great idea." He caught her eye before she twisted toward the next table. "Say, have you ever heard how Moses makes his coffee?"

"Moses?"

"Yes."

"No, how?"

"He brews it."

It took a second for the joke to register, but when it did, Madge let loose a laugh. "Hebrews. That's a good one."

Then she went on. "I do think we could use some help pouring coffee." Her chuckle came full-bodied and clear. "There's a reason so many pastors start to waddle as they age."

"So you see right through us lazy bums, eh? That's an outstanding quality in a newspaper reporter."

Her raised eyebrow almost disappeared beneath a hedge of auburn bangs. "Why do you say that?"

"The ability to analyze situations and people comes highly valued these days. Exactly what our armed forces look for in secret agents."

Her laugh delighted him again as she swung away, then half-turned. "If they come to recruit me, keep quiet about my talents. I just got my husband back, and I'm staying right here with him, thank you very much."

She took a step but changed her mind and turned again. "The offer stands—we really could use help pouring coffee."

Such a spunky lady. Aivars bid Harry *adieu* and followed Madge's bidding.

Thursday, April 6, 1944

Thursday morning, Aivars woke with Madge and Bill on his mind. Last night at prayer meeting, Vera mentioned the *Chronicle* article again, turning Madge's fair skin almost as red as her hair, but she maintained silence.

What would his father do in this situation? He had absolutely no idea.

Madge's article revealed the sharp edge of her wit, including the part about his *miraculous* rescue of the lily. He saw nothing offensive—if Vera had reason to be offended, so did he. But what good would it do to enter into the scuffle?

Maybe Vera suffered from insecurity effectively disguised by her brashness. Often more went on with folks than met the eye—usually the case when you really got to know someone.

But truth be told, you could put what he knew about women in his mother's thimble with room to spare. Why not write Dad for advice? This probably wouldn't be the only time he'd need some.

Careful to follow every step he learned years ago, he fixed his tie. Dad had explained the process as though it meant stepping into manhood. Aivars pulled on his vest before leaving for the short walk to Hank's Café—Dad's advice motivated this move, too.

"Support the local businesses when you can. People appreciate seeing you out in public—they like to know you're going about your work."

So, he'd sit for a few minutes, enjoy a cup of coffee and order some pancakes he could just as easily have made at home. Then he'd head back to the church to work on the Easter sermon—only two more days. The sanctuary would surely be full, and he'd likely meet some heretofore unseen members.

Such a quiet day in town, with school closing tomorrow for Good Friday. Later, he'd promised to meet some high school boys for a game of sandlot baseball over on Maple and Fifth.

With his hunger satisfied and another local name memorized, he retraced his steps, but noticed something on the back porch of the parsonage when he passed by. He veered over to find a casserole dish, still warm through its heavy towel wrapping. A white envelope lay nearby, so he carried them inside and opened the note.

An old family favorite.
Hope you enjoy it.

Vera Walters

"Great. Now I don't have to wonder what to fix for supper." Vera seemed to have ample time to cook and enjoyed sharing,

He placed the dish in his fridge and worked for a couple of hours in his study. Twenty minutes before his baseball date, he hurried home to change into khaki pants and grab his ball glove and bat.

Then he raced back to the church. No good being late for these fellows. He most likely had precious little time to let them know he cared about them. Still, guilt niggled at him—he'd made a little progress on his sermon, but not enough. After all, Easter Sunday came only once a year.

He pulled out his key to the side lock, but the heavy wooden door swung open at his touch. Odd. One of the women had promised to lock up last night, and he'd used the front door this morning. Everyone seemed so serious about locking the building—he'd have to devise a long-term plan to break the habit.

One step in, acrid odor assaulted him . . . strong tobacco? Possibly the kind Uncle Ander used in his pipe, but people never smoked in here.

Something else rode the air, a curious metallic smell. Aivars sniffed again—sort of like fresh-cut copper wiring.

A dim light from below drew him downward. Not only had someone left the door open, they must've forgotten to turn the light off. Mighty strange.

Aivars fumbled along the clammy, pimpled wall for the light switch. Why would anyone install it so far from the entrance? "One of those mysteries of history. . ."

As the bare bulb above the stairwell came to life, he made his way down, entered the kitchen and stopped short. On the floor, a dark stain spread before his feet.

A quick glance backward revealed another smaller one, and he twisted to see more trailing up the steps behind him. "Dad would just wipe all this away and chalk it up to his day's work."

Seemed like he'd seen some rags around here somewhere. The light above the stove had been left on, too. Curiouser and curiouser.

He started toward the pull chain, but something tripped him. "Wha—?" Catching himself on the counter, Aivars looked down. What he saw made him dizzy.

"Dear God!"

He could hardly take in the scene, starting with a female foot. He'd seen that shoe before. A woman's shoe almost as long as his own.

What could it be doing here? Unbelieving, he surveyed further and noted the rest of a tall, angled body sprawled on the cement in a pool of blood. Facing the dining room. A severe nose pointed toward the floor drain.

As if any of this mattered. These trivial details stood out to him like the details of his painting of Peter. Each one of them burgeoned with artistic meaning, but this scene—he couldn't make heads or tails of it.

Those stains on the steps must be blood. And he had walked right through the sticky mess!

Fighting back nausea, Aivars gripped the edge of the counter and forced himself to look again. Something protruded from a wet burgundy mass below—below a ribcage. Something thin, shiny, and about five inches long.

"Pastor Z, you down there? We're all here."

That would be Vern Barker calling from the top of the stairs. How long had he been standing here like a mannequin?

The boys mustn't come down and see this! But it took all of Aivars' effort to gather enough breath to yell.

"Someone's—someone's fallen down here, Vern. Run for the doctor, fast as you can."

Thankfully, the door banged. Then came the sound of footsteps pounding across the lawn.

"Vern, are you still up there?"

"Yessir."

"Go get the sheriff. Right now. Hurry."

From the silence, he sensed Vern's hesitation.

"No time to waste. Something terrible has happened down here." The door slammed, more footsteps raced off, and Aivars turned his full attention to the woman lying on the church kitchen floor.

Undeniably Vera Walters.

With all of this blood, could she possibly still be alive? He eased around the counter, taking care not to step in the dark puddle around her torso. Bending over, he held his hand in front of her mouth to detect any breathing. He nearly jumped out of his skin when her eyelids fluttered.

Then her lips moved.

He had to lean close to hear her halting words, laced with stale coffee. The ladies made it strong and were loath to waste any, what with rationing and all. Perhaps she had sipped some left over from last night.

Her pronouncement the other day when she'd replenished the coffee supply ran through his mind. They had discussed how much it cost now, but Vera voiced her determination to preserve coffee drinking through the war, no matter what.

"Harry and I can see to it. Shouldn't go without if at all possible. So good for our fellowship, don't you think?"

Now halting words issued from her mouth. "... hat ... Madge ... promissss ..." Vera's pale lips lapsed wide, a shiver took her, and a final feeble breath gurgled out.

Aivars sat back on his heels and attempted to digest what lay before him. This simply couldn't be happening, but the coppery tinge in the air, the sticky floor, and the knife hilt protruding from Vera's sternum told him otherwise.

For a few moments, a familiar sensation enveloped him, like what he felt during his Army physical. He was watching everything from a distance.

"Hurry up, Sheriff ..."

His next thought concerned that absurd Easter hat, such a bone of contention. Why should the silly thing come to the forefront now, with Vera's last breath?

Still squatting, he glanced around for the garish thing. What had she said about Madge? Could she still be venting her anger, accusing even with her final breath?

Surely not. He pressed his fingers to his temples as an avalanche of questions tumbled through his mind.

A definite throb began at the nape of his neck. He'd been going to write Dad for advice about women in conflict—now he'd have to ask how to handle a violent death in the church basement.

A murder.

Chapter Seven

A distant wail increased before coming to an abrupt stop. The Sheriff. Aivars slowly rose.

As Sheriff Dale Finley bent over Vera's still body, Vern called from the top of the stairs.

"We're all ready, Pastor Z."

"Z?"

"It's a lot easier than saying my whole name."

The sheriff twisted toward the stairway. Should've been a preacher—no problem with his voice carrying. "You fellas run along now."

"But what about our ball game?"

"Postponed. Got us an emergency here." Sheriff Finley stationed himself at Vera's feet. "Well, Reverend, would you care to explain?"

"I found her when I came over to meet the boys. The door was unlocked, and I saw a light, so I came to turn it off.

"That was when—" A cold tremble overtook him. "She—was still alive."

Finley's steely stare never wavered. "How do I know you just *now* found her?" He pointed to some bloody footprints leading away from Vera's body.

"Those aren't mine! Why would I—?"

"Step over here." Granite-faced, the sheriff gestured to a clean space. "Show me your soles."

Aivars lifted his right foot. His heart sank. Dark red—the same with his left.

"But I didn't step in the—I mean—"

"Then how do you explain this?"

"Maybe it's from the stairs?"

"Hmm. I'll have to compare your tread." The Sheriff let out a long breath. "Confound it all." He wiped a hand over his eyes. "Vera Walters—I can hardly believe this."

"I know."

The clock ticked away the minutes. "Okay, Reverend, suppose you tell me everything, right from the start."

"The boys and I were meeting here to play baseball. Oh . . . what did I do with my bat and glove?"

"By the door. "I might've broken my neck."

"Sorry. The side door's always locked . . ." Aivars bit his upper lip. "I—I tripped over her foot."

"I see. How did you know she was still alive?"

"I bent down. That was when she opened her eyes."

The sheriff pulled a pencil and notebook from his uniform pocket and began scribbling. "Did you touch or move her? Or touch the knife?"

"No, but her lips moved, and I leaned closer."

"She spoke? What did she say?"

"I . . . *hat* and *promise*. And *Madge*."

The sheriff's lips twitched. "I suppose the infamous Easter bonnet that made the *Chronicle* last week?"

"Maybe so."

"She also mentioned Madge McQuestion?"

"No last name, just *Madge*."

Heavy footsteps trudged down the stairs. "What's going on down here?"

Doctor Nils Lindquist could have passed for an old farmer, though he did tote a black leather medical bag. Aivars had met him in the café—he'd tended the Great War wounded and served as coroner here.

"The boys said someone got hurt." Doc panted as if he'd run all the way from his home office across town.

"Brought the ambulance just in case."

"I'm afraid it's worse than that, Doc. Reverend Zeven—what was your name?"

"Zevenbergen."

"Anyway, he found Vera Walters' body. Take a look."

"Doc took a cautious step and put a thick fist to his lips. "It *is* her. A knife . . . hmm. Who would . . .?"

"My question exactly. The Reverend says he found her alive, but then she died."

Doc shot Aivars a keen look. "How long ago?"

"Half an hour? I sent the boys for you right away."

Sheriff Finley jerked up his head. "Did they come down here?"

"No, sir."

"Thank goodness. That would've contaminated the evidence. Have you moved from where I found you?"

"No."

"Did you see or hear anyone?"

"No."

"Is there any other way out?"

"Yes, through the dining room." Aivars pointed beyond the serving counter. "But the main doors are usually locked."

"How do you know?"

"I use a key to get in."

Seemed odd the Sheriff wasn't more familiar with the building. Even the Catholics had attended weddings or funerals here, and some Brethren members probably sneaked into Bingo at the Catholic Church, too.

"Did you check?"

"No." He doubted he could have even if he'd wanted to. His heart still lodged in his throat. Those Army docs had been wrong—boot camp might have been less stressful than this.

Pulling rubber gloves from his bag, Doc examined the body and turned. "Judging by the bloody spittle, I'd say the knife punctured her lungs before entering her heart. Have to do an autopsy to confirm, but the killer knew what he was doing, I'd say."

The sheriff flipped a few pages before pinning Aivars again. "Vera mentioned a hat, right? Did you see one?"

"Yes. No."

He squatted. "There's something blue here and some pieces of straw. Could they have come from her hat?"

"I only saw it briefly, but the birds were sort of . . . unforgettable. I think one was blue."

"Birds?"

"Yes, two of them."

"She mentioned a promise. Mean anything to you?"

"No."

"Any idea why Mrs. Walters would come here this morning? And *how* she got down here? I assume that side door upstairs was locked too?"

"As far as I know, the ladies had nothing planned. But as the Ladies' Aid president, Vera has . . ." Aivars took a deep breath. "She *had* a key."

"Who locked up last night?"

"Agnes, I think."

"You left before that?"

"Yes, the Walters and some others were still here."

"Who, exactly?"

"Madge and Bill, Agnes and Percival Wellsby. But I think Percival went out to their Studebaker."

While Doc continued his examination, Sheriff Finley looked around. Aivars pulled out his handkerchief to wipe his forehead.

"Stay right where you are, Reverend."

The sheriff scrutinized a lady's purse on the counter's far end. "Who else has access to this basement?"

"Madge has a key. She and Agnes Wellsby clean the church."

Suddenly he remembered the casserole Vera left at his place.

"After I left the cafe, I found a dish on my porch with a note from Vera. She must've come here after leaving it."

"But you don't know why she came?"

"She took a lot of pride in her work here. You might ask some of the ladies."

Doc struggled getting up, so Aivars stuck out his arm to help. "Got your evidence kit, Dale?"

"Up in the car. Gotta dust for fingerprints. I'll get everything. Reverend, stay right here with Doc."

This *reverend* business was wearing. The word made him uneasy. But an even worse realization enveloped him. He had become the number one murder suspect. He not only found the victim, the Sheriff found him *with* her.

Another realization dawned as Doc scanned Vera's body. This would be his first solo funeral.

Sheriff Finley clumped back down the stairs. "Vera would've used her key. Could be in the purse or a pocket but searching might mess up the evidence."

"I'd take my key out before I got out of my car and put it in my pocket if I was just coming down for a little bit, wouldn't you?"

"I suppose so." Aivars swiped his brow again—such a violent tremble in his fingers. And those pancakes had started rumbling around.

"That key's on our must-find list, and the blamed Easter bonnet. Gotta have 'em both." The sheriff put his hands on his hips. "You're sure you didn't touch anything?"

"No . . . oh, wait! When I tripped, I grabbed the counter."

"OK, good."

Doc started hacking, which reminded Aivars of the smell in the stairway.

"I just remembered there was a strong tobacco smell in the stairway."

"Smelled that, too. Do you allow smoking down here?"

"I don't know if there's a rule, but I doubt anyone would."

"All right. First, some shots of the scene." The Sheriff pulled out his camera and focused on the knife, the wound, the blood, the footprints. Finally, he stepped back.

"Okay. Hold up one of your feet."

Feeling like a criminal, Aivars lifted his right foot.

"You can step away now. I need to check for blood spatter on your clothing."

A cold wave washed Aivars head to toe.

"For the record, you understand."

Grateful to finally move, Aivars stepped well away from Vera's body. Relief flooded him—every time he glanced at her, a terrible taste filled his mouth.

The sheriff peered, poked and prodded. So this is what a pat down felt like—good to know. Maybe someday, he'd visit somebody in jail.

"Okay, you can breathe now." The Sheriff pursed his lips. "You're clean."

Aivars closed his eyes, but the image of that knife hilt remained. He could never plunge a blade into anyone, yet soldiers had to do just that.

The sheriff removed a pair of rubber gloves, a white cloth and a brown paper bag from his kit. Then he squatted to pluck evidence from the congealing blood, put it in the paper sack and set it inside his bag.

"OK, Doc, you can take her now." He glanced down at Vera. "I'll come over to dust the knife for fingerprints later, after you're done."

Doc nodded. "I'll need one of you to help get the stretcher down here."

Good—something to do. Aivars sought permission with his eyes.

"Go ahead. I'll wait with her. You're gonna need help getting her up those stairs."

With Doc puffing at his heels, Aivars opened the door to a sudden gale. Rain pelted him, and the fresh onslaught filled his lungs. Odd—hadn't even been cloudy earlier.

At the back of the ambulance, Doc wheezed. Aivars lifted out a folded stretcher.

"Army issue. Brought it home with me years ago. Borne many

a hurting soul in its day." Doc slammed the trunk shut and Aivars started off.

Twenty minutes later, with Vera covered in white sheets, the three loaded the stretcher. All the way up the stairs, the Sheriff spewed, "Why did it have to rain? So much for footprints outside."

Visions of his buddies from high school, college, and seminary hit Aivars like the raindrops. Through all kinds of weather, they fought on.

Trivial in comparison, but right here in Caroline, a human being had passed into eternity—a slim hair divided the living from the dead. Those fellows saw death up close far more often, but what an awful way for Vera to die.

Doc scrunched his bulk behind the wheel, and the Sheriff started for the church.

"Now Reverend, let's get fingerprints so we can both leave." Aivars followed in his wake—he shook water off his shoulders like a dog all the way down the stairs.

In the kitchen, Sheriff Finley pulled a peculiar round brush from his bag, plus a jar of black powder, a roll of cellophane tape, several blank postcards, and some white paper.

"Show me where you touched the counter."

Rehearsing his stumble, Aivars pointed. Then he watched the sheriff go about his work.

He dumped some powder on one of the papers, twirled the brush through it, shook some off, and swirled in a circular motion across the paper. Like magic, fingerprints gradually took shape.

A few more brush strokes, and he carefully placed a length of tape over as many prints as possible. Next, he lifted the tape, stuck it to one of the postcards, and smoothed as he pressed down. He wrote something on the back, set it aside and turned.

"Have you ever been fingerprinted before?

"No, sir."

"Then we'll need to get a set for comparison. Are these I just lifted from your left or right hand?"

Nothing seemed simple any more. Aivars held up his hands to check. "My left."

"Come around here." The sheriff placed a new sheet of paper on the counter, well away from the corner. Then he peered at the card.

"Your left index, middle and fourth finger. Press them firmly in the middle."

Aivars obeyed. The sheriff repeated the same process with the brush and powder.

"Okay. I'll take all this back to the station and see what we come up with. You can leave now while I secure the murder scene."

Those two words bounced around like ping-pong balls. *Murder scene . . . murder scene . . .*

Still somewhat dazed, Aivars started toward the stairs, but the sheriff shot him one more look. "Go straight home. Don't leave town till you hear from me."

"Yes, sir." Out in the cool drizzle, Aivars thought he might collapse. All around, the grass sparkled fresh green—the farmers would be happy with this moisture, but its beauty was lost on him.

A murder. In the church kitchen, no less.

His church basement.

Impossible to work on his sermon—thinking about the Resurrection brought images of Vera rising from the stained linoleum. The idea of eating supper nauseated him.

Somehow, afternoon became evening. Sitting in a living room chair as twilight deepened into darkness, Aivars finally dozed off. Once, he awakened thinking about Vera's car. He hadn't seen it at all, and the Sheriff never mentioned it. Better call him in the morning.

Then another thought. Probably he had notified Harry by now. Ought to drive to their house to console him—but he couldn't leave town.

Harry, who enjoyed his food more than most. Harry, the council president. The town banker. Would Harry even welcome a visit from the number one suspect? After all, he was still the main suspect.

Chapter Eight

Easter Sunday, April 9, 1944

On a typical April Sunday morning in Iowa, even a perennial grouch could believe anything was possible. The bleakness of March gave way to Spring's coaxing, robins had returned to build their nests, and iris buds looked promising.

On these warming days, children cast off their winter coats and played hopscotch or pulled wagons filled with metal and rubber to the filling station kitty-cornered from the *Chronicle* office. A truck came by weekly to load up and deliver the goods to a central office for the war effort.

Besides that, Easter had arrived, and the war news was perking up. Surely, with the Royal Air Force dropping thousands of tons of bombs on German industrial cities, the enemy would soon capitulate. Without armament factories, how could they possibly continue for long?

Rumor had it the Allies were planning to invade France in the near future. That would surely end the horrid fighting in Europe. The young men who returned home with their war stories would someday enjoy their grandchildren, maybe even their great-grandchildren.

Things would return to normal and this typical little Midwestern town would grow and prosper. As the years passed, Decoration Day would remind people of their losses, but also of freedom's value.

But this was no typical town any longer. And no normal Sunday morning. Still, little girls primped about in new ruffled Easter dresses their mothers sewed for them, and little boys donned special tailored suits.

Many a woman had been hard at work for weeks on these new garments, stitching ever so carefully so as not to waste thread or yard goods. This annual celebration gave them a chance to sew new outfits for themselves, too, if they could afford the yard goods.

On this auspicious holiday, their husbands shined their shoes—even the farmers. The scent of aftershave flowed around spiffy Easter bonnets dotting the local sanctuaries like blossoms in snowball bushes.

But today a pall fell over parishioners as they entered the United Brethren Church. Old Otto produced a pathetic attempt at hymns he'd played hundreds of times—*Glorias* sounded more like dirges.

Pastor Zevenbergen looked as though he'd just bitten into a persimmon. The congregation, distracted by the empty spots in Vera and Harry's pew, had trouble following the sermon.

Questions plagued Madge. What had it been it like for Aivars to find Vera? And how many churches had ever lost a member right in the building? Surely not many. But to be the first on the scene—that amounted to something else altogether.

Straight as a new yardstick, Percival occupied his usual place, and beside him, Agnes wept silent tears. The way she kept reaching up with her hankie gave her away. Her own hankie in hand, Madge knew the feeling exactly.

The situation simply beggared belief. How could such a thing happen in their small town?

Of course, the Ladies' Aid would serve lunch after the funeral. Vera's funeral. Those two words vied with reality. Who would take Vera's place as president of the Ladies' Circle?

Another question followed. That impossible Easter bonnet—where the heck could it be? When Dale had come to notify her and Bill, he'd mentioned that outrageous hat. Gave her a strange look, too.

And she had fidgeted. Of course she had! That silly thing had been nothing but trouble right from the beginning, but she'd never dreamed a murder might be involved.

Pastor Zevenbergen's next words shook Madge back to the moment. "Many of us think the Holy Spirit either weird or to be feared. But the Spirit played a huge role during the week between Palm Sunday and the first Easter."

He held up his palm. "This Divine whisperer comforted the disciples in the loss of their dear friend, and now speaks to us, too. He says, 'Because of the Resurrection, I remember your past no more. Everything has been taken care of now.' Divine Love tells us we can forget our mistakes.'"

Forget our mistakes? It would be some time before Madge forgot hers with Vera. If she ever did. The weight of guilt nearly consumed her.

Did divine love envelope Vera right now? Had her worries and fears calmed at the moment of her passing?

Perhaps whatever had been troubling her fled away like late winter cold when warmth embraced the land. Perhaps all of her troubles disappeared in an instant.

Lying over at Twin Oaks Mortuary and Funeral Parlor, only her earthly body remained. Her soul, already passed into eternity, still lived. But not enough time had passed to try to picture her anywhere but here.

Down the pew, someone gave a heavy sigh that Madge echoed. Vera may have been sharp and bossy, but what lay behind that exterior?

Heaven only knew. Hopefully, the underlying motivations that drove her had now met with mercy. *Mercy*—such a profound word.

Just then Bill patted Madge's hand, and she moved closer. This must be so hard on him, yet he hadn't said much since hearing about the murder.

Did he know she pondered why had it been so hard to be kind to Vera? How did one forgive oneself for being small and uncharitable?

Then came the thought of the promise Vera had begged her to make. Keeping it would be easy—what purpose would it serve to tell Harry about the Easter bonnet's origin?

Interesting how one's perspective changed—before this, she saw him as a bumbling fellow. Now he became a little like a returning soldier, shell-shocked, grieving, vulnerable. His sister had come from Chicago, someone said. Good, this was no time to be alone.

But that anonymous admirer of Vera's—who could it have been? And where had that hat gone? Madge bounced from question to question, but a sudden throat-clearing from the pulpit got her attention.

"The past few days have reinforced our understanding of how short life can be. How fragile and out of our control—how shocking and disconcerting at times like this."

In spite of her melancholy, Madge felt an urge to grin. The other day, Aivars visited with Bill and disclosed that his first name hailed back to his family's Latvian moorings. Then he shared the nickname his classmates had called him.

Zeeb.

Something about it brought up an image of a bee buzzing around in the sunshine. A busy insect—and Aivars certainly kept himself occupied. Most folks had started calling him Pastor Z now, and he seemed to like that.

Now as he hesitated, an ethereal light radiated from the high stained-glass window behind him. Around his head, a soft halo formed as he paused to shuffle his notes.

"I . . ." He wiped his forehead. "I must admit that managing my own thoughts challenges me this morning." He navigated the two stairs to stand in the aisle.

"Vera Walters has passed from our midst in the blink of an eye, as we all shall one day. Many questions surround her sudden death, but let us keep her husband, Harry, in our prayers. We've grown used to checking the newspapers for the casualty lists, but never expected this grave loss here at home.

"We must continue the practical work before us. Right now, that includes planning a suitable service to honor Vera's life. And depending on our personal circumstances, it means completing our daily tasks and perhaps even helping the authorities solve the mystery of her passing.

"We all need to keep praying for each other. Only an extra dose of grace will help us grapple with this circumstance. We all need support and nonjudgmental friendship. It is my hope that our church will grow deeper in understanding and stronger through this terrible time."

It seemed the whole congregation held its breath as he dipped his head for a moment. Bill's fingers tightened around Madge's. She scooted even closer.

"Funeral arrangements are still pending, although next weekend is a possibility. I'll post a note on the front door when I hear, and a formal announcement will appear in the *Chronicle*. Now, for our final hymn. Let us carry its theme with us."

Otto played the introduction to "What a Friend We Have in Jesus," one of Madge's favorites. Not a normal Easter hymn, but a perfect choice for today. Bill's hand shook, so Madge held his fingers to her lips and leaned her head against his shoulder.

Just when things began to look up, why did this have to happen? *All our sins and griefs to bear . . .*

The massive lump in her throat forestalled all sound. Bill wrapped his arm around her as she stood there, awash with regret.

That night another nightmare visited Bill, worse than the last. Madge held him tight and rocked him back and forth. No tears this time—she'd cried herself out.

But the attack's severity left her shaken. Once he fully wakened, it had taken him much longer to quiet down. Finally, his breathing steadied, and Madge smoothed her palm over his forehead with a desperate plea.

"Lord, we're completely helpless. Please heal Bill—please, oh please!

She snuggled down against his chest, thankful to have him here beside her, no matter what.

Vera's funeral had been set for Saturday. The committee gathered to plan the lunch, and someone mentioned the need for a new president. All fingers pointed to Madge, who shook her head with fervor.

"Absolutely not—enough on my plate already. You'll have to pick someone else."

"How about you, Agnes?" Linda McDonald, who worked the local telephone switchboard, rarely spoke up.

"Not a chance." Agnes's shoulders shot up like a pair of birds on the alert. "Why don't you do it?"

Knowing Linda's shy personality, everyone enjoyed a good chuckle when she shrieked. Though all color drained from her face, laughing together brought a much-needed release from the tension. After all, they sat within mere feet of where Vera had so recently perished.

Eventually, someone nominated Wilma Stuempfle, a farm wife more used to butchering chickens than leading a group. But she allowed the unanimous vote and even gave a small speech.

"Somebody has to say yes, though you all know I'm not the leader type. I've learned something from everyone here, and considering what we've all been through, let's just try to work together, shall we?"

A chorus of nods and "Yesses" burst forth, so she continued. "When everything gets back to normal, we can elect a real leader."

"What a great idea." The other members echoed Madge's relieved sigh and got down to business. Would Maid-rites be suitable for the funeral lunch, or should they go all out and fix a beef roast dinner?

Someone asked, "What do you think would make Vera happy?"

A full dinner it would be.

Chapter Nine

"With this funeral now, do you think we'll ever get to put on our play?" Gloria's voice carried down the open stairway into the living room. She and Cheryl Akers had gone up to her room a while ago and left the door open.

"We've worked too hard not to."

"You're right. We'd better make a plan."

Bill caught Madge's eye just as she glanced up. "Th-that's our daughter, full of spice and organized, to boot."

"Sure is. She has so much spunk—if anyone complains about the play, I'd hate to be in their shoes. Gloria isn't about to let an opposing opinion stand in her way."

"Nope, and sh-she shouldn't."

Discussing their youngest always brought a smile to Bill. One way or the other, something Gloria said or did came into play each day, either here or at the office.

"I have no doubt she and Cheryl will make sure they get to act out that play. I just hope we get to be in the audience."

"Why w-wouldn't we?"

"Oh, I don't know. I suppose Pastor Z could tell them the time isn't appropriate, since everyone's still in shock. He might convince them to perform just for him or something."

"*Humph*—if that happens, I'll have a talk with Aivars myself."

His hearty response heartened Madge. During this gloomy week, light moments had become few and far between.

In time, perhaps, normalcy would indeed return. But the mystery of the murder wound around and around in Madge's mind until everything seemed hopelessly complicated. If only Sheriff Finley could ferret out the murderer, everyone would sleep a lot easier.

Bill threw out a similar thought. "Sure hope Dale can solve this in the next few days. I stopped by his office this morning, and he's having an awful time. No leads at all. Aivars feels awful bad, too."

"Do you call him by his first name to his face?"

"He asked me to. 'Course I won't in front of anybody else, but it's no time for formalities. That young fella needs a friend."

Just then, Gloria and Cheryl bounced down the stairs. "We'll be over at Cheryl's place for a couple hours, okay?"

"Sure, have fun."

Bill shook his head as they crossed the front porch. "Wouldn't it be something if we all could r-recover from t-trauma as quickly as those two?"

Letting a nod answer for her, Madge picked up her knitting. Her ability left a lot to be desired, but the local Red Cross director had just placed an announcement in the *Chronicle*. The troops were desperate for socks, and this would only get worse when European temperatures plummeted come autumn.

"If only I could knit like Grandma used to. She would never take a week to finish one sock."

Bill's chuckle warmed her heart. "You'd have to learn to sit still for l-longer, d-don't you think?"

"Right you are, Billy-Boy. And I'd have to get better at concentrating on one thing at a time, too."

Saturday, April 15, 1944

Light from the sanctuary window hit Madge full in the face, momentarily blinding her. In that transcendent space when time seemed to hover in midair, she imagined Vera's hat appearring right next to the altar and shook herself.

As if this past week hadn't shaken her enough.

Bill grasped her hand, something he never did in church before the war. While he was deployed, they'd missed so many Sundays together, including two Easters. For some reason, the hymns got to her back then, and "I Need Thee Every Hour," which Otto was playing right now, was no exception.

During Bill's absence, she'd also had to avoid other songs. The Andrews Sisters' release, "Don't Sit Under the Apple Tree With Anyone Else But Me," brought back the past. Years ago when they were courting, she and Bill sometimes sat under the tall maple in his parents' yard, and the memory erupted every time she heard that melody.

The same with, "In Your Easter Bonnet." Way back then, Bill sang the chorus to her a few weeks before their wedding.

Around her, women's hats were everywhere. Putting on a simple one had always made her feel special. Her modest straw fit this somber occasion. If she had to describe it in her column, she'd write *understated*. Not exactly intended for formal occasions, but still classy.

As if he could sense her angst, Bill pressed her hand. The best Madge could hope for during the funeral was that Vera's crazy hat would stay out of her thoughts.

As the fanciful image faded, the silver casket positioned before the altar riveted every eye in the place. After the viewing in the entrance, the funeral director had added a large spray of white Canna Lilies on the sealed lid.

Two stands of assorted flowers graced each side of the church, and various other arrangements lined the front. As usual, the undertaker would help the family take them to the gravesite when the service ended, leaving a few to use on the altar.

The pew Vera and Harry always occupied drew Madge, and several other heads turned that direction, too. People from out of town used that space today, since members of the congregation avoided sitting there.

Hard to believe Vera died right in this basement, where she

had reigned over the Ladies' Aid for so long. Just like that, all the pettiness vanished like an early morning mist. Instead, people mentioned her organizational skills and foresight.

"She really had a talent for making things happen, didn't she?"

Some honest soul offered, "She would've made a good army sergeant." Madge heartily agreed—Vera's talents had been wasted here, but she might have made a valuable contribution in some other arena.

Oh, why couldn't they have appreciated her while she lived and breathed? Why had she become such a thorn in the side of so many women?

As the prelude ended, the number one suspect in Vera's murder came forth—their new pastor. If someone had attempted to write a novel with bizarre elements, they couldn't have done a better job.

A sense of unreality cloaked this service, even more than at other funerals. In the midst of celebrating the Resurrection, this death forced everyone to ponder an unthinkable aberration in their little town.

Once, at an evening ladies' meeting at the Baptist church, a visiting speaker from another town had a heart attack. The women were horror struck, and Doc had to deliver her body home.

But a murder? Madge hardly dared whisper the word.

As Bill murmured in her ear just before they finally fell asleep last night, "Can't g-get it into my head that we're g-going to a crime scene for the funeral tomorrow."

The church kitchen had indeed become a crime scene. But though Sheriff Finley finished his investigation two days ago and removed the barrier ropes, Madge's own investigation had yet to begin.

Oh, she'd been down there yesterday morning with the committee to set up the luncheon. Most of them had cooked the food at home instead of using the kitchen. Madge itched to launch a search, but she'd just have to wait until no one else was around.

Did the same urgent desire also nag at Pastor Z? Surely he must long to clear his name as much as she did, since Vera's parting message had placed her—Madge McQuestion—squarely on the suspect list, too.

Obviously neither of them had stabbed Vera. Anyone in their right mind would never even consider such a possibility. What motive could they possibly have? But how could they prove their innocence?

The challenge had niggled at her ever since a sheepish Dale had informed her and Bill of her infamous status.

At his final declaration, Bill pulled her close. When he made his final declaration, Bill pulled her close.

"You'll need to stay around town, Madge, until we conclude the investigation."

Sensing her vulnerability, Bill took over. "D-don't worry, D-Dale. Sh-she will."

When Dale left, Bill shook his head. "D-don't know that I recall ever seeing you speechless before, hon."

Halfway through "Trust and Obey," a clear idea surfaced. Since Vera mentioned the hat with her dying breath, the blasted thing must possess some sort of hidden value.

The search had to focus on the hat, every insanely decorative element of the ridiculous creation. Near the end of the hymn, another of Madge's sighs reached Bill, who turned his dark eyes on her. Better conceal her fierce concentration on the murder—no reason to upset him. After all, he'd seen far too much dying at the Kasserine Pass.

On the other hand, how could she manage the burgeoning desire to figure this thing out? At times, she felt as though her head would blow up.

Then Pastor Z's opening words riveted her.

"We come to this service with a sense of ambivalence. Last Sunday, in the midst of death, we looked into the empty tomb. Now, in the midst of spring, we embrace winter once again, with a forecast of snow."

He paused to survey the overflowing crowd. People were even standing up in the balcony.

"But we're Midwesterners. We're used to snow in the spring. We know warmer weather will come soon. And in the midst of this conundrum, we cling to the one thing we know for sure—God never forsakes his own. He remains with us through every trial."

As he read the obituary, Madge leaned her head against Bill's shoulder for a moment. She already had the details memorized from typing it down at the office.

In the first row beyond the casket, Harry, his sister and brother-in law, their children, Vera's heretofore unknown cousin, and other relatives sobbed and sniffled.

Wait a minute . . . Helene? Hadn't she left for La Crosse the day after the welcome dinner? She had seemed so intent on her job for the war effort.

So why did she come all this way today? Or had she ever left town at all?

Madge didn't even realize she'd sighed until Bill enfolded her hand in his. What a comfort, in spite of his own challenges. He gave her strength, but at the same time, an insistent question harangued her. Why did things have to be so blasted complicated?

At Sunday worship the next morning, a cloud still hung over the sanctuary. For the first time, the permanence of Vera's absence struck Madge. The knowledge almost tore her apart.

No, they had never been fast friends and didn't even like each other much. But right now, strange as it seemed, she missed Vera's stringent ways. It didn't help that Dale paid another call to her and Bill at the office yesterday just before closing time.

Besides the hat, he told them another piece of evidence had gone missing the day of the murder. Vera's church key—which by rights ought to have been in her purse, on her person, or somewhere in the basement—was nowhere to be found.

Something else to search for, as if the bonnet weren't enough.

On this day when Madge surely needed all the sermons she could get, this one flew right over her head.

Later, she would return to search the kitchen. Somebody had to check things out, not that she didn't trust Dale to do his job. But he was, after all, a bachelor. With no one at home to brainstorm with, how could he possibly mull over all the angles of the case?

Anyone could see he needed help solving this mystery.

Chapter Ten

Monday, April 17, 1944

At six o'clock in the morning, Aivars awakened to five thick inches of spring snow. Heavy wet stuff. His first cognizant thought went to Bill. Would he be able to shovel out their place?

Maybe he should call, or just dig out his '36 Mercury and drive over there. He looked again at his watch. No, too early.

He lit the flame under a burner, filled his chipped enamel coffee pot with water, dumped in the coffee grounds, and set the pot on to boil. Then he got dressed, and after downing some coffee and two pieces of burnt toast, bundled up and went outside.

Bright April sunshine reflected from a pristine blanket of white. The sun's trek would eventually melt this snowfall, but until then, the streets would be a royal mess.

By the time he shoveled his sidewalk and freed his car from the downfall, enough local traffic had made the byways semi-passable, and he was sweating like a pig. Such a weird saying—did pigs sweat?

As he wiped his dripping forehead, the snowplow went by, creating a new pile to work through. Just what he needed, actually—he'd fought for sleep last night and could use a hearty workout.

One thing his professors had neglected to say: Funersls took a lot of preparation and drained the life out of a person. An Easter sermon, the funeral sermon, and last Sunday's—somehow he'd written and delivered all three, but the effort took a toll. Now he faced another one.

He attacked the fresh pile with vigor, stuck his shovel in the rumble seat and got behind the wheel. Snow had drifted onto the cracked leather seat—obviously, the windows needed to be re-sealed.

If he had suffered like Bill, the last thing he'd want to face would be five inches of slushy snow. This would be a day to hibernate until nature took its course.

Pulling up in front of the house confirmed his suspicions. No sign of anyone yet. But as he opened his car door, Madge appeared in the front doorway, fully dressed, and beckoned him inside.

"My, you're up bright and early. To what do we owe this honor?"

"Good morning. Thought I'd come over and see how you two were doing, and," he grinned up at her, "shovel you out if you need some help."

Her eyelashes glistened. "We've had snow in April before, even in May, but this one caught me unawares. You did warn us, though."

Much to his delight, she gave him an impulsive hug. "Bill had a rough night and could hardly get out of bed this morning, so I was about to tackle this mess."

"Oh, no. Brought my shovel, so if you'll excuse me, I'll get started."

"All right, but then you'll join us for breakfast, won't you?"

Doing something for someone else felt so good. True, he'd been intent on helping people all week, but this would be different— He'd be able to see a tangible difference.

Aivars could have gone on slinging snow forever. But a half hour later, Madge yelled from the porch. "That's good enough—the rest will melt. Come on in!"

Rubber galoshes left on the porch, he entered the warm kitchen stocking-footed. Bill sat at the table with Gloria, who looked ready for school.

"Good morning, Bill, Gloria. Thanks for the invitation, or was that an order from your wife?"

Gloria giggled. "You've got that part right, it *did* sound more like a command."

Bill laughed. "Sit d-down while Madge gets b-breakfast on the t-table." His stomach growled and everyone chuckled.

After eating, Gloria excused herself. "Time to head to school. See you tonight at Youth Fellowship, Pastor Z."

"Could I drive you? It's a long walk in all this snow, and there's a nippy wind out there."

"Oh, that would be wonderful." A bright smile lighted Gloria's face. Why hadn't he noticed how pretty she was?

"Come on then, let's go." He glanced at Bill. "I'll be right back."

The short drive gave little time for conversation, but for someone so vivacious, just one question sufficed..

"What are your plans after high school?"

"I've given that a lot of thought lately. Nursing, maybe. What do you think?"

"An excellent choice," Aivars drew up close to the curb. "Nursing takes dedication, and you have the perfect personality to deal with patients. Praying about decisions always clarifies things for me."

She opened the door and stepped out. "Thank you. Guess I could do more of that."

"See you tonight." Before pulling away, he relished her laughter carrying on the breeze as some other students joined her. Somebody launched a snowball. Gloria giggled and returned the favor without missing a beat.

In his rearview mirror, Aivars frowned at his image. "Don't even think about it, Zeeb."

Back at Bill and Madge's, with his shovel slung over his shoulder, Aivars rounded the house. Might as well clear the drift around the back door. As he began, Bill stuck out his head.

"Don't work too hard now. Didn't they say soldiering might kill you?"

"I think that'd be a whole lot worse."

"Naw. You'd dance your way right through it."

When Gloria came home after the youth meeting, she raved. "Pastor Z showed us the most fun game. Sort of a puzzle based on the Bible. You'd have enjoyed it, I know."

Then she frowned, so Madge asked, "What's that pout?"

"All of a sudden, Vern has started hanging around Missy Hansen. I was hoping he might ask me to the Prom."

"That silly Prom. I've always hated them."

Bill gave a warning look, so she softened her tone. "I mean, events like that put everyone in a bad position, especially girls without a date. I've been through it twice now, and it left a bad taste in my mouth.

"The girls in Lillian's class got possessive in the weeks before Prom, and with so many boys already drafted, it's bound to be even worse this year. Why don't you, Cheryl, and Audrey go together? Then nobody'll feel left out."

"I think that's a g-good idea." Bill reached over to pat Gloria's knee. "You've g-got all the t-time in the world to date f-fellas, even if it m-might not seem like it."

"Yeah. If this stupid war would ever get over, they all could come home. That is, if they survive."

"Well, I p-predict Rome'll fall to the Allies soon. And when that happens, our b-boys can storm on up into France and cross right over into G-Germany. Won't that be a g-glorious day?"

"That's for sure. We have to keep our hearts set on it." Madge eyed Gloria, hoping Bill's comments produced a good effect.

They did—their daughter's cheery smile returned.

"Hmm—I'll talk with Audrey." Gloria started toward her room. "Anyway, I sure had a great time tonight. Never thought Youth Fellowship could be *fun*, but Pastor Z says we're supposed to enjoy life. He sure is different from that cranky old—"

She left her statement right there. It wouldn't be the first complaint about their last visiting pastor. Gloria yelled back down as she neared the top of the stairs. "Hey, why don't we invite Pastor Z over for supper some night? Audrey said her mom already has."

"Okay, I'll get right on it."

Bill perked up in his chair, where he had snoozed through the last of the evening news on the big *Philco* radio sitting in the corner. Maybe having company would do them all good.

Should she fry a chicken or go with a pork roast baked with apples? Better check the ration book . . . her famous custard pie took plenty of sugar.

Chapter Eleven

Tuesday, April 25, 1944

A perfect custard pie stood at the ready, and Madge decided to whip up a batch of chocolate chip cookies in case Aivars didn't like custard. If he enjoyed it as much as Bill, she'd send the cookies home with him.

Or better yet, have Gloria stop by the church office after school tomorrow to deliver them. Bill would accuse her of matchmaking. And he would be right.

They used to socialize more, but everyone seemed to understand he needed quiet. This afternoon, noticing him come home a little early to wash up for their guest warmed Madge's heart. He even used his dad's remedy for the ink around his fingernails.

"Nothing like rubbing alcohol," he would say. Madge set a jar of baby oil near the sink to soften the drying effect.

Compliments on the roast beef and homemade biscuits seemed sincere. In a discussion on the state of the economy, Gloria chimed in with intelligent remarks, and Aivars turned her way.

"Do you follow these goings-on?"

"Dad and I talk about newspaper articles, don't we?"

Bill beamed.

"Sure do. I want my girls to know how to get along in this world."

"We've learned quite a bit about this in economics class, too. Mr. Pliny says the manufacturing boom has changed everything.

His brother works in Detroit, and the weekly wage has gone up almost fifty percent since '39."

"Sounds about right. Lillian's making as much in her factory as any man around here. 'Course, that's out in California."

Content to listen and observe, Madge sat back. Bill's points made sense. Something about Aivars calmed him—what a gift that he'd come to Caroline!

The nation's finances interested her, but human dynamics attracted her even more. So nice to see her family interacting—especially Bill.

At one point, the conversation turned to *Arsenic and Old Lace.* "Whose idea was that p-play, anyhow? You young p-people did a bang-up j-job."

"I don't remember, but I'd sure like to be in a play again sometime."

Bill's forehead puckered. "When was your drama teacher drafted?"

"Last summer. I'd looked forward to trying out this year."

The youth group had taken center stage in the church basement last night, drawing a decent-sized crowd. There'd been a few whispers, probably about the appropriateness of the performance, but lots of laughter, too.

The next comment from Aivars made Madge's hopes surge.

"Let's do another one sometime, maybe for the entire community. What do you think, Bill?"

"Why not? This town has always supported the school plays, and we need all the cheer we can g-get as this war d-drags on."

"Might be a way to draw in more people. Maybe you and your friends could help with the groundwork, Gloria ?"

"What do you mean?"

"Researching some plays would be helpful. We might also consider some old classics. Maybe you and a couple of the others can come up with some ideas. Would you be willing to organize things?"

"Wow. I'd be thrilled, sir."

"Please, I'd like you all to think of me as a friend."

Were lights flashing between them? This exchange reminded Madge of the summer fireflies in the pastures down by the river.

Maybe some evening the four of them could have a picnic. Gloria could show Aivars where she and her friends had spent their childhood summers.

Who knew what might come of that?

Chapter Twelve

The following week, Madge arranged for a meeting with Aivars. The investigation had still turned up nothing, and circumstantial evidence kept them at the top of the suspect list.

Such a lovely morning. All signs of that last snow had disappeared, and robins pecked in the grass for worms.

Aivars sat back after she blurted out her mission. "What do you have in mind?"

"I wish I knew. I just can't keep going with this *Damocles Sword* hanging over my head. I have to do *something*!"

"I know the feeling. By the way, I've been meaning to ask you to call me Aivars. You and Bill mean a lot to me."

"Oh, thank you."

His laugh filled the small office. "Most people don't realize I'm just like everybody else, except you and Bill."

"Yet with a different role to play."

"Exactly. It's just that people put pastors on a pedestal. I wish they wouldn't, because falling off is no fun."

"That Easter plant didn't help—your catch honestly looked miraculous."

Ignoring her remark, Aivars rubbed his palms together. "All right, where do we start, Madame Sherlock?"

"That silly hat bothers me most. Surely someone in the neighborhood saw Vera leave the casserole. Nobody could have missed that hat."

"But don't you think Sheriff Finley has already canvassed the neighbors?"

"Probably, but some folks shy away from the law—they get nervous, you know? Maybe to you or me, someone would open up."

"Hmm." Aivars steepled his fingers. "Would you mind if I talk to the neighbors myself?"

"Not at all. I'll just have to think what I can do in the meantime."

"I'm sure you'll come up with something." His chuckle ran deep. "Just don't get into any trouble, all right?"

After dinner, Aivars set out, starting with the Hansens directly across from the parsonage.

"Why, Pastor, what a nice surprise! Won't you please come in?"

"Thank you, Mrs. Hansen. I'd like to ask you a few questions."

"Of course. Can I get you some coffee or tea?"

"Oh, no, but thank you." He followed her into the living room and took the chair she pointed to.

He'd already gotten to know the Hansens during the evenings, even sat on their porch to chat with them. But this was different.

"Did you want to speak with Raymond? He's out back."

"No, that's all right. I was wondering if you happened to see anything the morning Mrs. Walters was killed?"

Alta frowned. "Sheriff Finley asked me about that."

"I was hoping you might have thought of something more after he questioned you."

"Like what?"

"Did you see Vera drop off a casserole dish on my porch that morning?"

"I'm afraid not." Her brow scrunched as though she wished she had. "Guess I was out back in my flower bed. It must be awful to be a suspect, but no one believes you could have killed Vera."

Aivars chatted a while longer before he stood and thanked Mrs. Hansen.

At the door, he turned back. "If you do happen to think of something . . . *anything* . . ."

"You can count on it."

The door clicked shut, and he ran a hand through his hair, debating. Some folks might take offense if they'd already been questioned once.

Halfway home, he decided to make one more visit. Sigurd and Clara Mae Andreesen had been the first to welcome him to town—such nice folks. Maybe, just maybe . . .

A quote he'd always liked came to mind. *Great works are performed not by strength but by perseverance*—Samuel Johnson, he believed. What did he have to lose?

Clara Mae was out washing her hands at the pump. "Why, hello, Pastor. I'm a sight to behold, been out hoeing the first weeds."

"You're fine."

"I just can't stop thinking about what happened. Such a tragedy, and in our own church, of all places!"

"Yes. But I keep remembering our troops. What they're going through goes way beyond our troubles." Aivars hesitated. "May I come in for a few minutes?"

"Oh, dear, where's my hospitality?" She swung open the back door. "Sigurd's late, out to the farm, helping Lester with the plowing." In the kitchen, she hung her work apron on a hook and led the way through the dining room.

The Andreesen home, like many here, had been built in the late 1920s. The closed-in front porches of these two-story bungalows spanned the width of the house, an instant respite from winter weather.

The east dining room wall boasted potted plants on a trunk and some wooden stands. The African violets impressed Aivars most. His aunt had a green thumb with them, though some women declared violets *touchy*. Aunt Mabel said they needed light from the East and watering from the bottom.

Her pots sat in saucers where she poured water every two or three days. In winter, she moved them to her cool upstairs, in eastern light but hibernating for the season.

Clearly, the upholstered armchair Clara Mae pointed out had

seen a lot of use. Was it true that people's houses reflected their personality?

"That chair was my father's. We've worn out the stuffing, but Sigurd still loves it." She clasped her hands, waiting for him. "I made a fresh pot of coffee for our supper. Would you like some?"

Ready to decline, Aivars changed his mind. "Don't mind if I do, thank you."

"Coming right up."

Soon, she returned in a fresh apron and set a tray with pound cake on an oak table between them. Doctoring his coffee to just the right shade of creamy brown, Aivars glanced at the clock.

"What's is it?"

"I may be grasping at straws . . . I'm sure you've already talked to Sheriff Finley about the day Vera died."

Clara Mae nodded.

"Well, because I found her, I'm the prime suspect in her murder."

"Pure rubbish!" Clara Mae spat out her opinion. "*No one* believes you killed her, even Sheriff Finley."

"But until the real killer is found, I'm trying to discover if anyone has remembered something new since he questioned them. Did you catch a glimpse of Vera on the morning she died?"

Clara Mae shook her head. "Sigurd and I left town early that day." She bit her upper lip.

"He had an appointment with a specialist up in Minnesota, and . . ." Her words trailed off.

"A specialist?"

Bright red spots adorned Clara Mae's plump cheeks. "He had an infected toenail. I tried a bread poultice and everything else I knew, and Doc Lindquist said it needed to be lanced, but . . ."

She lowered her voice and glanced away. "Doc is getting older, you know, and this required a steady hand. Sigurd was embarrassed to go somewhere else, so please don't let on I told you."

"Of course not." Aivars slumped back. "Ingrown toenails hurt so much. I hope all is well by now?"

"Yes. It's not that we don't trust Doc, mind you . . ."

"Oh, I understand. Well, I'd better be going. Thank you so much for your time. I appreciate your help."

She walked him to the door. "The sheriff's our nephew—we'd have told him right off if we saw anything."

In a small town, families crisscross. You have to step carefully to avoid insulting somebody's relatives.

Ah, Dad the prophet. Aivars tucked away this family connection for future reference.

"I keep thinking there surely must be some witnesses."

"You'd think so, since it happened in broad daylight. But nobody's said a word. I'll keep my ears open."

Crossing the threshold, Aivars lanced a parting word. "Thank you again. You're such a good listener."

"I always think there must be something I can do besides pray when I'm in a tight spot. That's human nature, I guess."

He went down a step, but Clara Mae still had to reach up to pat his shoulder. "I've prayed for years to be more trusting, but that's still the hardest thing to do."

"Need any help back there, Dad?"

Gloria's voice called Bill from the cavernous reaches of the *Chronicle* files. He retreated way back there from time to time—something about being in the aisle full of archives did his heart good. So much history here, and history often held the answer you were seeking.

This evening, his daughter might have spoken to him from across the Pacific Ocean. He hadn't meant to stumble across his army medals and wished he hadn't. He'd been searching through some boxes on a few rickety shelves behind the presses when a heavy gold envelope slipped to the floor.

Right now, he couldn't have told anyone what he'd expected when he opened it. He didn't recall putting it here at all. The outline of George Washington on his Purple Heart medal caught him unawares, and he'd have been glad for a nearby chair to sink into.

Cold in his palm, the circular piece made him nauseous as he squatted there. He tossed it to the floor and braced his head with his hands as a rush of memory raged through his mind.

If only he could toss away the reason for that medal as easily as he threw it from his hand. The commander handed the award to him and several other survivors in the evacuation hospital, where nurses scurried to prepare them for emergency surgery or transport.

Oh, the chaos in that pole tent sent up in the desert! Exhaust from a steady line of trucks carrying the wounded from the fateful Kasserine Pass mixed with a cacophony of sounds. Terse-lipped doctors snapped orders, nurses scurried from soldier to soldier, and every few minutes, stretcher bearers pulled back the tent flap to deposit more moaning GIs in the makeshift facility.

To put it bluntly, his unit's poor resources had been no match for Rommel's tanks, and casualties mounted as the men tried to save each other. They gave it their all, but their all wasn't enough.

That day, he watched enemy fire riddle more than one man. One young fellow's helmet flew thirty feet at the impact, and his lifeless body landed a foot from Bill. Since then, this scene and others just as dire haunted him over and over.

If only he'd been able to help those boys. If only. If only.

Seeing the medal sent him back into North Africa, complete with odors he'd never before encountered. Might sound prejudiced, but the nomadic people there *did* smell different if you stood in a crowd, and the open latrines stunk to high heaven.

He avoided those as much as possible, but sometimes had no other choice. *Choice*…the very word seemed out of place.

Stateside, the command had used him to train recruits, and in the field, his commander tasked him with writing reports. That meant he kept company with officers much of the time.

But in the thick of the fighting, he couldn't simply stand back.

He'd expected to take up arms when he signed up for the National Guard in the fall of '40, after President Roosevelt asked for huge supplements to his defense budget.

Not long afterward, Bill's old army buddy, still in the service, sent him a letter. Anybody with military experience knew that a program including 50,000 airplanes a year meant war down the road.

At that time, the War Department had begun supplying surplus arms to England in spite of the political divisions—isolationists versus non-isolationists. The America First Committee advertised in newspapers:

Save our sons…

No war, no convoys, no death for American boys.

Nobody wanted to officially enter the fray. Well, that wasn't true—some did, including FDR. And then in September, Congress passed the first peacetime draft and ordered the National Guard into active military service.

This signaled a year of preparedness training, they said, but there was no denying that mobilization lay ahead. His buddy saw through it all and was right on the money. Only a matter of time before the nation went to war.

Bless Madge, who listened quietly when he mentioned going back in. "The monthly pay isn't a lot, but it would help out."

He'd been foolish to take that particular tack. She scoffed. Life was good here—the *Chronicle* would never make them rich, but who cared? They had all they needed, all that really mattered.

He let some time pass before trying again, and they talked about him deploying several times, always leaving open the possibility. Throughout those weeks, the commander sent out several broad hints.

Finally, as tensions mounted in Europe and in D.C., he pulled Bill aside, "We'll need your maturity and experience. Not many still remember what war is like. It'll be mostly boys called up, you know, and men of endurance will have to make decisions on the spot."

Made all the sense in the world, and back at home, one good look at the Caroline football team in the 1942 season's first game told Bill he had no choice. It was one thing to fight the neighboring high school team on the gridiron, but quite another to face machine guns and tanks, and these boys would be the ones to face the enemy.

When it came down to it, even though he had laid the groundwork, it took some effort to convince Madge. She had plenty of good reasons for him to stay right here.

"Why? You're not between twenty-one and thirty-five."

"I know, but this thing isn't going away, hon. They'll be deploying men like me sooner or later, and it's better to get in there now so I'm prepared if war does come."

"How do you know what the boys'll need?"

He hadn't given her a good answer, because the truth was, he simply knew. His experience on the battlefield amounted to pure gold. Finally, he tried again. He asked her to trust him.

"I'd rather be situated with the Guard ahead of time than called up to any old regiment they choose. Don't you see? Then I'll know what's expected of us and can make a difference for all the privates."

The look in her eyes wrenched his heart.

"They'll lower the age once this thing gets going. My British friend tells me how dire the draft is getting over there, and the same thing will happen here. They'll start taking boys just turned eighteen, like they did in the last war, and men my age."

She smiled then. "But you lied about it back then."

"Yeah. And the army still thinks I just turned forty."

To her credit, she accepted his choice, although not without more questions. "Do you know something the rest of us don't?"

"Not really. It's just that I've been over there. We were a bunch of babes trying to figure out what to do, and I think—"

"What?"

"At the game the other night, watching those young fellas toss the football around, I felt . . . I don't know how to put it, exactly. Maybe the word is *called.*"

She fell silent, so he waited till later to try again. "Those football players will be drafted, no doubt about it. If we had sons who had to go, I'd want somebody with a level head to make decisions about their lives, wouldn't you?"

Her tears made him weak all over. She said no more, but he knew she was thinking. "*Why does it have to be you?*"

He knew because the same question plagued him. They were so nicely settled here, with all the reasons in the world to keep it that way.

Putting out the weekly paper kept him on his toes. Always something going on in town, always a challenge to meet. Keeping the press going required some expertise, too—breakdowns occurred regularly. But balanced with the way things were going in the world, his work seemed trivial.

He'd been following events in Europe, studying Hitler's rise to power, not to mention Mussolini's. The plight of those defeated in the Spanish Revolution ripped through him, and he wasn't alone.

He'd heard that some Great War officers had even gone over there to risk their lives in somebody else's fight.

In the Philippine Islands, a battle was brewing, too.

He didn't know what to think, but every sign pointed to the States engaging more and more. He'd rather sign up now and have some semblance of control over his assignment.

Blame the Boy Scouts—they taught him never to assume anything and always to be prepared. Prepared for what, Madge would ask, but it was the *what* that drove him to act. The *what* consisted of his World War I memories.

After minimal training, he'd entered battle with his unit at barely seventeen, and those months in France had proven unforgettable. He'd volunteered to be a dispatch runner on the Western Front.

His wound in the Meuse-Argonne offensive in September of '18 had sent him to a hospital and eventually to one stateside.

With the help of the Reconstruction Aides at Fort McPherson, Georgia, he conquered what the docs said would be a permanent limp. Those physical therapy aides were relentless about his progress—massages, hot water treatments, exercise regimens, and other methods he had long forgotten. But the tenacity of those women made all the difference.

Even after all these years, the face of one Aide named Gracie passed before him. She couldn't have been but a few years older than him at the time, yet she supervised all the other workers and demanded that he keep at his exercises.

Probably she had grandchildren by now. Wherever she was, did she recall those days, too?

At any rate, by the time the call came, Madge had made peace with his decision. He'd already been away twice for a couple of weeks' training, and everything had gone fine here.

Just Madge and Gloria would be left, with Judith married and Lillian about to do her bit for the war effort. A longtime friend of his Dad, a newspaperman in a nearby town, offered to man the press in his absence. Madge would bear up and make him proud, he knew she would.

"Dad? Where are you? Mom said I'd find you back here somewhere."

Bill took a deep breath and willed away the tight ball just below his diaphragm. Maybe he'd been wrong all along. He had lost his health and two years of Gloria's life. Worse, he wasn't at all sure he accomplished his mission.

Well so be it. Too late now.

When he stood up, George Washington's profile glinted at him from a corner. He hurried over and kicked the medal as hard as he could.

By the time Gloria found him, he had shoved his war memories back down where they belonged.

Chapter Thirteen

After meeting with Aivars, Madge considered her options. As she passed the garage, the front window of their 1932 Ford station wagon glinted at her. An impulse took her—why not drop in on Harry?

Every Sunday since the funeral he sat in the same spot, his demeanor bland. She tried to imagine what went through his mind. How would a numbers person process a loss like this?

Couldn't hurt to find out how he was doing, could it?

But of course, she mustn't appear empty-handed, so she ran into the house and filled a plate with cookies. The old wagon fired to life and she backed out. Two blocks down the street, she stuck her arm out to signal a left turn and headed to the outskirts of town.

Living in the country but less than a half-mile from Caroline seemed ideal—the best of two worlds. You'd be close to the grocery store and work but have peace and quiet.

Harry took some time coming to the door. "Hello, Madge. Come on in." His eyes looked dull, his face drawn and haggard, surprising in a man of his size.

"Thanks. I've been thinking of you every day. How're you doing?" She followed him through the back porch.

"I went to work this morning like usual but came back for a little lunch." He eagerly accepted the cookies.

"Can I do anything else for you or bring you something?"

"That's kind of you, but Trudy Rolfe and John have been checking in on me. Trudy brings over enough food to last a few days at a time. Good thing, since I can barely boil water."

His little joke eased an uncomfortable sensation in Madge's middle. One quick glance revealed that washing dishes fell outside his expertise, too.

"I'm glad someone's looking out for you. But if you ever need anything, please let me know."

As she spoke, Harry lumbered to the living room and dropped into a well-worn armchair. "Thanks. I appreciate that."

"I just can't . . . can't stop thinking about the . . . about Vera's death." Madge sank into a Queen Anne near the unlit fireplace.

"Me neither."

"Could I ask you a couple of questions?"

"Sure, what do you want to know?"

"Stop me if this is too painful for you, but I keep puzzling over the details. Were you home when she left the house that morning?"

Harry drew his large hand down his face. "Yeah, she rode with me, since I was about to leave for work. She'd made a casserole for Pastor Zevenbergen and was going to drop it off before going to the church. I was going to pick her up at eleven-thirty, but that's the last I saw of her."

"Was she going somewhere else after that?"

"She didn't say—sometimes she walks home. But she did answer a phone call before we left. I assumed it was one of her Ladies' Aid friends."

Though most businesses in town had telephones, many of the women had none at home yet. She and Bill used the office telephone when necessary, which wasn't often, and out in the country, the telephone company was putting in some poles. Clearly, Harry's position at the bank made a difference in their priorities.

"Was she wearing that . . . that hat?"

Harry *harrumphed*. "Might as well call a spade a spade. That thing was plumb ridiculous. Embarrassed me, it did."

"But do you remember if she put it on that morning?"

He coughed several times. Chest congested—better see Doc. "Can't rightly say. I wouldn't have noticed, I s'pose. Would've seemed strange if she wore it, wouldn't you think? I mean, after all, it was her *Easter* bonnet."

So he had no idea. At least the question about the car had found an answer. But Harry's cough sounded worrisome.

"Your cough doesn't sound good. Have you seen Doc Lindquist?"

"I'll stop by if it gets any worse."

So that was that. Nothing more she could do. Some men had to wait until they were on death's door to ask for help. She prepared to leave, but then inspiration struck.

"Harry, did Vera ever talk to you about that time we. . . About that scene in the basement that one night—you know—about the article I wrote?

"About you making fun of her hat?" For the first time since she arrived, a genuine smile appeared on Harry's face. "Oh, she was furious, all spit and fire. Nothin' I could do to calm her down. That woman could hold a grudge longer'n anyone I know."

His low chuckle gave Madge goosebumps. "Course it didn't help that I had no sympathy. Nothin' wrong with what you wrote. It was just plain funny, but my opinion irritated her, too. Guess I only made things worse."

"Well, I may have been guilty of overdoing it a little. But honestly, I never dreamed she would take it so seriously."

His jowls drooped again. "Don't fret yourself, Madge. Nothin' to be done about it now."

"I'm sorry, Harry, I never meant to hurt her."

He nodded but said nothing.

On her way to the back door, a whiff of stale bread wafted. As Madge reached for the doorknob, another hunch made her turn back.

"Do you know where Vera kept her hat? If she didn't wear it when she went out that morning, could it still be in the hatbox?"

Harry hesitated. "Well now, that's something I hadn't thought about until the sheriff asked me the same question. He came out here the day after she died."

"And?"

"She kept it in the spare bedroom closet down the hall." He threw up his arms. "Dale and me looked all around the house, but couldn't find a trace of the blamed thing."

Frustration cut like a bitter winter wind. With a sigh, Madge turned to leave.

Harry sat slumped into a chair at the kitchen table, eyes closed. He probably never even heard her say thanks. She walked through the back porch and let herself out.

"This just doesn't make any sense. Where else could that *blasted* hat be?"

Tuesday, May 2, 1944

"Hey, Bill. Good to see you." Tom Newberry tossed the *Des Moines Register* aside and leaped from his barber chair as Bill entered, bringing in a gush of rain and wind.

"Got time f-for a haircut?"

"You bet." Tom swept his arm toward the chair. "Humdinger of a day, ain't it? Durn nice rain, I say. Them farmers sure do need it, and so do I. Nothin' like a barber with no heads to scalp."

Bill shook the water off his coat and hung it on a hook beside the door. "Sorry it's a l-little wet."

"Um hmm, that's all right. Works out great for me. Already had four haircuts and two shaves, and it's not even ten o'clock. Rain always brings them farmers into town."

"I see y-your point."

Tom draped Bill's shoulders with a well-used canvas cloth. "'Magine you never saw downpours in Africa, right?"

When Bill gave no answer, he continued. "Well, then. What's the news these days?"

"I should b-be asking you."

"Nothin' much. The other day, Ned Pierce lost a calf n' the mother too. The vet from Osage tried to pull the calf, but it wasn't no use."

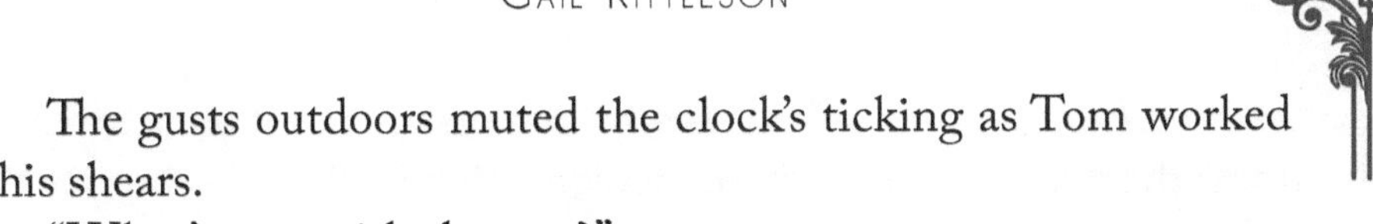

The gusts outdoors muted the clock's ticking as Tom worked his shears.

"What's new with the war?"

"Don't you listen to the reports?"

"Sure, and I read the papers every day, but all those places seem so far away. Like they're not real, y' know? I only pay attention to the stories about boys from here. The Wellesby's nephew or Betty's cousin, or that young fella that joined the Marines—what was his name, anyhow?"

He continued combing and clipping and Bill settled back against the crinkly barber chair. It had seen better days but still functioned, like much of the furniture in Caroline's main street businesses.

Bill took counsel with himself, since Tom's attitude had grated on him. But you had to consider the source, as Tom had never been accused of brilliance.

"Like the Battle of Sangshak. Seems the Japanese won that one. Mostly British troops, but Betty's cousin's ship might be in the area. Don't think I'd wanna be on one of them Navy boats. Too dangerous—enemy can come at you from all sides."

"B-but the B-British . . . held 'em off long enough to . . . s-send reinforcements to K-Kohima."

"Didn't realize that. Being a newspaperman sure makes a guy remember all the fine points."

"Maybe it's being a s-soldier?"

"That, too, I 'spect. Never went over m'self—too old for the last war. Heard any more about the *Tullibee*?"

"Sunk . . . full of Americans. Only one of the c-crew survived."

"How many casualties?"

"I heard s-sixty."

A few moments passed in silence, and then, "That's two times our graduating class, ain't it?"

The mirror reflected Bill's nod and a fresh crease in Tom's brow.

"Really thought this thing'd be over before now, to be honest. Seems like every campaign takes longer than they plan for. Went to war in '17 to make the world safe for democracy, but it seemed like it was the same then. Everything took way longer than we thought."

"But it d-did end."

"Yeah. And then them dictators started up—Mussolini, Hitler, and that Japanese fella."

"You mean the Emperor?"

"Yeah. What's his name—Hero somethin'?"

Bill let that one go and set his hopes on Tom hurrying up.

"They wanna control everybody, that's the thing. Just can't see why we couldn't do somethin' about all this earlier, before everything got so out-of-hand."

He rattled on for another full minute before pausing for Bill to say something. But what was the point of getting into all the complications leading to the present international predicament?

As he frequently did these days, Bill opted for a simple "Yep." And as often happened, that single syllable worked like magic.

Tom's face reddened as he peered closer at some strands of hair balanced in his fine-toothed comb. Then he changed the subject.

"Pretty soon, your Gloria's gonna graduate, ain't she? Can you believe it?"

Bill shook his head.

"Time flies, don't it? I s'pose then you 'n Madge'll keep on at the office, like always, and Gloria . . . What's she plannin' to do, anyhow?"

"N-not sure."

"Well, a girl with that much spunk'll go a long way, that's for sure. Pretty, too, and mighty friendly. She always waves when she walks by, y'know?" Tom took a broader vein, analyzing young folks these days.

The door opened, releasing another cold draft into the small shop. A woman stepped in, and it took Bill a second to realize Madge stood before them, drenched. A raincoat brushed her rubber boots and swathed her head to toe. Her hair had blown every which way, making her look like the wild woman of Borneo.

Wrist caught between the trim and the door, she held her umbrella outside. "Hate to bother you, but can you remember what day Merrill Alberts came into the office? I've misplaced my note about their farm sale, and if I knew when he came in, it would sure help."

"Hmm. Must've been T-Tuesday—he noticed I was covered in ink. And Mrs. P-Perkins skittered in r-right after he left, as I recall. Asked if it was too late to print a thank-you for all the food people brought when Herbert was sick. And you told her you'd find a way."

"That's right—must've been Tuesday." Madge's relieved expression reached to the depths of Bill's heart.

"I can always count on you to figure these things out. Don't know what I'd do without you."

"R-right. I'm your w-walking appointment b-book."

Widening the opening to the May onslaught, Madge repositioned her umbrella and sent him a big smile. Then she whisked out, leaving the door to shut on its own.

"Wow—quite the memory you've got. I can't keep track of things from one day to the next."

Still holding close the warmth of that smile, Bill shook his head. "N-not what it used to be, that's for sure. B-but sometimes it works p-pretty well."

Like a dog awaiting a morsel, Tom met his eyes in the mirror. A sudden impulse captured Bill. Why not give him something to chew on?

"Madge can out-think me any day. She invents things t-to make me feel better. She thinks I don't n-notice. But keep that to yourself, all right?"

With his forefinger, Tom zipped his lips, grazing his nose with the scissors in the process. Years ago, somebody described their town barber in a few words: *'Bout as sharp as a bowlin' ball, ain't he?*

Tom's eyes widened. "Not a word out of me, Bill. Not one word."

Chapter Fourteen

The day after his fruitless attempt to ply his neighbors for information, something took Aivars by surprise. In the Mercantile, he met Linda McDonald. Extreme shyness kept her home most of the time, Vera had informed him, so folks rarely saw her out in public.

To put her at ease this morning, he launched into a lighthearted account of his family in Bemidji. As they chatted, the tight lines around her mouth eased. Once, she even smiled and said, "Oh, really?"

As Linda moseyed on toward the front, a voice carried from the next aisle, over by the long wood cabinet displaying men's overalls, hats, and work shirts. Sounded like . . .

"You haven't heard? Why, it's all over town. That new young whippersnapper's getting our youth into acting."

"*Acting?*" Someone gasped, and Aivars strained to hear more. The agitated tone continued until he had no doubt about the speaker's identity.

Yep. Ingrid Tollefson. But hadn't she been there when the youth group acted out their little play? He thought so, since their daughter was involved.

It really didn't make much difference. Even if they hadn't come, she would have heard every detail about the play anyway—word traveled fast here. The *Caroline Express*, Madge called it.

His first impulse was to laugh. What was left of the youth group after the draft offered too few young people to pull off a full-fledged play. But didn't they deserve to have a little fun? One of them had already lost a family member to the war.

The mature thing would be to walk over and say, "Couldn't help overhearing you talk about the play. Did you enjoy it?" Or he could simply leave the store.

But curiosity got the better of him. What more was Ingrid going to say? He hunkered between the racks of men's jackets for more of a listen.

"I heard he lets *them* make the suggestions. An inappropriate idea in the first place, don't you think? I mean, they're so young and inexperienced, don't you know?"

The resultant titter issued too low and soft to discern. Even so, a warm rash started under the collar Aivars had so carefully ironed yesterday.

"Mustn't give young people too much free reign, no sirree. Why, before they left home to get married, my Virginia and Phyllis certainly never had anything to do with *plays*."

Eighteen-year-olds were *over there* risking their lives for Ingrid right now. Obviously, the gossiping old biddy hadn't heard the age-old truth that plays had been used to share Bible stories for centuries. Aivars had half a notion to write one himself and put Ingrid smack-dab in the center of the action.

Someone shuffled down the aisle he and Linda had just occupied, so Aivars nestled deeper into the hefty farmer jackets.

Scoot . . . shuffle, shuffle, shuffle . . . scoot . . . shuffle, shuffle . . .

Well, if it wasn't church meet-in-the-store-day. That had to be none other than Otto making his slow trek through the building. His cane clicked and dragged across the uneven floorboards in a unique pattern.

Peeking through the folds provided a glimpse of the old fellow apart from his organ for once. Age spots all over his neck, a hooked nose with a sizable wart, and ear hairs that begged to be clipped.

His permanent shoulder stoop completed the perfect image of Charles Dickens' classic curmudgeon, Scrooge. Did Otto ever step out of his house without a scowl?

Aivars checked himself. The old guy surely meant well, but after almost two months of hearing him search in vain for the correct organ keys, the patience his seminary advisors advised had worn as thin as the sparse hair on Otto's head.

Now, that was something Madge would say.

Had her astute sense of humor affected him already? Somehow, week after week, she came up with such pithy statements for her column. He'd have to ask her how she chose the title: *Talk of the Town.*

Bill had his own wittiness, too, although his speech hindered it. What a well-matched couple, those two.

Hovering there between the men's wear and Otto's shuffling feet, Aivars wished he could transport himself back to his study and forget all of this. Then Ingrid's next accusation heightened his angst.

"The other thing I heard, you just *won't* believe. Someone went for an evening walk last Saturday and saw *Gloria Harrington* out alone with that new pastor. Can you imagine?"

"Well, bless me, no. What on earth would Madge and poor Bill say about that?"

Talk about a head-shaker. Madge and Bill were *with* them the other night, walking just a few yards ahead. This confab was getting out-of-hand.

But who was Ingrid's listener? Some illustrious parishioner for sure, but which one? He focused on the two women's feet as they moved away, but could see only bony ankles partially obscured by low rubber boots.

Dirty ones, at that. He sniffed. Was that a tinge of chicken manure?

Oh, the joys of a rural parish—how it heightened one's senses! Visiting out in the country had taught him to identify the odor of chicken manure as opposed to cow, horse, or swine.

So those smelly boots could belong to Mrs. Penney or Harry Walters' neighbor down the road. Hmm. Aivars searched the new bank of local names in his brain. Might be a Rolfe. Yes, Trudy Rolfe.

"I must get going, but I'll keep you informed if I hear any more."

"Oh, please do."

"You can bet your bottom dollar, dear." Ingrid moved along, making it possible for Aivars to finally emerge from his cramped hiding place. She headed toward the checkout counter, while the smelly boots progressed in the opposite direction.

Trying to remember why he'd come in here in the first place, he checked to see if Ingrid's backside listed starboard. Yes, she was setting her purchases near the cash register.

He dithered a few minutes, but still couldn't remember what he needed. While the clerk helped carry Ingrid's purchases to her car, he slithered out and took an instant right.

Walking down Main Street, it hit him—he had a lot in common with Madge. He could picture her eavesdropping from a bunch of jackets. She always seemed to be on some escapade, and Bill allowed he had married a modern-day Miss Marple, a natural sleuth.

If you happened to find yourself on a suspect list, Madge certainly made a good companion.

Monday, May 8, 1944

When the town whistle blew at noon, Madge covered her ears. Why did the founders put that confounded thing just a block away? Friends of hers out in the country told her they could hear it, too.

Maybe that had been the point. In case of a tornado, even country folks would get the warning. And for a fire, they'd hurry to town to help.

As the eerie wail faded, her thoughts went straight to her talk with Harry. Not a completely satisfactory visit, but what else could she have done? She could imagine his shock if she'd mentioned searching the premises.

But how hard had he and Sheriff Finley searched? And what could it hurt to look again? One pressing question thrummed like a child's wind-up toy.

Vera's Easter bonnet wasn't where Harry thought it should be, so where *was* it? Had he and Dale even bothered to look anywhere else?

Perhaps he just said what he thought she wanted to hear. Something struck her as not quite right.

The office clock showed twelve now—no telling which was correct, the whistle or the clock, but did it really matter? Her morning's work lay barely touched.

This had to stop. With Bill slowly gaining ground, it would never do for her to fall off the deep end with the work here. The paper's success depended upon attention to detail week after week after week.

But even as she settled down in her chair, an image of Harry and Vera's big white house floated before her. She had half a notion to run over to the parsonage and ask Aivars if he'd mind sneaking around out there when they knew Harry was gone.

The longer she thought about it, the stronger the urge became. As the afternoon progressed, she began to feel sure tonight would be the perfect time.

Aivars had to be at the church council meeting with Harry, but that might be for the best. That fine, upstanding young man would never condone what she had in mind.

But she had an obligation to see this thing through. For Bill. Yes, to calm things down.

Recently, Aivars asked the council if they might include Bill in their meetings. He served as a member before he left, and his father had been a founding member.

What other reasons he gave the men, Madge had no idea. But whatever he said worked, because two members came by a week ago and asked Bill to join them.

"You have a broader perspective than all the rest of us put together, plus you know the building backward and forward. There's not a room where you haven't fixed something, is there?"

The other one added, "You headed up the building committee after the basement flooded that one spring. Don't know how you got the smell out, but it's been fine ever since."

From the kitchen, Madge had peered into the living room through the partially open door, just in time to hear Bill's heartening reply. "Sh-sure, I can come."

The two men shook hands with him. One said, "Good. You'll have a calming effect on one of our members, too."

Later, Bill asked her who they referred to, but Madge just shrugged. "I've lost track who's on the council but can think of several men who might get a little huffy."

A wonderful thing occurred then: Bill's lips turned up into his crooked grin. He looked downright pleased and allowed he'd had plenty of experience quieting upset people.

Then he went on. "I guess it wouldn't hurt to sit in on the meetings—they're just once a month."

And tonight just happened to be his first one.

Even as Madge tackled a pile of bills, the thought of searching the Walters' place kept surfacing. Ideas come to mind for a reason, and *this* surely had to be one of her best ever.

Even though she'd only been invited as far as Vera's living room at ladies' circle meetings, her eye for detail served her well. The house's layout was easy to visualize.

From the central living room, four doorways opened to other sections. To the right, an archway led through a short hallway to the second-floor stairway. Another door bordered the dining room, and from there, one went straight into the kitchen.

The third door led to the back bedroom, where Harry said he and Dale searched for the hat. And of course, the main entrance connected the front wrap-around porch.

Madge muttered to herself. "The hat's surely squirreled away in that house somewhere. I don't know how the feathers got near Vera's body, but she just couldn't have been wearing it that morning."

Men left something to be desired when it came to searching. You couldn't simply *look*, you must move things around and dig a bit. What if Vera hid the hat in the basement?

True, big old cellars usually harbored mold and mice, and smelled awfully musty, so she wouldn't have taken her precious possession down there, would she? But considering Harry's distaste for that bonnet, maybe *he* had.

Could he possibly have found out the truth? What if Vera let it slip that that someone gave the Easter bonnet to her?

Maybe— Madge got up and paced before the wide office window. She shuddered at her next thought, but what if that secret admirer had also been Vera's—? The phrase *secret lover* sent fire through her.

Good grief, how could she even *think* such a thing?

But what if it were true, and Harry's discovery of the liaison sent him into a rage? And what if, nearly out of his mind, he followed Vera to the church that morning?

After snuffing out her life, he took the gaudy thing with him because his fingerprints were on it. That's how those little feathery tidbits ended up in Vera's . . . in her blood. In his confusion after the . . . after he'd . . .

Oh, for heaven's sakes. Harry was too slow, too bulky, too— Long story short, he just couldn't be the killer.

But the brutality that took Vera's life replayed, just the same. A flash of silver, an unearthly moan as the knife found its mark.

Flopping in her chair, Madge dropped her forehead into her hands. "I just *have* to get busy!"

From the back room, Bill called for something, so she rechanneled her thoughts. A few minutes later, he said he had to run some errands, so she got down to business and cleaned off part of her pile.

But then she focused on the admirer, whoever he might be. Certainly not someone from here. Nobody had that kind of money to throw around.

Maybe *he* followed Vera to the basement for a tryst, and she refused him. A sick wave enveloped Madge's midsection. No. Vera might be as bossy as a heifer in heat, but she would never allow a stranger in the church kitchen.

And to think of someone making advances to her, especially

down there—inconceivable. Across the way, Bill stopped to talk with someone. Then he strode up the street to visit Bud Jensen at the hardware for the weekly advertisements.

"That's it, old gal. By the time he gets back, you *will* have these checks written out." Chances were, he'd be gone for at least a half hour.

As she sealed the last payment into an envelope and recorded the transaction, Bill came back. Soon he was busy again, and she called, "I'll be back in twenty minutes—going to deliver some checks around town."

As she followed her route, a plan unfolded. After supper when Gloria went over to Cheryl's, and Bill left for the meeting, she'd rev up the old Woodie and head out.

No two ways about it, this thing must be done. And she was just the one to do it.

Chapter Fifteen

A few rods short of the corner east of Harry's place, Madge coasted to a stop and shut off the motor. The engine coughed as dust swirled around, but the air settled down soon enough.

This field entrance seemed safe, hidden by a thick tangle of overgrown brush and trees bordering Teaser Creek. Thankfully, the bushes had broken into full leaf, making a great hideaway.

Harry would never spy her if he were late going to town. This unimproved road cut through the Tollefson's back forty. Bill had introduced her to these old *dead roads* years ago, and they always intrigued her.

The county deemed them unworthy of upkeep, but they drew her when she drove by. Somebody might have homesteaded down there decades ago. In the olden days, farmers had worked hard with horses pulling an iron drag to smooth these paths for travel. Now, even with tufts of wild grass growing in lines down the middle, these so-called dead roads might provide a shortcut.

Like an abandoned farmstead on the other side of town, this dead road still appeared usable. Why let it go to waste?

It wasn't long before a cloud of dust rose in the west. Soon, Harry's Chevy puttered by on the main gravel road. Just in time for the meeting—almost late. Vera would never have allowed this.

As soon as all trace of travel dissipated, Madge began her trek. With each step, she pleaded for heavenly favors.

Please let Ingrid Tollefson be busy washing supper dishes, looking out her kitchen window on the back side of her house. Direct her prying eyes toward the setting sun.

Such a serene scene she visualized, but there was nothing peaceful about the irregular thump of Madge's heart. This fell into the category of breaking and entering. Well, not breaking exactly, since no one ever locked their doors around here.

But she definitely planned to *enter*.

The thing was, most folks wouldn't mind, if somebody needed a drink or to use the telephone in an emergency. Most farms hadn't been hooked up yet, but no doubt, Vera had seen to that situation.

No sign of activity at the Tollefsons—still doing the milking chores. Didn't Ingrid make a point of letting everyone know what long hours they worked? And since the barn lay on the other side of the farmhouse, chances were slim she'd be looking this way.

Good. Madge started down Harry's driveway, thankful for no recent rains as she sneaked around the back of a corncrib. Such goings-on these days. With everyone growing victory gardens and hiring extra workers to weed and plant, tire marks showed everywhere.

Why, someone had even mentioned that a couple of hours west of here, and down by Waverly, Germans from the government Prisoner of War camp actually were lending farmers a hand. The thought produced a shiver.

Good thing nobody deemed Caroline an ideal spot for one of those camps—captured enemy troops would be one more thing to disturb Bill. Thanks to Aivars, he was doing better by the day.

Within minutes, the back door of the farmhouse appeared. "Well, old girl, you've always liked puzzles, so here's one as big as life and twice as scary."

Near the windmill, Madge slipped off her shoes and crossed the gravel driveway to the cool grass a few feet from the porch steps. She wiggled on the pair of gloves she stuck into her pocket before she left home.

The other day, Aivars told her how careful Dale had been with fingerprints—she dared not leave a trace. The lesson came home earlier when Dale stopped by the office that awful day a few weeks ago, to explain how Vera had died.

Right then and there, he insisted on taking her prints, as if she were a criminal. Even now, the humiliating memory incited tears.

Inside Harry's enclosed back porch, a shiny new Maytag wringer washer sat next to a deep galvanized sink. The washer's black drain hose hooked over its edge.

Rubber—rationed, but if you had enough money . . . Opposite the washer, a caned chair rested next to a large straw mat holding two pairs of boots.

On the wall above, several winter coats still hung on wall hooks. By now, Vera would have stored these away for next winter.

Obviously, nothing of interest to be seen here, but Madge scrutinized the corners before moving on into the kitchen. Once spotless, this room bore evidence of Harry's self-admitted lack of culinary skills. And plain old laziness.

A collection of dirty dishes peeked above the rim of the dishpan, and a china dish displaying dried-up remains sat on the counter. Crumbs covered the roll-top breadbox.

Vera would have a fit if she saw her kitchen like this.

Maybe Trudy came in and cleaned up after Harry every few days. Maybe she'd come over tonight . . .

"No—she's got her own family to feed about now. Keep your wits about you, Madge McQuestion. Check that back bedroom first. No use traipsing anywhere else if the bonnet's back there."

Hunching her shoulders, she tiptoed through the dining room and down the hall. The bedroom door creaked open at her touch and an onslaught of gardenia perfume caught her off-guard. She fell back against the nearest wall to catch her breath.

The light string must be here somewhere, so she fumbled in the waning daylight, found it, and pulled. Some farmhouses still lacked electricity, but not this one. Order prevailed here, Vera's brand of order, in every single fold of the chenille bedspread, each spotless floorboard, and every firmly closed drawer.

"Okay." Her voice sounded so small in this empty room, but she squared her shoulders. It wasn't as if Madge had to check every drawer, for heaven's sakes. That massive hat would never fit in any drawer made by man.

A drop-down secretary desk sat beneath the window. The hat would not be there, but something about the piece drew her. As she reached to lower the top, an inner alarm sounded.

"Now you're downright snooping," she whispered. "You came here to look for that hat. Get on with it and get out of here."

Despite the chastening, Madge still lowered the slanted wooden cover. Seemed as if it actually *wanted* to open. Inside, Vera's organizational nature prevailed. Each little cubbyhole held envelopes, monogramed stationery, or pens and ink jars.

In the slot on the far left, a postcard bearing a foreign postage stamp stood out. Madge gingerly pulled it out and noticed another like it. Then another, and two more.

Despite her sense of urgency, she simply couldn't stop until she read them all, postmarked London, months apart, over the past three years.

Odd. Who did Vera know in London? She bragged about everything, so surely the whole church, more likely the whole town, would have heard if she had a British friend. With the bombings over there, Vera would've had the Ladies' Aid sending care packages via the Red Cross. She'd have brought these cards in to show everyone.

No time to think about that now, so Madge reached for an envelope and stuck the cards inside. One last glance over the desk and—wait! What was that? Directly below the nook with the postcards, a punched, round-trip train ticket to . . . *Fort McCoy?*

"That's curious. Why on earth would Vera go all the way to Wisconsin?"

Adding the ticket to the envelope, she tucked it beneath her belt and shut the desk lid. The closet's brass doorknob shone smooth, as if recently polished, and Madge turned it.

That move plunged her into the source of the heavy gardenia essence. Opening the door produced two sneezes. Vera must've soaked her dresses in that perfume and sprayed it everywhere in this five-by-six-foot space.

Getting down on her knees, Madge swept her arm back and forth beneath the garments hanging from rods on three sides of Vera's famous walk-in closet. Must be a dozen pairs of shoes. With leather added to the war restrictions last year, how had she managed?

"There you go, judging again, and you're supposed to be figuring out who . . ." She still had trouble saying, *murdered Vera*. Besides the shoes, the closet floor offered nothing, not even a single dust bunny.

On the shelf above, deep enough to contain the bonnet, lay stacks of precisely folded blankets and a box of Christmas tree decorations. And an empty area—a large space where the hatbox must have rested.

Jostling the hanging dresses, Madge backed out. If Vera had worn the hat the morning she died, the hatbox would still be here, wouldn't it?

Then something fluttered to the floor. Bending over, she picked up a small blue feather. Proof! But only that this closet had once stored the notorious bonnet.

Something caught in her throat. Hadn't Aivars said the feathers in the pool of blood were blue? Adding the feather to the envelope with the postcards, Madge shut off the light and sneezed again.

The sound echoed into the living room, and she twitched her nose walking through. The stairway to the second floor beckoned, but she quavered. All of those rooms, all those closets.

Still, this deed must be done, and the hour had arrived.

Up she went, gripping the bannister with each step. The air seemed oppressive, even though summer's heat hadn't yet come in. Methodically, she searched each closet, the clothes chute in the hall, the sunny sleeping porch with its glorious bank of southern-facing windows.

Nothing.

All right, then, only one more possibility. She scurried back downstairs into the living room. As she passed the cluttered end table—something Vera would never tolerate—a now-familiar picture postcard peeked out from beneath the latest edition of the *Chronicle*.

Dare she take this? Would Harry notice? She doubted he'd find out about the cards missing from the back bedroom. Most likely, he'd not stepped foot in there except when he and Dale looked for the hat.

Maybe he didn't even know about those other ones. But this one was different, right here in plain sight.

"In for a penny, in for a pound." Snatching the card, Madge added it to the envelope and raced through the dining room.

The urge to rush to the car almost overcame her, but she steeled herself. "Keep your goal in mind, old girl. Clearing your names is worth whatever it takes. Somebody has to do it, and so far, the law has made no progress. Just get yourself down there like a . . ."

She almost said *man*, and the chuckle that rose in her throat felt good. "Are you a woman, or are you a mouse, Madge McQuestion?"

It might be forty years ago, standing before her brother, older by two years, as he dared her to do something dangerous. She rarely gave him the satisfaction of refusing.

"I'm a woman!"

She flung open the door so hard it clattered against a metal strainer on the wall. The banging increased the jittery sensation at the pit of Madge's stomach as she descended in feeble light. A solitary bare bulb dimly lighted hand sawn steps that turned at a landing halfway down.

One tremulous step at a time, she swallowed her trepidation and set out, pressing one hand against the clammy limestone wall for support. On the bottom step, she knew for a fact that Vera would never have brought her prized hat down here, for a lacey cobweb tickled her nose.

But she'd come this far, might as well finish the job, despite a growing certainty of wasting precious time. To her right, a stack of cardboard boxes sagged against the wall. Closer inspection convinced her they'd sat here undisturbed for years.

"Face it, you're not going to find anything down here. Might as well head home before you get caught."

Retracing her steps, she made sure to pull the cord for the basement light and shut the door. Then she slipped out through the back door. Full twilight had fallen, along with a thick layer of evening dew.

At the pump where she'd left her shoes, a glance to the Tollefson's showed lights still on in the barn. They had a large herd of cows, but she had no idea how long it would take to milk them all.

Still, even this one unpredictable part of her plan had worked out. Maybe Aivars had been right about her secret agent qualities.

She scooped up her shoes and galloped toward the car barefoot. Childhood experience had its advantages—the gravel didn't even hurt.

Something told her to look up, and as she did, the first faint star peeked down. Cool night air, heavy with the scent of sprouting seedlings, invigorated her. Definitely the best of both worlds out here.

Secure in the knowledge that if she drove slowly, the dampness would prevent any telltale dust trail, Madge poked her way home like a tortoise. During the time it took to retrace her out-of-the-way route, serenity prevailed.

But after she parked and retreated into the house, the enormity of her deed hit her like a slap to the jaw. In the security of her comfortable home, her bones turned to water, and her knees buckled. Fighting to stay upright, she staggered through the kitchen and collapsed in a heap on the living room sofa.

Condemnation overwhelmed her. How could she possibly have done what she just did? To her battered senses, the act seemed utterly unforgivable.

Still, she could ask for forgiveness, and did so with haste. Not much changed, but she had done what she could. Her next thought made her gasp, and her whisper launched upward.

"You wouldn't really ask me to do that, would you?"

The lead weight in her stomach told her the answer was, "Yes."

Chapter Sixteen

Friday, April 29, 1944

Aivars cut two thick slices from Agnes Wellesby's loaf of homemade bread and opened a jar of her thick homemade strawberry jam. The ladies of the church certainly kept him well fed. So far, he'd hardly had to cook a meal on his own.

Apparently, these dear souls believed he knew nothing about the kitchen. He chuckled at their shock if they ever discovered the exact opposite. His mother had seen to it he and his older brother Rognvald could fend for themselves.

Rog had married a wonderful cook, so his talent with a frying pan went to waste now, although he still whipped up a delicious meal whenever Alice gave him free rein.

"And I'm not so bad, myself. Fully capable of putting together a batch of cookies or a well-balanced dinner." But why dilute the joy of giving for these women? What they didn't know wouldn't hurt them.

This line of thought reminded him that what he didn't know about Vera's death *was* hurting him.

After cleaning up the cheery kitchen, he left the parsonage to work on his sermon. All week, he'd been pondering examples of people who met others' needs.

Now to organize them and choose the most pertinent. Many here were already motivated, already caring for people, and just needed some encouragement along the way.

Two hours later, he stretched his arms and pushed away from

the desk, that persnickety chair squawking every inch of the way. Despite his repeated attempts, the squeak refused to diminish.

"Might as well learn to live with it."

How many times had he said that in other circumstances? The most painful involved his heart condition. It had taken months to be able to mention it aloud. Thankfully, he'd finally become resigned—nothing to do except live with it.

Settling back down, he determined to finish the sermon when someone knocked. He glanced up, since he kept the door open as he'd planned. The old chair protested again as he rose.

"Madge, what a nice surprise!" He looked past her. "And Bill, too?" He swung the door wide as she lowered her head. "Come on in. Have a seat."

Palpable tension accompanied them. Bill's lips pressed together in a thin line, and Madge clenched and unclenched her hands. Hmm . . . strange.

After closing the door, Aivars returned to his chair. "So what brings you here? I'm always happy to see you."

"Madge has something to tell you." Had he ever heard Bill's tone so clipped? And no trace of a stutter. Something must really be wrong. But even the happiest of couples had troubles from time to time, according to Dad.

Bill's formality was troubling but he threw the ball into Madge's court. Nothing to do but wait.

Finally she met his eyes. He tried to gauge what would ensue— impossible, of course. She frittered with her hankie. So unlike her not to be straightforward.

"What is it?"

"You remember the other day when you decided to question your neighbors some more? About seeing Vera the morning she died?"

"Yes. A fruitless effort."

"I went out to look in on Harry. I told you later, I think."

"Yes." The clock suddenly seemed far too loud. Bill began tapping his fingertips on his knee.

"Well, I had the distinct impression he was holding something back, something I couldn't quite put my finger on. You know what I mean?"

"I do. My exact feelings the last time I talked with him."

"The more I thought about it, the more convinced I became that it must have something to do with that dreadful Easter bonnet. It seemed like a logical conclusion."

"Go on." Aivars leaned forward.

"Maybe it was the reporter in me, or some instinctive hunch, but I knew I had to get back into that house and look around for myself." Madge's tortured eyes implored him to understand without spelling everything out in graphic detail.

A glance at Bill relayed the message that he'd better make it quick. "You didn't!"

"She did." Bill's confirmation accompanied a grim squint.

"When?"

"Last night during the council meeting."

Not knowing whether to be amused or aghast, Aivars faltered. Amusement won, but he didn't dare let it show. Not in the face of Bill's obvious disapproval.

"Did you find the hat?"

"No, but I found evidence of it. Not to mention a few other curious things."

"What other things? No, wait. Let's start at the beginning. I want to hear the whole story of your breaking and entering escapade."

"There was no breaking involved."

Bill quirked an eyebrow, but Madge hurried on. "Harry left his doors unlocked, like we all do unless we're going out of town. Just entering."

A loud guffaw lurked low in his throat, and it was all Aivars could do to hold back. Bill sure had married one spunky lady.

"Suppose you continue telling me what you did. All of it, blow-by-blow." As those words left his mouth, his mind flashed back to Dale's interrogation after he found Vera. A shiver wriggled up his spine.

As Madge related the story, his amusement grew with each

detail. Yes, *entering* Harry's house without his knowledge qualified as illegal. And yes, she could be arrested if he pressed charges.

But first, Harry would have to find out she'd been there, and if no one had seen her, who could possibly tell him? Another glance at Bill during Madge's detailed recital revealed something vital. The poor man started biting his lips. Was he struggling to keep his own laughter at bay?

By the time Madge finished, Aivars could no longer contain himself. Once he let out a burst, Bill let go as well.

"Madge McQuestion, if you don't take the cake!" Aivars shook his head. "But there's something missing in your logic. Unlocked doors or not, what you did *was* illegal."

Still gasping for air, Bill added, "You should have seen her when I g-got home from the council meeting, all b-bunched up on the couch. She looked like the Raggedy Ann doll Gloria had when she was little."

He turned to his chagrined wife. "Red hair and all. Good thing Gloria was still over at Cheryl's or she'd have thought Madge needed a doctor."

That made Aivars burst out again. "My little sister had a Raggedy Ann too, so I can picture the scene."

Then he turned back to Madge. A lone tear snaked its way down her cheek. But before he could say anything, she brushed it away and squared her shoulders.

"What I did was wrong. I freely admit that. I asked for forgiveness even before Bill got home. And I doubt Harry will notice anyone has been inside."

"How can you be so sure?"

"The house is a terrible mess, a far cry from the perfect showplace. Vera must be rolling over in her grave."

"Well, I pray you're right." Aivars caught himself. "About not being found out, that is." Much to his relief, someone called from out in the sanctuary.

"Reverend, are you here? Anybody home?"

"Excuse me, folks." He crossed to the door and disappeared down the hall. In a few seconds, his greeting provided a clue.

"Why, good afternoon, Sheriff."

Madge's heart plummeted to her toes. She grabbed her throat and cast a fearful glance at Bill, who reached for her other hand.

Listening to the two male voices in the hallway, they waited. And then . . . *laughter?*

When Aivars ushered Dale inside, both men still smiled.

"Well, hello Madge . . . Bill. Didn't expect to see you here, but this saves me a trip."

Madge looked to Aivars, who gave her a big wink. What could be going on?

Dale put on his official pose. "Looks as though I'm interrupting something, so I'll get right down to business. The reports came back from Minneapolis regarding the murder weapon prints. I'm happy to say the tests detected no fingerprints in this room."

Madge's pent-up breath *whooshed* as she wilted against her chair, feeling every bit like Gloria's old Raggedy Ann doll. Dale hadn't come to arrest her.

"It feels great to know our names have been cleared." Aivars positively beamed.

"Not so fast. Neither of you is out of the woods yet. Your fingerprints weren't on the knife. I'm glad for that, but there's still the matter of Vera's last words."

He turned somber attention to Madge. "She said your name, something about a promise, and mentioned that durned Easter hat. Are you still sure none of this means anything to you?"

Madge cringed. How could she answer without telling an out-and-out lie—and what if Dale told Harry? Drat that promise!

Then inspiration struck. "I can't say for sure." Madge forced her shoulders back. The *can't say* part was certainly true enough, but would it satisfy Dale?

"You can't say?"

"I can't even imagine what Vera was thinking in that last moment. She must have realized she was dying, so it seems strange she mentioned me, since we really didn't have a lot to do with each other."

Finley held her gaze for a moment. Maybe he was expecting to hear more, but she sealed her lips.

"On another note, it has come to my attention that you, Reverend, have been asking your neighbors about seeing Vera that morning." Dale drew himself to his full height. "I'll have you know this is *my* investigation, and if you—"

He jabbed a finger at Aivars and twisted toward Madge, "or *you* do anything to hinder it, I won't hesitate to cool your heels in the county jail. Is that understood?"

Aivars added his nod to Madge's.

"I just wanted—"

"I know what you wanted. They told me. In plain and simple terms, Reverend, mind your own business and stay out of mine."

He turned to leave, and as his eyes swept Madge, outside Aivars's line of vision, he grinned. "And that goes for you, too. We've got a long history of working together, and I'd like to keep my respect for you intact.

"Bill, I'm sure glad to see you looking so much better these days. I'm trusting you to keep a keen eye on this wily wife of yours."

"You bet."

The door closed with a *snick*. Soon afterward, a car door slammed, and an engine roared to life.

Aivars cleared his throat. "I guess you could say we've been put in our places?"

"You m-might say that. The question is, will you stay there?"

Madge snorted. "Not on your life."

At their surprised expressions, she backtracked. "What I mean is, I won't step on Dale's toes or mess with his job. But what I found in Harry's house is burning a hole in my pocketbook."

"Something significant?"

Bill jumped in. "That depends. A postcard is a p-postcard is a postcard."

"But these aren't your ordinary garden variety penny postcards." Madge took the envelope from her purse.

"Is it okay to use your desk?"

Aivars squeaked back his chair to make room.

"I found these five in Vera's desk. This other one was on the coffee table in the living room."

Chapter Seventeen

Light filtered through the high study window in the back of the church—or the front, depending upon your perspective. One-by-one, Bill studied the postcards and handed them on to Aivars.

Scrutinizing each, Aivars labeled them aloud.

"Piccadilly Circus . . . hmm. Pretty typical."

"The Liverpool train station, the Tower Bridge, Trafalgar Square, and Big Ben with the Parliament buildings. All common sights—nothing peculiar that I can see."

The whole time, Madge kept looking, too. Finally, the the sixth card, postmarked Chicago, reached Aivars. "Why, I've been on this street with my brother. Wacker Drive, along the Chicago River."

"When?"

"Our grandfather taught at a college in Chicago, and we went to visit him a few times. Our last trip . . . let me see, maybe summer of '41, before rationing."

"Looks like these started arriving about three years ago." He looked up at Madge. "Did Vera know anyone overseas?"

"Not that I know of, and she'd never have kept that a secret. That's what makes this so strange."

Still holding the Chicago one, Aivars spread the rest out on his desk, message side up. "Someone named *Lea* signed these, and an *Albert* signed the others. But *Max* somebody sent this one from Chicago."

Bill fingered that one. "You say you found this in plain sight?"

"Sort of." She might have said it literally called to her as she passed through Vera and Harry's front room. "It was on the coffee table, beneath a recent copy of the *Chronicle*."

"Wonder if it arrived after Vera's death, and she never saw it? Hard to tell with the mail so inconsistent these days."

"I thought the same thing, because she'd have stored it away with the others. I tried to figure this out all night."

"Hmm—the message could have two meanings. *Take care, Mrs. Walters.* Could be a friendly wish. Or a warning. B-but about what?" Bill scratched his head.

"Do you think it has something to do with the murder? Vera seemed so anxious a few days earlier, and that's so unlike her."

"*Mrs. Walters*—why would whoever wrote this be so formal?"

"This all has to mean something. The day we met on the back stairs, Vera's fear seemed genuine."

"But she didn't say what caused it?"

"Not in so many words, but the Easter bonnet did have something to do with it." There. She'd come as close as possible to the truth.

"Some cards are signed Albert, others Lea—let me have a look at those again." Aivars read the *Albert* one out loud.

"*H'lo Vera. Bond's Pub wiped out. Checking for another that might have the real MacKay. ~Albert.*"

"Oh, my goodness—could that be Fort McCoy in disguise? *MacKay . . . McCoy . . .*" Madge remembered the train ticket and grabbed the envelope.

"There's something else here. In a nook below the postcards, I found this." When she fished out the train ticket, the feather drifted to the floor.

Aivars bent over to pick it up. "What—?"

"Oh my, I'm so rattled, I forgot. That feather fluttered from the closet shelves, so I brought it too. At least it proves the hat had been there, if nothing else."

Bill studied the ticket stub. "P-punched, so somebody used it for a round trip to Fort McCoy."

"So maybe this card told Vera to go there, and it looks like she did. Or someone did." Aivars could not have had more wrinkles in his forehead.

"It might not have been Vera?"

"Her name's nowhere on it, so anyone could have made the trip. But why would Vera have the stub?"

"Good question. Just speculation, that's all. Let's assume she used the ticket herself. Maybe that's when she got hold of that outlandish hat. But where would she come up with such a thing at Fort McCoy? Could she even get on the base, Bill?"

"Not without a military I.D. Locked down tight these days." He glanced into the distance. "But Fort McCoy has a POW camp."

"Is that so?"

"There's several around the Midwest. One at Algona, some up in Minnesota, smaller ones in Charles City, Waverly, and Eldora, and another down in Clarinda. Unless you live in one of the towns, you'd never even realize it."

Madge almost asked what the camps had to do with the investigation but decided to wait. Bill seemed to be working out something in his head. As usual, he came forth with a thought worthy of pondering, one that never had crossed her mind.

"Maybe . . . just maybe, there's a human connection—somebody from a long time ago, even someone she's related to . . ."

"In the camp? A German?"

Bill shrugged. "You just never know. Can't hurt to consider every possible angle."

"That's what a real sleuth would do. I'm wondering about the names. Lea—probably a woman. And Albert—I can't help but think they might have something to do with Albert Lea, Minnesota. That's where Vera told Harry she bought the Easter bonnet."

Oh my . . . had she said too much?

"She told you that?"

Madge pretended great interest in the cards.

"Madge? You think she got the hat somewhere else?" Bill's eyes bored a hole through her.

"I . . . I don't know. I'd never seen Vera desperate before—couldn't have imagined it. But now I keep seeing her face that way. It's even worse after going to her house last night."

Bill took a long breath and exchanged a look with Aivars. Madge's heart sank. In spite of her desire to keep her promise, she'd failed utterly.

"Hey, hon. Don't look so downhearted." Bill patted her shoulder. "Sometimes a vow has to be broken for truth to triumph."

"Well, at least I haven't told Harry. That's what Vera was afraid of—you won't let him know, will you?"

The two men shook their heads. The two men she trusted most in this world.

"To be honest, Madge, a secret admirer gave it to me, or so the card said—But don't tell Harry, please. He thinks I bought the hat in Albert Lea, and I'd like to keep it that way. Promise me?

"Just promise, Madge, please. I'll explain later."

Vera's nose came a quarter-inch from Madge's. Her eyes pleaded—begged. Not the Vera Madge had known all her life.

But, of course, that promised explanation had never come.

Fighting through a heavy cloud that bore down on her, Madge fought to open her eyes. Finally, she succeeded, and a suffocating sensation overcame her.

In the past twenty-four hours, she'd broken the law. Bad enough, but what price would a person have to pay for breaking a promise to a dead woman?

Beside her, Bill lay asleep. Quiet as a whisper, she eased out of bed and threw on the soft chenille robe Lillian had sent her for Christmas last winter. Downstairs, she checked her tea stash and heated some water.

"Certain times are made for tea, Mama used to say. My grand-mother swore that a cup could ease almost any complaint."

As she waited, recollections from yesterday flooded in. She and

Bill spent over an hour in the church with Aivars, poring over the postcards.

"This one says, *Greetings, friend. There'll be bluebirds over the white cliffs of Dover.* What in the world could that mean?"

"Well, Vera's hat had two birds, one most definitely blue." Madge pointed to the feather. "Vera Lynn is British—how many times have we heard that song on the radio?"

"Yes, although those cliffs are so fierce, I imagine only large sea birds can nest there. The song tells us nothing." Bill's tone carried a sarcastic tinge, so Madge grabbed his hand.

"I'm just thinking out loud like always. Seems to me the only way to figure out all of this is to brainstorm—like President Roosevelt and Winston Churchill."

"Yeah, well. I hope we come up with answers quicker than they do."

Aivars jumped in. "All right, then, let's tackle the next one. *A nightingale sang in Berkeley Square. Cheerio, dearie. Lea.* Spelled that way, it has to refer to a woman, don't you think?"

"Nothing has to m-mean anything. Did that c-crazy hat have a nightingale, Madge?"

She tried to call up the image. "I'm not sure, but nightingales are inconspicuous. Brown and grey, and there was nothing inconspicuous on that hat. Let me think. Now what color *was* the other bird?"

"Brown, I think. Maybe a house wren?" Aivars reached to the bookshelf behind him for a bird book and started thumbing through it.

"Or a purple finch?" He turned to a page of photos captured by some great nature photographer. "What do you think?"

Cute little birds—innocent and so captivating. Why, oh why couldn't she remember that brown bird better? Then the room started to whirl, and Bill grabbed her.

"Are you all right?"

"Just a little weak. You rushed me over here in such a hurry we didn't even eat breakfast."

"Well, come on over to the house. I'll put on a pot of coffee and whip up a fried egg sandwich." Aivars flung back some hair that had fallen into his eyes. "And bring along the cards."

So it was that they spent the next hour in the parsonage kitchen. And began to make progress.

Madge lit into those fried eggs and toast like she hadn't eaten for months.

"Sure you don't want any, Bill?"

"Thanks, but coffee will do me fine. I forgot breakfast is Maddie girl's best meal."

"It's all right—I've stopped shaking now."

"Back to the postcards, then. Bill, do you have any ideas what the Chicago one might mean?"

"Well, there's a Naval t-training center on Lake Michigan north of there, mostly air training. B-but what the connection is to Vera beats me."

"Okay, I'm grasping at straws, but what if Vera had a German relative who got captured in a battle and was brought to the POW camp?"

Bill had paled—maybe Aivars didn't notice, but she did. This was getting awfully close to home. But Bill's voice remained steady.

"Captured in Tunisia, maybe. The big base camp at Algona has a b-bunch of those officers—almost a hundred Hitler devotees, I've heard. Indoctrinated Waffen-SS Nazis loyal to the death. D-don't know if any of 'em were transported to McCoy, but it's sure possible."

A platoon tramped through Madge's chest. "You've never mentioned . . ."

"P-probably shouldn't have said anything. Some things it's b-better for the populace not to know. K-keep quiet about the camps, all right? No use getting f-folks all upset."

"But what if . . ." Aivars refilled their coffee cups. "What if some spy in England b-became a liaison for someone in the G-German army? Stranger things have happened. And this one card mentions the real MacKay, wasn't that it?"

Bill reread the back. "If this means McCoy, then maybe word

somehow got to this person in London that Vera's relative ended up in the camp there.

"This war has spies everywhere. The British have the Special Operations Executive, and our military has its own secret operations. Of course, the Germans have theirs, too. But wait a minute. Aren't we presuming a lot? Seems a bit of a stretch."

"You're right, we know nothing, really." Aivars rubbed his chin like something was nagging at him. A few moments passed before he burst out, "Wait a minute!"

Bill leaned forward as he continued. "I just remembered something. Years ago, back in Bemidji, one of Dad's parishioners battled a drinking problem. In spite of everything the local doctor tried, the poor fellow kept returning to his favorite, a Scotch whisky called MacKay! Somehow it survived through Prohibition."

"Interesting, but what does it have to do with Fort McCoy?"

"Nothing, I guess. The name just popped into my head—we're running wild here, aren't we?"

Bill tapped his fingers on the table. "Let's not get too c-carried away with this until we learn more, though how we'll do that is anybody's g-guess."

"Can I get you more coffee?"

"No thanks. Let's think on this some more." Bill patted Madge's hand absentmindedly. "Though I hate to admit it, little miss snoopy here may have discovered exactly what we need."

Chapter Eighteen

Neighborhood victory gardens provided rich sermon fodder. During these mild spring days, Aivars made a habit of walking past several prolific plots. Such promise here—and such hard work.

Sometimes if gardeners noticed him, they took time to chat over a fence, but engrossed in their work, often they never even saw him. This morning, one lady not too far from the McQuestion's house divided Shasta daisies on the sunny side of her home.

"Need any Shastas?"

"Thank you, but no. How do you know when they need to be divided?"

"They get to looking a little ratty. Last summer there weren't as many blooms as in other years."

No matter how full of vegetables, people's victory gardens sprouted wildflowers by the dozen. A good reminder that even a strict, hard-working gardener could never claim full control—weeds and wildflowers poked through the soil no matter what.

Last night's thunderstorm added another reminder. He'd gone to bed early, but a massive blast from the heavens shook him out of bed. Out on the front porch, he watched in awe. Rain drove straight into the earth and created rivulets along the sidewalks.

Lightning flashes in the north and constant deep rumbling magnetized him. He'd always loved storms, and this one bordered on spectacular. Cracks of thunder jarred his spine, and intermittent bolts revealed the water tower eight blocks away.

But as he stood there, another noise alerted him, like someone splashing up the walkway. Who in his right mind would be out on such a night? By now it was well after eleven. Yet the sound grew louder until a a close lightning strike revealed a shiny slicker.

Moving farther out, Aivars waited. Then suddenly the phantom leaped his steps and they came face-to-face! Lightning smote the sky again, revealing a familiar profile.

"Bill? Is that you under there?"

"Yep. In the army, you march rain or shine, and my orders came loud and clear." In the spell of his crooked grin, Aivars recalled his manners.

"Come on up and get dried off." He led the way inside while Bill hung his raincoat on a plant hook just outside the front door.

Time for a pot of hot coffee—there'd be no sleep for a long time, anyhow. He hadn't been able to doze off, thinking about those postcards Madge found. Then he began on Vera's key. What he wouldn't give to go through her purse, but the Sheriff kept it concealed in his office.

Next, her cousin came to mind, igniting more speculation. Impossible to turn off the flow.

Cups in hand, he and Bill retired to overstuffed living room chairs. Once settled, Bill started right in.

"I need to tell you something I'd rather not have Madge know. I told her I was coming over here, but not why. Just said I needed another man to talk to. She scolded me for going out, but I assured her I survived far worse in the war."

Not even one stammer. Aivars chalked up this information. "What's on your mind?"

"It's those blasted postcards. I think we're missing something, and can't say everything I'm thinking to Madge, though I probably should. She's as smart as Sherlock Holmes." He chuckled. "She's sure been acting like him lately. Stood by me through thick and thin, but ..."

No expert on marital relationships, Aivars did know how to listen. He'd barely taken a girl out during his seminary years. To be honest, he'd never met one that interested him that much, and it seemed wrong to date when so many men his age had to leave their sweethearts back here.

Gloria's profile flashed before him—not the first time since he drove her to school that day. At this point, he might be willing to reconsider his stance, but right now, he focused on Bill.

Watching streams of rain running down the windows like miniature waterfalls, his new friend seemed in no hurry. After a bit, the wind changed, and the onslaught slanted a little. Pungent coffee steam cleared his head—a parishioner had brought him an extra ration ticket for this luxury.

But here sat Bill, who had already sacrificed so much for the war effort. Gratitude for their new alliance swelled inside—Bill didn't expect him to say a thing, a rare treat.

"A buddy from my unit was wounded the same time as me, though not as bad. Anyway, he's working over at the McCoy POW camp now. Got another one over in Algona, but I don't want Madge to know—you've seen her in action.

"I do love her gumption."

"Me too. When I tend to hang back, she's rarin' to go. Sometimes, though, the less she knows, the less chance she has of stumbling into trouble."

A chuckle welled up. "Yes, I see that. But she's got such a good heart, as good as they come."

"In these camps, there's black market goings-on. The prisoners have it good compared to our captured troops over in Germany—that riles me. They've got a canteen where they can exchange scrip from working for farmers.

"In Algona, anyway, they keep busy with skill work, put on plays, play soccer, baseball, and all kinds of stuff. A far cry from the way the Huns treat our prisoners, I can tell you that."

Bill's face turned hard for a few moments, and Aivers maintained silence. "Anyhow, those blasted postcards got my mind going."

"You and me both."

"We all know the Luftwaffe bombed London ports without mercy, so why would someone send a postcard from there to a woman in Northern Iowa? Seems like this whole investigation revolves around Vera's hat, but what if we've focused on the wrong thing?"

"Could be. Got any suggestions?"

"That's just the problem—I don't. But the McCoy connection bothers me. I believe in Divine guidance—if I didn't, I wouldn't be here. So I keep asking myself how those postcards might be guiding us."

"Right. So far, I haven't had any brilliant thoughts."

Hail pelted the windows now. They sipped their coffee in comfortable silence until Aivars asked, "Want a refill?"

"Sure, why not?"

Maybe they could make some headway before this night, or the storm, ended. Bill still hadn't stammered once—come to think of it, maybe he hadn't the last time they were together.

Could it be that even this zany investigation might be used for a good purpose? Bill had come a long way since they first met. Maybe having something like this to concentrate on was precisely what he needed.

When Aivars came back with more coffee and some buttered toast, Bill's question surprised him. "Do you think Madge is still keeping something back? About her talk with Vera?"

"You know her far better than I do."

"Yeah, and she's about as loyal as they come. No way she'd break a confidence. There's no way to get more out of her than she feels right about. That, I know for darn sure."

"Well, then. We may just have to bide our time."

Madge had overslept, a rare occurrence. She woke groggy and a little stiff, probably due to last night's storm. Second one in a row but muttering about it would get her nowhere.

She pulled on a blue and white checked dress and tucked her

hair into a crocheted snood that pinned at the crown of her head. Great invention—kept those unruly waves out of her face without taking the time for a tedious victory roll.

Down in the kitchen, Gloria stood at the stove stirring scrambled eggs. At the table, Bill stacked several pieces of toast on a plate.

"Have a good night's sleep, Mom?" Gloria scooped the eggs onto three plates.

"Not really. The storm made me restless, especially with your father gone for several hours."

"The thunder woke me up a few times, too. Where'd you go, Dad?" Gloria sat down and passed the pepper.

"Oh, I got restless—needed a guy to talk with."

Madge rolled her head back and forth until something popped in her neck. That ought to help.

"I heard that, Maddie-girl. Bet it felt good."

"Sure did. Thanks for fixing breakfast, sweetie."

"You're welcome. Dad wouldn't let me wake you, so we got things started." They ate in silence until Madge tapped Bill's wrist.

"Have a nice visit with Aivars?"

He wiped his mouth and graying moustache, new since he'd returned home. "Yep. I really like that young man."

"We all do, too. He can even make reading the Bible exciting. And he told us he's thinking about writing a play about a Bible story." Gloria's bright eyes matched the excitement in her tone.

"Great. Did he say which story?"

"Not specifically, but he mentioned one from the Old Testament."

Madge glanced at the clock. "You'd better skeedaddle or you'll be late for school."

"Oh my goodness! I didn't realize the time."

"Go on, scoot. We'll see you this afternoon."

Hopefully Bill would volunteer more information now. After a full minute's quiet, Madge plunged in.

"So what did you and Aivars talk about?"

"Those doggone post cards you found."

"I know. It gets *curiouser and curiouser.*"

"You're right about that. But I'd better head on over to the office. Are you coming?"

"As soon as I clean up here. Oh, I had an idea for some future articles. What about a series featuring some of the older homes around town? We've got several real beauties. We could even take some pictures to go along with them. What do you think?"

"Something to mull over. We'll talk about it later, all right?"

Disappointed at his less than enthusiastic response, Madge kissed him goodbye and poured herself the last of the coffee. What was it Bill felt he couldn't share with her last night? Not that she envied his friendship with Aivars—not at all. But still . . .

Soon, her mind returned to the present. She thought he'd be all for her idea, and it would give her something to think about besides the war and Vera's murder. She drummed her fingers on the tabletop and considered another question.

Why was she so all-fired determined to solve this herself? She and Aivars were no longer suspects, so why not just step back and let Dale do his job?

"Who are you trying to kid?" She used this scolding tone with herself so often, it seemed natural. "You know you can't do any such thing."

True. She couldn't let go now, in spite of Dale's warning. A new angle niggled even as she finished the dishes, but she couldn't put words to it.

At the same time, she couldn't shake the thought that it could be important . . . might be a breakthrough. Was this how detectives in big cities faced each new day?

Chapter Nineteen

The bell jingled and Aivars walked into the office just as Madge finished typing the last want ad. They'd certainly changed during the war. In the past, *Wanted for Hire* had been uncommon, but now, establishments as far away as Iowa Falls and New Hampton advertised in the *Chronicle.* The largest demand, though, was for farm workers. The single men living at Elvira Tomlinson's boarding house must be hopping these days.

"Hello—what brings you here on this fine morning?"

"Thought I'd take a chance you'd be here before going over to your house."

"Too much to do for a day off this week. You look a little concerned. Is something wrong?"

"Mind if I sit down?"

"Oh, sorry. Have a seat."

"I've been doing a lot of thinking about those postcards."

"And?"

"You said you've known Vera a long time. Exactly how long?"

She started to answer, but he held up his hand. "Wait a minute, let me back up. Have you always lived in Caroline?"

"Born and raised. Why?"

"And Vera?"

"She moved here from Chicago when I was . . . after I graduated. Not long after she and her mother arrived, she and Harry got married. He grew up here, and from what I understand, met Vera in Chicago on one of his business trips."

"What was her maiden name?"

"I don't know. She never said, and I never asked. I could look in the archives. Maybe they didn't put an announcement in the paper, though."

"Well, it was quite a while ago."

"About thirty years, I expect. Her mother lived with them for about five years before she died. She kept to herself, and everyone referred to her as Vera's mother."

A wisp of memory tickled the back of her mind. "Now that I think back, I remember how miserable those two made Harry's life."

"Is that right? How interesting. Was Mrs. What's-her-name buried here?"

"No, they took her body back to Chicago. Why do you ask?"

"Just curious. I can't shake the feeling that we're missing something in all this."

Seconds ticked by. Then Madge couldn't stand it any longer. But just as she opened her mouth, the noon siren went off, and Bill straggled in from the printing room.

"Ready for some lunch? Aivars, care to join us?"

"That's an invitation that's hard to refuse, but I don't want to put you out."

"Not at all." Madge rose from her chair. "We were going over to Hank's Café. No dishes to do that way, and he appreciates the business."

"Sounds good to me."

In the back of the establishment, Bill chose an isolated booth, and during their meal, Aivars continued asking for details about Vera's background. Finally, Bill interrupted.

"What are you getting at?"

Aivars propped his elbows on the table. "Well, it's those post-cards—hand-written from three different people, addressed personally to Vera."

Under the table, Bill brushed his knee against Madge's, a

reminder to relax. How could he tell that her spine was tingling? But how could a person stay calm investigating a murder?

"You said you didn't know of any overseas friends or relatives Vera had, yet someone from there knew her, or *of* her. Right now, that's the only conclusion we can come to. What puzzles me most is that lone card from Chicago."

Bill jumped in. "That really strikes me as curious, too. Madge, you knew Vera lots better than I did. Did she ever say anything about having relatives overseas or a friend in Chicago?"

"She's never once mentioned anyone there or in England. She rarely talked about her childhood. I didn't even know about her cousin in La Crosse until she came a few weeks ago."

"But you wrote me something about her when I was in Africa. Something about her reaction to gas rationing—she thought Harry deserved a better grade sticker than the basic one for three gallons a week. After all, he was a *banker*."

"I can't believe you remember that. And sure enough, Harry found a way to get an upgrade. Didn't hurt that his banker friend from Albert Lea had connections with the Office of Price Administration. But that's all pretty recent.

"As far as I know, Vera never returned to Chicago except to bury her mother. That seems strange, come to think of it. It would make sense for her to make visits back there."

Bill folded and refolded a napkin. "What about that cousin—what was her name?"

"Helene. Odd that she came just days before Vera died. I only met her at church."

They tossed ideas back and forth. Once they burst out laughing over some outlandish speculation. Then Sarah, their waitress, came to their table.

"Pastor Z, I'm sorry to interrupt, but someone just brought in a note for you."

"Oh. Thanks."

Perusing the slip of paper, Aivars glanced up. "It's from Klaus

Hirsch. Berta is being rushed to the hospital in Decorah, and he wants me to get there right away."

Madge's hand flew to her throat. "Oh no! Did he say what happened?"

"No, only that I should hurry."

This sweet elderly couple that Madge had known all her life lived just a block away. Berta had been in ill health for several weeks.

Aivars slung on his hat. "See you later."

Before he left, Bill caught his sleeve. "Drive carefully on those curvy roads over there. We don't need *you* in the hospital. And keep your mind off those postcards, you hear?"

The Hirsches, such a kindly older couple, had won Aivars immediately. What a story they had lived, emigrating from Europe after World War I. He had yet to hear those particulars, but they'd starting milking cows, and reared nine children on a farm a few miles west of Caroline.

On his last visit, he couldn't help but notice the decline in Berta's health. Her bright blue eyes no longer sparkled as they had when he first met her.

Klaus had taken him into their home that day, and pride seeped into his introduction. "This is Berta. She probably has some cake for us." Indeed, she did, along with a fresh batch of butter cookies so rich they made your head swim.

After an eastward drive that seemed to take forever, some low hills peppered the countryside. And then more, complete with rocky cliffs. Just outside Decorah, Bill's curves appeared, with idyllic farm sites on either side.

Such placid scenes, dairy cows grazing in plentiful pastures as the occasional auto or truck flew by. Well, sort of—if you could consider the national speed limit of thirty-five miles per hour flying.

After what seemed like ages, Aivars circled the hospital and parked near the emergency room entrance. No car here from Caroline, so Klaus had probably ridden over with Berta in the ambulance.

Sending up a prayer, he pushed through the doors and approached the desk. "I'm Pastor Zevenbergen from Caroline. Could you please tell me where I might find Klaus Hirsch?"

"Oh, yes. He said to bring you back right away. Follow me, please." The nurse led him through the hallway to a curtained-off space at the far end.

She drew one side of the curtain back. "Mr. Hirsch, Pastor Zevenbergen is here." Quietly, she backed away.

Tears shimmered as Klaus lifted his head. "I'm losin' my Berta. The doc says she's not going to make it."

"I'm so sorry." Berta struggled for breath as Aivars carefully moved a chair next to Klaus. "Would you like me to pray?"

Eyes on his wife, Klaus nodded. His fingers clenched Berta's.

"Dear Father in heaven, please be with Berta now. Give her complete healing and rest in eternity, and make your presence known to Klaus in this difficult hour." He slipped naturally into the Twenty-third Psalm, and Klaus mouthed the words with him.

On the phrase, "And I shall dwell in the house of the Lord forever," Berta's lips twitched. Klaus stroked her hand, and within a few minutes, her chest rose one last time, before settling forever.

Klaus crumbled against her and bowed his head over her hand. Aivars simply sat there, thankful he could share this moment. He handed Klaus his handkerchief but might have used it himself.

In this sacred time, no human words sufficed. Klaus surely was expressing his love for Berta, and should his mother pass from this world first, Aivars could picture his father doing the same.

Women were the heart of a home, his childhood had taught him that. The man might *bring home the bacon*, but his wife prepared and served it.

Soon several members of the family arrived, and Aivars became engrossed in their responses to Berta's passing. One daughter wept openly, another sat quietly beside Berta. A son drew Klaus into the hallway.

Another funeral to lead. But this one surely would prove less taxing than the first.

Chapter Twenty

Monday, May 1, 1944

"Mercy me, Berta's funeral on Wednesday. At least this one had nothing to do with a murder." Madge sighed as she wrote up Berta's obituary, astonished to realize she and Klaus had been married for sixty-two years.

How would Klaus deal with losing his wife after so much time together? She'd heard how the surviving spouse often died shortly after their partner.

"Oh, c'mon, shake off these gloomy thoughts. Leave Klaus in God's hands."

"Talkin' to yourself again, Maddie-girl?"

"I didn't hear you come in. You caught me. Sometimes that's the only way I can control the wild thoughts in my head."

"As I well know." He tapped the paper rolled through her typewriter. "'Bout got that done so I can get it in the paper?"

"Almost." She handed him a pile of notices she'd typed earlier. "These other articles should get you started. I'll bring this in soon."

"Good. By the way, I think I'm going to give Linda McDonald's youngest boy Ethan the paper route for the eastern half of town. We've had an upsurge in subscribers, and it's a little too much for Joey Brentwood to handle alone.

"Ethan's asked me several times now, and I like his tenacity. Not pushy at all . . . just reminding like I asked him to. He can fill the newsstands at Jensen's and the Mercantile, too. It's getting too hard for me to climb in and out of the car these days."

"Oh, that's wonderful! I mean about hiring Ethan. I know your back's been bothering you. Linda will be so grateful, what with Danny still in the fighting. Ethan will be thrilled, too—nothing like a job to help keep his mind off his daddy."

"With summer coming on, neither boy is going to want to spend half their morning delivering papers, even if it is just once a week. Splitting the route will give them more free time."

"Makes sense to me. Now go on, so I can get this obituary finished—not one of my favorite tasks."

As he turned away, Madge had a second thought. "Oh, have you made a decision about the old home stories?"

"Sorry, I meant to tell you before. This would be a good time for something to distract the town from all the war news. Besides, maybe it will keep you out of trouble for a while." His teasing never annoyed her now, as it might have years ago. "Go ahead and dust off that fancy camera of yours. Might as well get started right away."

Ignoring his remark about staying out of trouble was easy. To be honest, curiosity had landed her in hot water more times than she cared to admit.

But no way was she going to give up on this mystery. Not only what happened to Vera's hat, but who gave it to her, *if* that occurred, or how she really got it. *And* finding the killer, but no use mentioning that right now.

"Thanks. Can't wait to get going on it."

What a perfect spring day—birds chirping as they searched out enough worms to fill hungry little tummies. Other familiar sounds enveloped the streets of Caroline, all seven of the ones running east and west. Someone had named them after trees, and the nine north-south ones recalled U.S. Presidents.

On his one day off work, Bill decided to see what he could do to help Madge with her new series—not that she really needed help. On a whim, he crossed Main Street to the Library on Chestnut.

In the quiet that only a library could offer, he browsed through the aisles and aimlessly thumbed the card files before spotting a stack of periodicals lined up on a table. Reference books, his favorite kind.

On the front cover of one, in bold face, the title *Names and Their Meanings* captured him. He carried the volume to one of the empty tables and flipped it open. One name jumped out:

Helene–light.

He almost laughed out loud, though the rules strictly forbade such emmisions. As he recalled, there was nothing *light* about Vera's cousin. If she weighed in under 175, he'd be surprised.

"Madge'll love this! I suppose maybe it really means "sunlight," but she'll get my drift."

Following down through the columns back to *Vera*, he leaned in. Slavic roots meant faith and the same in Latin. Now he was on a roll. Madge, short for Margaret, meant *pearl*—how accurate. She surely was a treasure.

"You're one lucky man," he murmured to himself.

Why not look up his own name—only took a minute. *Resolute protector.* Hmm.

For a while he sat staring out the library window. Had he been resolute enough in North Africa? Had he protected his buddies the best he could? And what about his family back here? Had he made the right choices?

Time passed, and his back pain eased a bit. He completely lost track of why he came in. When he came to himself, the day had altered—shadows leaned to the opposite side of trees and bushes out on the lawn.

By the time he started out for home, the purpose of his visit returned to mind. Ah, well. He'd discovered nothing about old houses or the history of this town, but Madge had things under control, anyhow.

While the postcards still drove Bill and Aivars to distraction, Madge diverted her attention and spent most of her waking hours thinking about Vera's key. Perhaps this had something to do with her new project.

Finding facts about the older houses here inevitably led to doors. What was a house, after all, without its entrances and exits? Doorways had always attracted her, anyhow.

So many types in this world—plain wooden ones like most in Iowa, but also arches and porticos. Tall heavy ones like those on old brick churches, short squat creations on sheds and chicken coops, and sliding ones with immense hinges on garages around town.

Maybe the process of going in and out defined the intrigue. Decisions were involved, even if unconscious. Maybe she'd never know why, and that was perfectly fine.

But Vera's key—they simply must find it. Not in her purse or pockets, so where could she have left it? Nobody had touched Vera's apron, still hanging in the church kitchen. Poking her fingers into that deep pocket made Madge a little squeamish, but someone had to do it.

After all, nobody but the other women had any idea this was even hers. Surely the thought of searching the apron pockets would never occur to Dale. No prejudice here, just common sense.

Every time she and Agnes went over to clean the church, Madge lingered behind after Agnes left and searched a little more. One day she worked a yardstick under the cupboards, stove and Frigidaire. What if the key bounced under one of them during Vera's struggle with her killer?

Or what if they'd all missed it in some obscure corner?

Today, she decided to retrace what would have been Vera's last steps, so she climbed back up the side stairs and paused outside. Then she pretended she was just coming in on that fateful morning.

Harry had dropped her off on his way to work, so it would've been pretty early. Would she have turned on the light?

Probably not, out of habit. You didn't waste electricity, and Vera knew these stairs like she knew her own face. Nobody traveled them more frequently.

Adopting a slower descent than normal, putting herself in Vera's shoes, Madge stopped to think. Deliberate and careful—she could almost sense Vera here with her.

With each step, she prayed. "Please, Lord—that day, what happened down here? Where is Vera's key? I know, I know. Dale's doing his best, but he's still a man. I really want to contribute."

Six steps down, her heel caught on something and the next thing Madge knew, she was bouncing down the stairs on her backside with her life passing before her. Like a rubber ball, she landed at the bottom with her legs splayed against the kitchen door.

Stars floated before her. Or were they asterisks, like the ones she'd been typing all morning between stories for this week's *Chronicle*?

Her tailbone hurt most, she decided, the left shin a close second. When her initial stunned sensation gave way to clarity, she wedged herself into the corner and propped up on her elbow. Just then, a glint of something caught her eye—not much of anything, she figured, but ran the side of her hand between the wall and floor anyway.

Hadn't she and Agnes bemoaned this ugly little space often enough? Trying to cut costs, they supposed, the original workmen had neglected to add the quarter-round here. Their frugality left a gap between the wall and the floor just wide enough for a pinky finger—or a family of mice.

Then something brushed Madge's fingers. Cool. Small. Flat, and narrower at one end than the other. Metal.

A warning ran through her mind. *Fingerprints—watch out.* If this was Vera's key, how had it landed here? Had someone been following her that day, causing her to hurry?

Until now, everyone thought she'd come straight in, but what if

Harry let her out at the parsonage, and she detoured to the alley behind the church after leaving that casserole on the porch?

No one would have seen her or anyone behind her—and no one had. *If* that's what happened.

Easing up to the bottom step, Madge gingerly flexed her legs and arms. Drat—a lump was forming on the back of her head. Must've hit the steps as she lunged downward. Other than that, her appendages seemed to be working fine.

Whew. What would Bill say? She stretched her left arm for the light switch. When she turned it and the light snapped on, waves reflected off that key wedged in the skinny gap between wall and floor.

The key. It must be! With Vera's fingerprints on it, one more piece of the puzzle would fall into place

But what if someone lost it long ago? What if it didn't even fit the side lock? Not daring to pick it up to compare with her own, Madge contemplated a while longer.

What had Aivars said about finding Vera that morning? Something about a light, she was sure. Yes, he saw a light from the kitchen and went to investigate. But did he mention whether the stairway light had been on? If it *had*, would he have been able to detect the kitchen light?

"Oh, this is getting me nowhere." Her words fell flat in the narrow cubbyhole. "Gotta go get Dale, that's all there is to it."

Joints complaining, she made her way back up the stairs and outside. Warding off a limp. she turned right toward Dale's office. Maybe hustling along would work out the kinks.

As she skirted the corner, an epiphany descended. She'd prayed, hadn't she? And if she hadn't fallen, she wouldn't have felt around on the floor.

Chances were no one else would have either, and that key could have lain there for months without being noticed. Years. Decades.

Chapter Twenty-one

Watching Dale pry the key loose and carefully lift it with a pair of tweezers, Madge held her breath. From a few steps above him and with her body complaining after her recent fall, appreciating his patience came easily.

When he turned and held out the new find, she reached into her pocket for her own key. He took it and compared the two, holding them up to light from the bare bulb hanging from the ceiling.

"They're not the same."

"What?" Her heart sank. "But they *have* to be."

"Hmm," he said, examining them again. "Maybe the one you found is for the main doors upstairs?"

"I don't know. I don't have one."

But the key didn't fit that lock, either. Following Dale down the aisle, she let go of the hope she'd entertained.

"Sheriff? Madge? What's going on?" There was Aivars, coming from his study.

"Hello Reverend. We're checking out a key Madge found downstairs." He held up the culprit. "Doesn't fit the side door or the front. Got any idea where it might work?"

"Those are the only two doors we lock, though I hope to take that up with the board one of these days."

"Is that so?"

"Yes. I believe a door should always be open. People should be able to come in whenever they need to."

"Isn't that a bit risky?"

"In a big city, I suppose, but here, I doubt it. My dad always kept the doors open and never had any problems."

"He's a preacher too?"

"Runs in the family."

"Is the side door always kept locked?"

"Only when I'm not here, or if the ladies don't have anything going on."

Dale ran his long fingers through his thinning hair. "All right, then. Any other doors with locks?"

"Just my office, though I've never tried the key." Aivars pulled out a ring of keys from his pocket and flipped through them.

"Here it is." Dale separated that key from the rest. "These two sure look the same. Better check it out."

The men led the way. Trailing along, Madge's pulse raced as though something grand was in the offing, but what could come of comparing two keys? Aivars stationed himself beside her as Dale wiggled each key into the lock.

His shadow hid most of the door, but when he twisted back after locking and unlocking the door twice, the vein in his forehead protruded more than usual.

"I'll be honest. This investigation has become a conundrum. I haven't had much experience with murders."

He stretched his shoulders. "But seems to me this finding deserves some investigation."

"Both keys worked?"

"Yeah. Now the question is, who dropped this one? If Vera did, what would she be doing with a key to your office, and how did she get it? You didn't give it to her, did you?"

"No, I've never locked the door."

"Why would somebody like Vera want to get into your office in the first place?"

"Maybe to leave me something she baked?"

"You're serious?"

"Well, she seemed to be all about baking. Since I've been here,

she's brought me several different dishes, although she's never left them up here."

"Do you know why she did that?"

"I can only guess. From my psychology studies, I'd say her insecurities drove her to seek affirmation. Her work in the kitchen, her baking, even her controlling tendencies would point that way."

"Hmm. I've heard that word *controlling* from several folks around here. She must've gone against the grain at times."

"I believe so. No one has said that outright, although I never asked. But it's tough to speak the truth after a death. I did notice tension among the women, but that's actually quite common."

"You think so?"

"Oh, yes. There were plenty of reasons my mother warned me to be careful in my first parish. And most of them involved the women."

Dale turned to Madge. "Would you agree with all this? Was Vera one to irritate other women?"

"I'd have to say so." Hopefully the shadows in the sanctuary hid her hot cheeks right now—they must be flaming. "We all get to know each other so well, personalities are bound to tangle."

"And Vera was one to tangle with?"

"Well—yes. She was opinionated, and it seemed like she thought her way was the best."

Dale uttered a long, "Hmm." He studied the pews for a moment. "I never gave a thought to it before, not seriously, I mean. But was there somebody—some woman—who clashed with Vera more than anybody else?"

Aivars gave Madge a raised-brow glance. If she were totally truthful, she'd have to say, "Me." Was that a slight shake of his head she saw?

"Umm, I'm not sure. She upset most of us at one time or another, and some women can suffer in silence better than others."

"Well, then." Dale peered her, then at Aivars. "I may seek your advice on some other investigations." His poker face made it impossible to tell if he meant this or was making an offhand joke.

Deep in following the conversation and picturing him bringing other cases to Aivars, Madge almost jumped when he addressed her. She could pen an article about Law Enforcement's Secret Weapon . . . *Behind The Scenes*—

"To your knowledge, does anybody else have a key to this office?"

"Not that I know of. We've always counted it off limits, I guess—I mean, you never know if somebody might be in there for private counseling. Pastor Tompkins pretty much worked with the door open—I doubt he locked it when he left, either."

"So. We've got a missing Easter bonnet that no one could mistake if they once saw it. And this key, with no idea how long it's been down in that crevice. We've got the knife, of course, and Vera's clothing." He closed his eyes for a second.

"Oh, yeah. There's Harry's testimony about Vera's frame of mind before her death, and her final words spoken in the Reverend's hearing. That promise she mentioned—I can't stop thinking about that."

He studied Madge and emphasized *promise*.

"I . . ."

"You wouldn't want to break a vow you made to a dead woman, do I have that right?"

Tears burned the backs of Madge's eyes. Why did Vera have to tell her about receiving the hat from a stranger? Why did she confide in her when they were so at odds?

Maybe Dale noticed her tears. For whatever reason, he muttered, "Right."

Aivars ventured in. "If there's anything else, please don't hesitate to ask." Was he attempting to rescue her?

Dale slapped his hat on his thigh before putting it on. "Until more evidence surfaces, we're stymied. I don't like this one bit, a murder right here amongst us.

"Wish we could call in the F.B.I. They're usually not interested in small town crimes, but what if this thing stretches further than any of us can imagine?"

He peered up at the vaulted ceiling. "It's wartime, after all, and there's plenty of international intrigue. Who's to say it couldn't enter our little community?"

Aivars brightened. "This keeps me awake at night, too. What if Vera had some connection with our enemies? What if somehow, maybe innocently, she got involved with the black market—that's a federal offense that *would* involve the F.B.I., wouldn't it?"

Dale's prolonged sigh ripped Madge apart.

She wanted to tell him everything. But even more, she wanted to discuss this with Bill. As soon as possible.

Dale flopped his arms at his sides. Surely he observed the deep flush rising up Aivars's neck. It was good to know that Dale saw this situation as anything but small and insignificant.

He was doing his level best. But how could they possibly tell him about the postcards without landing her in jail?

Then she recalled Aivars mentioning something called *pastor confidentiality*. What if she told him exactly what she promised Vera that day in the stairwell? Maybe instead of sharing what she knew with Bill, she ought to entrust it to him.

The disappointment in Dale's eyes traveled right to the pit of her stomach. A model public servant, he openly admitted his need. Aivars scratched the back of his neck but said nothing.

Finally, Dale handed him his keys. "Well, I'll see you two later. Thanks for the call, Madge. And you might want to put some ice on that shin of yours—quite the shiner you've got there."

Sudden shyness overtook Madge, so much so that her fingers trembled. She clasped her hands but found it even harder to avoid those remarkably blue eyes.

"To what do I owe this visit?" The usual friendly manner of the young man who had become her friend underscored how much she stood to lose. He'd only been here a few weeks, but already she held him dear.

Having someone from outside town enter Bill's world had done wonders, and she would never forgive herself if she ruined things. Not to mention her hopes concerning Gloria and Aivars.

This aspect complicated her mission—what man would want a dishonorable mother-in-law? Or better stated, what pastor?

The more the silence grew, the greater her urge to slink out. The trouble was, another day of juggling that promise against the need to come clean might send her over the edge. After hearing Dale share his anxiety about the case, she'd hardly slept last night.

In the meantime, Bill had started watching her like a child in need of supervision. After fending for herself and Gloria for so long, his wariness grated on her nerves.

So here she sat. This morning, the thought of leaving town had actually occurred to her. Ludicrous, for how could she miss Gloria's graduation?

"Madge?"

The concern in his voice startled her, but only two words emerged from her mouth. "Yes. Well . . ."

"I assume you wanted to discuss something?"

She closed her eyes with a sigh that verged on desperation.

"Do you have some questions for me?"

Questions—that was helpful.

"Yes. How does a person know if it's acceptable to break a promise? And if I told you what I promised Vera, you couldn't tell anyone, could you?"

Now his sigh joined hers. "First of all, my answer depends on the circumstances. For example, why did you make the promise in the first place? Was it to protect someone? If so, would keeping silent still protect that person, or have the tables turned? As things stand now, would sharing what you promised actually help rather than hurt that person?"

"Just a second," He stepped into the hall to straighten the picture of Peter and Jesus on the water. "This painting instructs me in difficult times. I can always see some fresh wisdom in it."

"I can imagine."

His chair objected to him sitting down and he shrugged. "Confidentiality has several significant angles. Let's say someone told me he wanted to express his love for his son who lived far away, but the son didn't make it back before his father died."

He fiddled with a class ring on his left hand. "The father wouldn't want me repeating his deathbed wishes, that goes without saying.

"But on the other hand, the son, very upset about their lack of closeness, might benefit greatly by knowing his father's deathbed profession. So do I tell or not tell the son? Which would give more honor to the dead? Would any good come from my silence, or would any come from speaking?

"Another possibility comes to light: what if the father assumed I *would* tell his son? He respected me enough to share those intimate moments at the end of his life, so did he assume I might share his sentiments with his flesh and blood?

"Of course, there's no way to tell for certain, but what if he did? Many families hesitate to express affection openly, but often send the message in a roundabout way. What if this father sent his message with me?"

The flow of his logic was not lost on Madge. Tears threatened as she saw how closely this imaginary predicament paralleled hers. The arguments swirling in her head quieted, and she glanced at that painting, a clear deliverance.

"All right. I only promised Vera I wouldn't tell *Harry* where she got the Easter hat." Getting that much out in the open brought such a release, she burst out again. "Some unknown person gave it to her, but she let Harry believe she bought it in Albert Lea."

"Ah, so perhaps this *someone* mailed it to her. Must've been quite the box. Sure wish we had the postmark from it."

Why hadn't she thought of that? What if the postmark matched that on one of the cards?

Aivars studied his hands for a moment. "It's worth considering." Then he fell silent.

Disappointment flooded Madge. What had she expected him to say? Maybe she expected him to absolve her.

"I've been struggling with this for days. It seems impossible to figure out what's right. Since I sinned by trespassing in Vera's house, I thought—"

"I think you're over-reacting a bit."

"What?" She hated the tremulous rise of her voice.

"You have no bigger claim on being a sinner than anybody else. Searching Vera and Harry's house, while technically illegal, was well intended."

Madge sat back against her chair. "You really think so?"

"Yes. And remember, God considers the *heart* along with our actions. If that weren't true, all of us would have to live frozen lives and would never follow our inner guidance. That's how I picture the Pharisees of old, and did their attitudes please our Lord?"

She shook her head.

"We have to do the best we can with what we're given. At the very worst, I would say the Good Lord supplied you with an extra dose of curiosity, wouldn't you?"

Madge swallowed a mountain. Could it be this simple?

"Most of the time, you use your innate inquisitiveness wisely. If you happen to slip up once in a while, especially under intense pressure, I would think God's mercy would kick in, wouldn't you?"

No, that's not what she'd been thinking at all.

"After all, He created you as you are, and by the way, that's in His own image."

All the breath drained from Madge's lungs. Her chair seemed to pull her deeper. She *had* been trying to do what was right. She had never meant to break her promise.

"Does this help?"

"Yes, I—I think so." She ought to get up but longed to hear more. Aivars seemed to realize this.

"Sometimes our consciences over-produce and fill us with shame for something we've done or haven't done even after we've sought

forgiveness. Chances are, this originates in being shamed during our childhoods.

"If we never experienced being forgiven, that continuing sense of shame can stifle our normal creative impulses. I would guess you've had trouble concentrating on your work this week?"

"That's an understatement. I haven't been able to write a column since—"

"I noticed that. I bet people are missing your humor."

"And Bill—he can tell something's wrong. You know I just can't ..."

"Do anything to upset him?"

"Yes."

"Of course not. Maybe it would be good to stand back a minute and consider the load you've been carrying. Have you patted yourself on the back lately for how you made it through all the turmoil of the past year—actually, the past three years since Bill left?"

No use even trying to answer that one.

"I thought not. Well, maybe you should. You've done a fine job of holding things together and welcoming him home. Because of your vigilance, he's gained strength since then. Gloria seems quite well-adjusted, and that's thanks to you, I bet."

"I really haven't done anything special, just kept on day-by-day, like everyone else."

"Surely it can't be easy for you to contend with his condition?"

"No. But having him home is worth whatever we have to face."

"Yes, indeed. But you're still under stress, and I'm here to tell you you're doing just fine in spite of it. Even in this short time, I can see progress—his stammer has all but vanished."

Now that she thought about it, she had to agree.

"So maybe now you can ease up a little on yourself."

The clock's rhythmic tick suddenly seemed less menacing. And then, tears stung the backs of her eyes.

"You know, we're all allowed to be weak sometimes. And imperfect. That's what faith is all about—we wouldn't need grace if we were perfect, would we?"

"N…" Madge meant to reply, but her shoulders started to shake. Her breath came hard and she dropped her head into her hands. She hadn't allowed herself to cry since Bill came home, except about Vera's death.

Aivars handed her his handkerchief and quietly left the study. At first, she held the deluge in, but then began to sob. When had she wept so profusely?

Finally, the flow let up. She blew her nose and gathered up her purse.

Passing through the sanctuary brought a renewed sense of serenity. Why had she gotten herself so worked up over all this? Her steps felt lighter than they had in months. Make that *years*.

Aivars waited outside on the steps, twiddling a stick between his fingers. He asked one simple question. "Better?"

"Better. I can't thank you enough."

"I'll see you later. We're still on for dinner tonight, right?"

"Oh yes. I got so caught up, I almost forgot." Madge hurried to add, "Don't worry, I put a pot roast in the oven on low. Like I mentioned the other day, Bill's excited about having you over."

She started away but paused. "So you'll—"

"Talk with Dale?"

All she could do was nod.

"If you want me to."

"Oh yes. That is, if you can make sure Harry won't find out about the stranger."

The sun struck the twinkle in Aivars's eye. "I do believe that can be arranged, and from what I've seen of Dale, I think he'll understand. He may come off a bit gruff, but he really cares about people around here, including you."

It wasn't until she rounded the corner that Madge realized she'd left her sweater in the study. And that the sopping handkerchief in her hand might never be the same.

Chapter Twenty-two

May 3, 1944

The train's movement created a soothing jiggle, but above the *clackety-clack*, passengers' voices rose like weeds in a cornfield. Humidity hung in the air, so wide-open windows ushered in soot from the coal furnace. Snitches of ordinary talk spiraled around Bill—people describing their jobs or chatting about the weather.

Inevitably, the war entered in. Someone asked about another passenger's son in the Army Air Force or offered a passenger a well-read newspaper, replete with headlines from the European Front.

"Do you think we'll really invade France?"

"Our neighbor says his son's unit is in England preparing for something big. It's bound to happen soon."

"Sure hope the commanders know what they're doing."

"An American's heading everything up now—that's good news."

"But we made all those mistakes off the African coast, don't you remember?"

"Hmm. But that was almost two years ago. General Eisenhower's a smart fellow."

The whistle announced a stop up ahead, blocking out the reply. Just as well—thinking about the Allies' strategic errors produced a sick sensation in Bill's gut.

He perused yesterday's *Daily Iowan*—somebody from southeast Iowa must've left it behind. Nothing piqued his interest like poring over articles, though some reporters got their wires crossed.

A cursory glance over the headlines underlined the situation: still dire but showing hopeful signs.

"*Allies Continue to Batter German Coast Defenses. Nazis Declare Invasion Near – RAF Night Bombers Carry Onslaught Into Nineteenth Straight Day.*

"*Empire Premiers Meet With Churchill –* 'We Need No longer fear defeat', says British Prime Minister."

"*Allied Planes Smash 20 Japanese Barges Fleeing From Wewak*"

"*Spain Agrees to Reduce Wolfram Sales to Nazis.*"

"*Poland—Soviet Bombers Destroy six Troop, Ammunition Trains at Big Rail Junction.*"

"*Lucky Boomerang Bomber Always Comes Back.*"

Settling in on the Boomerang bomber, Bill stretched out his legs. This Consolidated B-24 bomber's incredible record was a true marvel.

Its captain, Wally Stewart of Salt Lake City, had completed fifty-three missions. Unheard of. Good to see something positive, even though many other bombers had crashed early on, losing all aboard.

Closer to Waterloo, Bill relaxed. Soon he'd see Roger.

There was no way to express how he looked forward to meeting this buddy, even for a short time.

He'd run over to the school and found Delton Palmer there early this morning—didn't take long. Then Roger called, just in time to catch the seven o'clock train. His note would explain this to Madge.

The jukebox letters spelling *Rock-Ola* felt cold to the touch. Madge had been at the café for ten minutes, waiting for Bill. They'd planned to eat lunch here, but he was late.

Her mind traveled across the Mississippi as Helene came to mind. What did she do in La Crosse, anyhow?

Strangers plopped into an adjacent booth and one of them stuck a nickel in the slot behind the condiment rack. Some folks still found change to spend on music.

Her judgmental analysis softened as Bing Crosby's old hit, *Star Dust*, emanated. She could visualize him behind the cashier's counter. His bass-baritone transformed the premises into a dance floor.

She missed dancing, and who knew? Music might make a big difference for Bill.

Thinking of her friend Agnes, Madge poured a little more cream from the pint-sized pitcher beside her cup. Agnes had stopped by the office this morning when she was making order of last night's frenzy to get the paper out.

"Having a bad morning?"

"Sort of—I woke up late. Bill had already left, and I managed to knock some books off the nightstand when I stumbled out of bed. Have to straighten all that up."

Absently stirring her coffee, Madge strained to remember what Bill murmured last night before she fell asleep. He'd been going over their schedule. Something about interviewing the high school principal about graduation.

That wouldn't take long, though, unless he took pictures. But graduation day was the time for that, with the gymnasium decked out in crepe paper and the band playing *Pomp and Circumstance.*

Frazzled over her late start, she'd skimmed over items for next week's issue. The hatchery's baby chick ad and some local news that arrived too late for this week would make a beginning for the third page.

Mr. and Mrs. Barney Howard received a visit from their son, Private First-Class Richard Howard, of Bolling Field, Washington, D.C. Miss Genevieve Wells, a WAC stationed at the Capitol, accompanied Private Howard.

Another budding wartime romance.

Clifton Smith had been notified that Elmer, in a medical unit at Chickasha, Oklahoma, had been promoted to Sergeant. Felicia Corning transferred from one section of the Cornhusker Ordnance Plant to another near Grand Island, Nebraska.

Her mother added more information. "She's making eighty

cents an hour! Glad her cousin invited her out there to work but we sure do miss her."

The blurbs detailing people's lives went on and on. Three full columns next week, for sure. Made Madge's head ache to think of typing it all.

Then Agnes had walked in.

"I came to town because Percival has to check his seed corn order, and I've been dying to tell you something. We drove over to Decorah yesterday, and I saw someone you'd recognize."

"I don't know a soul there."

"Oh, but this is different. Percival's sister is having an awful rheumatism bout. Flared up since Jimmy left for the Pacific. They haven't heard from him yet at all. Can you imagine the strain?"

Agnes blushed. "Of course you can. What's the matter with me? Anyhow, she tries not to burden her other children with her fears, so she let loose with me while Percival fixed a pipe in the basement.

"But before we left for home, Vera's cousin from La Crosse walked by. Helene."

"Really? Are you sure?"

"Absolutely—I talked with her for quite a while when she was here. But when I hailed her the other day, she crossed the street. I called out again, but she cut through someone's lawn. Isn't that strange?"

"Didn't she say she was leaving for home right after our potluck for Pastor Z?"

"Sure did. She came back to the kitchen to thank us for the fine meal. Had to catch the four o'clock train to La Crosse, she said, so's she could get to work early the next morning.

"Important factory labor for the war effort. Makes me wonder if what Vera said about her was true."

"What?"

"That they'd lived in the same house in Chicago as children. Their fathers emigrated together and started a meat market. Eventually they set up separate households."

Meat market . . . black market . . . Red lights flashed.

The image they provoked set Madge's imagination on fire. She'd been thinking black market ever since Bill—or Aivars—mentioned the possibility.

What if Helene and Vera's connections provided the final destination for goods trucked by some black market group? What if . . ."

After Agnes went on her way, the tale became all consuming. Helene in Decorah? Why would she leave her important job in La Crosse? Unless . . . unless the ring needed her there, perhaps to supply truckers midway in their journey.

Madge's mind whirled until she simply could not sit any longer. She paced back and forth. Bill ought to be walking in any second. Where was he, anyway?

"Why must you always tell someone what you hear? Isn't that how gossip gets started?"

Her biting answer echoed through the front office. The ever-present ink smell prevailed out here, and blue fingerprints and smudges dappled her weathered oak desk.

"Because this news might shed light on a *murder*, that's why! Helene's supposed to be in La Crosse. Who knows how significant this could be?"

She fought the urge to run over and spill the story to Aivars. No, he must be worn out after his second funeral.

At 11:30, it was time to meet Bill at the café. "Might as well go over. I'm accomplishing nothing anyway."

By the time Bing Crosby's *I'll Be Seeing You* ended, her watch showed 11:45. Where could Bill be? Always on time, that man. Now she knew how he felt when she burst in late. A few minutes, that is, but nothing like this.

Another customer parted with precious pocket change to play, *It Had to Be You,* so Madge gulped the rest of her coffee and left a quarter on the table.

For some reason, that song always provoked her. Outside, the sunshine shone especially bright, and her stomach growled.

Maybe she'd stroll toward the high school. Perhaps Bill was still interviewing the principal. Soon, she'd meet him hurrying along, and he'd give her his special grin.

She'd say, "Can't believe you stood me up!"

He'd give her a peck on the cheek and they'd continue on together.

The beat of her pumps reminded her that graduation would be here before they knew it. And their youngest would step out into the world, although Gloria seemed in no hurry to figure out a plan.

Close to the red brick building now, Madge re-thought Bill's planning last night. "I'll go over to the school, and then . . ." What had he said? Oh, that was it—some other errands might occupy him until later this afternoon.

"How could I have forgotten that? Guess he'll grab a bite somewhere along the way."

"Madge! Good to see you—what a gorgeous day." Mr. Palmer, the principal, hurried her way.

"I thought maybe I'd cut Bill off at the pass."

"Bill?"

"Yes. Didn't he interview you this morning?"

"Yes, but it only took a few minutes."

"Really?"

"He's an early bird, always has been, right? I'm glad to see him doing so well, Madge. So pleased he can be here for Gloria's graduation. Well, see you soon."

He turned down his street, leaving her staring after him. *Early bird . . . just a few minutes?*

On the next corner, Madge eyed the church. Once again, the temptation to tell Aivars about Helene nearly overwhelmed her, but she checked herself.

"No. You *will* wait for Bill, even though he'll probably share it with Aivars. Might as well run home and make a quick sandwich while you're close."

As she did, a recollection arose. Helene had made a hasty retreat out the side door that day—yes the *side* door, after she gave them all a little wave. So she knew her way around the church basement.

Yes, she'd met the four o'clock train, which would put her in La Crosse late that night. The stylish, citified suit she'd worn that Sunday, along with her rather husky voice, already gave her a mysterious air. Now this sighting in Decorah.

Questions burned as Madge slapped a hunk of leftover roast beef between two slices of bread, grateful that Bill's uncle and aunt raised beef and split a half with them each year.

Must be rough in big cities . . . people had to change their eating habits. She poured herself a glass of milk and sat down. Normally, she'd have enjoyed the sweep of the giant oak that shaded the house on hot days.

When she and Bill bought this house, that tree had stood about fifteen feet high, way back in the far corner. Now, it towered forty or fifty feet.

But enjoying this lovely day was out of the question. What could be important enough to take Bill away like this?

He seemed just fine last night, so she ought not worry, but she could barely sit still long enough to finish her sandwich. Maybe she'd stop by the church after all. What if Bill's memory had taken a wrong turn, and he'd sought help from Aivars?

Tidying up the kitchen took only a couple of minutes, and then she recalled the mess she'd made upstairs. Such a strange start to the day—when had she ever gotten out of bed on his side?

Up in their bedroom, she reached down to gather up a book and surveyed the front cover. *Through The Wheat*—he must've started reading this World War I story. An uncomfortable sensation threatened, but she shook it off. He'd always liked military history.

Then a piece of notebook paper caught her eye. On one side, something had been scribbled. She turned it over—Bill's handwriting.

Madge, Roger, my army buddy at Ft. McCoy sent me a telegraph. He's going down to Waterloo to help his folks today, so I decided to make a quick trip to see him. Will bring the afternoon train home.

Relief battled with frustration as Madge sank onto the bed. Bill had never mentioned where Roger's parents lived. Irritation threatened, but not towards Bill. Her rush to get out of bed had kept her from seeing this.

He'd tiptoed in and left it on his pillow.

"Might as well get a head start on next week's articles while I wait." She clumped downstairs and headed back to the office.

"I felt bad not being able to tell you. But you were so sound asleep —"

Madge buried her face in Bill's collar. Over the past few hours, a nameless fear had hounded her. True, he'd come back on the four o'clock train, but not knowing the reason he left had wreaked inner havoc.

He sat down at her desk and pulled her to his lap. "I thought my note explained well enough."

Misery welled in her throat. "It did. When I finally found it."

"What do you mean?"

"When I woke up and saw you were gone, I hurried out of bed and knocked everything off the end table. So I . . ." She wiped her nose. "I didn't see it. When you didn't show up at the café, I came home and found it."

"Sorry, Maddie-girl. Guess I shouldn't have let you sleep after all, but I know you've been—"

She wrapped her arms around his neck. "It's okay. Now you're back. How'd it go with Roger?"

"Did me good to see him again. I'll tell you everything in a minute. But first, let's call Aivars—he needs to hear what Roger said, too. If you don't mind waiting."

"Me?" Madge gave a massive sniff. "Mind waiting? Where did you get that idea?"

His chuckle heartened her, along with the lights sparkling in his eyes.

"Good idea to call Aivars. I have news, too." Something Agnes told me this morning. But you're just going to have to wait along with me."

"Getting even, are we? Guess that's only fair." He helped her up. "You okay now?"

"Yes. I'm just so relieved to have you back."

"Glad you called. I needed a break to clear my head." Aivars closed the *Chronicle* door. "What's up?"

"Thanks for coming over. I went to see my Army buddy this morning, and he gave me some insights. "Did you know that Nazi youth camps spread through the States in the thirties?"

Madge's eyebrows spiked. "Where?"

"Mostly back East, in New York and New Jersey. But Roger mentioned one in a little town near Milwaukee."

"Seriously?"

"And somebody we've all met attended said camp in '34, in the town of Grafton." Bill pulled up a chair.

Grafton, Wisconsin, 1934. Who would've traveled all that way back then for summer camp? Aivars ventured a guess. "Would that be Vera's cousin?"

"One and the same."

Madge's mouth dropped. "So she might be inclined to pro-Nazi sentiments. But how did Roger know about her?" Madge's sputter ignited an explanation.

"All right. All right. I wrote him a couple of weeks ago when those postcards were driving me crazy."

He held up purple-stained palms. "Just couldn't sit around doing nothing. Roger's father broke his leg last week, so he got leave to visit his folks."

"Sounds like seeing him was worth your time."

"Yeah, well."

Madge and Bill shared a wordless communication. Wouldn't it

be wonderful to have this kind of relationship some day? "What else did Roger have to say?"

"Not much, except that Army intelligence already has its eye on Helene. The murder interested him greatly. Of course, I pointed out that we have no idea if she had anything to do with it."

"Did you mention that Dale . . ." Madge's voice tightened.

"Yeah, I said we wouldn't want our Sherlock Holmes activities known to our local law enforcement, and Roger assured me this was all completely confidential. Has to be anyhow, it's government-related."

"A Nazi camp for youth, right in Wisconsin. But then, anything's possible in America, the great melting pot. Room for all kinds of opinions—that's the beauty of our way of life."

Madge looked about to burst as Aivars spoke but held her tongue. How could decent, law abiding citizens have entertained Nazism that recently? He must have surmised her feelings and offered a response.

"I remember Dad saying how certain German immigrants were shunned during the Great War. Some changed the spelling of their names so they wouldn't sound so German, like taking double n's off the end."

"Oh yes, the Bruggemans did that, and the family that farms out on the bottomland. What's their name, Bill?"

"Wise . . . used to be Weiss."

"I'd heard about ship captains simplifying spellings in general because they were so hard to write and pronounce. But once folks settled, they didn't have to keep the change from their journey."

A fly buzzed around Bill's head. "Pesky things." He swatted again and it flew away, only to get caught in the roll of flypaper dangling from the ceiling.

"Gotcha!" Grinning, he picked up their conversation.

"Chances are the majority of them didn't even know how to write their name in the first place. When they switched to English, why not use the simplest version? Anyway, more fodder for the mystery mill, that's for sure."

What a tangled web. Suspicious foreign postcards. A used train ticket. And now, Helene's possible involvement.

"Okay, now it's your turn, Madge."

"Interestingly enough, my bombshell revolves around Helene, too. And would you believe, it came from Agnes?"

"Hmm . . ."

She explained about Agnes seeing Helene in Decorah and her peculiar behavior. "And Vera and Helene lived together as children—their fathers ran a butchering business."

Bill steepled his fingers. "So we've got some more clues, at least. But we really can't make any assumptions."

Madge pulled a paper from her desk. "But what about this? The Office of Public Administration sent out an article for next week's paper—about eating organs.

"They're calling them variety meats to make them more appealing."

"And?" Bill took off his glasses and rubbed his eyes. "Bound to be a shortage, with so much needed for our troops. The government expects us to promote liver and such to the public—works like the army."

"How so?"

"Somebody gets an inspiration and proposes it. The concept travels through the official routes until somebody higher up latches onto it and calls it their own."

"But this meat idea came from the top down, don't you think? And couldn't it have something to do with the black market?"

"Depends on what you call the top. Who knows where that phrase *variety meat* originated? Maybe the wife of somebody in the food administration whispered it to her husband one night, and he liked the sound of it.

"The next day, he mentioned it to his boss, who agreed and sent the idea on to Washington. Voila! The birth of an organ meat campaign."

"Just like that?"

"Yep. Kind of scary, huh?"

Another moment of quiet understanding passed between Madge and Bill. It didn't always work that way in a marriage, Aivars knew, but his parents enjoyed a similar quiet dialogue. A yearning gripped him—he couldn't even have put it into words.

He offered, "But there *could be* a connection. There's a big market for profiteers right now, and this will continue until the war ends. We never think of people we know getting involved in something shady, but I can see how someone might be drawn into a money-making scheme."

Madge's eyebrows disappeared under her tousled hair. "You can?"

"Sure. It's human nature. And what better way to disguise an operation like that than using someone from a small rural town?"

Chapter Twenty-three

Monday, May 8, 1944

One of those nights unfit for sleeping—hearing Madge's quiet breathing, Bill slipped down the stairs. No use fighting nature . . . must be some reason he'd awakened.

Then he heard it—a vehicle's unmistakable hum, not unlike the Army trucks that hauled supplies, troops, nurses—you name it—across the deserts of North Africa. 2:30 a.m., hardly the time for folks to be about, especially in a truck. Might as well go check around.

Grabbing his jacket and government-issue boots, perfect for garden work, he silently left by the back door. Moonlight shimmered on grass soft as lamb's wool.

Then the sound re-echoed as the driver shifted into low. Sounded like over on Oak Street, so Bill shinnied down the alley, over a fence, and sneaked along the Stringham's property line. No dogs here—the couple kept cats in their carriage house as mousers.

The one good thing about cats, in his opinion. Well, two. They liked mice, and they didn't bark. He caught sight of the truck, a typical Ford used for farm work, as the driver sped up and traversed Main. Two blocks ahead, it turned right and headed west.

Energized, he determined to keep up with it—had to be some good reason for somebody to be up in the middle of the night. A mission of some sort.

A shiver ran the length of his backbone as he followed the alley behind Tom's house and trespassed through the back yard. How many times had he said their dog was too old to raise a ruckus?

Not a stir anywhere except this truck, going slow to keep the engine quiet. But why? Instinctively, he veered right even before the truck turned the corner. Keeping an even pace, he wasn't even panting.

No pain in his back now. Not even a twinge. This solitary trek brought back a memory he'd held down for more than two years.

The Kasserine Pass. February of '42. By rights, he shouldn't have been there—should have been back in California training troops. But the Army doesn't always keep its promises. So in that stark desert land, unfamiliar terrain, their commander hadn't known much more than the rest of them.

Suddenly, the smells returned, as if he'd been transported across the Atlantic again. Guns blared, tanks creaked as they rolled closer, turrets squealed, and he was running, tripping. Then a shadow loomed directly above him.

Another GI yelled, "Come on, let's get outta here!"

That was when the *ping* hit him. Bounced off, he thought at first, before he tried to move. The next second, someone grabbed him by the collar and started pulling.

His jacket snagged on outgrowths. His teeth hurt. A rawness scraped right down to the bone. Nerves tingled, lights flared in his head, a boiling cauldron pooled between his ears.

A dog barked. Bill gathered his senses. Oh man—had it really been like that? He sucked in a mountain of cool air and then another.

They'd been out often at night back then, and the desert glowed in the moonlight, like snow in Iowa. But he had come home to solid black earth. Farm ground—the heartland.

This was his town, and he knew every street, every alley. He moved ahead—only one place that truck driver was headed.

A poster displayed front and center in the *Chronicle* window showed a somber young woman dressed in red. Holding up her hand, she vowed:

I will never purchase anything except
from local markets, and only with
approved rationing cards.
Here on the home front,
I will do my part to support
our troops in harm's way.

The girl's blonde locks set Madge pondering again. Such a shame if Helene's mind became twisted at such a young age. But her belief in the Nazi philosophy—if she did believe in it—didn't mean she had killed her own cousin.

If she had, what could have motivated her? Maybe some deep-seated reason, something to do with an old family grudge.

Yes, maybe that was it. Helene nursed hurt feelings about some past hurt, like many folks. Sometimes they carried their pain to their graves, but might also act it out. If only Harry were more forthcoming.

No use asking him. He'd light his pipe and peer at her until she felt uncomfortable enough to leave. He seemed to be getting along fine these days, anyway. He opened the bank each morning, left for lunch and returned, then closed up in late afternoon.

But what went through his mind?

What she wouldn't give to know!

The poster next to the rationing one showed a giant thumb smashing the words *black market*, while another boasted a beautiful young uniformed woman against a waving American flag. An enticing invitation completed the message:

Are you a girl with a
Star-Spangled heart?
Join the WACS now.

For a moment, Gloria's image rose. With graduation only a week away and several of the girls in her class heading off to other states to work in factories, what would she decide to do?

One of her friends was leaving with another girl for Arkansas, where they'd be threading bomb heads. The idea made Madge's stomach turn.

Somebody had to do this kind of work, of course, but the chemicals must be dangerous. Did the workers have to be young women with their whole lives ahead of them? What if a terrible accident happened in the plant?

She would never forgive herself if she let Gloria go and something horrible happened. But so far, Lillian had managed just fine. Good thing the rules required her to keep mum about what her factory manufactured.

But Gloria wouldn't . . . Madge shook herself. No, not after all they'd been through with Bill, she would never up and leave on a moment's notice. She wouldn't do something like that, especially after watching Lillian leave.

No. Or would she?

Bill's hand on her shoulder brought her into the present again. "Looking over our government poster collection?"

"Yes. Every one of the changes they advertise is for the war effort, right?"

"Yep, all for the cause. I'm just relieved that some, like rationing, don't affect us so much. Quite the black market springing up in those areas."

He kept mentioning that.

"Especially for meat. You'd think Prohibition was in force again and meat was as scarce as alcohol. One more thing for the authorities to keep an eye on. You know how Americans love our steak and roast beef."

He headed toward his domain but paused in the doorway. "Just like with alcohol, people will find a way. Makes me think of what Aivars said the other night about gasoline rationing in the South."

"I don't think I heard."

"When rationing began, people took offense when the authorities

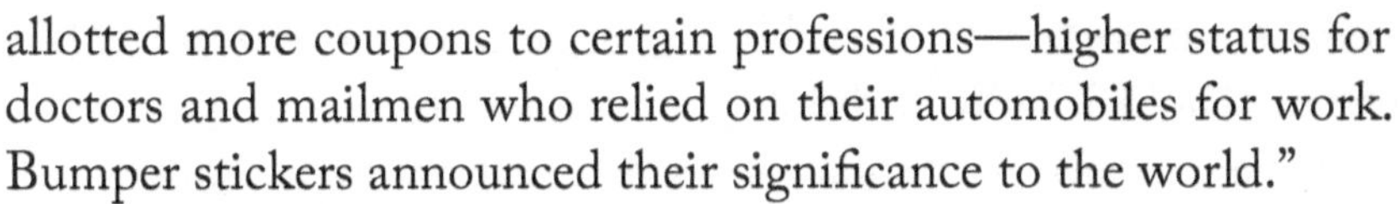

allotted more coupons to certain professions—higher status for doctors and mailmen who relied on their automobiles for work. Bumper stickers announced their significance to the world."

"Bankers, too."

"Exactly. Aivars said the board didn't include pastors in the so-called *higher class* at first, so some of them filed a complaint. Wasn't their work just as important? How were they supposed to make their hospital calls on three gallons per week?"

"Makes sense to me."

"Here's the humor in the situation—glad Aivars can see it. He said the rationing board faces an impossible job. He quoted the passage about serving instead of being served—said preaching about the concept comes way easier than living it out."

"Did the board change the pastors' ration?"

"That's my practical Maddie-girl." He entered the press room, so she raised her voice

"Well, did they?"

"Yep. Proves that, right or wrong, it pays to speak up sometimes."

Madge retraced her thoughts to what started her staring at the window in the first place. It was her concern for Gloria—but then she started thinking about Helene again, which made her remember what Bill had found at the library.

She snorted. *Little* woman? In a pig's eye, and *that* made her laugh out loud.

"What's so funny out there?"

"Oh, nothing." She stifled another giggle and forced her thoughts back in line.

If Helene were somehow involved with an underground slaughterhouse operation, what might motivate her? How would aiding the Black Market help the Axis Powers? And what did Vera have to do with it?

Once again, that garish Easter bonnet surfaced. What could it possibly have to do with a cold-blooded murder?

Try as she might, she just couldn't see how that hat ended up being so important to Vera. How strange to think of it as her life ebbed away. Literally at the very last moment.

But apparently, someone else valued that hat even more.

The knock startled Bill, who was drying the last of the supper dishes. Most folks came around the back when it was still light out. When he opened the door, there stood Dale Finley, looking fidgety. Something must be amiss.

"Why hello, Dale. Is something wrong?"

"Evening. Mind if I step in for a minute?"

"Of course not." Bill held the door open and waited.

"This . . . Well, I suppose this will sound highly irregular, but it can't be helped. You know how they've shipped in German prisoners captured in North Africa?"

"I'd heard that."

"They'll soon hit capacity at the main camps, which means they need extra guards. They're already using returned soldiers too injured to go back to the front."

"Yeah, an Army buddy told me about that."

"And now they're setting up more branch camps here and in Minnesota."

"Getting mighty close, I'd say." The uneasiness in Bill's abdomen was hard to ignore.

"From what I hear, the hard-core SS will stay over in Algona. That's a relief. But because the Army's so short on guards, they're dipping into local law enforcement."

"Oh?"

"I've been called up. Might be for a few weeks but could be longer."

Dale's sigh carried the faint smell of onions and whatever else he ate for supper. He glanced around the living room. "Is Madge here?"

"She's out working in the garden."

"Oh, I didn't notice her. I'd like to say what I've got to say with her present, if you don't mind."

"Sure." Bill led the way out, wishing he knew where this was heading, and Madge glanced up from the string bean row as he and Dale descended the porch stairs. They stepped over several rows and Dale began as Madge got to her feet.

"Evening, Madge. I came over to discuss something with you and Bill."

She pushed back a strand of sunburnt hair, even brighter in the prelude to sunset. "All right."

Bill hoped whatever Dale was going to say wouldn't disturb her. Curiosity rode her face like the freckles he'd always loved. Seeing her upset really bothered him—he would never leave a note to tell her his plans again.

"I've got to leave town for a time. Bill can explain later. I really have no choice, and as I considered who could handle things while I'm gone . . ." Dale swiped at his forehead with his handkerchief.

"The person who kept coming to my mind . . ." He twisted toward Bill. "Was you."

"Me?" Bill blurted out the word without thinking. The wild flicker in Madge's eyes made him gulp. She said nothing, but he had no idea what she was thinking. Sometimes he did—or thought so, anyway. But now she froze. The silence caused Dale to offer more.

"Thought about Harm Jenkins, but he's really slow on the draw, you know? And Clyde Heimers would be okay, but he lives a little too far out and milks that big herd of Holsteins morning and night. Other than those two, so many young men are gone, and what's left . . ."

The Chalmers boy went through Bill's mind. But he just wasn't cut out for this sort of thing—lacked the confidence.

"The town needs someone respectable and reliable, but quick-thinking at the same time. With your experience in the Army, I . . . Even though you've already done more than your share . . ."

Dale threw up his arms. "Well, what do you say?"

Madge crossed to Bill's side and took his hand. The grit on her fingers reminded him of her constant support. Her fiery green eyes met his.

"Hon? I can see Dale's logic. Who else could hold the reins as steady as you? That is, if you want to take this on."

Madge again, solid and steady. Bill gripped her hand. She was the solid ground beneath his feet.

A long breath escaped Dale's lips. "Then you'll consider it?"

"When would I need to start?"

"A week from today. Sooner, if they push. You could come over in your spare time this week and I'd show you the ropes, so to speak."

"What sort of authority would I have?"

"You'd act in my place, and if anything serious came up, you'd have the power to deputize another person." He shifted his eyes toward Madge. "Know anybody else around here who might have a hankering to investigate anything?"

Bill let go a laugh. "Around here? I couldn't say."

Chapter Twenty-four

"It's the Voice of Iowa, Jack Shelley, reporting to you tonight from Italy . . ."

Bill leaned back in his armchair. The mild clatter from the kitchen had a soothing effect. The melody of women at work took him back to his childhood, when his mother had run a tight ship. Hearing spoons and spatulas against bowls and pans indicated all was well.

Although his nightmares had stayed away for several weeks now, he knew he had to be careful. Still, he hungered for news of his unit. So tonight, he tuned in to the *Voice of Iowa*.

Troops still in harm's way—especially the guys from his unit—had become like family. Once he'd come through the worst of his injury, he'd wanted to know how they were doing. Needed to know. Tonight, he wasn't disappointed, since Shelley focused on the fighting at Anzio.

"Under Major General Ryder, the thirty-fourth infantry division joined the Italian invasion in late March. The Allies decided to by-pass the Gustav Line in order to establish a narrow beachhead at Anzio. But as you have heard, powerful German attacks have been preventing them from moving inland.

"I'm pleased to report that the long-awaited breakout finally came for the division yesterday, May 23. After much bloodshed, these brave men, members of the Red Bull line, who already have seen almost continuous dangerous duty since North Africa, now begin the drive on Rome.

"Looking ahead to Rome's liberation, those of you with loved ones

and friends in this fight can hold your heads high. Because of our boys'
steadfast courage, this brutal enemy will be conquered in Italy.

"After that, onward and northward. We shall eventually vanquish
the foe in its own territory."

Dangerous duty in North Africa . . . drive on Rome . . .

Faces of men from his squad filtered through Bill's mind, and he
blinked back tears. Jensen, Alberts, Carmichael, Schmidt, Peterson,
Cutler, Halvorsen, Taylor, Cominsky, Noelting, Morrison, Mitchell,
and so many others—they might be sitting right here with him
in this quiet living room.

How he wished they were. They'd landed at Algiers with the
Eastern Task Force and fought with the British Seventy-Eighth
Infantry and two British Commando groups through Sened Station,
Sidi Bou Zid, and Faid Pass, where the enemy took out Carmichael.

Then on to the battles at Sbeitla, where their squad lost three more
men, and from there to Fondouk Gap. Sites and names ran together,
but even now the closeness they'd developed enveloped him.

Of course, after weeks without opportunity to clean up, they
reeked. Here in their safe living room, the men's off-color jokes
and laughter sounded in his ears. Their grunts and groans as they
pressed on resounded, as real as the voice on the radio.

Through it all, they trucked on. Whatever the challenge, his
unit would meet it.

A slight pressure from Madge's hand reminded him of how far
he had come. "I'm going over to the school with Gloria to help
decorate the stage. You doing all right?"

"Fine . . ."

"Such a nice breeze tonight, maybe we can take a walk later?"

"Mmm . . ."

"See you later, Dad."

Through the screen door, the lilt of Gloria's voice carried straight
to his heart. His sweet little girl, about to graduate. How could
this be? He hated not being with his unit, but missing her big day
would be unthinkable.

After they left, he dozed off and dreamed about a guy from Red Oak—what was his name? They'd met in the officers' tent, with freshly transcribed records in their hands.

The Kasserine Pass proved to be a nightmare for those Southeast Iowa boys in the 168th. When news of their high casualties drifted to Bill's squad, he'd walked off by himself. The dreadful losses hit him hard, and he'd wondered ever since if the soldier he met had survived.

Then it happened. The next day, he was the one being carried on a grungy stretcher, fighting for his life.

Tap . . . tap-tap. "Anybody home?" A familiar mellow tone filtered through the screen and roused him.

"Sure, come on in. I was just—"

"Listening to the war news?"

"Yeah."

One thing about Aivars, he knew how to keep silence. Although questions traced his brow lines, he would never ask about the effect of the evening reports. And precisely because he did not ask, the truth came pouring forth.

"I don't listen every night. Sometimes it gets to me, but then I think about my unit and want to know what's going on. They've been over there so long and have fought so hard." Bill sat up straighter. "Of course, I don't want to make things worse for Madge."

"Yes, but don't they say, *Once a soldier, always a soldier?* I can't imagine how you'd get that out of your system. Besides, you're a newsman."

"Yeah."

"My dad never talked much about his Great War service, but I'm sure he can never forget those men he fought with."

"In France?"

A simple nod left Bill to trail back to that other war. If he were to write a memoir, he'd call it that—*The Other War*. But instead of meaning the Great War, the title would refer to his inner struggle.

He turned off the radio. "But I don't suppose you came over to discuss the war?"

Another thing he to appreciated about this fellow—his quick smile revealed genuine good will. Aivars liked people— wasn't just pretending because of his job.

"I really didn't have anything specific in mind. Just got the urge to see what you were up to."

"Madge went over with Gloria to decorate the gym. I ought to get out and do some yard work, or at least take a walk. Want to wander around town?"

"Sure. With the ladies' constant supply of desserts, I've gained a few pounds since I came."

Though Bill couldn't say how it happened, they ended up walking the gravel path through the cemetery. He pointed out certain names and recited their family connections. They skirted a low area still mushy from the last rain, and without meaning to, approached Vera's grave.

"Hard to believe, isn't it?"

"Sure is. The casualty lists we print, name after name, are one thing. But a murder—that's entirely another. Vera was your first burial, right?"

"Yes, and God willing, my last murder. Sometimes I'd like to ask Sheriff Finley what's taking him so long to close this case. But now he's not even here."

"When I consider the evidence—or lack of it—I wonder what else can be done. Finding this culprit is no easy task."

"Me too. Have you heard any more from your Army buddy?"

"Nope."

"No more inspirations about how the pieces all fit together?"

"Not really. But that reminds me. We did have a visit from Dale just before he left town." Bill kicked at a stone. "I should have told you right away, but it slipped my mind. He asked me to take over for him while he's gone."

"What? You're the sheriff now? That's great news—but how do you feel about it?"

"Glad I can still be of service."

"Oh man . . ." Aivars ran his fingers through his hair. "Now—"

"We can follow up on some of our leads with a clear conscience."

"Right. I keep wondering about that hair in the hilt of the knife."

"That's right—you saw everything up close. Sorry you had to. Not that different from battle scenes, I expect. Well, Dale mentioned that hair to me—the report came in one day while he was training me.

"Turned out to be blond, almost white. Not like Madge's at all. None of her fingerprints, either. Glad she's off the suspect list. Good thing, since she's married to the now-acting sheriff, wouldn't you say?"

"What a relief that must be for you both."

"You can say that again! But there's something else about that knife. The folks in Minneapolis identified it as a German-made switchblade."

"They did?"

"That's right. Dale rattled off the name of the company, but I can't remember it right now. Probably couldn't pronounce it, either. What do you think about that?"

"This gets more intriguing by the day."

"And Madge is more determined than ever to get the case solved."

A few steps closer to Vera's grave, Bill groaned.

"What?"

"Look—tire tracks."

He squatted and ran some soil through his fingers.

"I had to read way more than my share of tire tracks in the war. The tread tells its own tale."

"Oh?"

"These are from truck tires. Been here a while. Probably made just after that light rain we had about a week ago. Then it dried out, so they've stayed put."

"Oh yes—I woke up around four that morning, and the whole world was glistening."

But Bill was crawling around, intent on the tracks' trajectory. "Awful close to Vera's headstone. Then the driver backed up and turned around."

"What on earth? Maybe Harry was bringing some flowers—"

"In a truck?"

"No, I guess not. You'd think there might be some footprints."

A nasty sensation started in the pit of Bill's stomach. The other night, he'd followed that truck until he was sure it went out of town northward. Watched it make the turn and listened until its hum disappeared before the first drops of rain fell.

Satisfied, he made for home then, but maybe too soon. Had the driver turned around? For now, best keep these observations to himself.

They turned back toward town and soon arrived at the side door to the church basement. Aivars jingled his keys. "What say we do another search?"

"What could it hurt?"

"I know it was my idea to come down here, but I have no idea what to look for. Any ideas about where to start?"

"We both know Madge has been a beagle down here, sticking her nose in every possible corner. Maybe we should just look for anything everyone else might have missed."

"Her dogged determination did turn up that key, even though the result was disappointing."

"Yeah. And she got a few huge bruises, to boot. Well, let's start at the far corner." Bill headed toward the hulking furnace between the dining area and Sunday school rooms.

The weather had warmed up, so the coal-burner had been idle. The brooding thing looked ominous, with several fat pipes extending through the walls and ceiling.

The half-full coal bin and nearly empty ash bucket attracted Aivars. He started stirring through the ashes with a poker.

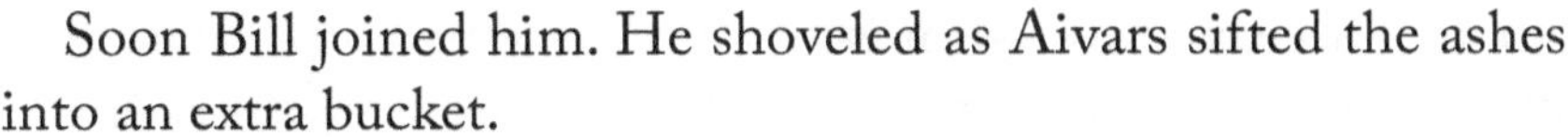

Soon Bill joined him. He shoveled as Aivars sifted the ashes into an extra bucket.

"Wait! What's that?"

With the tip of his finger, Bill nudged a clump of ash stuck to a solid round object. "I think there's a flashlight in the kitchen. It's hard to see anything in this poor excuse for a light."

When he found one and flicked it on, a tiny glimmer of gold shone through the ashes.

"Is that what I think it is?"

Out in the dining area, they bent over the shovel. "Looks like a ring to me." Bill went to pick it up but Aivars stopped him.

"Wait, don't touch it. Let me find something to set it on." He dashed to the kitchen and returned with a rag. "Here, dump it on this."

As Bill did so, some of the caked ashes broke loose, revealing the unmistakable shape of a ring. Aivars drew a pencil out of his pocket and used it to knock off the remaining ashes.

"A high school class ring. Maybe it has nothing to do with the murder, but you never know."

"We can try to find out who it belongs to, and the next question would be, how did it get in these ashes?"

"Yeah. How about looking a little farther —not inconceivable to hide a woman's hat in here."

Aivars nodded, banging his head on a pipe in the process. With a scowl, he rubbed the area.

"That'll leave a lump for sure. Pretty much everything in here's made of iron—I think that was a water pipe you contacted."

"You know this place well."

"My Dad got me started on a committee when I was still in diapers."

"He was a lifelong member, right? I've been reading some church history—wasn't it his father who moved the building to town?"

Bill wriggled behind the furnace and came out looking like a train engineer. "Nothing back here but a world of coal dust. What were you saying?"

Up to his ears in old paint cans, Aivars repeated his question, so Bill launched into family history while they made a throw-away pile. Seems his grandfather exhibited a fighting spirit by taking on objectors to his idea of moving the congregation into Caroline.

Most of the naysayers had passed by the time his youngest, Bill's father, came along. But the spirit lived on. Unlike many parents, Bill's Dad cheered for him when he signed up early for the Great War.

"Well, we've made a good start at cleaning out this mess." Aivars grinned at the sight of Bill's smudged face and shirt.

"But we're no closer to figuring out who killed Vera. Still, all this effort must count for something,"

Chapter Twenty-five

Thursday, May 11, 1944

Along the wall behind her desk, Madge pieced together her creation. No customers ever came back here anyway, and Bill's new authority underlined her sense of purpose.

No consequences of Dale learning the gist of her promise to Vera from Aivars. In fact, the sheriff knew her foibles and still thought she could contribute. He and Bill might exchange eye rolls, but deep down, Bill appreciated her finding the postcards, their sole lead so far.

Maybe being her own kind of secret agent wouldn't be so bad after all. That is, if she never had to leave him and Gloria.

With that weight off her shoulders, ideas flitted to her consciousness in the oddest ways and at peculiar moments. During Gloria's graduation ceremony, just as the band launched into the school song, a sudden inner vision developed.

The outlay of North Central Iowa, Southern Minnesota, and part of Wisconsin appeared. Just like that, the whole area spread out—a wider view than she'd been taking.

After Gloria's cake-and-punch party at the house, with a myriad of neighbors and friends bringing good wishes for her future and lingering in the yard to chat, Gloria went off to some of the other graduates' parties.

Bill decided to work in the yard, and Madge debated about helping him. Trimming branches, he looked so peaceful. He'd always enjoyed doing physical work—maybe he could find serenity in solitude again.

That map re-emerged in her brain, so she went out to the front porch and plopped on the swing. What could it mean? The question triggered a recollection. This past Sunday while in church, she'd had trouble focusing on the sermon, because there sat Harry.

He looked so miserable that all of the murder's unsolved aspects paraded through her head. Even though five weeks had passed, she still found it difficult to accept the idea of such a thing occurring here.

Why should their little town be visited with such evil? Up and down the street, she couldn't think of one family that didn't try to do what was right. The same with every surrounding farm.

Could the reason be something about Caroline's location, seemingly in the middle of nowhere? A distance from any big towns, they had no unique claim to fame.

Not to mention *where* that foul deed happened. People still avoided the church kitchen, even though the men repainted the walls and cupboards and someone donated new linoleum.

Yesterday at the Ladies' Aid meeting, they'd discussed the annual women's luncheon and decided on a Saturday in June. To everyone's surprise, Linda—usually the silent one—suggested a never-be-fore-heard-of concept.

"What if we turn this into a picnic? The weather should be perfect by then, so why not bring a few tables out to the back yard and eat outside?"

Eyebrows went up all over the place, but in the end, everyone voted for the idea. Madge had been the first to offer her support.

"You're right. Those beautiful maples in the side and back make the perfect setting, with plenty of shade. And being outdoors will give the little ones space to play rather than being cooped up downstairs."

Someone added, "Let's make the menu outdoorsy, rather than our usual meat and potatoes."

Agnes volunteered immediately. "I'll fry up a couple of chickens if somebody else will, too. That should be plenty." Wilma agreed to do the same and Madge offered to bake her favorite red devil's food cake. A huge bowl of potato salad, too—still plenty of spuds stored in her root cellar.

Somebody else offered four dozen deviled eggs, two people said they'd make pies, and Linda ended the planning with another great idea—homemade ice cream for after their meeting.

"My strawberries should be ripe by then. I'll bring plenty, and some buns." As Ingrid added this finishing touch, Madge let out a long breath. *Bless Linda for coming up with this.*

Agnes sidled up and muttered, "This sounds great, but we can't avoid the kitchen forever, you know."

"No. But waiting until fall might help."

"We could make some new curtains."

"Good idea. Anything to perk it up."

"I'll get started on some."

So that was decided—she and Agnes made a swell team. Madge tapped her foot on the porch floor as the swing swayed back and forth. Down the way, Mrs. Lawmaster whistled from her flowerbed.

What was that song? *Keep smilin' through…* Oh, yes. Another one that made her cry when Bill had been gone. She'd heard Vera Lynn singing it on the radio from Madison Square Garden, with all the troops joining in before they boarded ships to cross the Atlantic.

"I ought to start weeding, too. But why not take a walk first? Get some fresh air and stretch my muscles—then I'll come back and get to work."

The six o'clock whistle blew, startling Madge from her desk chair. "Oh, my goodness—have I been at this for two hours?"

But her handiwork sent a thrill along her spine. Splicing area maps she'd cut from an ancient, moldy Encyclopedia Britannica produced a large cardboard-backed creation that provided a bird's eye view from Fort McCoy to Albert Lea to Algona.

Brownish rubber cement stains showed here and there, but still. She leaned back from the strong odor to survey the result of her efforts.

Then something hit her like a grenade going off, to use a war metaphor. Placing a large enough compass with Caroline as its center point, one might draw a massive circle. Her pulse quickened. Did it just happen that Fort McCoy and Algona seemed equidistant?

Then something else struck her. In this part of Iowa, the Red Ball Route made up a large portion of roads passable year-round. That, plus Highway 218.

One day in '32, Gloria's teacher led the students down the railroad tracks to watch workers pour vast blobs of cement for the new highway. Aided by local farmers with horses and wagons, a new roadway came into existence.

Did she include the word *wonderful?* From this point on, traveling became possible even when the side roads were a muddy mess.

Awestruck to see such a huge outlay of smooth, still-wet cement, the children had oohed and aahed. Madge, who went along to help chaperone, gaped along with the youngsters. When Gloria came home from school later, she still gushed about the new road, and pronounced the word *progress* with relish.

Now where did Bill keep that book about the history of Iowa roads? Back in the bowels of the pressroom, Madge rummaged through a bookcase long overdue for a cleaning. Three sneezes after she began her search, her reward appeared.

Yes—the Iowa Transportation Authority did something right when they kept track of all these goings-on. Seated at Bill's desk, she started searching. Who would ever have thought anyone could write so much about roads, but several paragraphs were devoted to the Red Ball.

In 1913, work on the road began. At this time, surveyors called it the Red Ball Route *because the original route was marked with poles which had red balls, six inches in diameter, mounted on each side.*

In 1920, the Minnesota portion of the route was designated as Constitutional Route 40, as part of the Babcock Amendment that established the Minnesota trunk highway system.

This had to be important for their investigation. She just knew it. But why? At first, the answer seemed obscure, but when she retraced that imaginary compass line in a circle around Caroline, Bill's conjecture about the Black Market resounded.

If somebody wanted to transport contraband meat to more populated communities for a larger market, they'd need a truck. Normally, they'd use the train, but with guards on duty and so many urgent loads of military supplies and men, that would be out of the question.

The next inspiration raised Madge's temperature. If metropolitan Chicago—or Madison, for that matter—provided a market, they'd need to take the shortest possible delivery route. Or establish several stops along the way with enough customers to justify the unloading time.

The same would be true for trucking meat to Minneapolis. Or points west or south, for that matter.

Thinking like a criminal—I'm thinking like a criminal! Madge knew she should get home and make a little supper, but simply couldn't stop.

"Let's see. What if they used the Red Ball as far as . . . mmm . . . maybe Charles City or Waverly, both county seats? Fort McCoy's northeast from Charles City. Yes, and . . ."

How could a group of scoundrels make the most money in this process? What if they established a regular route, like those used by bakeries and canned goods factories out of Mason City or Waterloo–Cedar Falls?

The route would have to cross state borders. But why not? It wasn't as if you met up with a guard when you drove into Wisconsin or Minnesota—this was a free country.

The back door bumped open, and the next thing Madge knew, Bill stood arms akimbo, frowning. "Hey, I'm starving, but what happened to my beautiful cook?"

Hands on the desk, he leaned down and kissed her. "Couldn't stop thinking of Gloria while I was trimming. What a wonderful girl she's become . . . seems only yesterday, you were fixing her hair in pigtails."

"So true. Now, all three of our girls are through school." Madge took time to cherish the moment, but then her mind returned to her discovery.

If only she could frame Bill's expression at her next words. Shock. Wonder. And respect.

"Bill, think with me. If you had a load of fresh slaughtered beef carcasses to transport to Chicago or Madison, or maybe up to Minneapolis, which way would you go?"

He rounded the desk. "If the slaughterhouse were around Albert Lea, I'd . . ."

He pulled up a chair. "So, you're focusing on the overall view. Hmm."

"Instead of that silly fake bird. But this gives us some possibilities of what it might've been stuffed with that was so important. What if there's a ring of crooks—you know, a network—and everybody gets their share of the profits?"

"Yes . . ."

"What if they sent the records in something innocuous, like an Easter bonnet? And what if Vera truly had no idea they were using her as a pawn?"

Bill rubbed his chin. ". . . to undermine the war effort in any way possible. Including a black market network."

He stared at the ceiling as if imagining an even larger map. "So, let's assume someone had motive. What if Helene and her cohorts in crime realized that unsuspecting Vera lived right in the center of the action?"

"And what if Helene is the brains behind an intricate money-making web that stretches all the way to Madison, or even further?"

"What say you call Aivars, hon? His perspective might be helpful."

He hunched over the map. Then he made a comment that brought a chuckle, but also a sense of pride.

"I really think the Army could use you in its Special Intelligence Unit, Maddie-girl."

Chapter Twenty-six

In growing dusk, Aivars entered the office, his hair mussed by the wind. What would he look like in ten years? A bald spot would distinguish him even more, in Madge's humble opinion.

She pictured Gloria by his side, a proper pastor's wife in a fresh-ironed housedress, her hair tied back. There would be a couple of little ones hanging onto her starched apron when she answered the door.

"Pastor? Oh, he's gone out visiting. Is there anything I can do for you, ma'am?" Gloria would invite an anxious woman into her spic-and-span kitchen for a cup of tea and some cookies just out of the oven, and by the time Aivars returned, the woman would have forgotten what had troubled her so.

Aivars cleared his throat. "Sorry, I was deep into the readings for next Sunday, but a break won't hurt. What are you two up to?"

From the door between the two rooms, Bill gestured them in and Madge's heart did a flip. Gratitude for Aivars flooded her. How had she and Bill ever managed without him?

This reminded her how fast things could change—one day you were worried sick, with no recourse, but the next, hope fluttered in and made a nest in your heart. Things could still change without warning, true.

But on the other hand, Bill's nighttime attacks might have ceased altogether. He seemed so much calmer these days, so much more like his old self. Maybe Doc Lindquist had been right . . . time would tell.

Despite this war that dragged on and on, life moved ahead. She'd begun to dread the flow of government notifications she'd have to post tomorrow morning—every Monday morning. Whose son or husband or boyfriend would be on the casualty list next?

Convinced the Allies would soon launch an attack into Venice either from the north or the south, Bill spoke of the operation with hope. Just today at dinner he'd mentioned this when Gloria brought up the subject.

"It's been a hellish trek for us up through Italy, especially this winter. Our troops are dug in on the banks of the Senio River, with some of them being trained to drive Fantails, big armored vehicles sort of like tanks, but able to cross marshy country where tanks would get bogged down.

"Meanwhile, Patton sits in Sicily, itching to get back into the fight. Mark my words, the commanders'll put him there—he really knows how to lead. He's made mistakes, sure, but Eisenhower can't afford to let him idle out the war after all he did for our troops in North Africa and Sicily.

"He'll be in charge of a Division again. And when he gets back where he belongs, it'll make all the difference. But back to Venice—we have to remember it was the one part of Northern Italy Napoleon failed to subdue."

"You ought to be a history teacher, Dad. You've got as many maps as Mr. Masters over at school." That might work, but now, with the war so deeply ensconced in his mind, he'd been handed a murder investigation.

And here was Aivars, always ready to help.

Bill shook his hand and laid out the plan. "We may have some new insights and need your help." Bill plopped at his desk and Aivars pulled up a chair. "Look what Madge put together this afternoon."

It didn't take long for Aivars to immerse himself in the highways and byways of her map. Finally, he twisted her way. "What do you see here?"

"It occurred to me that Vera might have been caught up in a blackmarket network without even realizing it. Her cousin—"

Bill broke in. "She made Caroline the regional center with her compass, and the circle passes close to Albert Lea."

"So what are you thinking?"

Bill launched in. "Maybe we've been short-sighted, fumbling around with physical clues when *angles* might be most important. I've heard a little about the women working in London to figure out the Nazi underground.

"Sometimes solutions have more to do with mathematics than anything, and this map gives a fresh take on our puzzle. Add these dimensions to our slim physical evidence, Vera's personality, even Helene's, and what do you have? A broader view. New angles."

As he spoke, Madge visually traced the road from Albert Lea to Minneapolis to Fort McCoy and back. From Decorah to Fort McCoy to Madison and back. From Mason City to Charles City to Albert Lea. On a wider scope—from Fort Dodge to Minneapolis to Chicago, or to Waterloo and points east.

"Madge?" Bill tapped her hand. Both men were staring at her.

"Why, we actually have *tri*-angles here. So many of them, I can't keep them straight. I feel like I'm back in geometry class with Mr. Purcell. Obtuse—one angle is greater than ninety degrees, right angle—exactly ninety degrees, equilateral—all sides equal.

"What are the others? Scalene—no sides or angles are equal, isosceles—two equal angles . . ."

Aivars narrowed his eyes. "I see them, too. B equals base, h equals height. A equals one-half bh. But not one of your triangles includes Austin, Minnesota, with its big Hormel plant."

Bill burst out, "Maybe that would be too obvious with all the government inspectors around these days, and Hormel supplying SPAM for the troops. I bet the law watches their shipments pretty closely.

"The kind of network I'm visualizing operates in small ways—no huge slaughterhouse necessary because they can amass the meat from here and there. That's one of the basic principles of clandestine work. Takes a lot more effort, but the profit might be worth it."

Aivars folded his arms. "So, our task is to discover those small ways. It's the opposite of next Sunday's lesson. *He that is faithful in that which is least is faithful also in much: and he that is unjust in the least is unjust also in much.*"

Madge hardly heard him. "Oh wow! I just noticed something else. Draw all those triangles, and Caroline is still pretty much at the center."

"Right as usual." The admiration in Bill's voice made Madge's heart turn over.

"You know, I'm almost disappointed someone claimed that ring you two found in the furnace room so soon."

The day after he and Aivars made that find, Bill asked the high school principal if anyone had reported theirs missing. Sure enough, Vern Barker, who kept the church furnace stoked through the winter, claimed it. One mystery that turned out not to be so mysterious after all.

But now, they stood before this map that pointed to intrigue none of them had imagined. Vera, involved in the black market? How in the world did that come about?

Saturday, May 20, 1944

A picnic . . . the first of the season. Madge declared this the perfect way to welcome summer, and when she issued the invitation, Aivars offered to hold it in his back yard. "Someone just bought me a fresh chicken, so I've got to fry it soon."

Swell—one dish she wouldn't have to prepare, and the idea of getting Bill out of the house pleased her. The next evening beneath the shade of a huge maple, Bill sat in a metal lawn chair enjoying Madge's potato salad, a few deviled eggs, and some fried chicken. The evening turned out bright with only a slight breeze.

Nearby, Aivars sat cross-legged on a blanket. "I can't get enough of your wife's potato salad." From the yard bordering the church property, children's happy shouts filtered through a shoulder-high hedge.

"Is that the Smiths' grandchildren?"

"I believe so. Good to hear young voices, isn't it? What a rowdy bunch—makes me think of my brother and I when we were young. I suppose the whole neighborhood knew what was going on in our yard, and if they didn't, Rog told them."

Madge took her time joining them. As she pulled up a lawn chair, Bill pointed to her blouse, and she looked down.

"Oh my—I can't even get my food without spilling on myself. Ah well, nothing a little *Fels-Naptha* and the washboard won't take out."

About to ask after Gloria's whereabouts, Aivars paused when one of the children let out a war cry. Thrashing ensued in the hedge, and then a leg crashed through.

"Watch out!" Aivars sprang to his feet as two boys, obviously twins, wrestled through and smashed into the burn barrel at the back corner of the lot. The barrel toppled and the boys flew into the grass, so he gave them a hand.

"No harm done."

Like matching robots, they mouthed, "Sorry." Then they headed for home the long way around the hedge.

"I'll just set this barrel upright and—oh my—" Aivars gestured for Bill. "Quick, come over here!"

In seconds, Bill and Madge hovered near. "What's wrong?"

"Look." At their feet lay the slightly charred remains of Vera Walters' Easter bonnet. Limp after several spring rains, the thing couldn't have been more unassuming. As Bill nudged the fibers with the toe of his shoe, burned edges dispersed into the grass nearby.

"I can hardly believe it! Almost all of it is still here. Can't imagine why the whole thing didn't go up in flames."

Madge took a closer look. "Ooh! But the bluebird's missing."

"You're right. But how did this get in the parsonage barrel?"

"During my interview last February, someone asked if I'd mind having the church trash burned over here. That way, no one has to worry about animals or birds getting into it on church property."

"So someone conceivably walked over here across the whole back yard and lit this on fire?" Bill scratched his head. "But they'd have to be a member to know this barrel was even here."

"Good point." Madge shook away the shiver running down her spine. "And they'd have risked having you see them from the house."

"Hmm. Or maybe they just stuck the bonnet in the barrel and walked away. I've burned my trash maybe three or four times since Vera died, but it's snowed and rained a lot since then. The hat must've been so wet it didn't catch on fire down in the bottom of the barrel, and I didn't notice it."

"So now we have another solid piece of evidence." Bill held up his palms. "You just never know what'll turn up on a Saturday night, do you?"

Aivars spent half an hour cleaning out his car. Such a conglomeration he'd accumulated since he moved—he'd gotten into the habit of throwing things in the back seat, and after a while, a pile developed.

The heat soon soaked his shirt, so he ran inside to clean up again. Should have thought of sweeping the car out last night. Or the night before.

Ah, well. He straightened his tie—after all, he'd told the boys they needed to dress up for this cultural occasion. Seeing a play in a real theater wasn't their normal routine, but it might broaden their experience.

This afternoon, he used the gas ration coupons to fill up the car. All day long, his excitement kept rising. This excursion, only a half-hour drive each way, would satisfy the urge he'd had to get out of town.

The murder had something to do with it, and Berta's funeral.

He'd had no idea how draining it could be give grieving families a chance to voice their pain. Vera's sudden demise had exhausted him, and when Berta died, he went through the grieving process all over again.

By the end of that second service, he felt drained, but somebody had to prepare Sunday's sermon. And he was that somebody. Besides, the shock of finding Vera's body had taken a lot out of him.

That experience had convinced him his heart problem came as a blessing in disguise. He found himself imagining what it would be like to shoot men, to watch soldiers bleed and die in battle.

In the thick of it, the Chaplain Corps saw their fair share. Battlefield evacuees taken to hospital tents might be the worst. How would he convey hope to a man so wounded that the doctors could do nothing to save him?

Here, though, he'd been a murder suspect. Good grief! He could never have imagined such a thing, and didn't even want to think what life might throw at him next.

But he had to admit, all of these goings-on had bonded him with Bill and Madge, and finding true friends didn't happen every day. This line of thinking led him straight to Gloria. He stuffed down his wayward imaginations—she was just one member of his youth group.

That was all.

His focus returned to the murder. Last week, they came upon the remains of that confounded hat. Another puzzle piece, but where and how did it fit? Getting away from everything, even for an evening, came as a relief.

He donned his suit jacket, grabbed his wallet and checked to make sure he had plenty of cash, in case anyone ran short. These kids were sure a good bunch. Not a large group, but he liked their upbeat spirit.

All too soon, these boys would face far worse than finding a dying woman in the church basement. And the girls—who knew where they would end up?

Since the night they performed *Arsenic and Old Lace*, he'd wanted to take them to a real play and jumped at the chance to go to the Brown Playhouse. A feature story about it in the *Chronicle*, contributed by a reporter friend of Madge's who normally wrote for the county newspaper, had alerted him.

Amazing that one early Riceville settler had the foresight to build a theater above his hardware store. The town had nearly burned down before that, so maybe Mr. Brown realized how much a little diversion could hearten people. He'd like to meet that guy someday, although he might have passed on by now.

Walking out to the car, Aivars clicked off the names. Vern Barker, Gloria, Hal Tollefson, and Sarah, old Otto's granddaughter. He'd have the boys sit in front, the girls in back. Hopefully, they'd all feel comfortable.

As the engine rolled over, he once again checked his thoughts. Taking Gloria to school the day of that last snowstorm had probably been a mistake, since even that short time alone with her played with his mind.

He backed out of the garage between the church and parsonage and puttered down the alley. On his left, a mature apple tree showed plenty of green fruit for an ample harvest.

As he turned onto the street, he waved at Klaus out in his garden. How sad, all alone after so many years of sharing everything with Berta.

Parking his Studebaker in front of the church, Aivars spied a figure in a navy-blue flowered dress. Gloria, all by herself. The dark fabric lighted her delicate complexion, and she wore a perky red ribbon in her hair. Despite his best efforts, his heartbeat picked up.

But where were the others? He took his time getting out of the vehicle, but even so, no one approached when he reached the front steps.

"Hi, Gloria. Where's everybody else?"

"Oh, I'm so upset. The Army called Vern to Fort Leonard Wood today to do his basic training. An early slot opened up, his mother said, so he hardly had time to pack.

"Already? I'm sorry to hear that. Maybe the war will end before they send him overseas."

"Yeah. But his mom—it's so hard on her. He's her youngest, you know, and she had to sign off for him to go."

"Umm. Maybe I'll stop in to see her."

"Good—she's seen three sons off now."

"I can only imagine how hard that would be. Well, Hal is still coming, so—"

As Gloria shook her head, the sun's rays outlined her profile. Such a pert nose she had, a lot like Madge's.

"I'm afraid not. His folks let him drive Vern down to Missouri. I have this feeling another slot will open, and Hal will end up doing his training now too. Pretty soon, no one's going to be left in town."

Obviously, she meant eligible men. Aivars wanted to brush the worry lines from her forehead and almost groaned aloud at the thought of cancelling tonight's adventure. It took everything he had to maintain a cheery tone.

"Well, then, we'll just wait for Sarah."

The corners of Gloria's mouth drooped afresh. What now?

"They don't have a telephone, so I stopped by to pick her up. I knocked and knocked, but nobody answered."

Otto's son, a veteran of the Great War, had been called to Fort McCoy as a reservist. In that respect, Sarah and Gloria had a lot in common.

Word had it that Otto, set in his ways, clashed with Katherine, Sarah's mother. Sarah had grown up just across the way from him, right on the same property, but the family had nothing to do with Otto. That included staying away from church, but thankfully, Sarah still came to youth group meetings.

"Do you know her family well?"

"Not really. She's a freshman and works part time at the café, you know. I'd hoped to get to know her better tonight."

"We'll wait a few more minutes. She might still be on her way." They talked about Gloria's summer work for a local weeding crew, but five minutes later, Sarah still hadn't arrived.

"I just don't understand. She was so excited about seeing a real play."

"Let's drop by your house. Maybe your mom will know something."

"Good idea. My folks do seem to find out about things around here."

At a loss for a better course, Aivars shut Gloria's door. As he drove away, he peered into the rearview mirror and sighed. No one suddenly appeared.

Unfortunately, Madge had no idea what might be going on with Sarah or her mother. They'd found her at the kitchen table reading an old newspaper. Sleuthing again?

Her face crumpled at all the news. "Two more young men gone?"

"Vern didn't even have time to say good-bye, Mom."

"And Sarah missing. That's so strange." All of a sudden, Madge raised her eyebrows.

"Katherine stopped by the office yesterday to—Oh my! I wonder if this has anything to do with Sarah's older sister. Her first baby is due any second—Katherine's first grandchild."

Madge rubbed her forehead. "Doc Lindquist would know for sure. How about taking me down to the office, and I'll give him a call?"

"All right, might as well, and we'll make another pass by the church just to make sure Sarah hasn't come."

But she hadn't. They all went into the office while Madge made the call, but she hung up with a grim look.

"Doc's wife said they're all at the Osage hospital—he just got back from there. I bet everything happened so fast, Sarah forgot to let you know."

Gloria's shoulders slumped. "Well, shoot! I was looking forward to my first real play."

"Maybe you can still go."

"You mean, just …" Aivars stopped short of adding *the two of us*.

"Riceville's not very far, and you've been looking forward to this too, haven't you?"

"Well, I—" For some reason, he was struck dumb.

"You'll be home before eleven, won't you?"

Gloria clicked her tongue. "Mom, I'm eighteen now, remember? Shouldn't you loosen my curfew a little?"

"Maybe. But don't set your heart on it."

They all turned when Bill walked in. "Having a meeting here, are we?"

He put his arm around Madge's shoulder as she explained. Aivars attempted to remain calm while his grand plans for the evening crumbled.

He didn't know whether to laugh or cry when Bill exclaimed, "Why should you miss out? You can't help it if your youth group shrank overnight, can you?"

He looked Aivars in the eye. "I say go on over there. Don't be late. Enjoy yourselves—that's one thing my second war taught me."

"Wow! Look at the detail on that gorgeous stage curtain." Gloria's voice contained an element of awe. "Even the advertisements look enticing."

"Can you imagine how much time and effort the artist spent designing and painting it? We've seen three curtains so far, haven't we? And our program says three more backgrounds are still to come."

"This is all so fascinating. I can hardly wait."

Gloria exuded so much energy—her capacity to enjoy this evening knew no bounds. Aivars found himself wondering how much Bill's absence had affected her. Most likely, with a mother like Madge, she kept a positive attitude even during those years.

In seminary, he'd have graduated a semester earlier but for the delay caused by one of his seminary professors. At the time, he chafed at having to rewrite a long, involved psychology research paper. Such a persnickety prof—relating findings to everyday life in a parish seemed a bit much, but he decided to interview a couple more pastors. Plenty of resources for the future, but still he felt trapped, held back.

He'd journaled about this circumstance, and Dad had encouraged him through it. But now, besides gleaning strategies to help men like Bill, he could see some meaning in the delay.

If he had graduated earlier, he might not have had the opportunity to get to know Gloria this well. She would have been a year younger, and not as many young men would have left town.

Berating himself, he shook off this line of conjecture. How could he possibly be thinking this way? On the other hand, hadn't the Almighty brought men and women together through all of the ages and filled them with love for each other?

Peculiar how the present could make you question what you'd always believed. A year—even two months ago—Mom and Dad's example had been all the proof he'd needed for this belief. Now his confidence ebbed away.

During intermission, Gloria chatted with an older lady seated next to her. They'd just met, but this amazing girl—young woman— spoke with the stranger as if they'd known each other for years.

"So you're from Rochester and visiting your sister here?"

"No, she lives in Waverly. I came for a few days to help her with some things, and we decided to treat ourselves to a night out. It meant a drive, but we pooled our gas coupons.

"She's working at the county fairgrounds. They've made it into a prisoner of war camp now. Anyway, she's been at it dawn to dusk, and I told her she needed a break."

"Prisoners of war? You mean Germans?"

"Probably, and eventually Japanese, I imagine. Who knows who will end up there, maybe some disgruntled Americans, too. You know, some are against the war."

"Seriously?"

"You haven't met anyone like that?"

"Not in our town. We've sent a lot of our boys over there already. My dad went, too, and came home wounded. Our stores stopped selling German products years ago. Our neighbor lady had a hard time finding oysters for her Christmas Eve stew last winter."

"We had the same situation in Rochester." The woman stood. "So nice to meet you. We're going to walk around a bit before the show begins again."

Gloria turned to Aivars. "I should use the powder room while we wait."

His knee popped when he stood up. "Whoo boy, must be getting old."

"You?" The waterfall of Gloria's laughter struck a deep chord. During the rest of the intermission, he pondered. That woman's sister—what would it be like to work with enemy prisioners?

And then his thoughts squirreled into a question. Were seven years between a man and woman too many? The thought of his parents brought a little comfort. At twenty-nine, his dad married his mother. She was only twenty.

But eighteen—awfully young. He tucked his questions away when Gloria returned. How wonderful to see her exhilarated by meeting another interesting stranger and full of anticipation for the next act.

Since his dad let him take over the wheel on back roads from the time he was twelve or thirteen, driving had come naturally. Aivars prided himself in steering a straight course, like his take on life in general. If you abided by the rules and kept your head, you'd most likely do all right.

Fully expecting to be drafted, he'd felt that way the day of his physical. At first, he couldn't believe the Army physician.

"Can't I still go? As a chaplain, I won't be carrying a gun anyway."

"That's impossible, Mr. Zevenbergen. Chaplains have to be as physically fit as anybody else."

His words stung. It all seemed so sudden and final, but he'd gradually gotten used to the idea. Most likely, he would always feel like he'd missed out on his chance to do something exceptional, but he'd survive.

The play totally immersed him, and he lost track of time. After a standing ovation, he and Gloria followed the crowd out onto Main Street, but not before she noticed the clock above the door.

"Oh, my goodness—it's ten-thirty. We'd better get right back."

He rushed to let her into the auto. In the moonlight, it looked even more battered than he'd remembered. A dent here, a ding there, the back fender hanging a bit low on the left.

Time to start taking better care of it, especially if he was going to squire Gloria around. His pulse quickened at the thought.

Ten miles down the road, in the middle of discussing the play, Gloria's voice tightened. "We won't be late, will we? It's not that I . . . I mean, I'd love to stay out later, but Daddy and Mom have been through so much. I really don't want to worry them."

"We'll be there right on the dot. I'd hate for them to think I led you astray."

She giggled, and the tenor of that giggle must have thrown him. The next thing Aivars knew, the right front tire crossed the cement curb lining the highway, and he had to fight for control.

When they came to an abrupt stop on the edge of a rather deep ditch, the wheels had swung in a wide left curve that lighted Gloria practically in his lap. Stunned, he tried to say something, but nothing came out.

Having her so close, even in this haphazard way, stoked a fire within him. Finally, he loosened his death grip on the steering wheel and heard his own meek whisper.

"I'm so sorry. Don't know what happened there. We'll get back on the road in a second."

Meanwhile, Gloria slid to her side. "You look awfully pale. It's all right—it was my fault. I didn't mean for you to speed up."

"No, no—a grown man should never lose control of his car."

When he managed to get back onto the road, he was trembling all over.

But Gloria never missed a beat. "You know, Daddy has mentioned how hard the curb makes driving on these highways. He told us the same thing happened to the bus from Fort McCoy when he was coming home. They had a blow-out because of it, and the driver had to change a tire."

"Really?" This one word was all Aivars could offer.

"Yes. After the fighting he'd seen, and his stay back east in a military hospital, it struck him how ironic it would be if the bus had turned over. He might have died that close to home."

"Mmm."

"Are you all right?"

"Yes. I should be asking you."

"Oh, I'm fine. Say, what did you think about the guys who played Brewster's uncle and his homicidal brother? They both did such a great job—it wouldn't be easy to play a disturbed character, would it?"

"Might be harder than playing a normal person." Aivars thought a while as the divisions in the long concrete slab rolled by beneath the car. His heartbeat finally returned to normal, and perspiration stopped rolling down his back.

"Although maybe not. If you're trying to act like an abnormal character, nobody knows what to expect."

"You've got a point." Gloria turned quiet as the few dim lights allowed in blackout hours shone in the distance. One in front of Sheriff Finley's office, one near the telephone office, where the switchboard operator still worked, and another at the fire station.

"Thank you so much for getting the tickets for tonight and for driving over. I loved every minute of it."

Turning down Madge and Bill's street, Aivars silently agreed. Except for that slip-up on the curb. How could he have let that happen?

Before he shut off the motor, Gloria twisted toward him. "Looks like we're just in time. Dad's peeking through the window."

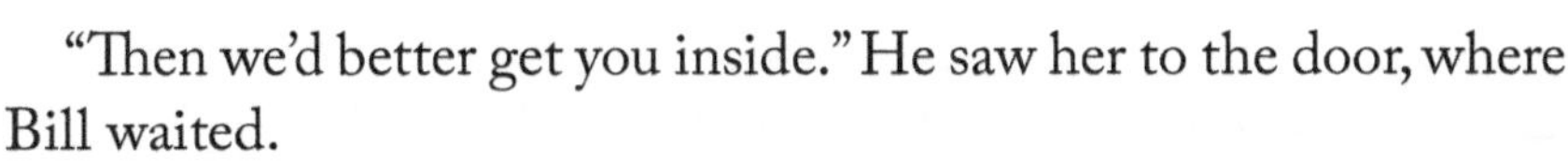

"Then we'd better get you inside." He saw her to the door, where Bill waited.

"Have a good time?"

"Oh, did we ever, Daddy." Gloria turned back. "Thanks so much, Pastor Z."

"My pleasure. I'm glad you enjoyed it. I know I sure did." He saluted Bill and whistled as he made his way down the steps. In the privacy of his Studebaker, he finally dared to draw a deep breath.

But the scene that accompanied him home wasn't from *Arsenic and Old Lace*. No, it was Gloria scrunched up against him in the front seat of this old jalopy.

Chapter Twenty-seven

Monday, May 29, 1944

With a pleasant late May morning breeze drifting across the Iowa countryside, Bill took an early turn down by the river before going to the office. Birdsong emanated from every tree and bush along the path—wrens, robins, cardinals, sparrows, and interspersed with all those melodies, the *Caw . . . caw . . . caw . . .* of crows on the alert.

Like guards on the perimeter of an Army encampment, they faithfully observed their territory and issued warnings of perceived danger. Their hoarse cries brought anything but serenity to the feathery populace. Necessary work, though.

After cutting through to the cemetery road, he passed Otto Depperschmidt's old house. In his squash patch stood Otto, leaning on his hoe. Every bit the scarecrow, his angular face and arched nose shone in the morning sun.

Bill waved and called, "Nice morning."

"Sure is. Right nice."

A few hundred yards east, Katherine's wash already filled the clothesline. What had caused the split between Otto and his son, anyway? Seemed a shame they couldn't come to terms.

When had the family moved to town? Bill couldn't recall exactly, but just before that, the church organist passed away and everyone had been thrilled to hear that Otto played. As the years passed, though, Madge began to call his services a mixed blessing. At this point, his playing had become no blessing at all.

Crossing Main at Jefferson Street, Bill entered the office through the back and cranked the windows open. "Gotta get some of that fresh air in here."

Last week's paper lay open, and he marked changes for this week's layout. Folks probably assumed things required little alteration from week to week, but an astute eye would notice subtle differences.

Each time he set the press, he aimed for perfection and a clean look. As he wielded his pencil across the pages, the bell on the front door jingled. Bill hurried to open up and Harry Walters meandered in, clutching a bulging box.

"Good morning, Harry. You're up and about early."

"Yeah. Well, I forced myself to go into Vera's room yesterday to, uh—sort through her things." He set his burden on Madge's desk with a thud.

"Getting rid of some of her clothing and the like, you know." He gave a nervous sigh. "I found something the sheriff might want to see. But since Dale's gone, well—here you go."

As the town banker, Harry maintained a low profile, spending his days in a back corner of the historic brick building across the street. Publicly, he always shadowed Vera and seemed at a loss these days.

"What do you have there?"

Harry picked up one of several fat leather-bound books. "I didn't read all of these—Vera 's fine handwriting wore me out, to be honest. But I figured you might want to look them over."

"All right, thanks. We sure need all the help we can get in this investigation."

"Did your time in the service give you experience at things like this?" The peculiar rise of Harry's heavy left eyebrow piqued Bill's interest.

"Well, we never called it exactly that, but just comprehending Army regulations and commands offered plenty of challenges." Bill chuckled to lighten the moment. No way would he admit to being attached to an Intelligence unit.

Harry's shoulders relaxed a little.

"And putting the *Chronicle* together can be sort of a puzzle too, you know?"

"I suppose." Harry straightened his tie and hitched up his pants. Had he lost some weight without Vera's great cooking? "I'll be on my way, then."

"Thanks for stopping in. I really appreciate your bringing these over."

Harry silently set Vera's diary down and left, crossed over to the bank, and opened the front door. Observing his gait gave Bill pause. He almost had a limp—some childhood injury, perhaps?

Going home to that empty house must be difficult for him, although Vera's death did little to change his everyday work routine.

Bill carted the diaries—at least that's what they looked like—to the back room and opened one. January 1, 1932–December 31, 1933. Vera's tidy handwriting formed a strict straight line in the top right-hand corner. He glanced at several more. 1933–1934, 1934–1935, on up to April of this year.

"Whew! If I needed a hobby, guess I'd have one now." Something niggled at him. Might be best to look these over himself, starting with the most recent. He'd share them with Madge later, but given how distracted she was these days, keeping them under wraps for a while made sense.

Or not. What if the golden clue they all sought lay right here within these pages? She definitely would be the one to discover it.

Though Madge made good friends all the way through life, she seldom received personal mail, except when Lillian or Judith wrote. When Lillian first left for California, she'd written every week, but her letters had fallen off lately.

Understandable—she was busy working overtime. Every time she thought of Lillian, she shuddered at the thought of her slender, sensitive daughter building grenades or bombs that could blow people to smithereens, and sent up a prayer.

The contents of their mail box in the Post Office entryway usually revolved around the newspaper. Tom, leaning over his box with his barber apron still on, saluted her as she walked in this morning.

"How's the good Major today, Madge?"

"Fit and fine. Thanks for asking." She eyed his apron. "You must've run over here in an awful hurry?"

Tom glanced down, and his face reddened. "Oops. No emergency, guess I just didn't think."

Madge mulled his admission as he walked out into the mid-morning sunshine. That was the way of it sometimes—people acted without thinking. Case in point, Gloria's story from her work crew yesterday.

She'd come home late, smudged with dirt from head to toe. But she seemed happy helping out the farmers and in no big hurry to seek other employment.

"Mom, you'll never believe what happened today. After we finished our regular work, Mrs. Bruggeman ran out of her chicken house in an awful state. She's Missy's aunt, you know. She said she'd gotten behind on cleaning the eggs, because the hens have been so regular lately, and the egg truck would be here early in the morning, so would a couple of us mind helping wash them?

"Missy and I volunteered, so she set us up with rags on a sawhorse table near the pump and told us we didn't dare miss one speck of—you-know-what—or the egg man would dock her pay. Have you ever washed eggs?"

"Sure. Every day from the time I was about five years old until I married your father."

"Oh. Well, it's nasty work."

"Yes."

"So part way through, after we'd made quite a pile of eggs with stuff that wouldn't come off, Missy thought of using a paring knife. She went in to get one, since her aunt was in such a dither and had gone off to load crates."

"A paring knife?"

"Yes. But it didn't work. Kept smashing through the shell. And when her aunt noticed, she had a fit. *Missy, you ought to know better—I'll go get you a—*"

"Let me guess—a razor blade?"

"How'd you know, Mom?"

"Like I said, I'm pretty experienced at egg washing. Too bad my folks didn't live closer when you were younger, so you'd have known how to do it, too."

Still chuckling about that, Madge turned the key in the *Chronicle* box and slipped out several envelopes. Missy had meant well, and who would ever think of using a razor blade, anyway?

Besides, weren't mistakes the stuff of learning? If Missy hadn't tried the knife, she wouldn't have found out what didn't work. As she neared the office, the investigation came to mind, as always. Wasn't that exactly where she and Bill and Aivars found themselves right now?

It wasn't that they hadn't put their minds to it, but so far, they hadn't hit upon the right approach. She dropped the mail in her inbox and spent a couple of minutes staring at her big map, but no fresh ideas popped into her head. So frustrating.

When Bill came in, he stopped by her desk and picked up the mail. Flipping through the envelopes, he peered closer at one.

"Say, what's this about? Postmarked Decorah—"

Madge started up. "Decorah?"

"Addressed to you. Return address, H. Miller. You didn't notice it? I can hardly believe that, Maddie-girl."

Almost always, she thumbed through the mail on the way back, to see if Lillian or Judith had written, but not today. When Bill handed her the letter, the envelope practically burned Madge's fingertips.

His eyes reflected the same question drumming inside her. Well, there was only one thing to do, open it. But with the envelope slit, she bit her lip.

"This has to be from Vera's cousin. But why on earth would

Helene write to me? We barely even had a conversation. Look, my hands are all shaky." She thrust the envelope at Bill. "Here, you read it."

"Nope. She wrote it to you."

"All right, then." Glad he stayed beside her, she pulled out a carefully folded letter.

May 30, 1944

Dear Mrs. McQuestion,

You may not remember me, but I'm Vera Walters' cousin from La Crosse. We met briefly at your church a while back. I desperately need to talk to you.

Please meet me at the Wild Prairie Rose Boarding House in Decorah at two o'clock on Saturday. I may have some information about Vera's murder.

I'll explain when you get here. I'll only be here a few more days.

Helene Miller.

Madge dropped into her chair.

"What's wrong? You're white as mashed potatoes."

She handed over the letter. Bill skimmed the few lines, his forehead like a plowed field.

"So she's not our murderess?"

"That's what it looks like. I'd better go talk with her."

"Agreed, but as acting sheriff, I'm going with you."

Chapter Twenty-eight

On Saturday, Bill and Madge set out to meet with Helene. Aivars offered to watch the office for the morning and close up at noon, like normal. Just as easy to work on his sermon there as in his office, he maintained.

Rolling down the car windows produced a breeze on this warm June day, and they rode in silence for a while. Talking over the motor proved a trial.

But finally, Madge spewed a question. "What kind of information could Helene have?"

"Beats me. But it had better be worth using up our precious gas coupons."

He sounded cranky, understandably so. He took this new job seriously and didn't like being away from Caroline very long.

"You know, you could have let Aivars drive me over here. He did offer."

"Not a chance. This case is my responsibility, and I need to hear whatever Helene has to say. I just hope we're not on a fool's errand."

What topic might smooth his ruffled feathers? The first that came to mind was dear to them both.

"I'm so proud of Gloria and the work she's doing. She seems to be enjoying it, even though she comes home bone tired and smelling like an old farmer."

"I'm proud of her too. Pretty appropriate that they call her *Glo.*"

Discussing her led to Judith and Lillian and the work they were

doing to support the war effort. Before they knew it, the outskirts of Decorah appeared.

"Which way to that boarding house?"

"I think it's on one of those streets near the Upper Iowa River."

Bill consulted his watch. "Well, we don't have time to wander around town looking for it. We need gas, so I'll pull into that station over there and ask directions."

The old Bill would never have never have stooped to ask for directions, but right now it made sense. The directions led them to a charming, two-story building with whitewashed boards above a brick first floor.

"Ready?"

Madge took a deep breath. "As ready as I'll ever be. Let's go."

Before they reached the front door, Helene came out to meet them. "Hello, Mrs. McQuestion. Thank you for coming."

"Hello—and this is Bill, my husband." Madge held out her hand, but Helene seemed too jittery to take it. "I can't help but wonder why you wrote to me."

"You're the only person I remember from Caroline—besides Harry, of course. Vera mentioned you more than once when I was visiting."

Bill caught Madge's eye. No use pursuing that line of talk.

Helene peered over the rims of her thick glasses at Bill. "I didn't know you'd be coming, too."

"As the town's acting sheriff, it was my duty. Now what is this all about?"

She wrung her hands and glanced around. "The walls are so thin inside. Could we take a short walk, maybe along the river?"

Bill started to protest, but Madge put a hand to his forearm. "That sounds nice. Why don't you lead the way?"

They followed Helene to a bench situated near the river, some-what low at this time of year. They might have been out in the country in complete solitude.

Madge plopped down beside their informant, and Bill, leaning on a tree, cleared his throat. "Miss Miller, you said you had information about Vera's murder. But why are you living here instead of La Crosse, as you told everyone?"

"When I arrived at the train station after my visit to Vera, a man in a brown fedora told me I should stop in Decorah."

"A man? The station in Caroline?"

"Yes. He wouldn't look me in the eye—kept his hat brim low and whispered what he had to say."

"Did he tell you why?"

"He didn't say, only that I was to get a room here and wait for a message. His tone frightened me, and I didn't know what else to do except obey."

"What did he look like?"

"He stood in the shadows after I visited the women's room. He was tall and had tobacco on his breath. That's about all I remember. But his voice scared me, and he gripped my wrist so hard, he left red marks."

"Did you get that message after you got here?"

Helene nodded. "I rented this room, and the note was in my mailbox a few days later. No one saw who left it—someone must have delivered it at night."

"Do you still have it?"

From her sweater pocket, Helene withdrew a folded paper and handed it to Bill. "It's very short, but it really frightened me."

Stay here until mid-July. And keep away from Vera's Easter bonnet. Verboten—only for her to wear. You are being watched.

Bill's raised brows said more than words. Madge hoped to find out his thoughts soon.

"Very interesting. So what did you take this to mean, and why would somebody think you wanted Vera's hat?"

"Believe me, I've thought about that every night since then. The only thing I can come up with is a conversation Vera and I had before we went downstairs to eat after the service on Sunday.

"In the vestibule, I reached up to touch one of the little birds on her hat when she leaned over for her umbrella. I said something like, *Someone worked very hard making this little birdie so pretty. I'd like to take it home with me.*"

"No one else was there?"

"I don't think so, although I didn't really look. Harry was already downstairs."

"You're certain no one was around?"

"I thought we were alone, but somebody *must* have heard me. Of course I was just teasing, you know. Why would anybody listen to two cousins chattering about nothing?"

"Very good question. Would you mind explaining why you stayed here, then?"

Glancing at the note, Helene shuddered visibly. "This message—I felt like somebody was watching me. I've always lived with my sister and brother in La Crosse. He's been paralyzed since the Great War, so my sister takes care of him while I work to make ends meet.

"I like my job there—factory work that pays the bills. But when I read this note, I was afraid I'd bring trouble to my sis and brother, so I did what it said and looked for work here. I'm making ten dollars a week more now, so I've been able to send what they need and still pay my rent."

Quite an outlandish story—could it be true? Bill gave no outward clue, but he seemed to have put two and two together. He asked Helene just two more questions.

"While you were visiting Vera, did she talk much about her Easter hat? Did she give any indication about where she got it?"

"No. I assumed Harry bought it for her. They seem to have plenty of money, so that didn't surprise me."

"Hmm. One more question: Would you mind if we took this note along with us? It could be quite valuable to our investigation, and we're grateful you showed it to us."

His whole manner had changed, but Madge determined not to probe. Maybe she could learn more by watching than by asking.

Had she been here alone, she would surely have mentioned that Nazi camp Helene attended years ago. Must be some reason Bill decided not to. He secured the note in his breast pocket and straightened.

"Thank you so much for your help. We'll be going now—perhaps it's best for you to wait a few minutes before you leave." He took Madge's elbow with a firm grip, and she barely had a chance to add her good-bye before he guided her along the path toward the automobile.

"Shall we eat our lunch in the park?"

Madge jumped at the chance for a closer glimpse of Decorah. Bill parked the car and spread his old wool army blanket under a shade tree while she gathered their sandwiches and drinks.

The quiet area made a perfect spot. The only other people here were a grandmother and her two fledglings who tossed a ball a few rods away.

"Picnics used to be our favorite date, Maddie-girl. We ought to take time for one more often."

"Yes, but life gets so busy."

Bill bit into a thick braunschweiger sandwich and chewed for a few seconds. "True, but when I was in Africa, I told myself I'd take advantage of things like this when I got back—especially the outdoors."

"The landscape there must've looked pretty bleak."

"That's an understatement. Day in, day out, sand, sand, and more sand. In your hair, in your ears, in your nose." He grimaced. "Never will be soon enough to see that much sand again."

Touching his knee, Madge whispered, "I'm ever so glad you're back."

"Did I write you about going out in the middle of the night one time, and the sand looked exactly like snow does here?" Without waiting for an answer, he grabbed another sandwich and changed the subject. "Well, what did you think of our meeting?"

"I don't know what I was expecting. Helene didn't give us a lot to go on."

"No?" His grin tantalized her, and she forgot her decision to ask no questions.

"Not from what I could see. How about you?"

"I thought you'd never ask." He patted his breast pocket. "I think this note gives us some big clues."

"Do tell."

"Number one, the handwriting. I'd wager somebody with arthritis wrote those words."

"Hmm."

"Number two, the use of *verboten*. These days, who would choose a German word to warn somebody?"

"Now that you mention it, that does stand out like a red light."

"And three, whoever wrote the note *really, really* had his or her eyes on that silly hat."

"True."

"Does it seem peculiar to you that Vera and Helene were talking about the bird that day she visited?"

"Not really—that's what I remember most about the bonnet. Both of the birds were so—you know—delicately fashioned. Very lifelike, and the blue one had more details than the other. I'd almost call it a work of art."

"That's where you have insight I lack. I never even noticed them. One look at that mountain of straw and decorations, and I wanted to vomit."

At her laugh, Bill bit into two cookies at once. "Never can get enough of these raisin and oatmeal treasures, hon." The gleam in his eyes reminded Madge of when they were young, just starting out. Whatever other questions had plagued her became lost for the moment.

June 7, 1944

Madge swung herself up on the heavy table in the pressroom, a little out of breath after hurrying over from home. Since Gloria was late getting in from the fields today, she'd left her supper on the stove.

Right now, her team still hoed, pulled, or cut weeds from corn, soybean, and hemp rows from early morning till late evening. Such a labor-intensive project sapped every single ounce of a person's energy and also fried one's skin. But Bill often remarked how cheerful Gloria was, even when exhausted.

Now, back to the pressroom. What could be so important for him to call her and Aivars over here like this after hours? Especially odd because the news reports overflowed from the Invasion of Normandy that began yesterday. Surely, Bill would keep this short so he could get back to listen.

Two minutes later, Aivars shut the front door and popped in his head.

"What's up?"

"We might've received a treasure trove. Have a seat." Bill reached to a low shelf behind the press and lugged over a box.

"I called you here as the acting Sheriff. Now, this may be just another in a growing line of clues that lead us nowhere, but on the other hand . . ."

One by one, he set a number of hardbound journals on the table. "You'll never believe who brought these in, thinking they might help in our investigation."

Our. What a lovely word.

"In my estimation, it'll take all three of us to pore through these entries and hunt for evidence—of course, I have no idea what kind we might find, if any. But a close look at Vera's diaries surely can't hurt."

Madge's gasp fixed his attention on her as Aivars reached for one of the books with awe in his tone. "Her diaries? Oh, my goodness!"

"Yes. Harry found them. Sounds like she stored them in that back room where she kept her Easter bonnet."

Madge bit her tongue. How could she have missed such a big

stash? Then again, she'd been bent on finding the hat. Only her insatiable curiosity had led her to lower the desktop. At the memory of that exploit, guilt once again assailed her, and the reassurance Aivars offered seemed flimsy.

Bill picked up a diary and began to read:

February 9, 1942, Caroline, Iowa. I can barely see out the kitchen windows today, what with the temperature so low. But through a small unfrosted circle on the right pane, I spied a cardinal lighting on the garden fence. If that's not a sign, I don't know what is.

And we surely need a sign these days. Yesterday the House of Representatives passed the Lend-Lease Bill, which Harry says will drive us deeper into the European side of the war. It's only a matter of time.

The Waterloo Courier says Admiral Husband Kimmel was appointed Commander of the Pacific Fleet last week, and a Lieutenant-General Rommel will lead the German Army in North Africa.

The whole thing makes my stomach turn, but all the better to concentrate on our Ladies' Aid meeting coming up. We may be small, but maybe we can still make a difference for the troops. Hopefully the ladies will agree that knitting sweaters and sending packages of goodies should be our top priority, with things going the way they are.

Maybe if everyone cooperates, we can even plan a fund-raiser for the war-bond drive. (That's a big maybe. The women make no secret of disliking my leadership.)

On another note, our town already mourns the death of a local sailor, a farm boy who perished at Pearl Harbor on the Arizona. Oh, this war is awful. But we must keep on.

Aivars let loose a huge sigh. "Seems more like a journal."

"Yes, so we'll have to try to remain objective." Bill sought Madge's eyes. "I know that won't be exactly easy, but as they say, we'll have to soldier up. I've read a little already, so I'm heading back home to see what happened today in France. But you're welcome to stay as long as you like."

"I'll stay a while. How about you, Madge?"

Finally, Madge contributed her first word. "I'm in."

When the front bell jangled, Bill emerged from the pressroom and was startled to see Fritz Van Zante. Had he ever stopped by before?

"Having a quiet morning over there at the post office?"

"No, with all the packages being sent overseas these days, I'm busier than a bee in a hive. But I was leaning over the sorting desk and happened to spot something stuck between the mopboard and the wall. I couldn't reach it, so I worked it loose with my handy-dandy yardstick from the hardware."

Fritz held out a postcard. "Since this is from overseas, I thought I'd better bring it to the law's attention. And, of course, seeing it's addressed to Vera Walters."

"Thanks. Did you think of delivering this to Harry?"

"I did, but then it occurred to me he might still be a suspect. Wouldn't want to jam up the works."

Bill jerked his head up. "Harry's a suspect? Where did you hear that?"

"Well, uh, there's rumors—" Fritz waited, head cocked to one side. Fishing for information. Probably a downside of his business—with everyone stopping in for their mail, he most likely heard a mountain of gossip.

"Mmm. Well, thanks for bringing it in."

Maybe Fritz thought he'd have made the best candidate to replace Dale, and his feelings were hurt. Just in case the possibility proved even half-true, Bill threw him an off-handed compliment.

"Sharp eyes you have. I appreciate your srwork. These days, we all have to put our heads together, don't we?"

"You can say that again. Who knows when some correspondence

might lead to solving a crime? Why, I heard the other day about a postman over along the Mississippi . . ."

Bill angled his head toward the clock. This was no time for a long story, and thankfully, Fritz followed his movement.

"Oh man! Gotta get back over there and make sure all the mail's in the boxes. People get pretty riled up 'bout this time of day if it ain't, ya know."

He would have gone down another rabbit hole, but Bill ushered him out the door. He might have reminded Fritz of the need to man his post at all times, a cardinal rule for any servant of the U.S. Government.

As Fritz loped away, Bill fingered the postcard. "Easy to understand how this could have gotten lost in the shuffle. Just one more in a vast slew of . . ."

He held it up to the light and tensed when a photograph of West Sandy Lake stared down at him. He recalled this place from his training. Actually, he might've drowned there, had it not been for Roger.

Those tough buck sergeants had a way of forgetting he and Roger had twenty years on the average recruit. Sometimes during those early days of training, he'd questioned why he volunteered in the first place. One of them occurred when his drenched boot hit the bottom of West Sandy for the second time.

He flipped over the postcard. If only the handwriting on the back would contain the final clue pointing to Vera's killer.

On this moonless night, Madge slipped out of bed and down the stairs like a burglar. When Bill said goodnight, he kissed the back of her neck and added a fatherly instruction.

"As your local sheriff, I suggest you leave that new postcard alone for the night. You need your sleep."

"Since when does a sheriff tell an investigator to stop pondering a clue?"

"Since now."

A while after he rolled over for the second time, his breathing deepened. Then he snored and turned onto his stomach. Some time later, Madge could tell he was out for the night. Thankful she was the one who couldn't sleep this time, she breathed a prayer not to wake Bill and eased one foot to the floor, then the other. Next, she sat up, found her footing, and slipped out of the room into the pitch-black hallway.

Seeing Gloria's door cracked a bit, she peeked in. Sound asleep, as it should be. Such a steady faithful girl, and the Green Giant Company had begun to see her worth.

How often did a crew chief stop to let a worker's parents know their daughter stood out from the rest? Not often, Madge was sure, but that had happened yesterday evening down at the *Chronicle*.

"Thought you folks might be here when I didn't find you at home. Yep. Just want you to know you can be proud of Glo, as we all call her. In a few weeks, one of the older ladies has to get back to her teaching job, so we're gonna promote Glo to crew chief for the fall picking crew."

He knocked the toe of his boot against the door, leaving behind evidence of his day in the field. That was, in addition to the same musty odor Glo brought home on her shoes each evening.

"No doubt about it, she'll come through fine with the new responsibility—better than some women way older'n her. We're countin' on it."

His visit came a few minutes after Aivars stopped by for an evening of diary reading. Bill thought it best the diaries stay in the office, which made a lot of sense—no use risking one of them getting lost.

So the three of them gathered after supper each evening to read. So far, they'd come up with only odds and ends, nothing particularly enlightening.

Now, hours had passed, and Madge ought to be sound asleep. Instead, she stumbled into the dark kitchen, brewed a small pot of tea, heated some leftover macaroni and cheese she'd heard advertised on the Kraft Music Hour, and sank into Bill's overstuffed chair.

Maybe down here, she could get her mind to shut off. Sometimes when Bill had been in North Africa, snuggling in his chair had helped.

She'd been there about three seconds when that new postcard came to mind. Now, what had it said? Try as she might, she couldn't recall a word.

But the picture on the face sat front and center in her mind's eye, one of those army-issue postcards for soldiers to send home. That lake must be somewhere right around Fort McCoy, a heavily treed area with gentle hills.

Ah yes. West Sandy Lake, the inscription read. Seemed like Bill had sent one a lot like it when he'd been in training.

Catching the time of my life.

The handwritten message on the back read: *Bluegill, Largemouth Bass, Yellow Perch, Black Crappie, and Channel Catfish.*

"So what might these fish be telling us?"

By the time she finished her snack and set the bowl on the floor, something came to her. Of course, this *something* might amount to nothing—she'd already learned that about other so-called breakthroughs.

This time, no thrill of excitement accompanied her discovery, only a quiet pause in the constant flow of erratic thoughts concerning Vera's death. What stood out was that the sender—or someone—had taken the time to underline *Channel Catfish.*

Not once, but twice. That might mean something significant. Madge closed her eyes and tried to visualize the writer doing this. Why would he—or she—emphasize those two words?

The first connection seemed to relate to the first five postcards from England . . . the *English Channel.* Of course, she had no idea if catfish even lived there.

Not the most desirable species, catfish were pretty familiar to just about everyone. But to be certain, she turned on a small lamp and went to the bookcase for the F volume of the Encyclopedia Britannica she and Bill had sacrificed to buy for the girls years ago.

"Grandpa used to call catfish bullheads, I think. 'Course, he didn't care what he caught—he'd eat anything." Recalling the way Grandpa's beard shook when he filleted his fish warmed her heart.

Sure enough, the main category of FISH led to a description of several varieties. She kept reading, and there it was! A full paragraph delineated between the two types. Channel catfish had deeply forked tails, unlike bullheads.

Bullheads had a rounded tail and head and typically a stockier build. The U.S. boasted something like twenty-seven different species of this breed.

The next thing Madge knew, Bill stood over her. Strangely enough, he was fully dressed for work and holding a cup of coffee.

"Been investigating all night, Maddie-girl?"

A bad crick in her neck made her wince. The whole world looked blurry, but his half-grin cheered her up. He massaged her neck—his touch felt like heaven.

"I know. I've gone overboard again. I think I make a much better office worker than investigator."

"And wife, and mother. You're good at everything. But some things don't seem to respond to our efforts. I'm thinking maybe this might be one. Makes me think of being in North Africa, when everyone called Rommel the *Desert Fox*."

They moved into the kitchen, where a sip of coffee helped Madge's perspective. "Don't you think that Fort McCoy postcard seems suspicious?"

"I have to be honest. I woke up early thinking about it, too."

"But at least you did it in bed."

"Well, I spent way too many nights *out* of bed trying to figure out how Rommel always seemed to know where our troops were going. Then he'd somehow manage to get there before we did.

"Often, he'd start his tank units out at high speed in one direction

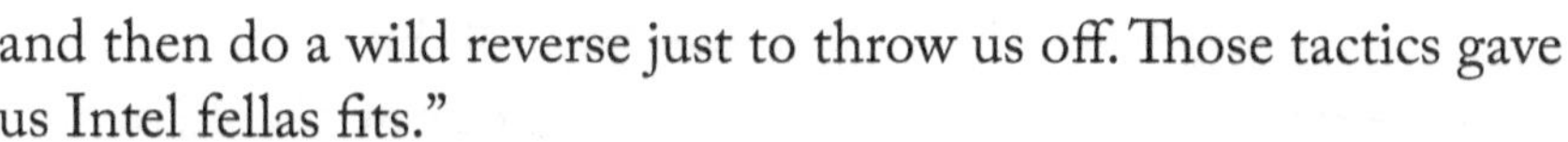

and then do a wild reverse just to throw us off. Those tactics gave us Intel fellas fits."

"And?"

"We found out that he had no special insight into our movements, after all. Turns out that one of our officers used a certain code in his reports back to Washington, and it just so happened that the Germans figured out the code, so they had first-hand knowledge of every action we were going to take. Basically, they knew as much about our strategy as we did."

"That's sickening!"

"Yeah. But at least we finally figured it out and got it stopped."

"So my lesson is . . ."

"*Our* lesson." Bill pulled his chair closer. "Sometimes I wonder if the postcards—the whole lot of them—actually have nothing to do with Vera's murder."

"But—"

He held up his hand. "I know, but hear me out. When I remember all the dead ends we hit trying to figure out how Rommel could be everywhere we didn't want him to be, I wonder if we might be wasting our time on the cards."

Madge's shoulders fell. "The catfish might not mean anything at all, or any of the other clues? So-called clues, that is."

"Don't take it to heart, all right? Maybe we *aren't* wasting our time, but on the other hand, there might be something else we're missing completely."

"How did the Army finally figure out what was going on with Rommel?"

"Unfortunately, it took time and lots of failures. After enough lost battles, people started to think outside the normal parameters, started to stand back and consider whether there might be an *inside job* going on. I was long gone when the solution came, of course, but Roger told me all about it."

"Do you want to talk to him again?"

"Maybe it wouldn't hurt."

That would mean a trip to Fort McCoy, and she wouldn't mind a bit. Bill had come so far since the last time he saw his old buddy. A few months ago, he never would have told her about his wartime experience in the desert.

This time, she wouldn't worry.

Chapter Twenty-nine

Wednesday, July 12, 1944

"**I**s Bill in the pressroom this afternoon?" The Fourth of July outing to Clear Lake looked good on Aivars—his tan accented the blue of his eyes. This time Sarah and another student had gone along for the day, and Gloria—of course, Gloria.

Oh, the look in that girl's eyes when she waltzed into the living room about nine o'clock that night. She really did glow after being with Aivars for so long. Madge turned her full attention to him now.

"No, he's gone for a few hours. Can I help you?"

"I was wondering if maybe we could put in an extra ad for the ice cream social. Something to entice nonmembers in town."

"You mean Sarah's parents?"

"You don't really think they're the only family in town that doesn't come to church?"

Madge jiggled her pencil between two fingers. "I'm thinking by streets. Do you know of anyone else?"

"No, but it seems highly unlikely they'd be the only ones. Of course, I'm including the surrounding farmers."

"Ah." She seemed to set aside his question. "You never know. An advertisement has worked wonders throughout the years, Bill would say."

"All right, let's try it. I'll pay for it myself."

"We'll see about that."

He turned to go but paused with his hand on the doorknob. It wasn't like Madge not to have mentioned Bill's whereabouts, but she just gave him a little wave as the phone rang.

"Oh, hello Evelyn. Sure, we'd be glad to—"

Thinking of Gloria still toiling away out there in this heat, Aivars made his way back to his office. The memory of that lovely day with her at Clear Lake hit him with full force when he stepped into a patch of sunshine—a perfect metaphor for her.

Radiant, warm, kind, and such a hard worker. Even though she'd graduated, she still attended the youth group and had the younger girls all excited about putting on another play.

His mind darted back to Bill, off on some mission. No, not necessarily. Maybe he'd just taken a few hours off and was casting a line into a placid pond.

But that seemed improbable. From what he could tell, Bill didn't operate that way. The rest of the way to the office, Aivars pondered, but had a little talk with himself as he climbed the stairs.

"Just because you and he have become good friends doesn't mean you have to know everything he's doing. And just because you and Gloria are . . ."

He stopped short on the landing. His gulp sounded loud in his ears. "Gloria and I are—what?"

From here, he could see the old paintings he'd moved to the hallway when he first came. The brooding evening sky in one overshadowed the Garden of Gethsemane.

"Thank you for praying *not my will, but Thine.* It would have seemed so much easier to become an earthly king."

A long breath brought an awareness of this building's deep silence, punctuated only by creaks and what people called *settling.* Having spent plenty of time in church buildings over the years, even these groans seemed comforting.

"I know the easy way isn't always the best." He closed his eyes. "Please guide me. Keep me in your way."

Bill got off the train and hurried toward the main camp. Finding Rudy Depperschmidt here might not be so easy. Should have contacted Roger first—he might have had a suggestion. The sheriff's identification in his shirt pocket gave him hope. Might not even need to show it, but at least he was prepared.

After checking at the main information desk, he felt foolish. Why had he thought he'd find somebody here easily? The clerk told him what unit Rudy had joined but had few more details on this particular afternoon.

"They're billeted in E-17. Maybe somebody over in that area will have an idea what they're up to right now."

Making his way toward the E row of buildings, Bill fought back memories. Every soldier he spotted might have been a man in his unit several years ago, and now . . .

The E row seemed even longer on this sweltering day. Nothing to do but keep moving—the five o'clock train wouldn't wait for him. He stopped in E-12 to find a water fountain and discovered more than he'd planned on.

"Is that you, McQuestion?" The call sounded unfamiliar at first, but then something jogged Bill's memory—why, could that be his old sergeant?

"Sergeant Morrison, what're you doing here? I figured you'd be bossing men through battle right now."

"Mmm. Would be, if it weren't for this." Sergeant Morrison lifted his folded-up right sleeve. "The war has made me left-handed. I'm just glad they still have jobs for the likes of me around here."

"Oh, sorry. I hadn't heard."

"Yeah, well. At least I made it back and can still contribute. After they hauled you away on a stretcher, several more followed. Taylor was too far gone, I heard, and Cominsky left an arm *and* a leg over there."

A burning started in the backs of Bill's eyes. Wow—two of the best soldiers he'd ever known.

"Those dirty Huns may have taken my arm, but I still can bark orders like a pro. And here you are walking around. I wondered if you stood much of a chance, to be honest." The Sergeant snorted. "Wondered when you almost drowned during training, too. So what brings you here?"

"Looking for someone from my hometown, Sarge. He's with the Twenty-sixth—brought in to help with the training."

"And old fogey like me, eh?"

"Oh, not *that* old!"

"You said it." Sarge cocked his head. "The Twenty-sixth—those guys should be back in pretty soon. Left on a forced march before dawn, if I'm not mistaken. You know, we even have a Japanese-American unit training here. Can you beat that?"

"This place has expanded, that's for sure. I remember back when it was mostly used by field artillery units. Now they've built a small city out here."

Someone stepped out of an office and gestured for Sergeant Morrison. "Okay, gotta go. Good to see you."

Sergeant Morrison, missing an arm. But that sure hadn't dimmed his spirit. Bill took another drink and decided to try for a quick hello to Roger. Probably a ten-minute walk from here, but who knew when he'd be back this way?

The truth was, meeting with his old buddy in Waterloo had buoyed him. He couldn't explain it, but all they'd shared in North Africa tied them together, even though at the time, they got on each other's nerves.

Halfway there, the distinct shuffle of marching men came into range, and soon a platoon appeared. The troops looked pretty haggard—could this be the Twenty-sixth?

As the marchers neared, Bill spied a shoulder patch. Sure enough, Rudy's unit's emblem. Better follow them—this might be his one chance to talk to Rudy. In one way, he hoped his hunch wasn't true. Hunches could make you feel like a fool, and this one seemed as unreliable as any of the ones he'd been following.

But just the same, something about old Otto ate at him. He'd learned long ago to pay attention to these intuitions, especially when they seemed to make no sense whatsoever. Feeling like a fool beat missing out on a clue.

It wasn't easy, but Aivars restrained his curiosity concerning Bill. "Be careful not to get involved with just one set of people in your church. Like any other organization, cliques get formed and others can feel left out." This warning from one of his seminary professors bounced through his mind. "I'd better get out and visit some other folks."

While he ate a quick lunch, Madge's comment gave him food for thought. If she was right about almost everyone around here attending church, and she usually was, then who should they reach out to?

One of his professors had joked about the *Lutheran heathen*, and here he was, in Lutheran country. This must be the only town for miles with only two branches of Lutheran churches. The other one, a synod unfamiliar to him, might as well be in another state. Bill described it as, *so narrow a straight pin couldn't fit in.*

Well, maybe it was high time he got to know some of those *narrow folks*, but how? If the group were that tight, they would be suspicious of him from the get-go. What if he asked about doing a joint Thanksgiving service? Couldn't hurt to try.

But an inner whisper forecast gloom. "Oh yes, it could."

Going where angels feared to tread had always enticed him. There must be a way, or maybe he was overlooking others out there who'd long ago given up on religion in general. People often got their feelings hurt or disliked a certain pastor or church member and decided they'd had enough. Hadn't he seen plenty of that in his growing-up years?

A memory of his dad lamenting to his mother came to mind. Some fellow hadn't gotten his way about a minor decision, like whether to paint the front steps green or gray. His ego rose up, and he swore he'd never come back, no matter how many visits Dad made to implore him. Seemed like it was often little things that pushed a certain button with sensitive people, and winning them back—what was it that Dad used to say?

Nary a word of the quote came to mind, but most likely something about never giving up. But a quip from Napoleon Bonaparte did surface. *Never interrupt your enemy when he is making a mistake.*

There must be some of those disgruntled folks around here. Maybe he'd just walk around town and see what happened. Out in the stifling afternoon air, he loosened his tie.

A longing to rip it off overcame him—and why not? Hadn't the Apostle Paul become *all things to all people in order to win some?* Who else wore a tie all summer long? Harry in the bank, maybe.

He tossed his tie over the porch rail and unbuttoned his top button. What a relief. Who decided how pastors should dress, anyhow?

Veering northwest on the shady side of the street, he hurried along. Not a soul out right now, and he couldn't blame them. A couple of blocks down, he turned down an alley—they'd always intrigued him.

You learned a lot more about people by walking behind their houses instead of in front. Their real lives showed—weed piles, peeling backyard tool sheds with garden tools leaning against an outside wall, and outhouses. About two-thirds of the town still had them in the back yard, though some had torn them down after opting for indoor plumbing.

Then a lone figure caught his eye. The fellow might have been one of those tall posts workers hoisted to hold the electric wires in the air.

Otto Depperschmidt. A cowardly urge nearly overtook Aivars. His first reaction was to duck through a yard and disappear. But then he recalled his prayer for guidance. Shouldn't he trust what came to him?

Just last week, three women visited one morning, clutching their purses after he took them out into the sanctuary to sit down. It didn't take long to uncover their intent.

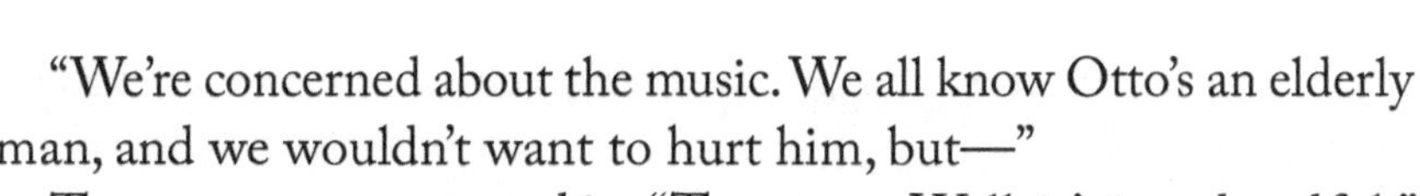

"We're concerned about the music. We all know Otto's an elderly man, and we wouldn't want to hurt him, but—"

The next woman started in. "The organ. Well, it's just dreadful." She emphasized the last word and made a sour face to boot.

"And we've been talking—actually *everyone* is talking—about it. I honestly think the music might drive some people away."

The third visitor leaped in. "One of our friends mentioned how her husband had started to come, but the slow pace drives him crazy." This particular voice stood out—Linda, the quietest woman in the congregation. Was she actually describing her husband?

"And you think . . . ?" He didn't want to finish his question, because it led down only one road: martyrdom.

"We thought perhaps you might approach Otto. It doesn't seem right for the entire congregation to suffer to save one man's feelings. Surely they taught you in seminary how to deal with delicate situations like this?"

No, they did not. He'd studied Hebrew, Greek, sermon writing, the history of the Minor Prophets, the context of Psalms, Proverbs, and Ecclesiastes, the Gospels, Epistles and the book of Revelation. Who knew how many classes he'd taken, how many papers he'd written?

But he had absolutely no idea how to deal with this *delicate situation.*

So he did what he supposed every pastor did at such times. He said he'd pray about it. To a woman, they looked relieved. But what had he done since? Pleaded quite a bit with his Maker, but that was about it.

I'll pray about it could sometimes be an acceptable way of avoiding responsibility.

Now, a couple of rods away, Otto's wide pin-striped overalls lapped against his long legs. Too late to scurry out of eyeshot. As trapped as a raccoon caught raiding a sweet corn patch, Aivars forced himself forward step-by-step.

He'd planned on being a soldier, and soldiers did their duty, right? But at this moment, he would much rather face a barrage from enemy guns.

The five o'clock train waited for no man, and Bill McQuestion was no exception. He reached the station just in time to watch the caboose disappear into what would become sunset in another few hours.

Exhausted from racing to the depot, he sank onto a bench and wiped his dripping forehead. A few years ago, this would have really bothered him, but today, he took the train's departure with patience. Worse things had happened, and somehow this would work out.

After what he'd experienced in North Africa, very little could raise his ire. He'd just sit here a while and see what happened.

His conversation with Rudy gave him plenty to chew on. He hadn't realized until now that Rudy had changed his name. What kind of town sheriff would miss that vital detail?

When he'd approached the trainer in charge of the marchers, strong family resemblance had declared Rudy's identity. After the *Dismissed* order, the men scattered, and Rudy held out his hand.

"You're Bill from the newspaper, right? Is something wrong back home?"

"No, no. I just need to talk with you a few minutes." Bill licked his lips. "But I was looking for Rudy Depperschmidt."

"I changed my name a couple of years ago. Don't do much business in Caroline anymore, since I'm out driving trucks most of the time, so I'm not surprised you wouldn't know."

"Interesting. May I ask why you decided to do that?"

"Well, *Depperschmidt's* about as German as you can get, and—" Although no one stood anywhere near, Rudy gestured toward an isolated bench in the shade of tall oak.

Once they sat down, he continued. "It's not a good time to be plastering a German name on your truck when you're just building up a business, you know? Driving into farmyards with

that name painted in big letters—well, a lot of those folks have boys over there.”

“Yes, I see.” Plenty of folks minimized their German ancestry these days, especially if their livelihood depended on name recognition. “Tell me about your family—all I know is that your father plays the organ for our church.”

“Never could understand that—his hands shake so much, it can’t be good.”

“Well, he tries hard. And when he first came, we were desperate.”

“Yeah?”

Bill sought a way to learn more about Rudy’s background, but all he came up with sounded flimsy. “So you were in the last war, like me?”

“Guess I never realized you were in, too. Where’d you see duty?”

“France. Marne.”

“Both battles?” When Bill nodded, Rudy sucked in his breath. “Small world—I was in the last one, too. But you didn’t come all this way to discuss that?”

“No. I’m curious about your father. I’ve never spent any time with him, but maybe because I’m in the newspaper business, he puzzles me.”

Rudy looked off into the distance. No help at all.

“What did he do before he came to Caroline?”

“Odd jobs around Chicago—delivering meat, for one. Then his Iowa cousin died. He’d never married, so he willed Dad the place we’re on now. By that time, Kathryn and I had a growing family, and times were tough—no work, and food lines in Chicago.

“The offer of a free place lured me, even though I had my doubts about living so close to Dad.”

“Doubts?”

Rudy’s sigh came from down deep. “Yeah.” He checked behind them. “Look. I don’t mind talking about this, but I need your word our conversation won’t go any further.”

“Of course. I should have said that right off. I’m here because

Sheriff Finley was called to help out at a POW camp and appointed me temporary sheriff. I'm a little slow on the draw at times. You've heard about the murder in our church basement last spring?"

"Word like that travels. Got any leads?"

"No. I'm grasping for straws at this point, but this thing is keeping me from sleeping. Can you help in any way?"

Rudy uncrossed his arms. "I've done everything I can to distance myself from my dad. He's an unruly old codger—never know what he'll do next. Even though we live a stone's throw away, Kathryn keeps the children on our side of the property."

"Otto has a mean streak?"

"You might say that. But because of the war, I— His past scares me sometimes. I'm afraid the older he gets, the more he'll ..." Rudy fidgeted a bit. "See, in the early thirties, he got involved with the *Bund* back in Chicago."

A shiver traced Bill's spine. He remembered reading that in '39, it took 1,500 New York City policemen to hold back the anti-Nazi protesters at the *Amerikadeutcher Volksbund's* "Americanization rally."

"Your father became a member?"

"I hate to admit it, but yes. He even sponsored several young people to attend summer camps here in Wisconsin. Thankfully, our children were too young at the time. The group was a lot more active back east, but Chicago had its share of members, and Dad—well, he took to their line, heart and soul.

"After the Great War, he and my mother suffered so much at Germany's expense, you'd think he would've wanted to put the old country behind him. But for some reason he didn't—or couldn't."

"As I recall, our government deported the *Volksbund* leader. That must have made little impression on your father?"

"I guess not. I believe Dad would still say Hitler has the answer the whole world needs. He saw how Germany changed in the thirties—people finally found work, and they built the autobahn. It all looked pretty good if you didn't dig much deeper, you know?"

"Yeah. So at this point, you think your dad . . ."

Rudy massaged the back of his neck. "He still believes in the Nazi cause. I think he'll die that way, no matter what happens. The last time I talked with him, he kicked me out because I mentioned some of those camps I've heard about over in Germany.

"He doesn't want to hear how the Reich has treated the Jews. He denies that *Kristallnacht* ever happened. I tried to tell him straight out, but he wouldn't even listen."

"Hmm."

"Nope. Said I was spouting Roosevelt's propaganda, stories he invented to get us into the war. Dad's as stubborn as the day is long—I don't know what could shake him."

Bill gave a long sigh as Rudy continued. "My brothers have all changed their names, too. I'm the youngest of nine, including our sisters, and none of us wants anything to do with him.

"When they called me here I was glad, because they feed and house me. I can send every dime from my paycheck home, and after the war, we'll be able to move to another town. I want to get as far away as possible from that *Bund* stuff, and that includes my dad."

He gave another furtive look around. "If anybody here heard that somebody this crazy is in my family, they'd—" He crossed his throat with the fingers of his left hand.

"You can rest assured they won't hear a thing from me."

Rudy gestured toward a row of barracks. "Do you know that right down there, we've got over a hundred German Americans imprisoned as potential enemies of our country? Dad could so easily be one of them."

"Don't worry, I won't say a word. But I will have to look deeper into your father's activities."

"Yeah, I can see why. Well, I hope he had nothing to do with that . . . that murder, but . . ."

A squirrel started a racket in the branches above them, and Bill waited. Seemed like this man had more to say.

"Guess I have to say that nothing would surprise me. This

investigation will have nothing to do with Kathryn and me and our children, will it?"

"No, absolutely not. I did just think of another question, though. Do you recall your father mentioning anyone named Max?"

"Max? Hmm. He has an old friend by that name. Or at least, he did. Don't think he ever left Germany, but he and my dad used to write each other."

Lost in thought, Bill hadn't even noticed the station clearing out. Alone with his ponderings, early evening shadows overtook him. Ah, well. He'd be all right. Wherever he ended up tonight, he had followed his hunch. A satisfying sensation filled him.

But Rudy's information stirred such foreboding thoughts. What if old Otto *did* have something to do with Vera dying? What if— He could have gone on in that vein all evening but did need to find a way to get home, or let Madge know he'd have to spend the night here.

He stood for a moment, uncertain which way to go. Then someone shouted, "That you, Bill? Miss your train?"

Someone slipped up and slapped him on the shoulder. Bill turned to see Roger, who held out his hand.

"What're you doin' here, buddy? Need a place to spend the night? I don't have much to offer, but we can rustle up a hamburger, and at least you'll have a roof over your head."

"That's just what I need right now. I'm sure whatever you have'll be better than the cold desert floor."

"Come on, then." Roger slapped his shoulder and led the way.

Chapter Thirty

Though she'd be exhausted after her hard day out in this heat, Aivars longed to see Gloria. But almost more, he wanted to know what was going on with Bill.

Maybe he'd been following a lead, but it wasn't like him to stay out of touch for so long. Besides that, the so-called chat with Otto had turned out to be fruitless. Sometimes he wondered if Otto chose what he wanted to hear and what he didn't.

And today, he certainly did not want to hear anything Aivars had to say. The conversation hardly proceeded beyond, "What did you say?" and "What was that?" to "Speak louder—you can see I'm an old man!"

Aivars finally gave up the effort. Easy to tell his flock to avoid discouragement, but almost impossible to follow the same advice.

Being ignored was no fun, but he found himself in good company. Just this week, he'd been pondering how the Pharisees ignored the stories Jesus told them. Not quite the same, true. But back in his study, the parallel cheered him, anyhow.

But the failure with Otto still troubled him. So much for his efforts to reach out to the community and his visions of making a difference in this woebegone world. Those women who asked him to do something had too much faith in his abilities.

The rest of the afternoon he accomplished not one single meaningful thing. Ah well, his stomach growled anyway, as though he deserved a decent supper. Over in the parsonage, he downed a quick sandwich.

The whole time, he pictured Bill doing something significant, while his beautiful daughter faithfully carried out her contribution to the war effort. Madge would have manned the newspaper office all day, too. Everyone did their part.

"Might as well go on over there—I'll never sleep until I find out what's going on." Aivars washed up and changed into some khaki pants, a comfortable alternative to the trousers that had clung to his legs all day in this awful heat.

The cold water he splashed on his face helped his attitude. If only he could take Gloria back to Clear Lake for another wonderful splash in that cool water. All by herself this time.

Madge wasn't home, so he backtracked to the newspaper office. Maybe something was wrong. Maybe that's why he'd been so over-concerned about Bill all day—he had experienced some kind of trouble.

When the *Chronicle* door swung open, Aivars stopped short. The expression on Madge's face sent his heart into a spiral.

"What is it?"

She wrung her hands. "Bill's been away so long, and the evening train's come and gone. I just can't imagine—"

The words no more left her mouth than the phone rang. She lifted the receiver and held up a finger.

"Yes, of course I'll accept a collect call." Pause. "Bill? Are you all right?"

A longer pause, then a nod. "Oh, all right then. It's getting so late and the train has come and gone already, so I . . ."

Madge leaned over her desk, and Aivars walked into the print room to give her some privacy. Something about this room brought forth Bill's image, so earnest, so faithful to his duty.

"I'll see you in the morning. Love you, too." A scramble to the door, and Madge heaved a great sigh.

"Whew! He's fine. I shouldn't have doubted. Years ago, I wouldn't have, but this darn war—"

"It does change us, doesn't it?"

"Yes. Well, now I can go home, but I just couldn't leave without hearing from him."

Aivars held his tongue as she locked up. She still hadn't mentioned where Bill went.

He fell in step as she began talking about how she'd managed in the past. "I suppose I took him for granted. He always came home eventually, usually with some story to share. But since he was gone for so long and came back so—"

Suddenly she looked up. "Sorry—guess I got all caught up in my anxiety. Not a very good example of faith, am I?"

"You waited all that time for Bill—I'd say you kept the faith. Besides, I'd be the last to judge. I've been a pretty rotten example today myself."

"Oh, I doubt that."

"Believe!" Aivars raised his fist as if preaching, and Madge laughed out loud. She set such a fast pace it took no time at all before they reached her front porch.

"Have you eaten yet?" She gave him no opportunity to reply. "Would you like to come in? Gloria should be home in a while, although maybe she'd rather have a chance to get cleaned up first."

"Of course. Right. I'll mosey back over around seven, how's that?"

"Okay, see you then. I think we have some apple pie left—made one yesterday from our early-bearing Winesaps."

She raced up the stairs and inside, so Aivars turned back toward home, still pondering where Bill might be. Every step underlined this fresh mystery, since Madge still hadn't mentioned any details. Halfway home, a parishioner greeted him, and they passed the time of day. Nice to live in a town small enough for this kind of encounter.

As he started off again, a single thought held his attention—why hadn't he considered this before? Maybe Madge had no knowledge of exactly where Bill was until he called, so she couldn't have told him if she wanted to.

The early train took Bill straight into the Charles City depot, where he checked to be sure another one would pass in an hour to get him to Caroline by noon. Then he started for the Floyd County fairgrounds and searched for Dale, whose commanding voice and height made him easy to find.

"Why Bill, good to see you." Dale gave instructions to someone and pulled Bill to a quiet corner of the former livestock building. He leaned against the wall and crossed his arms. "What's happening? Did you catch the murderer yet?"

"No, but I might have found a decent lead. I might need a search warrant."

"Good."

"It's a little hard to explain."

"Things like this are never very straightforward, in my experience. Give me the highlights." Dale glanced at his watch. "I've got about five minutes."

"Well, I just came from talking to old Otto Depperschmidt's son Rudy. It seems that Otto followed the German *Bund* pretty closely back in the day and might still communicate with a friend over in Germany.

"Hmm."

"The guy's name is Max, and we've found that signature on a postcard Vera received. That is, if it's the same guy.

"I was surprised to hear how strongly Otto supported Hitler. Rudy tried to convince him against the Reich, but Otto's so set in his ways, he wouldn't hear of it. Says it's all propaganda. Rudy even changed his name to distance himself from his father—did you know that?"

"Yep. The papers came through a year ago, maybe longer. So many Germans are doing that lately, it didn't strike me as odd. So you talked to Rudy at Fort McCoy?"

"Yes, and the more he described his dad's devotion to Hitler, the more I began to wonder. Then when I asked if Otto happened to have a friend named Max, Rudy answered in the affirmative."

"Looks a bit suspicious to me, and you're right. Searching Otto's house is the only way to find out if there's any connection. Come into my office and we'll fill out the paperwork. I'll sign everything, and you'll need to get it to the county attorney. He'll take it to the courthouse."

Dale led the way to another building. A few minutes later, Bill had what he needed, and Dale shook his hand. "Sure hope what you've found leads us to the killer. I've written down a phone number here if you need to reach me."

"Sure wish you could be doing this instead of me. I'm fumbling around in the dark."

"Oh, so am I a good share of the time. All we can do is give these things our best effort."

In spite of his better instincts, Aivars found himself pouring out his troubles to Gloria as they walked under low-hanging maple trees. She'd suggested this stroll after they finished supper, and by then, a half-moon was rising. Madge begged off to clean up the kitchen and get ready for tomorrow.

After describing the situation with Otto, Aivars added, "Sorry, here I am telling you about my bad afternoon when you're so tired. I bet you can hardly follow what I'm saying."

"Oh, it's okay."

"Don't your feet hurt?"

"No, we rode on the back of the cultivator most of the time and jumped off whenever we saw a stray corn plant or weed. I actually like being outdoors all day, and it's been fun to get to know the other workers."

"Tell me about them."

"One has two brothers overseas, and she's scared to death for them. Their letters are mostly blacked out, and only come every few weeks. There've been times I wished I had brothers, but right now, I'm glad I don't."

"Yes."

"Anyway, I'm happy Dad went to see his old Army buddy today. I'm sure that'll do him good."

"Mmm."

"What you said about Otto—I've had kind of a funny feeling about him for a long time. One day, I stopped in to pick up something Mom had left in the church kitchen, and he was down there looking around."

"He maneuvered those stairs with his cane?"

"I assume so—he was standing by the counter staring down. Mom told me that's where you found Vera, so I backed away. Must have been showing his respects."

"He just stood there?"

"Yes."

"Did he hear you?"

"If he did, he didn't show it."

"Interesting." They walked a full minute in silence before Gloria asked a question Aivars didn't know how to answer without stepping into unknown waters.

"Are you and my parents investigating the murder for Sheriff Finley while he's away?"

So Bill and Madge hadn't told her. If he said no, he'd be lying to the woman he hoped would one day become his betrothed. As he had with Otto, he waffled.

"Does it look like that to you?"

"That's for sure. Their behavior leaves me no doubt. After all, their voices travel, even when I'm upstairs. But you—would you get involved?"

"From what you know of me, would I?"

She grasped his arm under a leafy arbor near the Sheriff's office. "You would. You're all about justice and getting things right."

The light in her eyes strummed through his veins like liquid gold. "Besides that, you were Vera's pastor, and even on the suspect list. I would think you'd want to solve this crime in the worst way."

He gulped. "You know me pretty well."

She took a half step closer. "And I love you for it, Aivars Zevenbergen."

That did it. Without checking to see if anybody was coming, Aivars gathered her in his arms—what else could he do? Before he realized what was happening, her lips lay right under his, warm and tender and inviting.

He ought to have pulled back, but couldn't move, couldn't think, much less analyze the situation. When he finally took a breath, Gloria leaned against him, and he might have fallen over if it hadn't been for the sturdy fence Tom Newberry had built around his property.

Holding this amazing, perfect girl, he scarcely kept his wits about him. He'd never experienced anything so, so enthralling. He'd dreamed of this moment, prayed about it, yet never planned for it to come so soon.

Gloria leaned her head back, her lips rich and full, and he nearly drowned in the adoring gleam that filled her eyes. Then their lips met again—he hadn't moved, had he?

All he knew was that somehow, he still found the strength to stand. And he wanted to stay right here forever, until the very end of time.

Chapter Thirty-one

August 7, 1944

The train ride from Charles City to Caroline gave Bill time to prepare. Sometime soon, he would have to go through Otto's house. What would the old man do if he knocked at the door and presented the warrant?

Instinct told him that would never work. Men like that, who'd come through the Great War and the Great Depression—and Otto had accomplished part of that in Germany, where people literally starved to death—weren't about to let the law traipse all over their property.

No, he'd have to do the search when Otto had gone off somewhere. He'd post the warrant on Otto's door when he left the house, and when Otto discovered the notice, who knew what the old man would do?

But there was no other way to further this investigation. Every so-called lead had gotten them nowhere, even though he and Madge and Aivars entertained such high hopes with some of them.

Once in a while, Otto walked down Main Street at a snail's pace—until now, there'd been no reason to pay any attention. But those times were purely random. Every Sunday, rain or shine, minus-zero temperatures or snowstorm, Otto trekked to church..

Never missed, much to the dismay of so many. Otto's playing was getting on people's nerves more and more. Once, when he discussed his questionable contribution to the services with Aivars

252

and Madge, Aivars made light of his miserable accompaniment.

"Well, he gives new meaning to the verse about *the left hand not knowing what the right hand is doing*, don't you think?"

But more than humor lay beneath his joke. How do you guide an eighty-year-old man out of your church, especially when he isn't even a member?

The three of them commiserated that day but reached no conclusions. Life sure had changed since Aivars came to town. It wouldn't do to be glad for his heart problem, but that was, in a way, what had brought him here.

If not for those Army docs, Aivars would have been crawling through Normandy's hedgerows these past weeks or defending a small French village from fierce gunfire. What a terrific cost they had paid, but soon, the Allies would have liberated all of Northern Europe.

Yes, a nightmarish cost. Nonetheless, the headlines predicted plenty of fighting still ahead. That was the thing with war. You weren't given the luxury of changing your mind and backing out halfway through.

Watching the Iowa countryside roll by, Bill replayed Rudy's comments about Otto. What a sad situation—sons at odds with their father.

Nothing to do about Otto right away, not until that search warrant appeared in the mail. But the evidence seemed to be mounting. The old fellow loved Hitler and was still devoted to the *Bund*. The murder weapon originated in Germany, and Otto had a friend named Max.

Strange how he, Madge, and Aivars had assumed the worst of Helene, but had no idea the culprit might be front and center right in their own sanctuary every Sunday morning. A shudder ran through Bill at the very thought. But then, stranger things had happened—he had caught wind of spies pretending to be men of the cloth.

How Vera got in the middle of Otto's blind loyalty, he had no idea. Maybe she hadn't, either. Hopefully this search would bring in some new facts to tie everything together.

Dale said the county attorney, known for doing his job without favoritism, would be Johnny-on-the-spot processing the warrant. And by then, there'd be a plan, which meant he'd better come up with one.

The first question, of course, was whether he ought to go alone or take somebody along. Two sets of eyes were better than one, no doubt about that. But how could he justify taking both Aivars and Madge?

He couldn't hurt her feelings by choosing Aivars, not after the way she'd stood by him. And nobody had worked harder than her on this investigation.

Ah well, it would all work out—worrying about it would do no good whatsoever. As he observed fields of deep green corn pass by and hay being harvested into bales, a group of workers all dressed alike stood out—POW camp internees. Bill's blood ran cold to see them out there so hale and hearty,

On the other hand, the farmers really needed help these days. With their sons and other young men gone off to war, it seemed only reasonable to employ these able-bodied prisoners. Might as well have them aid the war effort in some way.

From his vantage point in the safety of this train car, they looked like young Iowa men, sleeves rolled up or backs bared to the July sun. Sweat glistened on their deep tans.

Could these men really represent the enemy his unit had fought against? For all he knew, some of them might have manned the tanks that rolled down on them to the glory of the Desert Fox.

Seemed impossible. Besides, most of the ones captured in North Africa, Hitler's elites, had been sent to Algona. That main camp, out in the middle of nowhere, boasted stronger security.

Soon Caroline lay up ahead, her outskirts appearing rather lonely. For now, best let go his ponderings about the search warrant and the war. Madge would be waiting for him, and he hoped she'd see that he was returning a little stronger.

These times with Roger did that for him. All he knew was, there wasn't a memory or a flashback, not a grimace nor a grin that Roger failed to understand. They'd trained together, each of them older than most of the eighteen-year-olds who'd been drafted.

They'd each signed up long before the Pearl Harbor attack on that December Sunday, as if sharing the same premonition. Seemed so long ago already, but that awful news only increased their desire to play their parts. What good was a man if he wouldn't fight to protect his homeland?

Though leaving Madge and Gloria behind had almost killed him, and he'd returned home a different man, Roger had it a lot rougher. He returned to an empty house. His wife ran off with somebody else and took the children. She sent him a letter to that effect while their unit lurked under Rommel's fierce shadow.

Bill's heart still lurched at the heartbreaking details Roger poured out when her letter arrived. He'd had every confidence she would be there waiting for him when he returned, and no idea she could be so fickle.

Then there was Madge, whose face rose like an angel's before him as the train neared the depot. From the first, she understood his desire to do his part. And she'd sacrificed so he could—so had Gloria.

The train drew to a stop at the station. There his lovely wife stood, here for him as always. Always here for him.

The last time he'd succumbed to feeling like he'd failed during his final battle, she held him and whispered, "You *did* protect those young men, you *did* save some lives. That's why you went in the first place."

Seeing her waiting for him again, something eased inside him, and he finally embraced that benediction. Maybe he had done the right thing after all. Madge caught sight of him and waved as though they'd just gotten engaged.

What a woman—her love went on and on and on. He'd have to think of a way to show her some extra attention soon.

"She loves you, man. She's head over heels for you." Staring into the mirror above his bathroom sink, Aivars shook his head. How could this be true? The most beautiful girl in her graduating class, and probably the smartest, had told him she loved him.

This wasn't how it was supposed to go. He ought to have been first to vow his devotion. But when he tried to remember how it all happened, his mind buckled.

Had he kissed her, or had she kissed him? How long had they stood there, lost in their own magical world? What happened after he walked her home? He remembered hearing her say good night and the touch of her fingers on his, but that was about it. He might have fallen into a ravine on the way back to the parsonage, for all he knew.

That one enchanting moment had also snuffed out his curiosity about Bill. His own incredibly charming youngest daughter had seen to that. Emphasis on *youngest*—only eighteen years old.

Should he be discussing what happened with Bill and Madge? No—not yet. That would seem presumptuous. First, he had to talk with Gloria again. But he really didn't want to talk, he wanted to kiss her. Over and over and over.

No, no, no! He was an old man, and men of the cloth in other denominations took a vow of chastity, disciplined their masculine desires for their whole lives. Some of his seminary mates figured they'd never marry, but although he hadn't dated much, he'd never felt led that way.

After last night, though, he began to wonder if he could survive the rigors of love. But then, what did he know? Maybe loving someone so deeply would somehow strengthen his heart. After all, love originated with God, didn't it?

Coming out of the post office, he almost ran smack into Agnes Wellsby. She toppled to the side and grabbed at her hat.

"Are you all right, Agnes? I'm so sorry—guess I was preoccupied."

"Sure looked like it, Pastor. Well, it's all right. I expect you're concentrating on your sermon for Sunday." Agnes straightened her coat. "Or the murder. Have they made any headway on that?"

Aivars muttered something about being in a hurry and rushed on toward the church. If Agnes only knew his selfish thoughts. He simply wasn't himself, but had better shape up.

"I must get started on my sermon—can't put it off any longer. Gotta shove everything else out of my mind. Good thing Agnes reminded me."

But when he arrived at the church, he thought he heard someone on the back stairs. Recalling what Gloria had said about Otto, Aivars ran around to the front, crept downstairs and stepped cautiously across the basement to the furnace room. There, he smashed himself in next to the massive coal-eating iron monster and held his breath.

From the side entrance, someone creaked open the kitchen door. He would've given a month's paycheck to know who it was. Such a long silence followed that he was tempted to slither into the hallway and peer around the corner but controlled his urge.

Controlling his urges—yes, that was his calling right now, in more ways than one. Time crawled by, minute by everlasting minute.

And then finally, whoever was here shut the side door and started up the back stairs. Aivars raced across the basement, up the front steps, and plastered himself behind one of the pillars at the illustrious entrance.

Silence. Was he imagining things now? Then slow steps sounded in the distance. Very slow. And was that a cane clicking? He drew in a breath and shrank against the pillar as, about fifteen feet below and to his left, a scuffed black leather boot came into view.

Next, blue striped overalls, a wooden cane, and a beak-like nose. Otto. A chill took Aivars. Traversing those steep stairs had to be tough for the old guy, but something must be drawing him to the kitchen.

Once Otto passed out of sight, Aivars returned to the basement and looked around, as he'd done umpteen times before. He paused close to where he'd found Vera in her death throes.

What connection did Otto have with her, anyway?

For some reason, the narrow hallway's open closet attracted him—he'd barely noticed it before. That jacket hanging there, an everyday men's spring coat. How long had it been there?

He'd never known a church not to have at least one of these, usually a man's, left behind after a meeting or a funeral. Sometimes, a hat occupied the shelf above the hooks, too. Easy enough to forget with Iowa's weather sometimes turning from chilly to warm within minutes.

Trepidation tightened his chest as he advanced toward the garment. First, he stuck his fingertips into the far pocket. Nothing but fuzz. He bit his lips and tried the other side. Ah, something soft and smooth, almost downy. He closed his eyes, got a good hold on the thing and brought it out into the dim morning light.

Seeing what lay in his hand, he caught himself on the wall. A bird. A little stuffed bird to match today's glorious summer sky— the very birdie that had perched on Vera's Easter bonnet. Aivars grasped the framework of the door with his other hand as wild imaginings convulsed in his head.

Had Otto been searching for this? The dank basement started to close in, and a tingle ran the length of his backbone. He must get this evidence over to the newspaper office pronto. By now, Bill had probably gotten home.

Not one to enjoy summer's heat and humidity, Madge fanned herself at the desk. Three notices of fall weddings had come in this week, two for wounded soldiers expected back from the war. The bride in one, Twila Smith, had taken the train out to Washington, D.C. at word that her Ervin had arrived at a hospital.

Her mother popped in yesterday with an article written out in pencil on the lines of a notebook. Smudges from Mrs. Smith's palm made it difficult to read in spots, but she jubilantly filled in the blanks.

"Twila's so happy she could burst. Ervin's a little slow in his thinking, she says, but shows improvement every day. The doctors say he'll be released in about a week, and she'll bring him home on the train.

"They'd get married out there, she said, but want us all to be with them for the big day. Now, isn't that nice?"

"How wonderful for you, and how thoughtful of Twila. So many couples go ahead and tie the knot wherever they are these days. Such a pleasant story, love blossoming in spite of this old war."

"Old is right. Honestly, sometimes I wonder if it'll ever end."

Madge nodded in commiseration. Indeed, the war seemed endless. Back in the press room, Bill whistled away as he worked on the next paper, and her heart swelled to the tune of *Don't Sit Under the Apple Tree With Anyone Else but Me.* Bill had heard Glenn Miller's rendition first, at a USO station somewhere in early 1942, and asked her to listen to it down at the cafe.

She still kept that letter in her top dresser drawer. No need, really, since she'd memorized the message.

"This is our song, honey. I'm so worn out that when I get home, sitting under the apple tree may be all I'll be able to do, but I want you beside me."

Worn out. He certainly had been.

Seeing him come home from Ft. McCoy late this morning, feeling his arms around her, she'd given thanks again for his safe return. Luckily, she was still here at work when he called last evening to tell her he couldn't make it home.

His voice sounded so strong, so clear. He hadn't stuttered for . . . how long had it been? He seemed almost like the same fellow she'd married—almost, because once in a while, especially when the war report came on, that far-away look in his eyes still troubled her. But those times of seeming lost in another world had decreased.

Shoving her chair back, she picked up a stack of notes to show him, but just then the door crashed open and Aivars bounded in. What did that wild look in his eyes mean? She set the papers down and hurried over.

"Are you all right?"

He croaked, "Is Bill here?"

In the pressroom, Bill raised his head to peer at them. Then concern overtook his features. "What is it?"

"I think maybe you should lock the front door for a few minutes. If you don't mind."

Madge complied and when she hurried back in, Aivars held out his hand. Seeing that bit of blue nestled in his palm. Bill emerged from behind the press.

"You found—"

"Yes."

"Where, for heaven's sakes?"

"Sit down. You'll never believe it."

Madge pulled up chairs, and Aivars launched in. "I heard someone on the basement stairs this morning and snuck down the front way to the furnace room. I couldn't tell who was rummaging around but had my suspicions. When they started up the stairs, I ran up the front and outside to watch."

"Who was it?"

"Otto."

Madge scooted to the edge of her chair. "How did he get down there?"

"It seems our organist might not be as lame as we've always thought. Gloria told me she found him down in the kitchen one other day, staring at the spot where Vera died."

"Oh, my goodness! She never said—"

Bill held up his hand. "And the bird?"

"After Otto left, I went back to the kitchen and stood there trying to figure out what he's been looking for. And then I noticed that unclaimed jacket hanging in the hallway near the furnace room. It's been there forever, you know. Something told me to check the pockets, and that's where—"

He dropped the small feathered thing into Bill's hand with a sigh. Bill laid it on a table. Madge turned on another light so they could get a better look.

"Wait." She held up her hand. "Let me get a magnifying glass."

When she returned she brought her letter opener too. "Just in case you need to—"

Bill nodded. "Thanks, honey. Exactly what we need."

He jostled the feathers a little with the tip, revealing a small slit on the belly near the tail. "Right here. Can you see it?"

Aivars nodded in tandem with Madge.

"Shall we cut it open or not? It's evidence—maybe we should wait for Dale."

"But he gave you his authority, and if there's nothing inside, we really haven't found much at all." Aivars angled his head for a closer look. "There *is* something, though. Isn't that a little piece of paper sticking out? See, down here at this end?"

"Yeah." Bill bit his lip. "Well, then." He inserted the opener into the slit and Madge held her breath. Someone knocked on the office door, but no one made a move.

"Whoever it is will come back," she whispered. They'll think I've just gone for the mail or something."

Bill wedged the opening a little wider. "Can you get ahold of it?"

Making a tweezers of her thumb and forefinger, Madge reached in and pulled. Little by little, a scrunched paper wiggled out.

"Go ahead, bring it into the light." Bill wiped his forehead. "And read it to us."

"Oh my. I feel like Miss Marple. "Why, it's a tiny scroll!" Unrolled, the paper matched the size of a recipe card, and Madge squinted as she read.

"Neshanic—San Pedro, Ca 6/19/43. Logistical support for ADAK, Attu and Shemya . . ."

Bill interrupted. "Navy operating bases in the Pacific. The Neshanic's a petroleum tanker—keep reading."

"GOC Marquette WI/ 24 hr. observation over raw IO transport."

"Ground Observation Corps. IO means raw iron ore. The Upper Peninsula supplies most of it for the steel the Navy needs to build its ships. What else?"

"GLNS – RAIVARS/over 100,000 in trng/air obs in effect."

"Great Lakes Naval Station – Recruit Training Center—100,000 in training."

Aivars gaped, and Bill's eyes trained on her like an eagle's. "I'm afraid that's it. That's all there is."

"Whew—that's plenty. I need to report this to Sheriff Finley right away. Glad he gave me his phone number down at the camp. Bet you ten-to-one he'll call in the F.B.I."

Aivars positively gaped. Then Bill let out a long breath. "Friends, if I had to bet, I'd say we've got a war crime on our hands."

Chapter Thirty-two

Monday, August 7, 1944

"I wonder what all this means about Vera?" The last rays of sunshine slanted in through a high window in the back of the *Chronicle* office as Aivars conjectured.

Bill had summoned him back after supper. Gloria hadn't come home from work yet, so Madge left her a note. She even left the supper dishes unwashed.

"I have no idea how she got in the middle of this. But a search warrant for Otto's house is on its way. It seems he's been a long-time supporter of Hitler."

Madge felt her mouth drop open at the same time as Aivars's. "Otto Depperschmidt?"

"The same. His sons have had nothing to do with him for years. They've even changed their names."

"Ah, yes—it's *Sarah Sweeney*. I did wonder about that."

"And her dad, Rudy, Otto's youngest, is saving up to move his family away from here as soon as possible."

"I finally reached Dale by phone late this afternoon, and he said he'd wait until after our search to contact the F.B.I." He shifted his weight and glanced at Aivars.

"We're going to have to do the search when Otto's not home. Do you know when he'll be gone for sure besides during church services?"

"The music committee meets this Wednesday at seven. But I think they would wonder if I didn't show up."

"It's all right—we want to keep everything looking as normal as possible. Go ahead and do your duty. I'll have a professional sleuth at my side." Bill raised his arm, and Madge slid underneath.

"If my wife can't sniff out the evidence, no one can. She started us thinking about that ridiculous Easter bonnet in the first place."

"And she was right as rain. What I don't understand is, how could Otto—" Aivars rubbed his chin. "I mean, how long has he been plotting this?"

"Who knows? I'd like to find out how he decided to use Vera to get that little bird here. And who was he supposed to pass this information to?" Madge gestured to the note. "And how would he have accomplished that?"

Bill shrugged. "The answers might be really simple. Maybe he was looking for someone in town who had the means to travel. Vera did, right?"

"True. Maybe that's how her train ticket fits in. People have been known to carry contraband without realizing it. Otto may have sought someone who was vulnerable—hungry for attention?"

At these words from Aivars, Madge pounded her fist against the table. "Makes me sick to think of him up there on the organ bench, analyzing which woman would work for his purposes."

"Yeah. I'm sure glad he didn't pick you, Maddie-girl. He must be pretty shrewd, and he did a good job. It's no secret how much that hat meant to Vera. She sure did fight for it."

"So between the furnace room and the kitchen, you believe she struggled with her killer, and this bird flew off and somehow landed in that jacket pocket?" Incredulity laced this question from Aivars, and Madge jumped in.

"I can picture Vera putting up a fight. I bet she scratched him with her fingernails, but none of us knew to check his face or arms. He must be way stronger than he appears—but then, he works in his garden a lot."

"How far is it from the kitchen counter to that coat rack…maybe six feet? I guess stranger things have happened." Bill squeezed

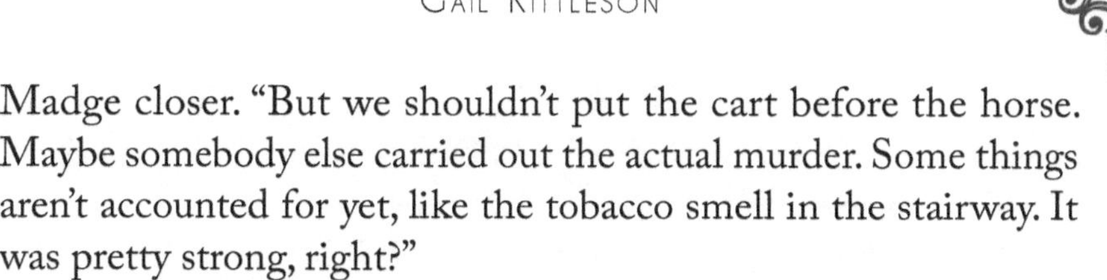

Madge closer. "But we shouldn't put the cart before the horse. Maybe somebody else carried out the actual murder. Some things aren't accounted for yet, like the tobacco smell in the stairway. It was pretty strong, right?"

"Right. That was the first thing I noticed. Unless Otto smokes. Maybe your search will reveal that."

"At any rate, we've got the motive. We'll need prints of Otto's shoes."

Aivars lifted his foot. "And his fingerprints. Say! We've got them in spades on the organ keys." Everyone chuckled, and he added, "Whatever he was being paid for this information must've seemed worth it to him."

Madge turned to Bill. "Do you think this *Max* was supplying the payment?"

"Seems likely. Perhaps in gold—I've heard the Nazis have a fortune tucked away." He jotted something in a notebook. "Can't hurt to take prints of any other shoes in Otto's house—probably all he has are his garden boots."

"Maybe we'll have to sneak in when he's in the garden to print his Sunday shoes?"

Bill gave Madge a grin. "Oh, my dear, I'm sure you'll find a way."

"Absolutely she will. I can't wait to see what you find. Oh—and how do you think those tire marks we saw in the cemetery fit in?"

"Tire marks?" Madge crossed her arms.

"Guess I forgot to mention that—we came upon them one day on a walk. Someone drove right up to Vera's grave, turned around and backed out. That was back when we thought there might be a black market connection. Still might be."

"Hmm. And what about Helene?"

"I'm afraid we got off on a tangent there. Her innocent comment about the hat must've been enough to bring on that threatening note. My guess is that Otto overheard her say that. Not sure who wrote the note to her, though."

"But what was she doing in Decorah?"

"Like she said, the note scared her, and she didn't want to bring trouble to her brother and sister. She may have gone to that Nazi camp as a child, but probably had no choice. No anti-American wears a *Remember Harbor* pin on her collar."

"What? She had one on that day, and I didn't notice?"

"Wonders never cease!" Bill's lopsided smile softened the blow. "Oh, I should let Roger know about this—I imagine they're still keeping an eye on her."

Madge's thoughts bounced ahead to the most exciting part. "I can't wait for the F.B.I. to get here. Imagine having agents right in Caroline! Maybe we can invite them over for some of my potato salad and I can bake raspberry pies—"

Bill burst out laughing. "I doubt they'd accept an invitation. But wouldn't Sherlock and Agatha be proud of our efforts?"

The plan was for Bill to leave at six-thirty and wait out behind the lilac row east of Otto's yard until the old man left for the church. Madge was to close up the office and start for Otto's no sooner than twenty minutes later.

Although time dragged, she obeyed but blazed a new record getting there. As he promised, Bill had left the back door ajar, so after sneaking along the edge of the corn field bordering Otto's property to the north, Madge whisked straight in.

On this second entrance into someone's house without their knowledge, her breath came more regularly. Sure helped to have a partner in crime. And a search warrant.

The back doors of these big old houses often opened into a small space at the top of a stairway that led to the basement. It was as if the builders did their utmost to make entering difficult—if you didn't realize the stairway existed, you might take too big a step and end up on the cold, unforgiving cellar floor.

Putting her hand on her chest to calm herself, Madge paused just inside the door. Dirty fingerprints decorated the partially opened basement door, and heavy mustiness seeped up from the cavern below.

A hoarse whisper reached her. "I'm in here." Up two steps on her left, she entered what might have been a spacious kitchen. So much light filled the curtain-less room that she blinked. But the amount of objects in the room made it into a maze.

Bill bent over a large table shoved against the north wall. He gestured her closer to some official-looking documents written in German.

Behind the table hung a framed likeness of Herr Hitler and several small Brownie photographs pinned to a haphazard bulletin board. Leaning closer brought into focus gatherings of young people in Hitler youth shorts and shirts.

Meanwhile, Bill thrust a letter her way, with some parts translated into English. Otto's signed name filled the bottom section.

"This seems like some sort of contract." Bill straightened as she glanced over the page.

"Yes, I'd say so."

"I haven't found any mention of Max yet, but this whole place is a treasure trove. Maybe you can keep an eye out. How much German do you remember from your high school classes?"

"Some."

"Why don't you start in the living room? It's a carbon copy of this mess."

"All right." Madge circled the table and passed under an archway with peeling tan paint. The south half of the ceiling boasted a brown stain shaped like the state of Iowa. The entire large piece had slipped from its moorings.

"You think it's safe in here?"

"What?" Bill popped in his head. "You mean the ceiling? Probably been that way for decades."

Still, Madge started on the other side of the room. Looked as though she could spend a year in here and not read everything.

"Good thing you told me to wear my gloves. The last thing I need is to be hauled in by the F.B.I." Her cheeks warmed at the memory of being a suspect.

Beginning with a grungy envelope near the edge of the table, she launched her investigation. Thirty minutes and three envelopes later, she came up for air and found Bill eyeing her intently.

"Can you read any of this?"

"Yes. There's one letter that might give us a big clue. It's written in such a fine hand, I had to read it three times, but one sentence stands out. *Wenn etwas passiert, sind sie Max.*"

"It mentions Max? Great! What does it mean?"

"'If anything happens, you are Max.'"

"Hmm. I never thought of that."

"And see here. Beside it there's a note in handwriting a lot like Otto's signatures."

"*Ich bin Max.* I am Max?"

"Exactly."

That might have been the highlight of the search, although Bill took several prints of Otto's boots. But then, just when he announced they ought to leave in five minutes to play it safe, Madge made another discovery.

On an old high chest of drawers stacked with letters, one that bore Max's script stood out, so she pored over it.

"*Sie müssen alles tun, was nötig ist…* You must be willing to do . . . Drat! Wish I'd studied harder back in Mr. Haupt's class." Rereading the context, a paragraph stood out—instructions about making sure the message reached its destination. The meaning suddenly sprouted in her brain.

"Ah! *Whatever it takes*—that's it. You must be willing to do whatever it takes."

"That's what it says?"

"I'm pretty sure. The message absolutely must reach its recipient, and Otto must be willing to do anything to make sure that happens."

"Including murder?"

Madge shrugged. "I imagine so, if that's what it takes."

"I still have a question. If Otto was the murderer, how did that strong tobacco smell get in the basement stairway?" Aivars leaned his office chair back on two legs and fiddled with his pen. "Did you see any tobacco around his place, or a pipe?"

"Plenty of both, and paper for rolling cigarettes. The tobacco smelled European—strong," Bill rose and crossed to the door. He paused with his hand still on the doorknob, and doubt pressed at his mind. He turned back to Aivars. "I wonder why we never smelled it on him?"

Aivars shrugged, and Bill left, closing the door behind him. Aivars pondered the puzzle for a moment, but found no insight. He tried to clear his mind to work on his sermon. But not ten minutes later, someone was walking up the sanctuary aisle.

Thud, thud, thud. Someone was walking up the aisle of the sanctuary. Slowly, Aivars lowered his chair and froze. Someone with a little extra weight, from the reverberation in the walls.

That was the trouble with having his office up here, essentially right behind the altar. People had to trudge through the whole church to find him or else use the side stairs. But since Vera died, almost everyone avoided them.

Whoever it was took a few more moments to ascend the stairs and pass through the squat hallway.

Then came the knock. Tenuous.

"Come on in."

Harry Walters met him face to face, since he took up most of the remaining space inside the doorway.

"Would you have a minute or two, Pastor?"

"Why sure. Have a seat."

With a little huffing and puffing, Harry settled into the seat, a tad tight for his width. The neighbor ladies must still be supplying him plenty of food.

"So, how is it going for you these days, Harry?"

"Oh, fine."

The expression on his face belied his brief statement. How to help him relate whatever had brought him here?

The chair creaked as his visitor sought a comfortable position. Harry kept his eyes on the floor as though something quite interesting had alighted at his feet. At times like this, Aivars had taken to studying the portrait on the hallway wall. Something about that depiction of the Savior reaching out to one distraught follower touched him, although his perspective had changed since he'd hung it there.

At that time, he saw himself as the one offering solace. Now he had become the desperate one, and parishioners would be helped only as he received guidance. Besides that, sometimes *they* would bring *him* help.

That predatory eagle soaring overhead epitomized the war—always bad news pending. So far, most visitors to his study shared troubles relating to the dire state of things around the globe. They felt helpless with loved ones deployed who-knows-where and feared the dreaded notification of a son or husband's death.

Mostly they needed a listening ear, for pat answers simply wouldn't do. Aivars shifted his focus to Harry, who was wiping his brow in the growing heat. What was it he needed?

Might as well get right to the point. "What can I do for you today?"

Harry blinked. "Well, I . . ." Something must really be troubling him. Nothing to do but wait.

"It's . . ."

Aivars throttled his urge to blurt, "Come on, just spit it out." Instead, he asked, "Is this something about Vera?"

"Yeah." Harry's deep sigh was laced with such feeling, Aivars leaned forward.

"Something has upset you?"

"Oh, that's for sure."

Okay. A bit of progress.

"Sometimes regrets surface when we're grieving."

"Regrets. That's it exactly." Harry's bushy brows rose and fell.

"Is this about something you did, or something you wish you had done?"

"Yeah."

Good grief! This was getting them nowhere.

"Something you did?"

"Something I wish I hadn't done."

"Mmm. Do you think you can tell me about it?"

"I resented her." Harry's deep flush increased by the second.

"Oh. What in particular did you resent?"

"She was always so hoity-toity, I think you call it. Anybody in town would tell you that. She used my position to make herself seem better than other folks. You know how she was."

Whoo boy. How to reply? "Did something specific bother you most?"

"Yeah." Harry's inhale seemed gargantuan. "It was her going over to Chicago. A man's supposed to be able to trust his wife, but I just couldn't." His face flamed, even his forehead.

Finally he spewed the words. "I had her followed." Getting that out, his shoulders released, and he leaned into the chair back. "She'd been getting mail with foreign postmarks. I s'pose she thought I didn't notice. It happened so many times, I was afraid she might've gotten mixed up in something underhanded."

Fishing for something to say, Aivars came up with a neutral, "Hmm."

"So I feel bad about that. Guilty, I guess."

"But you must have thought something was amiss."

"I did at the time, but looking back, I think she really just wanted to visit her relatives. The only thing the detective I hired discovered was Vera buying Woodbines and smoking them in a park."

"Woodbines—that sounds familiar. Weren't they handed out to soldiers in the Great War?"

"Right. But those gaspers were so harsh, I don't think many

women smoked them. Vera started young, and her smoking always bothered me. I've got weak lungs, you know, and she—well, it seemed like she didn't care."

Now that he'd gotten started, it was as if a well gushed up, and Harry let loose. Meanwhile, this revelation about Vera switched on an inner light for Aivars.

"So way back, I told her never to smoke another one inside the house. She said she wouldn't, or I don't know what I would've done. To her there was nothing wrong with it, but she only smoked out in our old milk house.

"Even in winter, that was the first thing she did every morning and the last thing at night. Walked out there through the snow or rain and had her smoke.

"Here's the funny thing, though. She always kept her Woodbines a secret. Loaded up when she went to the city, never bought a one of 'em here in town. I don't think she could have if she'd wanted to. They're made in England, you know."

Giving a nod, Aivars waited while Harry drew a breath.

"So like I said, I feel bad for having her followed. She just needed her nicotine, that's all. Like some folks with their liquor."

"The detective never found her doing anything suspicious?"

"She went to a certain place for the smokes, he said, and spent quite a while in there sometimes, but nothing else. He checked on the owner of the tobacco shop but didn't find anything that made him wonder."

"This is all so interesting."

"Yeah, and she was all about making sure nobody knew about her habit, you know? Morning and night, she smoked in her nightgown and robe. During the day, I don't know—maybe she had a few more, but she must've changed to go out to the milk house, because her clothes never smelled.

"She used Listerine to clean her breath. That stuff's pretty strong, so I hardly ever noticed anything at all."

A mental note—better purchase a bottle. Couldn't hurt to make sure his breath smelled fresh for Gloria. Aivars kicked himself inwardly and leaned nearer to Harry again.

"It sounds as if you did what any concerned husband might have. Seems to me as though you were thinking of Vera's welfare."

Harry pursed his thick lips. "Maybe, now that you put it that way. It's true, I didn't want her to get into trouble, what with all the racketeering going on these days.

"But then that big box came for her with that monstrous hat, and she got rid of the address before I could check it. I almost called my detective friend again, but how could he find out anything about the U.S. Mail?"

"That bonnet certainly did arouse some antagonism."

"I just don't understand it. Probably never will. It's funny how a man sits around in the evenings with all these questions in his head."

"I understand. It's probably best for you to keep as busy as possible."

"I thought about playing Bingo over at the Catholic Church, you know? But I wasn't sure how they'd take the bank president dropping in."

"Seems like a good idea to me. And perhaps you could take your dinner at the café some nights, spend more time getting involved in community affairs—"

"The café could use more cash coming in, that's for sure." Harry bit his upper lip.

"I'm sure they would appreciate your business."

"Suppose I could be a little looser with my money, now that I'm not paying for expensive clothes and trips to Chicago." Harry released a lighter sigh. "Thank you. You've given me some things to think about."

"Oh, you're so welcome. We all have regrets and anxieties, and the only way to get them off our chest is to share them."

"Yeah. Well, then. I'll be going. How's your sermon coming this week? Hope I didn't get you off track."

Aivars stood and shook Harry's hand. "Oh my, no. Don't even think of it."

Harry plodded through the hallway and down the stairs to the sanctuary. Thoughts scurried through Aivars's head like a pack of wild rats. And they had nothing at all to do with a sermon. At least one puzzling piece of the murder scene had been solved. He could hardly wait for the front door to close so he could head down the side stairs and make a beeline for the *Chronicle*.

Chapter Thirty-three

Aivars did't mean for it to go this way, but then, that's kind of how this whole relationship had developed. He never meant to date Gloria, and in all truth, barely had. He didn't mean to fall in love with her and couldn't have been more shocked when she professed her commitment to him first.

And now this: the morning after their latest meeting, Bill and Madge were on the way to his office. The moment he spied them on the sidewalk as he came to work from the other direction, he knew their intentions.

Last night Gloria had given him fair warning. She'd told them about him, she said. Told them about *them*.

Aivars kneaded the area over his heart. "About *us*." All of his analyzing about whether he should meet with Bill and Madge disappeared, and for a fleeting moment, he considered avoiding the church altogether.

"Coward!" He squelched that thought and raced through the side door and up to his office.

The sanctuary door protested, and by now Bill and Madge had covered half the distance up the aisle. Only seconds away.

Most of the night, Aivars had gone back and forth about initiating a talk with them today. He had all but proposed to their daughter last night—he simply couldn't help it! What would any normal man have done in his shoes?

There stood Gloria, her eyes big as the full moon, glittering with adoration. His heart bounced around in his chest. Then she kissed him and his senses went blurry. All of his determination to move slowly, with mature consideration, vanished like summer's heat.

He still couldn't believe it—they'd taken a walk to the very edge of town, and just around the corner from Otto's property, Gloria practically shoved him into the lilacs. The straggly bushes still carried a heady fragrance from spring blossoms shed months ago.

"See here," he attempted to maintain control. "We need to—" But once again she sealed his lips with her own, and he was a goner. Electric current jittered up his arms and through his shoulders. His stomach did jumping jacks under his ribs.

"Gloria, you're very young, and—"

Her knowing look bespoke her intuition. "And what?"

"I have feelings for you, deep feelings, but we must consider your age, your parents, your—" He was about to utter "your future" when she swept him off his feet once more.

This was not how it was supposed to be. He knew that for sure. The man ought to do the sweeping, ought to take the lead. That's how it had been when his brother courted his bride.

But now as Madge and Bill climbed the steps, a vision befell Aivars. He had no idea how it happened but could not doubt the scene.

Suddenly his father and mother appeared before his mind's eye. Mom had always maintained her rightful role as her spouse's partner—his helpmeet. At least in public, so no one outside the family knew her real role in the home.

By comparison, Dad was by far the meeker, milder one. Why had he never realized this before?

With Madge and Bill closing in, Aivars waited at the door, and could see the expressions on their faces through the short hallway. The lines in Madge's were sharper, more defined than Bill's.

Maybe the same thing held true in their marriage. He had no more time to ponder, for now they were upon him.

"You're out early," he offered.

"Yes. We have to get the paper out today but thought we should talk with you first."

"Would you like to come inside?"

Bill gestured to the sanctuary. "How about out here?"

Aivars studied the wall as if it suddenly appeared out of nowhere. But Bill awaited his response, so he burbled, "Okay, sure."

He managed to follow them and took a seat facing them. The comradeship he'd felt with them all this time teetered on the brink as Bill opened the conversation.

"That was quite a revelation you brought over yesterday about the tobacco smell. We may never know if Vera or Otto left that smoke trail." He waited, but once again words forsook Aivars.

"And then last night we had quite an interesting conversation with Gloria."

"Mmm." Aivars almost choked on this singular emission.

"Yes, indeed." Bill glanced down the aisle as if the most exotic automobile in the world had cruised into the sanctuary. Then he started again. "We talked about you. You and her."

Hot coals lanced Aivars's throat. His efforts to clear them made little difference.

Madge took up the cause. "So we thought it best to face what Gloria said head-on."

In a croak not unlike his grandfather's voice on his deathbed, Aivars whispered, "What did she say?"

"She said she loves you and has told you so. And that you as much as said the feeling was mutual."

"Well, I—er . . . Yes, that's about it."

Bill leaped back in. "We think highly of you, of course, but Gloria's our baby, and we—" He tipped his head, waiting once again.

"You'd like to . . . you need to hear it from me?" They both nodded, and something inside Aivars crumbled. Words poured forth like rain.

"I was going to come over today. This wasn't the way I envisioned things at all, but Gloria's so sure of herself. She's so clear about her wishes, so—"

"Forward?" Madge threw out the word like bait.

"Cock-sure of herself?"

Bill's addition stunned Aivars. "Well, sort of—in a good way, you know. She knows her mind and seems to see the road ahead before I even realize it's there."

Nothing could have encouraged him more than Bill's belly laugh. "That's our girl. We trained her to be confident, to say what she thinks, and she sure does."

"She had to fight for her way with her older sisters at times. But we didn't suppose she would—well." Madge fingered the smooth edge of the pew. "I mean, we thought in this instance, she would wait for you to take the lead. She's grown up so fast, with the war and all."

"Yes. I surely didn't mean to take her away from you like this. So soon, I mean. In the past, I've always hung back on matters of romance. I have to say they actually frighten me a bit, and it takes time to conclude that . . ."

Bill and Madge sat there like the silent baptismal font. No help from them this time.

"At first I couldn't believe that what I felt for Gloria could be the kind of love required for a lifelong marriage. And I'm well aware of our age difference, but then . . ."

There, he'd almost said it, but not quite. So he made another attempt.

"People get married overnight these days, it seems. But when it comes to confidence, I'm not always so sure of myself."

Madge held her tongue. Bill chipped at his thumbnail with his other thumb. Something squeaked over by the organ—a mouse? Finally Bill offered something for Aivars to cling to.

"Nothing's the same as it used to be, we realize that. We want you to know that we trust you and Gloria. She's young, and we don't want her to be hurt, that's all. But there's never a guarantee against that, is there?"

"I guess not."

When Bill stood and held out his hand, Aivars rose and shook it.

"Thank you for coming over. I want you to know I've been debating how to talk to you about all this. But then things happened so fast, I could hardly believe it."

He rubbed his hands together. "I think I've . . . Actually, I feel as though I've been in shock."

"I understand. Gloria's a lot like Madge—she thinks fast, feels fast. But her instincts usually prove better than mine." Bill gave Madge a quizzical look. "As I recall, you may have known I was the one for you long before I figured that out."

Her grin warmed away the tension. "That's an understatement. I thought you never would get it."

"You see? We men are in the same boat."

"I guess so. That helps a little." Aivars felt as if his breathing were finally returning to normal as Bill turned to go.

"All right, then. We'll leave things up to you, Aivars. You know we'd enjoy having you in the family. You've already become such a good friend."

"And fellow detective," Madge added with a distinct twinkle in her eyes.

"Speaking of that, the F.B.I. agent should be here tomorrow. Dale called about that last night."

"Wow—they must be so busy these days. How can that be possible?"

"Obviously, when military information gets included in a note, they perk up. And the info about Vera's fondness for Woodbines sure came in handy, by the way. That smell you noticed has bothered me all along, and finally we've got an answer."

"Although it's still hard for me to imagine Vera smoking in the stairwell." Madge shook her head.

"Yes, I thought of that, as well. And for all we know, it might've been Otto. But please, please—no mention of this to Harry. Confidentiality, you know."

As Madge and Bill neared the door, they paused, and Aivars continued. "Harry emphasized how careful Vera was about her smoking habit. Maybe that underscores how anxious she must have been the morning she died."

"Definitely a nervous reaction. I saw plenty of that in the military—guys shaking for a smoke. Maybe by that time, Vera had some inkling of the danger she'd gotten into."

"Maybe so. Well, I'd better get back to my sermon. It's been a tough week for controlling my thoughts, and today's my last chance to pull something together."

"Good luck." Madge stepped back and gave him a hug. "We're pleased as punch about Gloria and you!" Her whisper had such a calming effect, and Aivars headed back down the aisle with a massive weight lifted.

Leaves crackled underfoot. Aivars relished the sensation of Gloria's hand in his. During the past few weeks, taking walks had become their favorite activity.

With the F.B.I. taking over the murder investigation, another weight released. Gradually—if you could call anything about this month-long courtship gradual—he had come to believe that he and Gloria were meant for each other.

That talk with Madge and Bill helped the most, and then these wonderful strolls, full of secrets and revelations and tenderness. Most of them occurred after dark, after Gloria returned from the fields.

Knowing he'd get to see her later somehow increased his capacity to concentrate during the day, so he produced some powerful sermons, if he had to say so himself. Parishioners commented on this as they shook his hand on their way out, which solidified his sense that all was well.

"This had to be your best yet!"

"I never thought of Jesus walking on the water in this light before. Thank you."

"My daughter's coming this week, and I'm going to tell her what you said about prayer being like crying, *Help!* Sometimes that's all we can do, and the Almighty doesn't mind our helplessness at all."

Not one comment went by the wayside—Aivars recorded each of them in his diary on Sunday afternoon, and it seemed his confidence grew along with his love for Gloria. No longer a feverish thing, it had settled down inside him as if meant to be there.

All of this had led him to this moment, this evening. He felt in his left pocket with his free hand—yep, that little box his mother had sent in response to his letter waited right there.

Please help me to make this special.. I really want Gloria to be pleased and cherish this memory as long as we live. His silent prayer accompanied her stories from the long day's work.

Past Main Street, he guided her east beyond the old mill, and down a curve into a grove of cottonwoods. He'd come here earlier to prepare and hoped no furry creatures had disrupted his plans.

Who would ever have thought a real live F.B.I. agent would cross the threshold of the sheriff's office in Caroline? But today one did, and when Bill came back to the *Chronicle* after speaking with him and Dale, he had a message for Madge.

"The agent wants to talk with you, since you knew Vera pretty well."

"Oh no! I didn't know her any better than any of the other women."

"But it's in the record that she told you she was worried. There's no way around it. Besides . . ." He gave her his endearing grin. "You said you wanted to meet the F.B.I. when they came."

"But I didn't mean—"

"I know. Just tell him the truth. It'll be all right, hon. Do you want me to come along?"

"No, you've got so much work piled up here. I'll be a big girl and face the music alone, but pray for me, okay?"

As she grabbed her purse and opened the door, Bill patted her shoulder. "You'll do just fine."

A few minutes later, with a sense of impending doom, Madge

took a seat across from the agent. Strange how this middle-aged fellow looked as normal as apple pie.

"Mrs. McQuestion, you were a good friend of the deceased?"

"Vera Walters?" Madge squirmed. Why did he have to use the word *good?*

"We worked together in the church with all of the ladies. I honestly don't think Vera had any *good* friends, because she could be very bossy."

"About what?"

"Whatever we were doing. Any project brought out the leader in her, I guess, and the critic. But most of us are capable, too, so she came off as thinking she was superior."

"But she confided in you?"

"Only one time. Otherwise she always acted as if everything was fine. Just that once, she hinted at something being wrong."

"I see. And that was just before she died. Exactly what did she say, and under what circumstances?"

"I was leaving the church basement by the side door and met Vera coming in. We were all working earlier, and she had left but came back. I thanked her for her work, and she said I resented her leadership. I noticed how pale she looked."

"Anything else?"

"She seemed quite worried about something. She said, *You have no idea what I've been* . . . That was all, and she kept moving down the stairs. I asked her what, but she didn't answer. I did notice a shudder pass over her, though. I called, *Good night,* but she was already in the kitchen and didn't answer."

"Would you say Mrs. Walters had enemies, then?"

"No, but she ruffled feathers a lot, over things that seem trivial now. That was just her way."

"Can you give me an example?"

"Oh, she liked to tell people how they should mash the potatoes, or what ingredients make the best pie crust, things like that. She was so opinionated, it grated on us at times."

The agent made a notation on his pad and peered into Madge's eyes. "Is there anything else you'd like to tell me or anyone else you think I ought to interview?"

"No, I don't think so."

"All right, then. Thank you for your time."

Madge practically ran back to the office, where she raced to the pressroom and collapsed in Bill's arms.

"Everything all right?"

"Yes. But remind me never to do that again."

The glade couldn't have been more beautiful, a respite from the humidity that still draped over unharvested cornfields across the river. Shadows played off each other under a giant cottonwood ceiling, and the last rays of light mingled with encroaching twilight.

With his hand on the small of Gloria's back, Aivars aimed to where a fallen log created the perfect seat. Gloria sat before he did and pulled him down as if she knew every move he was going to make.

"Oh, what a lovely evening. There's nothing more beautiful than the leaves changing color, don't you think?"

"Yes." His voice came out a bit ragged.

Her furrowed brow matched the concern in her voice. "Is something bothering you tonight?"

"No, not really. It's just that I have something important to say to you." He searched his memory for the little speech he'd prepared and rehearsed before the mirror, but at the stricken look that passed over Gloria's face, he backtracked.

"Don't be alarmed. I'm only—" He reached down inside the log where he'd hidden a bouquet of roses he had scrounged through his backyard fence a few hours earlier.

What a sight they'd been this year, peeking through the white picket, and miraculously, they had blossomed again this week, completely out of season. Mrs. Smith had been admiring them the other day and wondered at this late blooming.

"If you'd like to pick some, feel free. They won't last long this time around."

Today it occurred to him that they still might look pretty good, so he checked and was happily surprised. At about four o'clock this afternoon, he cut several and wrapped the ends with a water-soaked dishtowel, carried them down here in a paper sack, and eased them ever so carefully into the log. Hopefully, no varmints had discovered them, and they still looked fresh. Fresh and glorious.

They did, and Gloria's "Ooh!" spurred him on. Though he had determined to weigh every word, the deepening color in her cheeks and her silence, except for that one exclamation, instilled an urgency to get on with his proposal.

In the end, he jumbled together, "I love you and want to live the rest of my life with you by my side," with "Gloria, I hope with all my heart that you will see fit to accept my proposal of marriage."

Unsure what he had actually blurted, he fell to his knee and beseeched her. "I love you so much, Glo. Will you marry me?"

Suddenly, the birdsong that had welcomed them to this abode fell silent, as if a storm were brewing. For far too long, Gloria stared into his eyes with raised eyebrows.

"Gloria?" In his ears, his tone resembled a cry for help. Then tears sprang into her eyes, making her look so young and vulnerable. Could she have imagined their growing relationship would lead anywhere but this? Had he gotten in too big a hurry?

Just when he felt his heart would crumble to bits, she fell into his arms and half-sobbed. "Oh yes. Yes, Aivars. I will marry you."

His ears unblocked. The tight cords around his heart unwound, and the mourning doves and meadowlarks proceeded with their evening melody.

Aivars felt as if all the entire vault of heaven replayed their chorus. Immersing his senses in sweet Gloria's embrace, he wondered that a human being could ever possibly experience such joy.

Chapter Thirty-four

Monday, December 18, 1944

November wreaked its vengeance on the countryside. Farmers still harvesting their crops froze their fingers in the frigid weather and more than the normal amount of accidents occurred.

Tom Newberry's brother fell prey to the gears in his tractor. When he reached to clear away some cornstalks that had gotten stuck near the power take-off, the machine reminded him he should have taken time to turn it off.

As Tom put it, "He never even realized what had happened until his hand got cold. He saw his glove was gone, along with his little finger. But he's a tough fella, and drove himself home for Marlene to take him in to the hospital in Osage. Needed a few stitches, he did."

He told this story the last time Bill sat in the barber chair, swinging his scissors around like a pointer. Finally, Bill took matters in hand.

"Set those things down until you finish the story, all right?"

Tom gulped and obeyed.

Before they knew it, December swept in with a fury. This was true everywhere, it seemed. Just yesterday in the Pacific, a vicious hurricane struck General Halsey's fleet. Although the final count was still forthcoming, word had it that the storm took many American lives.

Madge found herself praying with a bit of sarcasm. "Really? As if the Japanese threat wasn't enough—"

She kept busy posting thank-you notes from families who suffered an accident. Neighbors took time away from their own work to help out in the cornfields or heft pots of potatoes and beef for lunches for neighbors harvesting for farmers who'd gotten hurt.

Three of them so far this year, and many would be working in the fields for weeks yet. Nothing like misfortune to bring out the best in people.

While she typed, Madge muttered to herself. "You'd have thought this would've been an easy fall, according to the *Farmer's Almanac*. But that just goes to show it's not always right."

Being busy didn't bother her one bit. In fact, with Gloria at home sewing her wedding dress and arranging for food and decorations, coming to the office proved to be a good thing. She might have stuck her nose into every little detail, and the newspaper allowed Gloria to make some decisions on her own.

After all, it was *her* wedding, a Christmas wedding, to take place at two p.m. on the twenty-third. That left plenty of time before Christmas Eve services the next evening. It seemed strange that Aivars would still be leading them, but the next day he and Gloria would take some time off.

They were going to drive up to the Twin Cities so he could show her where he took his training. Then they'd go on to visit his home further up North. People would talk, no doubt about that, but let them. Didn't everyone deserve a honeymoon?

Since Christmas fell on a Monday, the wedding would be on Saturday. Perfect. Madge's mind swam with all the preparations, even though wartime scaled down everything. But people had been so kind and generous.

Elsbeth offered one of her out-of-this-world wedding cakes as a gift to Gloria and Aivars. Agnes noted their abundance of pork this year, so she was cooking up enough to feed all the guests.

Even though it wasn't normal winter fare, Madge would whip up several batches of potato salad, Gloria's favorite. Others offered

sweet and dill pickles or green tomato relish, and the church ladies said they'd bake four or five big bowls of scalloped corn.

What a feast! The main job was making the house ready. Good thing Aivars' father was retired, so they planned to drive down from Minnesota with his brother and family on the twenty-second.

Hopefully the unpredictable weather would cooperate. The *Old Farmers' Almanac* normally inspired confidence, but this year, even this reliable resource had issued a caveat.

1944: *"With the Almanac staff at present in the armed forces or in war service, this edition [was] born in the all too few hours of evenings and Sundays . . . in candlelight."*

Although Gloria hoped Lillian and Judith could make it, trips from California and Michigan had been rendered nearly impossible. The war altered things in drastic ways for normal families throughout the land, and they'd all gotten used to making allowances.

But looking on the bright side, their daughters' absence made it easier to find room for the Zevenbergers. The parents would use the girls' old room upstairs. The younger couple would camp out in the downstairs bedroom and let their children overflow onto the sofa.

She'd need to work herself into a cleaning frenzy this week before the big event, but what else was new? Soon, Gloria would be finished with her dress and offer to help. My, how that girl could clean when she put her mind to it!

The door crashed open, and a dripping Agnes swept in. "Sorry, Madge, it got away from me in the wind."

"That's all right." Madge had already leaped up to show the storm who was boss. She gestured Agnes to a chair. "Glad to see you. What can I help you with?"

"I don't know. Sometimes I think I'm beyond help."

"How about a cup of coffee? I brought a full thermos."

"Oh, yes. I was so sure the war would be over last year at this time, and now another twelve months has passed, and Jimmy's still over there. My sis is fit to be tied."

While she poured Agnes a cup and refilled her own, Madge

clucked with her tongue. "Isn't it awful? I heard his unit is still along the German border—is that true?"

Agnes nodded as she sipped. "Oh, hon, this hits the spot. Thanks. Yes, and it's terrible cold over there, too. I can only hope someone's offering Jimmy a cup of hot coffee right now."

From the war report last night, that seemed about as unlikely as Hitler suddenly deciding to surrender. On the Western Front, the Battle of the Bulge began two days ago when the Fifth and Sixth SS Panzer Armies plus the German Seventh and Fifteenth Armies launched a surprise attack on the Allied forces in the Ardennes Forest.

Bill did a lot of head-shaking during the broadcast last night. "After all the German casualties this summer, Hitler must be sending boys into the fight. Don't see how they can hold on like this."

Gripping her cup tighter, Madge tried to shake off the memory of his gut-wrenching reaction as the newsman rolled out the details. Bill squeezed his eyes shut and dug his fingers into the arms of his chair.

He could visualize the troops in such a miserable position, surprised by this relentless foe. On some excuse, Madge got up and left the room—seeing him this way made her stomach wrench. But of course, the grim details of the newscast followed her into the kitchen.

Now Agnes reminded her that boys they knew were trapped in the thick of a horrendous last-ditch battle. A sense of hopelessness had plagued her all night, and Agnes understood. Nothing like a good friend during trying times.

The gentle silence brought a sense of comfort, though the wild wind continued to wail. Some worries were meant for friends to share, even if the sharing was all they had to offer.

The actual service flew by, with Gloria's new father-in-law pronouncing the couple man and wife.

Bill whispered to Madge just before they walked down the aisle, "Take a deep breath." His murmured message came just when she needed it. Soon the entire wedding was over. The vows had been spoken, dinner eaten, the lovely cake sliced and devoured, and rice thrown over Gloria and Aivars as they left the church.

True, they were only headed next door to the parsonage. But during the past few years, many young couples spent their wedding nights in their parents' homes. Far too often the bridegroom had to leave the next day to meet a troop train, and the bride needed to be back at work making bombs or packing parachutes.

Still, seeing her youngest child go off with her new husband made Madge's heart palpitate. Gloria looked absolutely radiant in her white satin gown. Aivars seemed like any groom, delighted with his new estate, yet relieved that the ceremony had ended.

A friend of his from seminary had preached the short sermon, and another came, too. They left immediately afterward, needing to get back to their congregations.

Later, back at the house, everyone sat around and chatted. The groom's fingers were trembling before the service, his brother reported.

Mr. Zevenbergen agreed. "Of course. Mine were too, and they were when we said our vows forty years ago. As I recall, you did a little shaking on your wedding day, as well."

"You're right. Marriage is such a big step."

"Absolutely. Bill was trembling on our wedding day, too."

Bill allowed as how Madge had a better memory than he but was probably right. She turned quiet as the others talked, holding fast to these fresh memories. Standing together, they had witnessed their daughter enter a new life. At the same time, an era ended.

When she turned to Bill as the young couple crossed the church threshold, his eyes glimmered, too. She pressed her head against him, and he wrapped his arm around her.

After the meal, the whole Zevenbergen family plunged in to help them clean the church. Of course, the kitchen ladies did their share, so this merely involved sweeping and scrubbing the dining area, moving chairs and tables back where they belonged, and tidying up anything left astray.

When everything was nearly finished, Madge left the rest of them and went upstairs. She dusted the floor until the lights from the small Christmas tree reflected on its glassy surface. In this quiet place, she took some time to reflect.

What a day this had been—she never would have believed Gloria would be married by Christmas. Who knew? Maybe by next year, there'd be a grandbaby to play the infant's role in the nativity pageant.

But no use getting head of things, not that she didn't do that constantly. No, Gloria and Aivars were a couple now, and she would stay out of their business. She sank onto a pew on the right side of the aisle and took in the scene. The black-out had been lifted, so thankfully, she could relish the glow of candles on the leaded windows.

"I *will* stay out of their business, even if it kills me." Yes, she did like to be in charge, but acknowledging this was a start to changing her ways. This past year had taught her so much. In spite of all her foibles, the Almighty still cared for her and had work for her to do.

Yes, even investigating a murder.

Her sigh carried over the silent pews. What a year it had been, with Vera's murder right here in the basement. The impossible reality still produced a shudder. Last year at this time, she would never have believed this if someone had told her..

But one never knew what lay ahead. She'd experienced this time and again, especially with Bill going off to war.

You just had to let life lead you on day by day and accept whatever showed up. That seemed to be the secret. Take each twenty-four-hour period with grace and do your best with the responsibilities given you.

Someone was coming up the front stairs, and she turned to see Mrs. Z. She waved her forward, and they sat together for a few minutes.

"I can't say how glad I am we were able to come, Madge. You've been such a good hostess."

"I wouldn't have had it any other way. Hopefully the weather will hold, and you all make it back safely tomorrow."

Mrs. Zevenbergen leaned back against the pew. "A son's wedding is so much easier than a daughter's. We've had two of those, and now you've managed three."

"Only two—we couldn't be there for Lillian's. And this one was the simplest, honestly. Rationing made things that way. You can't serve your guests something that's not available."

Someone entered the sanctuary from the front.

"Ready, ladies? Everything looks so spiffy downstairs. Vera would be proud!"

"Vera?" Mrs. Z looked puzzled for a moment, but then the truth dawned on her. "Oh, yes. How could I forget the way Aivars mentioned her in his letters last spring?"

Bill grabbed Madge's hand and pulled her up. "Come on, let's go home."

Everyone changed clothes and quickly settled in for the evening. Rog's children started a card game with their parents and grandparents, with Madge and Bill observing from the sofa.

"Nice to hear younger voices in the house again."

Bill had barely spoken when someone knocked on the front door. Madge answered and invited in an apologetic-looking Dale Finley. Bill stood to say hello, and Madge gestured them both to the kitchen.

"Starting to snow out there. Sorry if I'm tracking in."

"Oh, don't worry about it. This old house has seen plenty of tracks in its day." Madge took a seat.

"I realize you've had a big day, folks. I debated coming over, but thought you'd want to hear some news."

"Thanks, as long as it's good." Bill took his usual chair at the head of the table and Dale shrugged off his coat. As he started to drape it over the back of his chair, Madge pointed to a row of hooks on the wall.

"How about a cup of coffee?"

"Sure. I never say no to that offer." He glanced toward the living room. "Gloria's new in-laws?"

"Yes. Nice Minnesota folks."

With the coffee, Madge brought over a piece of leftover wedding cake for their guest, who tackled it right away. Must be hungry and in no huge hurry to deliver his news.

Her thoughts returned to Gloria's expression as she repeated her vows today. *For better for worse, for richer for poorer, in sickness and in health, till death do us part.*

A wave of sympathy flooded her for Dale. Imagine having all the stress of being a sheriff and working with enemy prisoners of war, but having no wife or family to come home to.

He'd been single his whole life—Bill said Dale dated one girl in high school, but she broke off their engagement after graduation. Bill glanced her way with understanding in his eyes. Could he know what she was thinking?

He slid his wedding band around on his finger, still meeting her eyes. He did know, she would bet money on it.

"This must be one of Elsbeth's cakes."

"Yes, it was her wedding gift to Gloria and Aivars."

"She makes the best ever." Dale wiped his mouth. "Well, here's what I came to tell you. Today, the F.B.I. finalized their report on our murder case."

Bill's intake of breath matched Madge's.

"I never would've put all this together myself, and considering everything else they have to do these days, those agents worked pretty fast."

Dale nodded when Madge refilled his cup. "I expect that's why I'm the sheriff here, and those agents work for the big guys out of D.C."

"I know what you mean. We all have our work to do, and this

time, what happened here might have affected the war." Bill reached for Madge's hand.

"Yeah. Well, here's the gist of the report." Dale pulled a stack of folded papers from his chest pocket. "First of all, it was Otto who killed Mrs. Walters."

At Madge's gasp, he angled his head. "I knew you—and the other women—didn't exactly like her, but I'm sure no one would have wanted her dead."

"The thing that still baffles me is how Otto could carry this out right in the church kitchen. When we made the arrest and they hauled him away, he walked off without even a cane. He sure knew how to put on a good act, didn't he?"

"I'll say. I guess a person can do whatever they think needs to be done if they're motivated enough."

"You were on the right track, and the evidence you found in Otto's house led the agents to search further. They found a stash of gold this fellow named Max had siphoned to him over the past few years. Regular payments, and would you believe he sent them by parcel post?"

"You don't say!"

"Yeah. 'Course, that means they came in by train, and before the war, who was checking on things like that? Even now, who would have thought gold that originated in Germany would end up in our little burg?"

"Fritz didn't have any idea down at the Post Office?"

"Nope. But how was he to know? As long as the postage is paid on the mail that comes in, his job is just to make sure it's delivered."

"Otto, he . . ." Madge shook her head, ". . . he killed Vera for money? But what did he do with it? He never made improvements on his house, wore the same old clothes year after year, and could have used a little more soap."

Dale leaned his chair back on two legs. "There was more involved than meets the eye. He did it for money, true. But I'd say loyalty was the bottom line. When misplaced, loyalty can lead a man down dangerous roads.

"Seems Otto's first loyalty was to the land of his birth and to the Reich. Those lessons he had drilled into him at the Bund gatherings made a deep impression, and he never veered from believing Hitler had the answers for the whole world."

He took a gulp of coffee. "Makes me a little sick to my stomach, folks. And you ask what he did with the gold? He stored it away. Considering what happened during the Depression, I'd have to say that might have been a wise choice.

All along, Otto made choices—decisions that drove his sons and his grandchildren away. A fella doesn't change his name without good reason, and your interview with Rudy did a lot to convince the agents."

"Mmm. Did they say how that information made it into the bird on Vera's hat?"

Dale scanned the papers for a minute. "Not specifically, but other names appear here, ones we've never heard of. Looks as if quite a few folks had their hands in this operation, and hopefully they're getting their just desserts.

"The report does state that someone sent the bird—the whole hat, remarkably—from England, through a German spy. Glad to say the Brits have already nabbed him. If he hasn't been executed by now, I'd guess he'll sit out the war in custody on the Isle of Mann, like a lot of other questionable customers."

Bill steepled his fingers. "So, piecing this together, someone here must have inserted the little scroll in the bird."

"Yeah. They obviously infiltrated the naval base at Great Lakes somehow. I guess they passed the info through some Chicago connection. Just seems so implausible that that they chose that infernal hat as the vehicle." Dale shook his head. "Don't this whole thing beat all? No wonder we needed help solving such a mess."

Bill nodded. "I still keep wondering how Vera got involved."

"What I have here doesn't specify how exactly, but says she was instrumental in moving some of the information to the next recipient. Whether she had any concept of her role remains a question."

"It's hard to believe she did." Madge couldn't help herself. "But at least we know why that silly bird was so important, why Otto saw it as worth a human life."

Bill studied her for a moment before chiming in. "So he killed Vera because of the bird and kept searching for it. If he had found it, he would've gotten it to the Nazis somehow, I expect."

"Or passed it on to the next person in the chain. But that part of the investigation has been sealed, so we're left to surmise who instigated the treachery and was waiting for it. And to the best of our knowledge, we can assume that Mrs. Walters played her role unknowingly."

"But she sure fought for that hat."

"Yeah. Maybe in the end, she was only fighting for her life. Maybe when she mentioned the hat to your preacher in her last seconds, it was an attempt to help us understand. We'll never know for sure, I guess."

Ruminating on these possibilities, Madge asked, "Is it always like this in an investigation? Do you ever find out all the details?"

"Let me think." While doing so, Dale accepted a third cup of coffee. "Can't say as I've ever investigated anything this serious before. You know how it is around here, minor incidents of theft or infringements on property rights . . ."

"And with those, either the person committed the crime or they didn't."

Dale agreed with Bill's summary. "Yeah. Our cases are usually open and shut, pretty straightforward, sometimes downright cut and dried. But this one, whoo boy, was it ever different."

He leaned back in his chair again. "One thing we do know for sure, we've got our murderer, and that's what matters. Should set people's minds at rest." He took a long chug of coffee. Perhaps he might not want to go home.

"Actually, I tried to deploy with the military this time, like you did, Bill. But the higher-ups said I was needed more here. Took me a while to get over that, but this case makes me feel as though we did make a little difference in the overall picture.

"Who knows what might have happened if that message had made it to its destination? Maybe more of our boys would have been killed."

When Dale finally rose to put on his coat, Bill shook his hand. "Thanks for letting us know the outcome."

"You betcha. There's nothing so itchy as a story when you don't know the end."

"You'll be heading back to Waverly now?"

"Nope. I'm back in town for good. The Army has enough returned soldiers now to man the camp. Which reminds me, you can turn in your badge on Monday, if you don't mind."

"Don't mind a bit. I'll be there bright and early."

Epilogue:

Thanksgiving Day, 1945

A tiny squall rose from the wicker cradle a few feet away from the table. Madge sat back to observe everyone eating—Aivars and Gloria, Lillian and Marcus, Judith with her husband and family.

The room felt so small with all of them around the table. She couldn't even recall when they'd all been together, but the war had finally ended, making this gathering possible.

One of Judith's girls leaped up. "Aunt Gloria, is it okay if I check on little Billy?"

"Sure, but he might go back to sleep. Sometimes he cries out like that for no particular reason." Since the baby's birth, Gloria's cheeks had only grown rosier. She was the picture of health, and Aivars was bursting with pride at his growing family.

Then there was Bill, finally reunited with everyone after so long. When Aivars and Gloria announced they would name their firstborn after him, he shed a few tears. But not a day went by that he didn't appear at the parsonage to spend a little time with his namesake.

Right now, he engaged in conversation with Judith's husband, something about a new business venture.

"You mean you might be coming to live in Iowa?"

Catching that bit of the dialogue made Madge's heart soar. The details flitted by—something about a new company spreading through the Midwest and needing someone to oversee several state representatives.

What if they did move back? All of these cherub faces around the table today would be here for every holiday. Getting to know them better would be a dream come true.

Now travel was possible for Lillian and Marcus, too. They had made this long trip even though she was expecting their first baby in a few months. Surely they would all get together at least once a year?

Maybe she and Bill could even take a jaunt out to California someday. They'd never imagined such a thing, but minus the all-encompassing war, the world seemed full of new possibilities.

Noting the satisfaction on Bill's face nearly brought her to tears. In May, she had wept with him on V-E Day, and then in August, oh, the relief when the Japanese Imperial forces surrendered at last!

Bill had run such a huge headline in the *Chronicle* that week, she'd had to scrunch in everything else, and even left some for the next edition. That had been a first. Remembering, she set down her fork and folded her hands in her lap.

"Grandma, this turkey is so extra special good, and your biscuits are so yummy. Aren't you hungry?" Seven-year-old Patricia's eyes met Madge's.

The child's red curls brought out her freckles. "Just like yours, Mom," Judith had proclaimed as Patricia ran into Madge's arms when they arrived two days ago.

A minute later her brother, another freckle-faced urchin, made his entrance. "Gamma, Gampa!" His cries nearly made Madge's knees buckle.

"Yes, honey. But I'm eating in spurts today. Right now I'm taking time to enjoy another kind of feast. I guess you might call it a feast of the heart."

About the Author

Words have always been comfort food for Gail Kittleson. After instructing expository writing and English as a Second Language, she began writing seriously. Intrigued by the World War II era, Gail creates historical fiction from her northern Iowa home and also facilitates writing workshops/retreats.

She and her husband, a retired Army chaplain, enjoy grandchildren and in winter, Arizona's Mogollon Rim Country. You can count on Gail's protagonists to ask honest questions, act with integrity, grow in faith, and face hardships with spunk.

Visit Gail online at: GailKittleson.com

Discussion Questions

- Does Caroline remind you of any community you know? How so?

- What unique family dynamics play into this mystery?

- How does World War II enter into the plot?

- What surprises await Aivars when he comes to Caroline?

- How does his education prepare him for what he faces?

- Imagine what rationing would be like. What family stories come to mind?

- What would it be like having your high school graduate make grenades for the war effort?

- Describe how local history and geography affect the characters' view of the world.

- What role does friendship play in Bill's recovery—and in Madge's journey?

- We don't hear a lot about the black market or people like Otto during this era. What created his unique perspective?